MILT MAYS

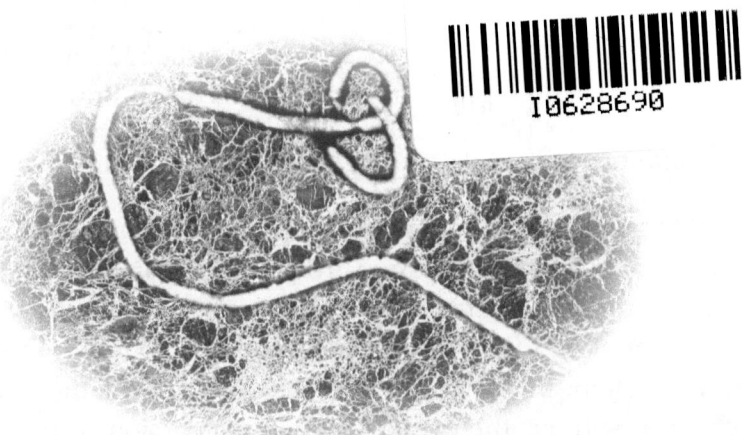

THE
NEXT DAY

ALSO BY MILT MAYS

Novels
Dan's War
The Guide

Short Stories
"Thanksgiving with Riley"
"The Dry-Land Farmer"

Humorous Poetry Book
Take the F…ing Fly

DEDICATION

To: Tolerance.

ACKNOWLEDGEMENTS

This book was my first effort at a novel and has undergone countless edits and taken almost ten years for me to get the courage to publish it. It has been a labor of love, frustration, and several dumpster dives to rescue it from death. I started writing it because of all the intolerance I witnessed after 9/11, both in others, our government, the world, and myself. It was born in cursive writing on a college composition binder, graduated to WordPerfect, then finally to Word. The formatting changes alone have driven me crazy. The final copy here could never have been possible without many, people, and many, many reference books and material.

As a physician, I had some basic microbiology knowledge, but this required a major step up to learn about retroviruses, viral DNA manipulation, antiviral drugs, making of vaccines, and genetic modification of viruses and bacteria, including possible key diseases in Near Eastern theaters of operation. Viral DNA admixture into animal DNA is fascinating, and could result in an Alex or Jabril sooner than you might think.

I am not really a history buff, so this required research into the several areas: WWII and the Jewish state, military documents on the wars in Afghanistan, Iraq, the Jicarilla Apache Nation, the Navajo Nation, Christianity and the Muslim wars of old, and of the new religious animosities after 9/11.

The Colorado research was a bit more eyes-on and personal. I stayed at the B&B in Moffat, CO, and have travelled many of the roads, rivers and areas, including the Royal Gorge Park before the fire of recent years.

Thanks to Google Maps, and numerous other YouTube and Internet references of geographic areas I've never been, to give me a direct flavor.

I spent twenty-seven years in the Navy, from my time at the Naval Academy to various tours throughout the world, once even planning a tour at the US Navy Preventive and Environmental Medicine Unit in Brazil that closed in 1999. I have had several friends in the NSA and Navy Security Group who gave me insights into the clandestine services before and after 9/11.

Specific thanks goes to my editor and book designer, DeAnna Knippling, for her patience and whipping this novel into its current state. Whew! Thanks to my writer's critique group: Jane and Jean and Beth, for keeping me straight. There have been numerous beta readers, my brother Forrest and his wife Pat, my sister in law Trishia, my deceased stepfather, Peter, and numerous friends, especially Lee. Finally, of course is my wife, Lynn, who has read this so many times she probably knows it better than me. We did it, Babe!

As a final note, this book and my other novel *Dan's War* have one character in common, Sam Houston, and the two books then meld into a sequel, combining many characters from both novels into the finale, which takes GMO to the nth degree. It should be out soon.

Then I saw a new heaven and a new earth; for the first heaven and the first earth had passed away...And he who sat upon the throne said, "Behold, I make all things new...It is done! I am the Alpha and the Omega, the beginning and the end. To the thirsty I will give from the fountain of the water of life without payment. He who conquers shall have this heritage, and I will be his God and he shall be my son. But as for the cowardly, the faithless, the polluted, as for the murderers, fornicators, sorcerers, idolaters, and all the liars, their lot shall be in the lake that burns with fire and sulphur, which is the second death."
—Revelation 21:1-8

And those who believe in Allah and His messengers, they are the loyal, and the martyrs are with their Lord; they have their reward and their light; while those who disbelieve and deny Our revelations, they are owners of hell-fire.
—Koran 57:19

We have no government armed with power capable of contending with human passions unbridled by morality and religion.
—John Adams

A sovereign cannot raise an army because he is enraged, nor can a general fight because he is resentful. For while an angered man may again be happy, and a resentful man again be pleased, a state that has perished cannot be restored, nor can the dead be brought back to life.
—Sun Tzu, *The Art of War*

CHAPTER 1

September 10, 2001

Alex Smith awoke in a cold sweat. His heart hammered.

Holy Crap. That dream had been way out there, even for him. He lived for the edge. Job, hobbies, even his habits put him teetering on a knife blade, sharpened daily.

Yeah. So what? He was young. He could take it.

A jarring thump announced the 737 landing, bringing him totally back to reality and ending the first five-hour leg of his journey from New York.

A humid haze cloaked Caracas, Venezuela. The buildings were dulled and grainy, the sun merely a meager white orb with a brightness as bland as the moon, only without the friendly face. The entire panorama was a surreal vision that made him wonder if he were still dreaming.

It was 12:30 p.m., Caracas Weird Time—a half hour earlier than New York. Who would choose to be a half hour off New York? They should call it Caracas Idiot Time. Though on a per capita basis, New York had more idiots, and most of those had PhDs from Columbia University. Who needed a PhD? Only someone with a desire for three dumb initials after their name and to do their research on biogenetics in some university-sponsored, white-coat lab. He was already doing more cutting-edge biogenetics in the lab in the Amazon than most PhDs would do in their entire lives. Probably change the world soon.

The exit door opened and he walked down the stairs. The air hit him like a sweaty net. Fetid aromas and distant ramshackle lean-tos reminded him of where he was. Another plus of traveling down here: experiencing the ambience of the fair city right away, instead of walking across a nice air-conditioned connecting ramp.

Even though he'd been here several times and knew what to expect, he wanted to leave, go home, have a beer, forget the whole thing. Now. If anyone found out what he was carrying, the USA and Venezuela and the one hundred and sixty-seven countries that ratified the Biologic Weapons Convention over thirty years ago would have him jailed. But they had to catch him first. It was one thing to ratify an important treaty, another to enforce it. He was pretty sure no one would find what was inside the 1.5-cm-thick false bottom of his metal coffee cup. Keeping the cup full—preferably with double-strength espresso—helped. If they wanted to inspect it, he could pour out the coffee, and they'd still find nothing. It required a few tricks to unlock and remove the bottom. Even so, he'd love to fit in with the locals better. All he needed was to lop off six inches at the knees, dye his curly blond hair darker, take off fifty pounds, and get rid of the Hawaiian shirt, blue jeans, and the green eyes that ladies found so memorable.

Customs was usually easy. A little pocket money to the familiar customs officer, a stamp on his passport, and he was out of there. But soldiers sometimes haunted the terminal with machine guns and suspicious looks. Reminded him of Mexican Federales. Only these guys were worse. Last time, one actually walked up to him and asked to see his passport. Dark eyes had coldly inspected every wrinkle of his clothing, so close that personal space was more than just violated. The smell of sour sweat and garlic had gagged him.

This time customs was as easy as ever. Hand over the bribe money, grab the bags, and start down the hallway to the taxis.

Except, at the end of the hallway, two soldiers waited—silent, staring vultures. *Holy Crap.*

Every movement slowed. The end of the hallway seemed a mile away. *Stay calm. Move casually.*

Their eyes scrutinized every nervous lick of his lips, followed each drop of sweat down his forehead.

Any second they would raise their guns and—*blam!*—right between the eyes.

He walked past them, slow and easy. Just another turista on vacation, in no hurry. Time straggled by on crippled legs.

They didn't move.

At the exit, he hid his hand next to his chest, slowly stuck up his middle finger, and whispered, "Fuck you, assholes. Made it again!"

Next was a short cab ride to a smaller airport. The young driver was unshaven yet dressed in new Levis and an immaculate white tee shirt. He spoke excellent English, trying several times to start a conversation. But Alex let the words die. The dream from the flight barged in.

He is a child in a two-bedroom house in Wyoming. His father, Joseph, a small man with gray eyes, mousy hair, and a thin, acne-scarred face—but whose rare smile could melt ice—is hurrying in the door from the garage in his underwear. To please his wife he's taken off his work clothes in the freezing garage and put them in a plastic bag before stepping inside. Oily fumes would not come into her house!

His clamped jaw keeps his teeth from chattering. A warm shower and warm clothes should come first, but he stops and ruffles Alex's hair with callused, oil-stained hands of an oil field roughneck.

"Hey, buddy." Joyful voice. Sad eyes.

"Hi, Dad."

A grating female voice streams out of the kitchen. Her words hang in the air like frozen fog. "You know tonight is Bible club. Couldn't you be on time just once?"

His father runs up the stairs.

She whips around the corner, white hair up in a bun. Amber, laserlike eyes pierce Alex. A semi-smile shows gleaming shark teeth. Painted-on, arched black eyebrows and Bing cherry lipstick are sinister above a bright orange and green clown outfit.

She grabs his arm, and her words come out as a hiss. "You're going with me tonight to learn about God. I am not leaving you two here to talk fishing."

She drags Alex outside and slams the door.

His father's voice is muffled but audible. "Love you, Alex."

———

Alex closed his eyes and shook his head in a spastic shudder, trying to end the images.

Was Mom that bad?

The clown in Stephen King's *It* had given him nightmares and a wet bed for months as a child. If the clown-suited Mom of the dream had said, "Beep, beep, Alex! Beep, beep…" Goose bumps crawled up his back and he touched his groin to make sure his pants were dry. Stephen King must have had a really weird childhood. Or maybe he hated kids.

Alex's head bumped the roof of the cab, jarring him to look outside. The dusty back road ended at a shack with a dirt landing field cut out of the jungle. A lone Cessna amphibian plane waited, motor purring.

He gave the driver a tip, bigger than usual. "Sorry, dude. Shoulda talked more." Most of the locals were interesting, and usually Alex enjoyed talking with them.

The driver perked up. "No problem, Mr. Smith. Perhaps on the return trip you can tell me all about the Amazon."

The door shut and the cab wheels spit dust. Alex frowned at the cab's rear window as it disappeared around the bend. He didn't remember telling the driver where he was going, or his name.

It would have been nice to catch up on more sleep, but the flight to the Amazon Lab west of Manaus, Brazil, was a turbulent carnival ride. Once, his shoulder crashed against the wall so hard that he had to stifle a scream. Did the pilot even care about his lone passenger? Alex held on tighter. The jungle below was green. Leafy and green. Forever.

At 6:00 p.m. Brazil time, one hour later than in New York—at least the Brazilians liked whole numbers—the plane slid into the water of the Amazon river, and coasted to a stop at the pier—if you could call it that. They were surrounded by—what else—more leafy green jungle. Only this place was even more surreal than Caracas, a humid, hot Twilight Zone. He grabbed his pack and stepped out onto a narrow pier, a sharp-edged puzzle of mismatched wood. One misstep and…busted nuts.

Next was a murderous uphill path to the lab. There were side walls of thick green jungle (of course) and a quarter mile of cobblestones laid by a madman: ankle-busters.

He was young. He could take it. Yeah.

The end of the path marked the divide between local workmanship, shoddy as it was, and the twentieth century—boring but modern. On the other side of the gate, a smooth cement driveway led to a one-story, gray cinder-block building. Metal doors, barred windows. He panted and sweated and stopped at the gate.

He studied rolls of concertina wire fringing the top of the twelve-foot tall chain link gate and fence that surrounded the building. *Tell me again. Why do you do this?*

A barely audible hum of high voltage coursed through the fence and gate. *So comforting.*

In front of the gate stood a four-foot metal post topped with a square keypad. "Angled for easy viewing," they'd said on his first trip. He wiped sweaty palms on his shirt and typed in the code. Below the keypad, a metal shield whirred open. He placed his thumb on the glowing red pane of glass. A beep sounded. He jerked his thumb back to avoid the carnivorous metal shield zipping down and closed. The thing was getting faster. Must have developed a taste for him after the last nip.

The security camera inside stopped its preprogrammed roving and swung back to point directly at Alex. The gate opened with a loud click. He walked through, waiting for the gate to close and the electric hum to resume. What exactly would he do if the gate didn't close?

Turn around and leave. No doubt about it.

A similar procedure opened the metal door to the cinder block building. The door clanged shut behind him and there it was again—the same prickle at the nape of his neck he always got at this point. *Will I ever get out again?*

The high-speed elevator descended so fast he felt weightless for ten of the fifteen seconds. He jumped up at the end, as usual, though he was too tired enjoy the usual rush. He yawned. No sleep any time soon. He trudged to the sleeping quarters—some "bedroom"—dropped off his pack, took off his shirt, and sighed, placing a cool, wet washrag over his chest and face. The sweat came off and he felt a tad more awake, though when he got up again, his eyes in the mirror looked like some kind of zombie's.

Coffee.

Before sleep, in the break room, there was the customary two-hour "briefing" on the new viral codes so he could get started first thing in the morning. Why was he so tired? He'd slept much less so many other times and felt way better. It wasn't even 7:00 p.m. in New York. Maybe he needed a beer. Might help with the aches in his muscles.

Almost felt like he was coming down with something.

He drained the still-warm cup of espresso left in his carry-on cup, padded to the break room, and nodded through most of the videotaped briefing. After a quick snack, he went back to his Spartan bedroom. Without turning off the light or undressing, he lay down on the small metal-framed cot that jutted from the wall, feeling like a lonely book on a solitary bookshelf.

A brief thought of his dream from earlier slipped through his mind, and he murmured, "Miss you, Dad," then slept.

It was dark when something woke him. Was the bed vibrating? Probably another tremor. He'd been told the tremors here were not nearly as bad as the ones in Peru, and not as dangerous. He took off his clothes and went back to sleep, peripherally registering that his tee shirt was more than a little damp and that his muscles ached all over.

Shrieks, whistles, and nails scratched on a chalkboard. Alex bolted upright. What the hell? Oh yeah, the new Memory Stick Walkman alarm. Better than Colombian espresso.

He shut it off, feeling drained, his tee shirt still damp from yesterday. 7:30 a.m., September 11, 2001. New work hours was probably the reason he felt so tired. Reset the internal clock. Get used to it. The last several weeks he'd been doing research in New York, finding the right DNA proteases for the viruses between about 9:00 a.m. and 4:00 p.m. That left the whole evening for hops and barley research. Way too many Irish bars. He hadn't seen the early side of 8:00 a.m. in…yeah, six weeks at least. 7:30 was *way* early—6:30 New York time. Jesus.

He took a shower and took stock of who he worked for: La Riva Labs did *some* things right—good food, movies and music. Of course, they had to. Worse than a nuclear submarine: no contact with the outside world for a month.

What had they said? *You must concentrate on your research.*

They did supply outstanding equipment. And they hired great people. No amount of great food could ever make up for working with assholes.

He finished the shower, still achy but better, and dressed in the "Uniform of the Day," as M.C. would say: blue scrubs and Nikes. M.C.,

Master Chief, was their retired Navy Class IV bio-procedure manager. A short walk and Alex was in the small—make that tiny—break room, hoping for a quick bite to eat before getting started. The break room fit M.C. to a tee. But the sterile, white-walled room pinched Alex's Wyoming psyche. It was a mere closet made into a break room. He sat on the cold, metal picnic table bolted to the floor.

For easy cleaning—my ass! Just plain cheap, and uncomfortable. Have a nice break, only be quick about it!

He recalled the Amazon Lab had once been a Navy base—Tropical and Preventive Medicine. It was one of the first bases closed in the late '80s, and La Riva scarfed it up. Funny thing, though, the government fully funded La Riva. It was the Washington shell game: take one pot of money and move it to another.

Pays your salary. Don't knock it.

Jesse pressed into the seat next to him. "Hey, Alex. How's it hangin'?" The blue scrubs she wore barely contained all of her six-foot-two and well over two hundred pounds. Jessibelle Yanaha Macallan was beautiful, sexy, and one of the smartest microbiologists Alex knew. He liked her even more because she'd been a rebellious youth at the University of Arizona, once being jailed as a grad student for protesting sanctions against Iraq. She was responsible for decoding parts of the Ebola DNA and was helping him transplant viral codes from smallpox-like monkey viruses to the middle of Ebola DNA.

She always liked to sit close, too close. Okay, maybe he liked it a little.

"Hi, Jesse. I'm good. Except I think my mind is still an hour behind." Truth was, even his eyes ached. But he had to get going. Work meant money. "Give me a few minutes, though, and I'll be multitasking as usual. Right now, how about some of that good old Colombian?"

"Sure, baby." Her smooth voice was nonchalant. "But you know I don't bring any of that stuff with me to the job."

"Right...just pass the coffee."

Macallan was a weird last name for an Apache. She'd explained it as a Scottish trapper hired by James Kirker to tame the northern New Mexico Jicarilla Apaches. Raised on the rez, she hated government oppression. She'd told him Yanaha came more from distant Navajo relatives, and translated to *One who confronts her enemies*. Fit her perfectly. Y this. Y that.

Fuck this. Fuck that. Oh, yeah. Alex also loved it that "Y" fit right in with the D.C. acronym game. The best part: it was only one initial.

"So how's Lora?" she asked. That was a new one. Not like Jesse to care about the competition.

"Good."

"Just good? Come on! This is her big day, right?"

"Yeah, she was a little nervous. But like I told her, all she has to do is strut her stuff and she'll get a Nobel."

Alex wished he'd stayed to see Lora do her thing. She was an amazing woman. Amazing. Hmm…why did he not think of her as "my dream come true"? Was it because he really loved someone else? Was Lora only a rebound after Rachel? If Rachel hadn't been a coworker…

Lora was good, though. Yeah. Good. Then there was Jesse. What the hell was wrong with him? Lora was it. He wondered what she was doing right now.

In New York City, Lora Livingston stepped out of the shower, slightly less nervous than when she'd awoken an hour ago, and more determined. Black hair and blue eyes of a Scottish father topped a tall, athletic body of a Viking marauder mother. The morning four-mile run had almost rid her of the butterflies.

She'd been working in the North Tower of the Trade Center for five years now, and today's presentation was the culmination. Her brother's senseless death due to a medication error had infuriated her, spurring her to develop software that should eliminate all medication errors—a certain Nobel Prize, according to her boss.

But first they needed funding. Today was the day.

She donned the pale blue blouse, the new gray business suit, and added black heels and onyx ear studs. She held up her grandmother's pearl necklace. It always gave her luck. Placing it around her neck drained a bit more tension. It was like playing tennis—after the first few serves she loosened up. Maybe Andre Agassi was right: image *was* everything.

She scowled and addressed the mirror: "Screw that! There's a lot more than image under this suit, and I'm going to show them."

A deafening sound permeated the room. She jumped, then remembered Alex's alarm.

They'd met last year at an Internet café and it was love at first sight—Alexander Smith, curly blond hair she could run her fingers through and mischievous green eyes that twinkled like new aspen leaves fluttering in a spring breeze.

She strode into the bedroom, shut off the eighty-decibel alarm, and wished he was here. She could still see him yesterday, waking up, rubbing his eyes like a little boy, apologizing for oversleeping again with his usual, "Holy Crap!" His one minor flaw was his inability to wake up without "noises from hell." She could live with that—and his lack of time sense. But how all those OCD scientists in South America tolerated him was beyond her.

Maybe they liked his ability to do three things at once. But it annoyed her. Like yesterday. Before she'd left for work, he was talking to her, dressing, finishing his packing, and eating. All at the same time.

Now she wished she hadn't scolded him: "Are you really listening to me? Why do you always try to do three things at once? It is a proven fact that if you do more than one thing at a time, then all the tasks get short-changed. So you're really better off doing one thing at a time."

He didn't flinch. "I get too bored doing one thing at a time. Anyhow, I had a professor who said the world is changing so fast that the next major mutation will favor survival for those with the quickest ability to adapt to change. Maybe I'm the first with the mutant gene!"

He'd looked so pleased with himself. If only she'd hugged him instead of rushing off to work. Maybe she would call him right now, to make up for it.

Except there was no phone number for him in Brazil.

When she had complained about his working there, he'd said, "You can't get those monkeys up here, so South America is perfect. And when we find out how to make monkey viruses suppress human melanomas, I might join you for that Nobel Prize."

She still hated it that she couldn't contact him for the next month. Rachel Lane, his ex, probably could. And there was also the possibility Rachel might visit the Amazon Lab. Alex had assured Lora it was over with Rachel. But how many times had Lora heard that from other guys?

Maybe she would surprise Alex in a month. He'd be in Patagonia on a fishing trip. If this deal succeeded, she'd have the money, and certainly deserved some time off.

The taxi honked.

She grabbed her laptop and shouldered her new black Prada purse, a birthday present from Mom. Locking the door, she remembered yesterday as she was leaving—Alex grabbing her and starting to undress her.

She yelled at the door, "Dammit! I should have let him."

But she'd have been a half hour late. At least. And *that* would not have been a good example to her crew. Yeah, but it might have taken his mind off Rachel.

She climbed into the cab. In four weeks, she would undress him on a Patagonian river. Well, maybe back at the cabin. It was cold down there.

She opened her laptop and said to the cabby, "Twin Towers."

CHAPTER 2

Afghanistan, September 11, 2001

The word had come down from the superiors: watch the TV tonight. In the mountain desert they had few TVs, but all eyes would find one. This was it.

The razor-thin man wished he could celebrate with his comrades all night, but his plane left in a few hours. What would be on the TV was important—it would cripple the infidels. But his mission would bring them *to their knees*.

And he, Jabril El Fahd, would deliver the ultimate weapon. Finally, revenge would be his.

First he must prepare. The trip to Jakarta had many legs and he must be ready to flee at any moment. He picked up the dossier on his cot and sat to study it and learn as much as he could about the scientist he would soon confront.

The microbiologist who had discovered the secret, Rashid El Hammed, was now isolated from the world in their lab in Jakarta, at Jabril's request. None of Rashid's research had been published for a year, so his most recent secrets had been kept from the world. Since then, his only contact with the outside had been his frequent calls to his wife, a small price to pay for continued work. Otherwise, the lab had been his only world.

Jabril had sent Rashid a "helper," Jorge, really Jabril's inside man. Jorge was tasked with surreptitiously finding the most lethal and contagious

virus, and secreting it for Jabril. To accomplish his task, Jorge had pur-
posefully acted like a bungler, and Rashid had insisted he leave. Before
Jorge had left, however, he'd labeled Jabril's lethal virus with a special
code—a blue dot. As far as Rashid knew, Jabril's visit tomorrow was to
get an update on Rashid's progress and to ensure he was still on task after
Jorge's bungling.

But Jabril's visit had another, much more important purpose.

Rashid El Hammed loved his work, yet now, bathed in sweat in this hor-
rid place, he felt something was terribly wrong. He had been recruited
when he was twenty-six and had worked for three glorious years close
to his home in Baghdad. Then, in two days, they had moved his lab to
Jakarta, explaining the rapid move was necessary because any experiments on viruses would be considered work on a biological weapon. But
this was not a weapon. So, he'd asked, why the move?

The government officials had raved about his work: a medical break-
through, too important to stop. It would show everyone how Iraq led
the world in humanitarian endeavors. But first he had to complete it.
Any manipulation of viruses would be viewed as suspicious by the
U.N. peacekeepers, and they would halt his work for possibly years. So
to Jakarta he went. Halfway around the world, from the arid desert to
the humid, sticky jungle of Indonesia, he had toiled with hope in his
heart.

Now fear replaced hope, catching in his throat with each swallow of
the lukewarm water. He spit out the water and again dialed his wife on
the cell phone.

No Signal.

It had started yesterday, September 10, right after they restricted him
to the compound.

"Your project is on hold," they'd said, "too much scrutiny right now.
But in a few days, when all the attention dies down, you can return to
work and finish your great discovery."

But why stop him now? His published papers on the subject had been
out for years. The scientific community already knew what he was doing.

Maybe it had to do with Jorge's screw-up last week. Jorge was new,
but he was supposed to know what he was doing. And even though he

had helped with the cleanup after his bungling, the bosses had sent him packing. No wonder. It had been a very bad mistake, and it confirmed Rashid's opinion that Jorge was one of the dimmest candles he had ever worked with. The new viral combination Jorge thought so important would be of no medical use and could potentially be very harmful. Rashid had quarantined all those vials in the freezer.

Rashid dialed the number again. He needed to hear his wife's voice—reassuring him that everything was all right.

In the desert, Jabril put the dossier on the ground and lay down on a cot, wanting a few hours of rest before the event. But sleep did not come.

He is a child in his village of Karbala, Iraq, in their home of many years, sitting at a simple wooden table. White cotton napkins and brown clay plates are arranged neatly. He bows his head as Mother whispers a prayer before evening meal. "I pray that Allah will bring love and food to our children, spread caring and tolerance throughout the world, and give my son a gentle heart that will help others." Then louder "Eat your food, Jabril. You are too thin."

Father's dark eyes flash at her, his voice loud and angry. "Care and tolerance? Is that what we need? No! Jabril, who is my son too, will not do these things you wish. You are a nurse. Have you not seen the pain of your patients? Do you not think we have tolerated enough? This American embargo is killing our country. It has taken away our food, our very home. And you think we should be more tolerant?"

Father smashes his fist onto the table. Dishes clatter. Jabril flinches. Mother watches the floor, her hands in her lap, meek as a mouse. Father looks at Jabril. "You can help them more by ridding the world of those that caused their suffering. The jihad is the highest calling in the Qur'an, and your name...Do you not realize how fate has given you the name of Gabriel—Gabriel, the angel through whom God revealed the Qur'an to Muhammad? You must live up to your name—the avenging angel. You must make your life a sacrifice to Allah. This you will do, my son." He rants on for another hour while Jabril and his mother cower and the scant food grows cold.

—

That was how it had gone since Grandfather lost an arm in the bombing of Baghdad. Father started going to weekly jihad meetings and came home spouting all the facts he'd learned: "The American embargo made us paupers. Before the infidel embargo, one dinar was worth three U.S. dollars. After it, two thousand dinars wasn't worth a single dollar. Disease killed our chickens, so we have no meat. Now we eat like starving Africans, only rice or bread."

Mother had been the opposite. She was a nurse and every day took Jabril to the hospital. She showed him how compassion and love helped even those who were doomed to die, and how proper knowledge could save many more. She had wanted him to learn, to be more than his father, to be a healer, a doctor. Like her mother before her, Alexandra, who had died helping others in World War II, she made sure they prayed together. She taught him that a true Muslim was tolerant of others always favoring love and compassion over hate and revenge. "Your father is not himself. He has let his anger take over his soul. But he will come back. He will come back."

Then Father's brother was killed by a sniper bullet and Father became a leader at the secret jihad meetings. He all but quit his job and spent the days raging about infidel Americans and how Allah would avenge the suffering of all Iraqis. He took Jabril out of school and taught him fundamentalist beliefs, quoting the Qur'an about how infidels must die if they don't become Muslim. He ended Jabril's trips to hospital with Mother. Yet Jabril still resisted Father.

Thinking about it now, he wondered why.

But he knew why. His mother. He could still see her beautiful dark eyes looking at a dying child as if she could will him to get better. Her gentle hands seemed to heal merely by touch.

She had courage as well. The last argument, he remembered it so well. She had stood up to father.

That day, in hospital, she lost five children to starvation and disease. Her prayer before meal begins, "Please let Saddam spare the children—"

But Father interrupts, "Let Saddam spare the children? Saddam? He is not responsible for killing half a million of our children over the last ten years. It is the Americans and their embargo, keeping food out or their mouths and antibiotics out of our hospitals."

She coughs, a persistent cough that Jabril has come to worry about, then stands, angrily staring at Father over the table, "It is Saddam taking the oil money meant for food and medicine. He buys gold for his palace."

Father stands, frowning, his voice a dark, ugly sound. "It is not Saddam, my wife. It is the infidel Americans causing the pain you have seen. They pay billions of dollars to the Israelis, funding the murder of Muslims in Palestine, Lebanon, and now Iraq. All they want is to take our oil for their cars." His voice sounds strangled and his eyes water. "They kill our babies, our brothers, and maim our fathers so their cars can run."

Mother coughs more and grows visibly weaker during father's harangue. Her hands grip the table, at first shaking, then giving way as her dark eyes flutter. She faints, falls forward, landing prone, her head bouncing off the table like a wooden ball.

Jabril had not realized how frail and weak his mother had become until he and Father picked her up and took her to hospital. She was as frail as a china doll, only with real bones and skin. Over the next several weeks, Father and Jabril would care for her in hospital.

She had pneumonia. Every day Father would say, "See what the infidels have done with their embargo. They have starved her. The doctors cannot get the correct antibiotic so she cannot get better. Do you understand now? Even if you were the greatest doctor who ever lived you could not help her Jabril. You will help her more by destroying the infidels."

Love—hate. Help—destroy. It felt better to love and help than to hate and destroy. But Father was the man, the leader, the head of the family. As Allah had proclaimed, so it must be.

How had she become so thin? She must have given up her food for him. If only he had paid attention to her instead of going to jihad meetings with Father. Over the following weeks Jabril had ignored his hollow stomach. He became thin, so thin. Yet he thrived as she weakened. His angular features, gaunt dark eyes, and jet-black hair mirrored a razor-sharp yet emotionally starved mind.

Father taught him that a man who could think well but not express himself might as well be born in a cave. Father took him to auctions, not only to learn how to express himself, but also, how to *sell* himself.

Iraqi newspapers announced that the embargo killed fourteen Iraqis each hour.

That late September morning his mother became one of the fourteen.

Coughing and suffocating on her phlegm, her face twists, eyes plead for more air. He can still feel her hands clutching at his shirt, as if she could pull oxygen from the very fabric. All he can do is hold her, screaming inside at the agony on her face.

The lines of pain soften; her breathing fades to nothing. She will have no more pain.

Yet his tears pour out like a cloudburst in the desert. Sobbing, he pleads with Allah to make her well—bring her back.

In this desert land filled with dry hate, she had been his water. She had taught him never to hate. As the Qur'an had taught her to love, so had she lived, every day of her life.

Hungry, tired, and immeasurably sad, he has never felt so alone.

But then all of Father's teachings hit him.

As her final breath fades, his tears dry to another feeling, so strong he prays for Allah to forgive him. But soon it burns white hot, filling him.

Hate became his mantra—jihad his crusade.

Thinking about it now, Jabril hardened his heart for the task ahead, even as he wiped a tear from his cheek.

They will pay!

He paced for an hour, then walked through the desert, the late-afternoon shadows of each sand dune touching the next. The air was cooling fast. A fresh-killed lamb was roasting on a spit outside the brick hut. It was crowded inside, but he found a place in the back and watched the small TV. The jets flew into the Twin Towers and everyone cheered. Everyone else. It was not enough. He had to finish them. He was the Sword of Gabriel.

The others celebrated, hugging each other like long-lost friends, running outside and shooting their rifles at the sky, eating the roasted lamb. Jabril returned to his cot and thought about Jessibelle and her report of the American's research in the Amazon and how closely it followed Rashid's. Everything was in place. Jessibelle would keep her promise and help Jabril. Jorge had discovered the best virus. Allah was pleased.

At sunset Jabril took his prayer mat outside, faced the setting orb, and went through the surahs his father had taught him.

Before he ended, he said, "Allahu akbar, Allahu akbar." *God is great, God is great.*

And, finally, "Ameen."

He took his mat inside, picked up a book that was ragged and dog-eared and written by a Chinese infidel. Though he enjoyed Sun Tzu's original thirteen chapters, the passage he most came back to was the one in the introduction by the American infidel, Samuel B. Griffith. Even though he had been a brigadier general in the U.S. Marine Corps, his words rang as true as the Qur'an. He would have understood Jabril.

Jabril lay down on the cot and read the passage, though he knew it by heart:

"Philosophers and kings distinguished between a righteous and unrighteous war; an enlightened prince was morally justified in attacking 'a darkened and rustic country,' in civilizing barbarians, in punishing the willfully blind, or in dealing summarily with a state going to ruin. Such chastisements were in accord with the Will of Heaven, and were properly inflicted by the ruler in person, or by a specially deputized minister of state."

CHAPTER 3

Two days earlier. 2:00 p.m., September 9, 2001

Rachel Anne Lane arrived at Denver International Airport totally pissed after three hours of screaming kids kicking the back of her cramped 737 seat. And then no luggage. It took all of her control to keep from strangling the impolite politeness out of the scrawny lost-luggage clerk. She wanted to scream obscenities at him, but instead she seethed for another two hours, gagging down stale coffee. Never again would she check luggage.

On one bathroom trip she washed her face and brushed the knots out of her thick black hair, though it was a little long for her taste. Going into the back country with shoulder-length hair was not ideal. With all the waiting, at least she was comfortable in her rust-colored cargo pants and mid-level hiking boots. She looked in the mirror and straightened the collar on her beige, polyester shirt. Grandma's simple gold necklace shone.

Walking back to the lobby she replayed Scott's words: *I'll be unavailable the second week in September.* Long hours at the Pentagon, special project for the Army. Same old story. She would teach him. And have fun at the same time. At least that was the original plan.

What fun was this, though?

Finally, she wheeled her *found* luggage out of DIA to a yellow taxicab.

"Hey lady," the cabby asked, "Okay if I play some music?" He looked like a Wyoming transplant: white, cowboy hat, brown tobacco stains on his teeth. Nothing like Alex, though.

"Sure…but if you play country you're dead meat."

His eyes widened in the rearview mirror as he flipped through CDs.

"Livin' on a Prayer" played and her smile relaxed the cabby's tense face. Not her fave but it would do. A bit of metal like "Here I Go Again" by Whitesnake would be better. She thought about giving the cabby her CD, *Whitesnake,* but it *was* their best album and that cowboy wannabe would probably scratch it with his first touch.

The taxi dropped her off at the old one-story brick house on Logan Street in Denver: a simple two-bedroom house with kitchen, living room, and dirt-walled basement. Not that it mattered to her grandparents. They had been simple people, Swedes and Scotch-Irish, with family, friends, and work their main priorities, and in that order. Thirteen people had lived under this roof during the Depression. No one complained, just happy to have a roof over their heads. Granny Lane had left it to Rachel knowing their priorities matched. It was great having this hideaway, far removed from D.C.

She wasted no time in loading up gear from the house into the Scout in the back alley. Dents and rust added character to the washed-out yellow finish, belying the finely tuned V-8 under the hood. It started on the first twist of the key, and the motor purred.

She patted the steering wheel. *That's my baby.*

She flipped and rubber-banded her hair into a pony tail and glanced in the rearview. There always seemed to be a slight crease in the center of her brow. Yeah, there was hardness. Needed it to balance the too-feminine oval face, full lips, and pixie nose. She frowned hard, then harder at brown eyes flecked with green, then laughed. This was going to be fun. She put the Scout in gear.

Big-city claustrophobia eased as she drove north on I-25, then west on Highway 34. Snaking up the Big Thompson River canyon, each curve quickened her pulse. For the next two weeks she would be doing something she had dreamed of for months. Forget La Riva and viruses and DNA. Instead she would concentrate on wildlife, film speed, and f-stops while camping in the wilderness of Rocky Mountain National Park.

Arriving after dark, she stayed in Estes Park, hoping one night would be enough to acclimatize her to the higher mountain altitudes. After checking into the hotel, she called Scott and got his answering machine.

"Scott, if you're there, pick up…" She waited. "Scott?"

Nothing but phone void—worse than outer space. She left a terse message, hung up, then eyed her cell phone.

Working late. Right? Maybe he'll call me back in a minute.

But someone else might trace the cell.

She turned the cell off.

No traces, no interruptions. Period! I earned this vacation.

Only Scott and her mother knew her real location. She was only to be interrupted for true emergencies, the kind requiring last rights. La Riva didn't count. They would think she was in British Columbia, where her good friend and look-alike, Tasha Flanders, had taken a flight from Denver in Rachel's name. A deal they had worked out last year after La Riva had shortened yet another vacation from a week to two days. Tasha liked Canada. And in her job Rachel needed to know how to evade others, so a fake ID was practice. Merely practice.

Hope they don't give Tasha a hard time when they find her.

Thoughts of La Riva brought thoughts of Alex Smith. What would her life have been like if she had continued dating him? He had those green eyes and a hot bod. But Scott was more…dependable? No. He wasn't a work colleague, like Alex. She didn't date colleagues. Her game, her rule. Scott was it.

The next morning, September 10, she felt good when she woke at 5:00 a.m.—no headaches, shortness of breath, or other signs of mountain sickness. After an early breakfast, she picked up her backcountry camping pass at the Beaver Meadows Visitor Center and entered the Park, determined to put every minute to good use. Though anxious to begin, she took her time on the hike from the Lawn Lake trailhead up into the Mummy Range, pacing herself, letting her body adjust to the altitude.

Autumn in the Rockies was perfect for photography. Cool clear air made for sharp pictures. Labor Day had been two weekends back, so the summer crowds were gone, making the animals less afraid to wander out.

She camped that night and was up before first light on September 11, a little stiff but ready for a more strenuous day. She had worked hard preparing for her hikes with spinning classes and strength training. As a result, she'd lost a little weight and gained muscular curves. She started hiking and felt great—breathing hard and sweating. This was where she belonged.

The soft morning light added to the quiet solitude. She focused on three Rocky Mountain bighorn sheep. Each click of the camera was a mantra melting away her tension. The months of planning were finally paying off.

At the Pentagon, a low rumbling interrupted Scott's second cup of coffee. Not quite sure what he was hearing, he looked up. Then a tearing, shearing sound made him leap from his chair, too late. His office was at ground zero of the new improved kamikazes—larger planes, bigger boom.

The warm sun felt good on Rachel's face and the stiffness in her calves loosened as she hiked higher. The morning mountain air smelled of pine and heightened her senses, making the sky so blue she wanted to fly into it like the hawk that soared overhead. By stretching only a few more feet, she was sure she could touch the orange glow in the east. Her breathing quickened as she walked up a steep path into wild country where even her NOAA weather radio had no signal. This isolation was exactly what she wanted.

Too bad her *real* job couldn't be a hobby, and vice versa. Though she loved them both, she much preferred this working environment to the sterile top-secret D.C. lab.

"Screw this," she said too loud, startling the nearby elk.

"Shit!" This time a hoarse whisper.

Forget about work, stupid, or you'll scare your next shot.

She quickly gathered her pack and followed the elk, wanting a few more clicks before the light was too harsh.

CHAPTER 4

Jesse squeezed Alex's thigh a little too high and brought him back from thinking about Lora.

"Where'd you go? Thought I lost you." She got up, brushing a breast against his shoulder as she poured him a cup of coffee.

With flawless, tawny skin as smooth as a doe's belly, jet-black hair, and walnut-brown eyes, she sometimes made concentrating on DNA difficult. The extra weight she'd gained in the last year sitting behind a computer softened her previously hard Apache edges and made her even sexier. Despite her bulk, she moved like a big cat, and was always flirting with Alex. If they passed in the hallway, she made sure it was close enough to touch, and whenever she could, she would pat his butt.

She touched her pink tongue to her upper lip. "Yeah, I know you want a little of this brown and beautiful. Never did like yours blonde or sweet back in Wyoming, didja? Just strong and dark…kinda like someone I know. Right baby?"

She emphasized *baby* with another firm squeeze on his left thigh, high enough to tickle his imagination, though hard enough to cause pain.

"And if that don't wake you up, you need to go back to bed."

He winced, not so much at the pain, but at the thought of what Lora would do to him if she knew this Apache Wonder Woman was giving him a raging hard-on. *Holy Crap, I need to talk to Doc about this.*

He glanced sideways at Jesse's cleavage, the top two buttons always open for a generous look. *Maybe there's an anti-Viagra drug Doc can give me. Need to find out what's causing me to be so tired and achy, too.*

"Yeah, yeah," he said. "Pass the coffee. And keep Wyoming out of it. I left after high school and never want to go back, except maybe to fish. Anyway, we need to get cracking on these viruses. The sooner we're done, the sooner I'll be fishing for Amazon dorado and Patagonian trout."

"I've been trying, but the viruses won't do the snake dance without you. Maybe they need your male influence to complete the mating." She gave him an evil grin. "So bolt down some of that high octane and put those little gray cells in high gear."

She moved toward the door with an exaggerated sway of shapely hips. "You know, if we finish early, we could take a week in the Peruvian Andes together before your piscatorial adventure. But then again, that might remind you of Wyoming, all that snow and cold. I know, I'll show you some private streams in a warmer place, like New Mexico."

"Okay, enough already. You must need a hormone adjustment. I'm seeing Doc today. I'll ask him to put something in your soup so we can get more work done."

Her repeated dig about Wyoming had almost goaded him into a return comment about Indian reservations and New Mexico. But he stopped short. She'd been raised on a "rez" and was a little touchy on that subject. Lucky for her she had an aunt who tutored her. This allowed her to get a special Native American scholarship to University of New Mexico for her undergrad, then did so well she transferred to Arizona University for her graduate work in genetics.

Mentioning Doc had seemed to cool her a bit. She enjoyed teasing Alex but liked to keep it a secret. Also, any father-like male figures seemed to quiet her immediately. "Finish your coffee and come to the lab. I've got some interesting stuff to show you." This time her words were terse and she disappeared from the lounge like a grizzly in the bush: quicker than anything that big had a right to move.

He dialed sick bay on the wall phone. "Hey, Doc, I need to see you sometime today. A lot of weird stuff is going on in my bod and I need your help."

"Stop by about eleven-thirty, and we'll dissect the problem. And bring a good scalpel, Alex, or it could get messy."

Doc's preferred "scalpel" was a new fly-tying recipe. He tied flies to pass the time while waiting for the mostly healthy researchers to get sick.

"Okay, Doc, I got a real sharp Bard-Parker for you this time." That would get Doc's mouth watering.

On his way to the lab, Alex recalled fishing last month with Lora. She had loved it, though she had argued about how best to cast. Then, in his mind's eye, he saw her smiling at him yesterday before he left, just before the strange feelings started.

He'd told Lora a lie, that he was working with monkey viruses to discover a cure for human melanomas. *She'd freak if I told her the truth— and, anyway, I can't.* He'd almost undressed her at the door. *Almost had her, too.* She'd left; he'd drunk his OJ and put on his backpack. *Gotta pack lighter.* He'd run down the stairs to the taxi. That's when…

Something tried to pull away in my chest and…I couldn't breathe.

But he'd run down six flights of stairs.

Did Dad have heart problems?

He pinched the skin around his middle. No fat there.

Nah! I'm in great shape. Outrun Lora, and she's a jock.

Maybe I was stressed about being on time. Last time they were pissed about holding the plane.

But this time he'd been ten minutes early. *Brownie points!*

He sighed and muttered, "Probably too many double-shot espressos."

To be safe, better let Doc check me out.

He put it out of his mind as he entered the lab, where Jesse was already "plugged in" and working behind the Plexiglas walls of the top-secret Class IV bio-safety lab. The protective moon suit worn inside the lab required constant cooling and positive pressure through an air hose attached to the suit. If anyone tore a hole in a suit, no nasties got in, but were blown out of the way until the technician could get into the debugging station for wash-down. To allow maximum movement with minimum interference, the air hose "plugged in" at the side of the butt of the suit—resulting in many sexual innuendos.

Alex placed the hockey-puck titanium disc from the false bottom of his Starbucks cup into the air-locked slide drawer on the outside of the Plexiglas room. One touch of the green button above the drawer and the drawer closed, making a hissing sound. Sterilization started. He suited up, plugged in, and joined Jesse inside. The suit was bulky, his walk slow and careful. He stopped on his side of the work box and studied her.

She was manipulating a container of mosquitoes inside the airtight work box, which looked like a huge aquarium with holes on either side for arm-length, accordion-type gloves.

"So, Jesse, what's the deal with the bugs? I thought we were looking at aerosols."

"M.C. asked me for a more directed attack vehicle, something that could be contained and destroyed after the initial delivery. So we started working with the combinations of smallpox and plague, and smallpox and yellow fever. In tropical countries like India or Southeast Asia, we could use the mosquito to deliver the smallpox-yellow fever combo. In most other places, we could use the rat flea to deliver the plague combo. So the idea is to get a type of smallpox that is not airborne but only infects those bitten by the mosquito or flea. That way we can have a more controlled biological weapon. Kill the big bugs and we stop the little bugs."

A voice crackled over their headsets. "That's right, Jesse."

The voice was that of their procedure manager, M.C., also known as Master Chief George Baar, a retired E-9 Navy corpsman. His training had been in Environmental and Preventive Medicine, but as an independent duty corpsman he'd delivered a baby in Germany and put chest tubes in Navy Seals while stationed in Scotland. His claim to fame came when he almost single-handedly developed a better vaccine for smallpox. It had virtually no side effects and was effective for twenty years.

M.C.'s bald, bullet-shaped head beamed as brightly as his humor. Built like a fireplug, he was stronger than two oxen. Yet his Jay Leno comments over the intercom kept the tedious work from becoming stale, getting maximum work out of everyone in minimum time. Despite constantly cracking jokes, he never missed anything.

"All right you two, quit yabberin' and get to work. We got miles to go before we sleep. I checked out everything early this morning. It seems like all systems are go after that tremor we had last night. So move it."

From Alabama and with a deep, slow, Southern drawl, M.C. fooled many into thinking he was just a slow, dumb good ol' boy. Alex had seen many a surprised face when they discovered too late that M.C.'s knowledge of viral microbiology left them in the dust.

Jesse glanced over her shoulder. "Hey, M.C., Alex just got here. Give him a break."

"Oh, the poor baby. Maybe I should get him grits and eggs, fresh-squoze OJ, a cute little señorita, and let him go back to bed."

"He's almost married. He wouldn't go for another woman."

"That never stopped *you*. Maybe we should give you a new Apache name. I got it—*Mare in Heat*."

"Hey, you two," Alex said, "I can talk for myself. First, the señorita is a nice touch, M.C., but Lora would castrate you first, then me. Second, I prefer Y. It leaves more up to the imagination. And third, I'm wide-awake, ready to rock and roll. What's the problem sequence that's keeping us from getting this splice?"

"It's the two nucleotides from the tag end that are giving us problems," Jesse said. "For some reason we are not able to break off the guanine cleanly."

"Let's try this new enzyme I brought you from Main Lab. It should do the trick." Alex put the disk from his coffee cup into another air-locked drawer. The drawer closed and hissed and the disk was now inside the work box. He put his arms into the accordion gloves and grabbed the disk. After he pushed one of the top squares, a drawer opened in the disk, revealing a small capsule. He opened it with precision hemostats and dropped the contents into the soup inside the metal test tube containing the recombinant agents.

During the concentrated work that followed, M.C. noticed Alex constantly used more air conditioning than Jesse. When M.C. confronted him about it, Alex passed it off by saying he might have a little cold. M.C. got more concerned when Alex's voice became strained and his movements quick and fidgety.

At 9:43 a.m., M.C. noted Alex's forehead beading with sweat, and at 9:45 a.m. Alex cried out, as if in pain. His knees buckled, and he fell over onto Jesse, unconscious. She was looking right at him and caught his fall.

"M.C.!"

"On my way, Jesse. I been eye-balling him all morning. Not good. Not good at all."

—

Forty-five minutes earlier, at 8:00 a.m. New York time, Lora had finished her preparation and decided to go up to the roof of the North Tower to clear her mind.

The cool air and cloudless sky was exactly what she needed. In the distance, cars drove over the Brooklyn Bridge like toys in an erector set, some slow, other stopped. Planes took off from La Guardia. Their distant roar made her wish she could be sitting inside, sipping bottled water, travelling to visit Alex.

But she must stay. This meeting was extremely important. All the doctors she had interviewed agreed: The insurance companies, Medicare, and coding had changed medicine from a helping profession to a multibillion-dollar business, and everyone wanted a piece. To get any of the pie, doctors had to be more concerned about "getting the code right" than taking care of the patient.

Her project could change all that, starting a new era in medicine. Doctors and pharmacists would have time to talk with patients about their medication. Insurance companies would get the formulary medicines prescribed the first time. And most of all, the errors prevented would save countless lives and heartache.

The beta test sites had gone smoothly. The encryption was finally working well. This morning was the finale. She needed to get the Palm Pilot and other PDA gurus to fund a major trial.

If there was no Nobel Prize in this, Lora would at least know in her heart that she had changed the world of medicine for the better.

One last look at that New York City skyline and she walked down the stairs. No elevator for her. Get her heart pumping before the meeting.

Promptly at 8:30 a.m., the meeting began. Lora started her slide show.

At exactly 8:45 a.m., she was just beginning to present the connecting link for the software when there was a loud crash, a flash of light—and the room split in two. Lora and her crew were on one side of the split, the PDA guys on the other. Lora screamed and managed to grab her laptop just before the floor dropped into oblivion.

A large silvery convex surface replaced the middle of the floor, moving up and through the room like some futuristic conveyor belt. Only, this belt was impossible to stand on because it was disintegrating. Then Lora felt the heat. The PDA guys' clothes burst into flames.

Lora's backward tap-dance became a pivot and dive for the exit stairs. After slamming the door shut she ran down the stairs. They started crumbling under her feet. After two flights, the stairs disappeared completely, ending her dream to save medicine.

CHAPTER 5

M.C. suited up and entered the chamber. Jesse stared at him. "You don't think…?"

"We always have to think that, Jesse." M.C. rolled Alex onto his side, feeling for a pulse and watching for breathing.

"Infected with one of our viruses? That's not possible—not with the precautions we take. Call it woman's intuition, but I think it has something to do with Lora. Though he did say he was going to see Doc today for something."

"Doc's on his way." M.C. log-rolled Alex onto the special sickbay gurney. He pulled the straps tight and activated the gurney-buckling mechanism. The gurney buckled slowly until Alex sat in a wheelchair, the butt hose ready for easy detachment. This had been developed for the tight quarters they worked in. Wheeling him into the sanitizing vestibule, M.C. quickly popped off the butt hose and moved Alex down the hall through a very tight turn to a ten by ten-foot cubicle with white walls, floor, and ceiling; one dangling shower head on a flexible hose; a metal chair; and an IV bag of fluid hanging from a hook and metal shelf of sterilized emergency equipment. Doc stood by the equipment, already suited.

Dr. Michael Fox had met M.C. years ago when working on the DNA sequence of smallpox. Short, chipper, and from a small Mississippi town, Doc was immediately nicknamed "Doc Hollywood" by M.C.

Doc hit a button and the wheelchair unbuckled. He and M.C. lifted the gurney to waist height while the legs unfolded and locked. They stripped away Alex's suit.

"M.C., I need the video of the event. Now!" Doc started examining Alex.

M.C. responded in rapid-fire sentences. "There's not much to see. I was watching him like a hawk. He started sweating, made a little yell, then fainted. Pulse and respers were 45 and 24. Pupes reactive and equal. He was acting a bit fidgety and used his A/C more than Jesse., which was pretty unusual…said he had a cold. Jesse said she thought it was something to do with Lora, not a cold. Not that her little 'woman's intuition' thing means anything to me. But I've known a lot of Indians in my time, and they could pick up on things I couldn't."

"You know I'd trust your observation any day. But I still want to look at the video. Those hi-res recordings pick up more than human eye or ears."

"No prob. I'll get it." M.C. left.

Doc took Alex's pulse again, and murmured to himself, "Your pulse is coming up, mine coming down: symmetry. I like that."

"What the f—" Alex's speech was slurred and he was tugging at the oxygen mask. "Hey, no needles. I'm fine."

Alex sat upright.

Doc jerked back the IV he was about to insert. "Take it easy, Alex. Tell me what happened in there. You scared the heck out of us."

"I don't really know. Something in the pit of my stomach, like bottoming out in a roller coaster. Lora's face flashed in my mind, I felt real hot, and then everything went black. I guess it must be this cold."

Was it a cold? Alex thought. He squinted, trying to bring a distant object into focus in his mind.

Doc lifted the head of the gurney and gestured for Alex to lay back. After Alex was settled, Doc pulled the metal chair around, the legs making a harsh chattering sound. He sat and looked at Alex.

Alex knew that look. Doc's breathing was inaudible, his face calm. Almost like he was in a trance. But Doc was actually hyper-vigilant, keenly aware of any change in the emotional current of his patient, calmly waiting for the best approach.

Alex closed his eyes and sighed.

"So," Doc said, "has this got anything to do with your call earlier this morning?"

Alex opened his eyes. *He's going to think I am crazy. But I've got to tell him.*

"You know I said my bod was sending out messages I didn't under-stand?" He paused. Doc's eyes were calm and friendly. They helped you… no, *made* you tell your darkest secrets. "Well, I think this is like…like a signal. When I left New York a few days ago, I felt the same sensation in my stomach when I said goodbye to Lora. Like that was a warning and this is the real thing. Only…I don't know what the real thing *is*. But now I feel like there is an empty spot in my chi." He placed his fist on his sternum. "Right here."

"Did you ever feel this way before yesterday?" Doc's words were soft, yet firm and very distinct. As he spoke he focused intently on Alex's eyes.

Alex felt like when he'd been caught smoking in the bathroom in high school. "Maybe." He half-closed his eyes, and a faint, almost impercep-tible hum resonated from his throat. "Doc, I haven't had these feeling since I was a kid. My mom said I kind of knew things."

"Knew things?"

"When I was little, my mom always said I could predict the future, at least for people I was close to. Like my Aunt Macy. When I was about ten, I had that same feeling in my gut, and in my mind I saw a car crash. So I told her to be really careful when she drove around the bend at old man Caruthers's place. She looked at me like I was nuts, and told me that she had no intention of driving there. But later that day, she *did* drive that road. When she came around the bend, a deer ran in front of her. She told me she was thinking of what I told her, and slowed down a minute before the deer jumped out. She gave me a big kiss and thanked me for saving her life."

Doc said nothing.

"Mom said I'd known things before. But that's the only one I really remember. I don't remember anything quite as strong as that until now. I had a few twinges, sure, but nothing that ever knocked me out."

Doc sat still and looked at Alex.

Alex shook his head. "I know I'm supposed to be a scientist and not believe in mumbo jumbo crap like seeing into the future. But it's the only thing that makes sense. What do you think happened to me, Doc?"

Doc raised one eyebrow.

Alex sat up again. "No. Definitely not. No way."

"Alex, you know we have to treat this like an infection. Probably hallucinations caused by viremia. You're still emotionally tied up with Lora, so you naturally went there."

Doc shook his head and sighed. "But after that damn dog Fang… He was… Well, I don't know what to think."

"Oh yeah. Fang. But he got bit. I never did."

"You work with those screwy viruses all the time."

Alex shook his head. "Jesse's been working with them more than me, and she took care of Fang. She's not having any problems."

"Jesse's all right. But you're not. You're going to lay low in isolation for a little while. We'll see how you feel in a couple of days. Okay?"

"Yeah, okay, Doc, whatever you say. I still feel weird. Maybe I just need a little rest." He laid back down, disappointed. He wanted to finish this job quickly. Patagonia was calling.

"I'll be back in a bit." Doc said. "After I check on Jesse."

As Doc entered the lab, Jesse jumped up, dark eyes searching his face.

"How do you feel, Jesse?" She studied his lips, every word.

"Fine, Doc, just fine." She glanced nervously towards Alex in the other room, then back again. "It's not only him. There is something…else."

"What do you mean?"

"The circle has been broken."

Doc scratched his head. "Circle?"

She glared at him. "You know exactly what I'm talking about."

He shook his head and left her to work.

CHAPTER 6

Alex was like a big cat in a cage, pacing back and forth in isolation for a week. But the entire compound was isolated. Though the "little tremor" Alex had felt the night he arrived was not unlike others over the last year, it had knocked out communications and killed the elevator so they couldn't get to the one working satellite phone on the upper level. One measly sat phone. La Riva Labs was indeed cheap. When M.C. had pressured them for a back-up, they sent one two months ago, a lousy one that had been used in one too many jungle missions. It had stopped working a week ago.

M.C. worked on repairing the elevator and every day said they were closer to getting to the phone, though it was taking much longer because of toxic gases in the shaft.

It was always some damn thing in South America. Last year, a downpour had shorted out the radios and the sat phone. They'd had no word from the outside for two weeks.

Doc checked on Alex twice a day and tried to get him to relax, without much success. Doc usually started talking fly tying and fishing. Alex always ended with Lora.

On September 18, his last day in isolation, Doc finished his examination on Alex and said, "It's a little funny really."

"What do you mean?"

"Fly tying. It's bizarre. Tying feathers and fur on hooks and then throwing them out on the water."

"Yeah, it's even stranger when you talk to someone who doesn't have the passion."

Doc nodded.

"I think you said it best when you explained it to Jesse." Like most Apache, she did not understand catch and release. Apache only fished for food.

"What do you mean?"

Alex imitated Doc, placing one hand on his hip and tilting his head. He spoke with his best Doc voice, distinguished and erudite: "It gives me great peace, casting my inspirations into currents and eddies, besting the wild trout."

Doc paused, his eyes seeming to focus on reading a distant river for signs of a rise. He sighed. "Yep…"

No chuckle. No, "That was a good one, Alex." Nothing.

Alex squinted and frowned. "Damn, Doc. You gotta get out more."

Doc shrugged. "Right. All your blood tests and exams have been normal. I'll let you out. But stay away from the live viruses for now."

Alex buttoned his shirt, still smiling. "Thanks, Doc. You're my hero." He tucked in his shirt and zipped up his pants and stuck his hands in his pockets. "Sorry to keep bugging you, but I really feel like something happened to Lora. Any word on the phone?"

Doc typed on the computer keyboard.

Alex took his hands out of his pockets and watched Doc type. He put his hands back in his pockets. "Hello."

Doc looked up as if unsure where the voice had come from. "Sure. Yes. M.C. said the elevator might be fixed today. Let me give him a call. And if it's fixed I'll personally get the sat phone. I think it's in the admin office. In the meantime, you help Jesse with the sequencing on the computer—the *computer*, no suiting up. I'll give you a buzz on the intercom when I'm ready. Stay away from the live viruses. Okay?"

Alex went to Doc and gave him a hug. "Thanks, Doc. I'll get with Jesse. But I don't think you need to worry about the viruses. I'm not infected."

Alex found Jesse in the computer lab, an eight by twelve room with three state-of-the-art computers lined up on a shelf jutting from the long wall, a printer on a shelf on the far wall, fluorescent ceiling lights, three metal chairs, and Jesse sitting in one facing a monitor.

"Hey, Jesse, Doc says I need to help you."

She frowned at the computer screen and kept typing.

Alex spoke louder, in his best John Wayne imitation. "Whatcha doin', liddle lady?"

She kept typing. Maybe he really wasn't here and this was a dream.

He was about to do the unthinkable, actually touch her shoulder, which might end up with her and him…

She glanced at him and rolled her eyes. "I've been wondering if your little fit was caused by infection with an airborne virus. So I'm checking to see if any of our little babies have airborne qualities."

He smiled, wishing she had let him touch her. *That's Jesse—always trying different angles—and usually my angles too.* "You know, I've been mulling that over too, but I don't think that's it. I think—"

A strong tremor shook the room. He stumbled forward and grabbed her by both shoulders.

Doc had to go through several levels of decontamination before he could leave the lab; during the last two levels he had to be naked. The drying breeze on his bare skin made him think of beaches and one particular woman: tan, long legs, and still waiting. After that last air lock, he snatched street clothes from his locker and almost jumped into them to cover his excitement.

He picked up the in-house phone. "M.C., Alex is about to drive me nuts. Is the elevator fixed? I need to get the sat phone so he can call Lora."

"As it turns out, I made an empty trial run a few minutes ago. It should be fine. You want me to go with you?

"I think I can manage, thanks. When will the com lines be back up?"

"That's still a day away." M.C sounded dejected.

"Hey, we all know you're doing the best you can. At least we'll have the sat phone."

Doc ended the call and entered the elevator. A jolt halted the elevator halfway up. After a few minutes of failed button pushing, he mumbled, "Earthquakes and old elevators: a bad combo." Being this close to Peru, they got their share of quakes. He hoped it was only that.

He pushed up on the roof access panel and crinkled his nose at a rotten-egg smell. The haze in the elevator shaft obliterated all but twenty feet of visibility.

The only thing to do was climb the ladder in the shaft. It would only take a few minutes.

CHAPTER 7

It had taken a long, frustrating week for Jabril to get to Jakarta. The celebration in the desert after the Great Event seemed like months ago. At the last airport he had watched a television commercial of a woman in some sparkling U.S. city, placing a Band-Aid on her son's skinned knee at a playground, kissing his forehead and hugging him. Jabril had squeezed his eyes shut and clenched his fists and nearly punched the TV. The infidels had ripped his mother from him. No more Band-Aids. No more kisses. No more life. For that they would die. All of them. Women. Children. Every last one. End the West. Now!

He had unclenched his fists and taken in a few deep breaths, letting them out slowly. But the frustrations of the last few days would not disappear. He had waited so long, had planned so carefully, from Iraq to Europe to Arizona to Afghanistan. Yet it seemed he had to wait a bit more. All international air travel had been slowed to a snail's pace. And with the heightened security, he had to arrange for smaller planes in private airports.

He had finally arrived in Jakarta International Airport early this morning with washed face, combed hair and tailored suit, expecting an immediate pick-up. And here he was, waiting again. One of the security guards kept glancing at him. The sun would soon be up and Jabril needed to pray. His anger grew by the minute.

The limousine arrived and the driver shuffled out, eyes downcast.

"What kept you so long?" Jabril said. "I have been sweating here for over an hour. The water is putrid, and the food is only fit for dogs."

The driver bowed his head. "I am sorry, sir. I have good food and drink in the car. I was held up by all the new inspections since the Great Event. Even in Jakarta the infidels are powerful. We must be careful. There is a file about the new holy weapon on the back seat. And we have a woman for you. She was chosen from many at the auction in Manila and flown in last night."

"Hey, you!" The security guard yelled. The guard really wanted to smile at the dark man's frown of frustration, but he kept his face stern. Timed that yell perfectly, though—just before the guy got into the limo. You just had to be patient. The guard was a big man, tall and muscular, which by itself was threatening. And even though he had shaved clean only hours ago, he knew he already had a heavy shadow, which he also knew made him more threatening. This and his dark eyes and hair might give the thin man the impression he was from India. With better light the man might see that the guard's eyes were too hazel, his face too square, his body too solid, and his close-cropped hair too curly. If the guard were to take off his shirt, the man would become even more alarmed at the Special Forces tattoo on his inner left biceps. And even though the guard would enjoy even more alarm in this dark, definitely Arabic-looking fellow, Salvatore Sebastiano Rocca was damn sure not taking off his shirt.

Rocca, or Rock to his friends, was a former U.S. Army Special Forces sergeant and, though usually pleasant, was dehydrated, tired, and edgy. After Desert Storm, he'd left the service and joined a security agency that guarded Jakarta International Airport, looking for "anything suspicious." And now, after a brutal week of sixteen-on and eight-off, he thought he might have something.

Besides being beat from the long hours, he was punchy from diarrhea that had kept him up the last two nights. Yet he was sure this dark thin man was up to no good.

Why would you fly into this hellhole at 0100 and wait for an hour, ignoring all the taxis?

This guy, with only a small briefcase for luggage, had sat outside, sweating and swatting at the moth-sized mosquitoes, looking more pissed off with each passing minute. Then the limo showed up—black instead of the usual white. The license plate had some unusual symbols—a sword and a long rectangle.

Rocca repeated himself, louder. "Yeah, I mean you. I need to see some papers or identification."

The man turned slowly, and looked so scared and meek that Rocca immediately felt a slight twinge of regret at raising his voice. Had he misjudged this Arab?

Behind Jabril the driver whispered, "I will deal with him, sir."

Jabril spoke under his breath at the driver. "You are not capable. Do not move."

Jabril walked toward the guard, calm and deferential, holding up his papers, smiling, with steady eye contact. "I am sorry, sir. My driver was late and I should have immediately presented my papers to you. I am here on some pressing business trying to get more oil for my American friends. We have some wells here that my cousins in Scotland wanted me to look into."

Rocca scrutinized the papers. *It all checks out. BP does have some wells here. Photo matches. George Issam? Have to let him go. Check out the license plate later.*

"Okay, Mr. Issam, sorry I got so uptight. Where do your cousins live, anyhow?"

"Oh, they are from around Aberdeen. The weather will get nasty up there soon, so we need to get more oil flowing from our southern wells. Since I have connections down here, I was elected to come to this sweat box. I prefer Aberdeen myself."

"Yeah, I visited there once. Getting cool in Perthshire this time of year."

"You mean Aberdeenshire, don't you?" corrected Jabril.

"Oh yeah. Sure. My bad. Weird names to those counties. Guess I mixed them up. You have a nice trip. And don't forget to check back with us on your way out. How long are you going to be here?"

"A day or two should complete my business. I will be sure to look you up on my way out." Jabril nodded, then turned to get in the limousine.

"You do that, Mr. Issam. Look forward to seeing you then." *You may know Scotland, and your papers look good, but you're still on my list, buddy.*

Rocca brought his clipboard up a little higher, feigning making notes, but really allowing for a better angle to snap a picture with a hidden camera. He made sure he got a good face shot.

I've seen that face somewhere...

He would send the picture and the license plate back to headquarters. *Right after I catch a few hours of sleep.*

CHAPTER 8

Rachel was finishing her last day in the back country, rested, happy and ready to get back to work. The ruse with Tasha had paid off—no interruptions for a week.

Yet there was a tickle of concern. Three days ago she'd found a hill where cell coverage was adequate and tried Scott again—still no answer. The low battery light blinked and she left a message, but the phone died before she was done. *He did say he would be busy.*

Goose bumps prickled her arms from the chill of the early predawn hour. Fall had set in last week, with aspens starting to turn and the occasional morning frost. There were even two gray days of sleet and a dusting of snow. But the last few days had been a true Indian summer, with crisp nights and warm days. She was in short sleeves by the afternoon. The brook trout had been rising to hoppers, big flies she'd tied last week. She kept a few of the fish and fried them for supper, the most delicious pink meat she'd ever had. It was a good thing, too. Four days ago she had had a misstep and slid a good hundred feet down on loose shale, losing half her supplies over a cliff. If she hadn't caught those fish she'd probably have packed out two days ago.

Those days of gray cold and sleet had made her hunger hard to bear, and her concentration had waned, and thinking about food instead of f-stops, she'd missed it.

A mountain lion.

After waiting an hour in a camouflaged blind before dawn, she had dozed off and missed it. The biggest cat native to North America, it was one of the big three animals she admired and feared most in the high country. Moose and grizzly mamas with young were unpredictable, and mean when encountered. But the lanky, tawny-colored cat would calmly stalk you for miles, moving like wind through grass, waiting for the right moment. Then, *wham!* You were cat food.

At least, that's what all the land-locked *Jaws* movie buffs said.

Usually, though, in her series of somewhat under a thousand cases—five, to be exact—the cat had come and gone so fast that she was lucky to get two photos. They were so nocturnal that it was rare to get a shot of them, except maybe at false dawn or by accident. That's when she'd got hers. The first shot was of the back of a head when she'd been hiking up to Dream Lake for a dawn shot. A year later, she had taken a group of star gazers up Royal Arch Trail at Chautauqua Park in Boulder, and on the way down a deer ran across their trail. She'd had her camera out for sunset, and was adjusting it for the deer when the lion appeared on the trail, probably chasing its favorite meal. Before she had a chance to think of the danger she clicked off three photos. Luckily the flash scared the lion and it fled. The stargazers clapped. Her heart started pounding and they almost ran the rest of the way down the trail to their cars. The photo was framed on her mantle at home—a full side view with the cat looking into the camera the second she snapped the shutter. Still a bit of white and red in the pupils, but who cared? It was a mountain lion.

She'd not been as lucky with this one. She'd been so hungry and cold that, by the time she fumbled the camera up, all that was left was the flicking black end of its tail as it rounded a boulder and slunk off.

Then there were the dreams. Maybe it was from seeing one too many bighorn ewes mounted by a ram, but she was getting horny. The dream last night was *too* real: everything but the face. She'd felt him inside and the slow but gradual tension, mounting. His face had been close, his smell wonderful, his sweat slick. But when she looked at his face it was a blur. Or was it? It was too much like Alex to be Scott. She had awakened with goose bumps.

Mmmmmh! That was really good, whoever it was.

Alex… There was something about him. The song "Bad Boys" by Whitesnake played in her head. She'd hated ending it with him six months ago. But she'd already had trouble dating a previous coworker. Not this time.

And now she was committed to Scott. Or was she?

One thing was for sure—whoever was in that dream had made her morning more complicated. Airing out the sleeping bag would take extra time. She was used to her slow, easy morning routine, and now she'd have to hurry to break camp, cover her tracks, and get down the mountain to catch her flight.

Ah, shit. Wish I could stay longer.

Her mind was fresh, like a beaver pond after a mountain thunderstorm, ready to get back to her little creatures…and to some serious sex.

Was the dream of Alex?

She wondered how he was doing down in that hot, humid shit-hole in South America. Why did he go down there? Maybe it was to get away from Rachel. Maybe it was to get closer to Jesse. She oozed sex around Alex.

Forget Alex. You're almost engaged to Scott.

Next week was already planned: a stashed bottle of Pinot, a hot, spaghetti-strapped red dress, and a black thong that could barely be seen through the dress. It should drive Scott wild while they were eating.

Why eat first?

Then she remembered the sleeping bag needed airing. It could wait.

She packed quickly and trekked down the mountainside.

Walking out of the last clump of pines at 7:00 a.m. on September 18, she was greeted by the sight of her trusty old friend, the Scout, parked in the shade of several pine trees. It had never let her down, despite many bumps in the road.

But who is that standing around my truck? A park ranger and someone else…Jesus Christ! Is that camouflage?

CHAPTER 9

"Rachel Lane?" the camouflaged guy asked. He was medium height with short, sandy hair, graying at the temples, and interesting tan eyes that had a hint of sadness.

"Who are you and what the hell are you doing in this park dressed in camouflage? Don't you know it's against the law to hunt the animals here?"

She willed her gaze to cut into his brain. Despite her love (surely it was that) for Scott, she was not fond of the military. And hunters in camouflage? In her park? Shoot 'em. Better yet, hang 'em.

"Miss Lane, I'm Sergeant Prescott, and this is *desert* camouflage." He showed her his ID "I'm from the Pentagon. You've been out of touch. Why don't you sit down? We have chairs. How about over here in the shade?"

"Can't this wait? I have to hurry to catch my flight at DIA. Maybe you could tell me on the way."

"Please, Miss Lane. Please, sit down. You won't be late. We have a jet waiting for us at Buckley. Been a long two days trying to find you. Things didn't add up 'til we talked to Ms. Tasha Flanders. She led us here. Luckily a ranger remembered your photo, but as 'Toni Jasper,' a photographer on a back-country pass. You really wanted to stay hidden, didn't you?"

She looked him over. *Seems genuine—clipped hair and speech of an army sergeant.*

The park ranger eyed the fold-out chairs as if they were the answer to everything.

"Okay, I'll sit. It was a long hike anyway. Now, what the fuck is going on?"

Prescott waited for her to sit. Then he sat, looking very much like he was sitting on tacks. "Would you like coffee or water?"

"Look! Would you stop the social niceties and get on with it?"

He looked her straight in the eyes. "I have bad news. Scott Jacobs was killed in a terrorist attack on the Pentagon. He was working on some pretty top-secret stuff…stuff related to what you are working on at La Riva. The DoD thought you needed protection. Did you know that Scott was working on the same things you were?"

She stared at the sergeant. "What?"

"Your fiancé, Major Scott Jacobs, was killed in a terrorist attack on the Pentagon. They dove a plane into it."

She blinked a few times, stretched her back and shrugged and wrung her hands. "That's not possible."

He handed her a bottle of water. She unscrewed the top, started to raise the bottle, stopped, then blurted. "Scott was killed? Jesus. What the hell happened? I thought he was safe in the Pentagon. You said a plane hit something. What? And don't tell me the Pentagon. That…no way."

Prescott's eyes softened. "God knows it's hard to believe, but terrorists hijacked a 757 and rammed it into the Pentagon. Scott was working there and died instantly. I've been ordered to take you back until we can sort this out."

As he talked, Rachel focused on the distant hills. She got up. She sat. The water sloshed out of the bottle onto her legs. She continue to gaze into the distance. Prescott gently took the bottle from her. She put her head in her hands and sobbed.

As suddenly as the tears started, they stopped. Lifting her head, she caught Prescott's sad look, gritted her teeth and stared him down. She wanted to reach out and strangle him.

Prescott sat straighter and looked away.

She began a continuous, staccato verbal assault. "Scott's dead? You're sure? How could a plane run into the Pentagon? Don't they have some kind of early warning radar or anti-aircraft guns to prevent that? For Christ's sake, didn't they think someone might try something like that? After all, the Pentagon has a fair concentration of military intelligence, if you want to call it that, not to mention *personnel*. And what—you think Scott would talk about top secret work with me over dinner? Or maybe

I would make him whisper secrets during sex? Boy, you guys have a lot to learn. No wonder Scott was planning to get out soon. Let me see that fucking ID again. And the ranger's too, if I'm going to be your prisoner."

She stopped and rubbed her forehead with three fingers, trying to force her brain to work. Her head felt detached, floating. She put her elbows on her knees and leaned over, covered her face in her hands, but would not allow herself to cry in front of these two. Not again.

Prescott felt a smile begin, but he quickly stiffened his face. This woman was not only beautiful, she was strong and he liked that in her, but if he smiled she might think the wrong thing. "Why don't you examine our IDs until you're comfortable? You are *not* my prisoner. I'm here to protect you. I'm not sure that's necessary, but I have my orders. The ranger here will take care of your vehicle if you will give him the keys. I can explain it all on the way back."

She wiped her nose on her sleeve and examined the cards and waved them off. *Probably handcuff me if I say no.*

She handed the keys to the ranger. "That is not just a *vehicle*. That is a one-of-a-kind Scout, considered an antique, but it can out four-wheel any other modern vehicle today. So take care of that Scout for me, Ranger Ricky."

"Actually, I go by Richard. And I know all about Scouts."

"Of course you do." She eased into the Sergeant's car.

Prescott smirked at the ranger's reflection in the rearview mirror and shifted his weight to make the cuffs in his back pocket more comfortable. He wondered how the hell he would have cuffed her if she had refused to come.

CHAPTER 10

Jabril glared at the back of the limousine driver's head. *Fool! You're all idiots. But that guard was no fool. I will need another way out, and soon.*

He looked at the doe-eyed woman sitting across the seat in a green silk gown and light blue head scarf.

This woman…beautiful. Ash-brown eyes. Appropriately covered. Seen and not heard. Refreshing. They had chosen well at the auction.

He put down the report on El Husam, the new weapon. He could not concentrate. The woman stared out the window, her curves inviting.

How long had it been? Two months? The women at camp had been harsh and unyielding. But this one is quiet, and seems obedient.

He pushed a button, rolling up the opaque, soundproof divider between him and the driver. He yanked the gown off the woman's shoulders, laughing at her astonishment. Her breasts were small, but oh, how perfectly formed, with skin a wonderful, tawny gold. He devoured her, squeezing and sucking until she cried out, then undid his pants and demanded she take him in her mouth. Forcing her head down he roared with pleasure even as she gagged. He was still so excited he flipped her over, ripped her panties down and rammed her from behind. She screamed with alarm. He grabbed her head, twisting it around to clamp a hand on her mouth, muffling her screams. She wriggled, trying to escape. He squeezed and twisted her head further, and, despite feeling a *crack* in his hands, he came again, over and over. He pulled out. Her body was limp, head flopped to the side. Lifeless doll's eyes stared at him. He must have broken her neck.

What have I become?

Her sphincter let go. The smell was overpowering. He covered his nose with his sleeve. *Must wash. Must pray. Must…No matter.*

NO MATTER!

She is part of the path to power. I do have the power. It is good.

Is it?

Yes.

Moving robotically, he covered her with her gown, opened an alcohol wipe, methodically cleaned himself, and then gently laid the towelette on her face.

He zipped his pants, buckled the belt, sat up straight and said a prayer over her body. Without thinking, he took out his checkbook, wrote one for twenty-thousand dinar, tore it out, and placed it in his shirt chest pocket. He returned the checkbook and went back to reading the report, now able to concentrate perfectly.

An hour later the car slowed, passed through a fenced guard house, and stopped in front of a one-story gray brick building.

When the driver opened Jabril's door, he peered at the woman and covered his nose.

Jabril got out, smoothed his pants, and then held out the check.

"She performed Allah's will. Unfortunately she was too frail. Please give my apologies to her family and deposit this check in their account. Make sure you tell them she was instrumental in the creation of a new world. She died doing Allah's will. Her ministrations helped me become more alert so I could discern this new weapon in its fullest glory. Is this the place?"

Jabril fixed the driver's gaze in his own, willing a look of complete calm. He could not afford emotions. There were too many things to do.

The driver froze, his eyes wide, forcing his answer, "Y-y-yes sir, the door to the right. They are waiting."

Jabril chose his words and tone carefully, observing the driver's response to each syllable. There could be no mistakes now. "Get rid of her body and clean up this mess quickly. This must not be discovered. If it is, you will die, too. Also, I cannot risk going back to the airport. Call Mustafa. I will be ready for his helicopter in four hours…make that three-and-a-half. Do you understand?"

The driver nodded. He closed Jabril's door and covered his nose.

Though the volume of his voice remained quiet, the tone became acid: "Answer me. Do you understand?"

The driver blurted, "Yes, it will be done as you wish, sire." He bowed to Jabril.

Jabril smiled. *That is good: "sire" and bowing.* "Don't forget the food in the trunk. I will need it. Now, go!"

The driver was already scurrying around the limo.

Jabril turned and tapped in the code on the keypad lock by the door. As he opened the door, an armed guard greeted him with a deferential lowering of eyes and nod of his head. Jabril pointed to the package of food the driver had unloaded from the trunk. The guard grabbed it and led Jabril to the next room.

Though there was a window air conditioner, the room was close, humid, and pungent. Fear exuded from the man sitting alone in a chair.

CHAPTER 11

For the better part of an hour Rashid had been sitting on a high-backed aluminum chair sipping a glass of water. He stared at his laboratory through a pane of Plexiglas. Even though the laboratory was only three by four meters, it was his. Usually it gleamed with his efforts to keep it spotless. Today there were a few dirty test tubes, a Bunsen burner was on its side, a rubber hose dangling over a counter, splashes of water on the counter and floor. He wanted to clean it, but still he sat, holding the cell phone next to his heart. Though the battery was dead, holding it reassured him that there was another world outside. Perhaps his wife would feel his heartbeat through it.

He had not bathed for a week, losing interest in anything but talking to his wife. Before that, all he had known was work and the little shack he lived in next door. That had been enough, as long as he could talk with his wife. When that stopped, he became anxious. Then a fearful cloud enveloped him, paralyzing any action except staring into space.

Today his sweat oozed so much fear that he could taste it. Although he wanted to make a good impression, he had been unable to even comb his hair this morning. He felt like a lowly street cleaner from his home in Iraq.

A man entered the room. Rashid turned his eyes to him, eyes so dry and matted he could barely see. He vaguely remembered the purpose of this visit: a man of power, here to take Rashid's discovery to the minister and give Rashid his reward.

He stood, wiped his eyes with the heels of his hands, and faced the man. "Good morning, sir. I am Rashid El Hammed. I have made much progress and hope you will let me return to my homeland. Why can I not talk to my wife?"

Jabril could barely contain his disappointment. This was the scientist they had pinned their hopes on? Greasy hair smashed flat on one side, eyes dull and defeated, arms tightly wrapped over his chest. What should have been a white shirt was gray, the armpits and chest dark and outlined in a yellow map of old sweat stains. *Allah be with us.*

The loving father approach might work. He spoke softly to the scientist, "I am Colonel Jabril El Fahd, head of operations. Rashid, you have done important work here. Allah will reward you handsomely. We believe it is almost time to release these results to the rest of the world, and I am sure the world will also heap well-deserved praise on your shoulders. Security has necessitated that there be no contact outside the compound due to the sensitive nature of your work. But now that you are almost finished, it will be only days before you can talk with your wife. If all goes well, I will take you to her in my private plane, tonight. But I must see your work with my own eyes."

He let that sink in, then added, "But first, let us get you clean and fill you with food from home. You look like you have been working too hard. Have you lost weight? I have brought wonderful food from Baghdad, meticulously prepared by an exquisite chef."

He watched the scientist closely, pleased at the spark in the man's eyes. *Yes, be happy. Focus. I must know if your invention will work before moving forward.*

Rashid looked around the room and took a deep breath. The mention of seeing his wife was like a shot in the arm. He felt rejuvenated. The name *Jabril* sounded a chord through his haze—a very powerful man indeed. High enough in the government to make things happen. Perhaps a shower and good food would get him the boost he needed to impress this colonel. Long hours had weakened him. Sustenance would certainly improve his energy. He would then give Colonel Jabril a tour of tours so he could see his wife tonight. Oh how he missed her. She would be so proud of him.

"Thank you, Colonel. I will shower and shave. Forgive me for not being more presentable for your arrival. I was worrying about my work and my wife. The food here has been so stale and poorly cooked that I have not been interested in eating."

Jabril smiled. *Better.* He oozed empathy. "I understand perfectly. You have done much for your country and you are to be commended. I think you will enjoy the food. Go now, and return for a meal and discussion about your work. I must stay on a fairly rigid schedule, so could you be back in, say, thirty minutes?"

I must get out of Jakarta before that guard interferes.

Rashid bowed slightly. "Yes, Colonel. I will hurry. My stomach looks forward to good food, and I will give you all the information you need on my work."

He left quickly, a new lightness to his step, excitement he had not felt for a week.

Jabril watched Rashid leave, enjoying his power to transform this man so easily from a disheveled, dull-eyed crony to a servant who would climb a mountain for his country.

He addressed the guard, "Prepare the food."

After the guard left Jabril retrieved the tape recorder from his briefcase. A record of every word would be needed to reproduce this work in Baghdad.

Looking through the glass walls of the laboratory, he saw his mother dying in his arms with only the cold hospital walls surrounding them. Oh, how he yearned to see not thousands, but millions of Americans dying on CNN.

As Rashid showered and shaved, the shadow of doubt crept into his thoughts. Why would they send such a powerful man to go over his project? Then again, why wouldn't they? Rashid's accomplishment was unique. He had finally found the link between the Marburg virus and leukemia. The latitude he'd been allowed with failures had proven how important at least someone viewed his research. The Borna virus mutants were a failure. The Smallpox/Ebola combinations had only killed all the monkeys. After these failures, Rashid had worried that Jorge was sent to end his research. But he was only help, perhaps to prevent other failures. What a mistake. Jorge thought he'd found something, but it would never be used for medical purposes: Ebola that was spread by airborne particles—very nasty. Praise Allah for the quarantine freezer. He must ask the colonel to transfer those mistakes to an appropriate disposal unit. He wondered if the colonel's plane would have proper storage for the quarantine and separate containers for his new virus. Maybe he could name it after himself, the new Rashid-Marburg anti-leukemia virus. It had a certain ring to it.

Oh, to be home again. He dressed and glanced at his watch: only twenty minutes had passed.

Jabril was ready: the recorder plugged in and hidden, the laptop and scanner ready to immediately copy and upload the laboratory logs.

When Rashid entered, Jabril nodded at him and showed him the food. "Please enjoy."

Rashid sat and looked up at Jabril, timid.

Jabril opened his arms. "It's all yours. I have eaten."

The scientist began filling his plate while Jabril sat across from him, crossing his legs: patient. *That little Russian, Jorge, had better be right. He said a month with Rashid was all he needed. Then El Husam would be ready to strike at the very heart of the infidels.*

He sighed deeply; comfort filled him. *And I will twist the blade.*

Rashid devoured the food.

If Jorge was right, then Rashid will be…unnecessary. Especially with this recording and the scanned files.

He uncrossed his legs and sat forward. "I see this meal brings you pleasure. And you have returned looking refreshed from your shower. Please, if you can slow down in your meal, tell me of your accomplishments."

Rashid began his discourse. Jabril started the tape.

CHAPTER 12

Doc used the safety banister inside the elevator to boost himself up and open the ceiling door to the elevator shaft. He pulled and pushed himself onto the top of the elevator. It was hazy and hard to see. There was a dark scratch on the sidewall by the exit, probably a reminder of a measurement by an installer. His flashlight penetrated about five feet above his head into the grayish yellow mist. The odor reminded him of his dad and how his work clothes reeked of the paper mill, that slithering smell that got into everything—but mostly the gag center. "The smell of money in the South," Dad had said. That was the year he'd finished paying off Doc's college, then died of influenza. Viruses were hell.

Doc's eyes watered. He coughed. He wanted to throw up, but he had to get the sat phone for Alex. He started climbing. The temperature rose with each step. The quake must have opened a volcanic vent.

He stopped and blurted, "The viral containment systems." If the containment system had been knocked out by the power outage and the viruses had leaked into the ventilation system…

All the more reason to get the sat phone.

Another several steps and he was breathing hard, too hard, like he'd run a mile with a thirty-pound pack. Concentrating on every step, he pushed himself to climb one careful step after another. The sat phone was their lifeline.

He remembered the dark scratch on the side of the shaft. How far up had he come? He should have counted his steps.

Above, haze obscured any view. Or were his eyes not functioning? He gritted his teeth. Must go on.

His foot slipped. His forehead banged on two rungs before he caught himself with one hand. *Dang!* He wheezed out a cough.

His feet finally steadied on a rung. This was not good.

He moved back down, one careful and slow foot after another. They'd have to figure another way to get the sat phone.

"Aren't you satisfied yet?" Alex tried to sound as impatient as possible.

After he'd grabbed Jesse's shoulders during the tremor, he thought she might snap out of her research funk. But nothing seemed to work.

Jesse stared into space. There wasn't much of it in the computer room. Four close walls, three computers and a printer.

"Jesse, can you hear me now?" Alex asked louder, in the same tone as the Verizon TV commercial.

She turned her head, "Yeah. I keep thinking there must be something we missed."

"We've gone over this at least three times. No way we missed anything. My little fit, as you called it, was just a brain fart and won't happen again." He paused. "Enough about me. Let's get back to the real problem. The sooner we get these little gems doing the tango the sooner we can get on with our vacations. Where were we when I so rudely interrupted our progress?"

Jesse shook her head. "I know you don't want to think it could be one of these viruses, because that would mean you're contaminated and you'd be sent back to Main Lab. You would be studied, poked, prodded, bled, and MRI'd until you attracted metal. But if you're infected, we need to know sooner rather than later. Let's backtrack. When did you first start feeling funny?"

"Let's see. I guess my first funny feeling was when I was three years old. Those guys, Bert and Ernie, were hilarious. And then there was Big Bird."

Jesse's eyes widened and her lips scrunched. She shouted, "I—am—serious!"

"Come on, Jesse. I just want to forget about some of this stuff for a while…lose myself in the work, you know?"

"Yeah, I know. I also know you see my point. So, once again, when did you start feeling funny?"

Alex shrugged. *An Apache and a woman.* "If you insist. I first felt strange about a month ago. I was dizzy then, too. Thought I maybe drank too much the night before. Went away, so I was right. It happened again when I was leaving, right after I kissed Lora good-bye. But, like I was telling Doc, I had some of the same feelings when I was a kid, and back then I would say something ridiculous. I've literally had these weird feelings all my life. Maybe I got some heavy metal poisoning in Wyoming living next to oil wells. No way it could be from some recent infection."

Jesse squinted one eye. "Okay, so you've had funny feelings like this your whole life. But were they exactly like the one you had last week? Did you notice anything different?"

"I never fainted before. I only spouted my mouth off after the feeling came on, everybody made fun of me, and that was that." Alex tried not to look uncomfortable, but he was beginning to feel odd again.

"What do you mean you spouted your mouth off? When it happened to you as a kid you would say…what was it? 'Something ridiculous.' Did you say anything ridiculous to Doc?"

"Look, Jesse, I really would like to wait and go over this with Doc. He's the medical guy, and you are…a friend. Can you understand? Maybe we could get back to work while I'm feeling okay. If you want to put me back in isolation, I don't think it's necessary, but I'll go along with you until Doc gets back. Right now, though, I need to work."

All this talk about Lora. I don't feel so good. It wasn't that he missed her so much—and maybe that was what bothered him. He should miss her more. He should not be thinking about Rachel. He should not be wanting to touch Jesse. He sat down.

"Alex, you're *not* okay."

"Maybe I do need to stay in isolation."

"Lie down. I'll get Doc. Where did he get off to, anyhow?"

"He was going topside to get the phone so I could call Lora. He left a while ago, though. Should've been back by now."

Alex's legs gave out and he caught himself falling to the floor onto his side.

"Alex! Jesus! You are definitely *not* okay. Maybe M.C. can find Doc."

He closed his eyes. All he could think of was the dog Jesse had saved and then "sacrificed," the PC lab term for kill in order to autopsy. The "sacrifice" was not being able to continue studying a live animal. After being bit by one of their lab monkeys the dog had changed...changed into something awful and almost killed her.

Was he going to be like that dog?

CHAPTER 13

"M.C., are you there?" Jesse queried into the intercom wall speaker, keeping one eye on Alex.

No answer. M.C. had said he wanted to check on a few things and left pretty quickly. She'd been so engrossed with Alex that she'd missed exactly what he said. She tried again.

Nothing.

She frantically punched one button after the other, buzzing every room in the complex. Finally, he answered from the main control room. "Master Chief."

"Goddamn it, M.C. Where the hell have you been?"

"Taking care of problems." His tone was not the usual assuredness with a touch of jest. "The latest tremor screwed everything up, again, and more."

"What now? This is really getting old."

"We…" His voice was garbled. "The el…tor…is…st… And I think Do…s…in the shaf…"

"M.C.!" She shouted into the intercom. "I couldn't quite get all of that, but it sounded like you said the elevator is stuck and you think Doc is in the shaft. Is that right?"

"Yep, you go…it. And…op yelling wo…you. I can he…you jus…fine."

"M.C., I can't understand you. Change over to the sound-powered phones." She hated to use those antiquated phones, but they were exactly for this situation: backup.

"Aye, aye, Jesse. I tho…yo…never as…"

She released the sound-powered handset from a special bracket on the wall that kept it from being jarred loose. It looked like an ordinary black wall phone from the '60s, but in order to hear someone on the other line, the other operator had to push the handset button and speak loudly, slowly, and distinctly. The phones were all connected, so everyone on the circuit could talk and listen at the same time, like one of the old party lines.

To avoid confusion, there was a special operating procedure that M.C. had taught them. The first thing you said was your station or location; the second thing, who in the circuit you were addressing; and the third thing, your message: short and to the point.

When they first started practicing it sounded like this:

"Hey M.C., it's Jesse, in the main lab, and I want you to bring two cups of coffee as quick as you can."

"You have got to be kidding me," M.C. had scolded.

They finally got it down to the right sequence. "Main Lab, Admin. Please bring two cups of coffee here ASAP."

M.C. had answered, "Admin, Main Lab. Sorry, coffee is gone. Drink water."

And so it had gone, with M. C. drilling them each week with a refresher.

It was automatic now. "Main Lab, Control Room. Do you read?" She released the talk button.

His answer was crisp and easily heard. "Control Room, Main Lab. I read loud and clear. I repeat previous message. Main elevator stuck. Doc not in elevator. He may be in shaft. I will ring elevator shaft now. Stand by and stay on-line."

She glanced over at Alex who seemed to be getting his color back. "Are you feeling better?"

"Yeah, I'm good. What's going on with Doc?"

She held her hand up. "Wait a minute. Main Lab, Control Room. Okee-dokee."

She knew M.C. wanted to growl at her for not answering *aye-aye*, but instead he said, "Control Room, Elevator Shaft. Do you read?"

They both waited…

M.C. tried again. "Control Room, Elevator Shaft. Doc, do you read me?"

—

Doc was gradually moving down when a sound like a bird whooping echoed in the shaft.

He peered around briefly and climbed down twenty more feet. The sound came again, this time deafeningly. He jerked his head to the right. On the wall, there was a metal plate with hinges and a flush handle. The *whoop* was coming from inside.

Then he remembered. There was a sound-powered phone in that box for emergencies in the shaft. M.C. had made sure of having one at every level.

Doc turned the handle, yanked open the door and snatched at the phone, but it resisted. He pulled harder to release it from the lever-action spring holding it fast. "Hello?"

No answer.

"Hello?" He looked at the phone. "Push the button, you idiot." He shook his head so fast he almost dropped the phone, but he needed to try to clear his thinking. What was wrong with him? He pushed the button on the phone. "Hello, this is Doc. Is anyone there?"

"Control Room, Elevator Shaft. This is M.C. Doc, you don't have to yell, just talk louder than normal. Can you get down the shaft to the control room?"

"I'm trying. The elevator is stuck and without power. The shaft is filling up with some kind of gas. The earthquake must have caused a vent." Doc paused. "Sorry, M.C., I'm having trouble remembering the right sequence of using this phone."

"Control Room, Elevator Shaft. Doc, get down here as fast as you can. That gas is toxic, probably affecting your mind. It could get a lot hotter and more dangerous any minute. As soon as you get down here, we have to seal the shaft so *we* don't get any of that gas."

"Uh…Elevator Shaft, Control Room. Aye-aye, M.C. It may take a few minutes, but I'll hurry."

Jesse broke in, "Main Lab, Elevator Shaft. Doc, I need you here right away. I think Alex is having another attack. "

There was no answer.

"Control Room, Main Lab. Jesse, I heard you. I'll get Doc there as soon as he comes through the air lock, if he's able."

"Main Lab, Control Room. Thanks, M.C. I am *so* over this phone-speak. Out."

She turned her attention back to Alex and put on a mask, gown and gloves. He was unconscious.

Mom has blown her top over something stupid—throwing dishes, scream-ing, and generally acting like a madwoman. Dad grabs Alex and they hop in the old Ford truck. Always loaded with the fishing gear, it almost drives itself to the river.

While his dad readies the fishing gear, Alex blurts, "Hey, Dad, why did you marry Mom? You two are so different."

His father looks at him with his sad eyes and then smiles, his whole de-meanor changing, like he's a kid again. He laughs, looks upriver, then back at Alex. "Guess it's about time."

Replacing the gear, he gets into the truck, beckoning Alex while he pours two mugs of coffee from the thermos. While Alex sips his very first cup of coffee, his father lights a cigarette and faces him. "Alex." He looks around the cab of the truck and slowly blows out smoke. "Your mother and I were raised Jewish."

"Is that like in the Bible—like Jesus?"

"Yes, Jesus was a Jew."

"So, what does that mean?"

His father rubs the scar on his forearm and gazes out the window. "It means you have to be careful who you tell."

Alex thinks for a minute. "I won't tell anybody, Dad. I can keep a secret."

"I know son. I know."

"Are you okay, Dad?"

Tears drip down his father's cheeks. He takes out a handkerchief, wipes his eyes, and blows his nose. His eyes smile again. "Yep. I was just remem-bering 'bout your mother. You see, we lost our family 'cause we were Jewish. Your mom didn't handle it too well."

He puts his hand on Alex's shoulder. "Someone spared her and me and planted us in Wyoming. There weren't any Jews here, but the Baptists helped us out a lot. We became Baptist and never looked back."

Alex takes in Dad's smile. "So you married Mom 'cause she was really Jewish like you?"

His dad squints and nods. "Huh." Then he looks at the seat. "I guess that's part of it. But mostly it's 'cause I loved her so much."

"But she throws stuff at you."

His father laughs and flicks the cigarette out the window. "You forgive someone you love, especially if you've shared heartaches."

They sip coffee and watch fish rise on the river.

"Hey, Dad?"

"Yeah?"

"I don't want to be Jewish. I don't want to lose my family."

Alex awakened to Jesse shaking him.

"Alex, Doc will be here soon. He's gonna need vital signs and blood. No more work for you today."

Alex was as compliant and quiet as a well-trained dog, making Jesse even more worried. She had to have him finish the work on the vaccine. He was the key to her plans. He could get things working when the others were still guessing, including her. If he finished soon she could get the vaccine and leave.

As she readied the venipuncture equipment, she noticed his blond hair seemed to glow against his flushed temples and golden pearls of sweat studded his forehead.

CHAPTER 14

Rocca awoke with a start. The two-inch mattress on a metal-framed rack in this hole-in-the-wall rental room wasn't exactly the Jakarta Marriott. But it had a kitchen and was quiet and close to the airport. He could have slept on the floor last night and not heard a 747 land next door.

The phone was ringing.

He picked it up. A male voice hammered out. "Hey, Rock, we need to talk about this guy at the airport."

Now there was a blast from the past. "Jack? That you? What time is it? Wait one sec." He rubbed his face, shook his head, and looked at the clock. "Jesus. I need more sleep. I've had Montezuma's revenge keeping me awake the last week. What guy at the airport?"

Jack Dillon had covered Rocca's back many a time in Desert Storm, sometimes without a gun. "It's 6:00 a.m., Rock. Rise and shine. You know, the guy's mug you faxed us at 2:00 a.m., the guy you said was suspiciously familiar. It turns out he's very familiar to us. But we can't use this line. Get dressed. I'll meet you at the Betavia Marina. They have good food, great coffee. I'll bring Kaopectate."

"You damn spooks. Probably think it's Elvis. I'll be down in five unless I have to do another Jakarta foxtrot."

He hung up before Jack could respond and addressed the phone on the hook: "You think I'm a dumbshit, Jack? Like I haven't already tried Kaopectate, Pepto-Bismol, and about every antibiotic in the local store. Damn viruses."

Jack was waiting at a nice table in an almost empty dining room. There were chandeliers, a bar in the corner, and a windowed view of a pool, beyond which was the harbor, filled with various moored boats. On the table sat a bottle of brown liquid and a cup of black coffee. Jack's face was worried. He'd let his hair grow some and was dressed in a typical CIA gray suit and dark tie. There was a guy with him: darker suit, shorter hair.

"Hey, Rock. We need to plug you into an IV? You look a little peaked for an Italian Stallion."

Rocca did something he hadn't done in a week. He smiled. "Man, it's good to see you. This bug I got is about over, so forget the brown stuff. I could use something besides coffee, though. How about eggs and a bagel? Maybe a banana and OJ, too. You were right about the food being good here. It's the airport food you gotta watch. Shouldn't have eaten there last week."

"My trusty assistant, Jonesey here, will get food for you while we get started. The boys up top want to move quickly on this guy. Oh, by the way, Salvatore S. Rocca, meet David Jones, my partner."

Rocca shook Jonesey's hand. "Pleased to meet you. So, is it Jonesey, Davie, or just Locker, as in Davie Jones's?"

"Cute. Jonesey is okay, but I've been known to answer to Dave."

"Okay, Dave, call me Rock. Thanks for getting the food. I could really use bacon, too. 'Preciate it."

Jack guided Rocca to an outdoor poolside table. "Okay. Let's talk."

"Hey, I get enough of this heat every day. How about inside with the A/C?"

"Come on, Rock, you know the drill. Bugs, ears, cameras—there's more inside than out. Besides, there are those hot babes out here by the swimming pool to keep our minds quick. Am I right?"

Rocca lowered his voice to a whisper, "Jack, trust me on this. Inside, outside doesn't matter here. Talk about old times for now."

Jack nodded. "A/C it is. I'm sorry you've been so sick. Let's get back inside."

As they sat, Jonesey returned with the meal. Jack made small talk while Rocca wolfed his meal and made a few grunts and nods.

Finally Rocca placed a palm on his stomach. "For a while I thought that virus was going to kill me. Now I think I might survive. What do you say we go down to the dock and check out those boats? I've been thinking about buying one."

They all walked to the dock and began inspecting each boat: some wooden sloops, some huge fiberglass yachts.

They were a good hundred yards from the restaurant when Rocca stopped, looked up and down the dock, then nodded to Jack. "It's okay down here. So let's hear it. But keep your voice down."

Jack whispered, "Okay, Rock. Let me tell you about the guy at the airport. He is Jabril El Fahd, one of Bin Laden's right-hand men. We need to know what he's doing here."

Hidden in the shadow of a boat, a dark bearded man wearing headphones listened intently, pointing a small parabolic dish antenna at the three Americans.

The surgical mask made it difficult for Rashid to read the colonel's feelings during the two-hour tour of the lab. But, when Rashid reviewed the final results with him, he saw the colonel's eyes brighten and his hands clasp as if it had been the answer to his prayers.

Rashid raised his eyes to heaven and thanked Allah.

Yet when he turned to face the colonel, he realized his prayers had not been answered after all. The bullet penetrated his frontal cortex, taking with it all conscious thought and any chance of improving the world with his research.

Jabril felt the gun go off before he was aware of it. It had become a reflex. He had killed without thinking. His mind tumbled like a dry weed in a sandstorm.

What have you become?

His mother must think him a killing machine.

I am what Father and Grandfather wanted.

Grandfather visited often during the last few weeks of Mother's illness. He was devastated by her death and swore an oath to carry out her wish for Jabril to get a good education. Only, after the American bombings of 1991, half of all the Iraqi schools were gone. The remaining schools were so poor that Jabril learned nothing.

A member of Saddam Hussein's highest circles, Grandfather used his influence. He had Jabril tested. His score was the highest the school had seen. Saddam needed smart men. Jabril would have to move away to a special school. Father resisted, arguing that without his son's help he could not survive.

But Grandfather prevailed. Jabril went away at the tender age of thirteen.

He visited Father a year later, in a new town: a beautiful home on a large estate with many servants and a new wife—Jabril's aunt, Mother's sister. Father had done very well.

Jabril overheard Father and Grandfather laughing over the deal they'd made, and how profitable it had been. At first he did not understand. But as the conversation continued, he realized that Father had sold Jabril to Saddam, gaining money, land, and…*power.*

Money was power. Jabril burned for enough power to save the children of Iraq, and to never have to sell his own son. But most of all, he wanted enough power to destroy the American infidels and avenge his mother's death.

It was truly amazing what three meals, regular sleep, and a burning life goal could do for one's progress. He excelled in physics and political science, soccer, and tennis, and became fluent in Spanish, French, Russian, and—of course—English. Military training with the most dangerous terrorists in the world. He was totally immersed in the Qur'an: "We must convert the world to Islam, and if the infidels refuse, then tax them with Jizya, and if they refuse that, pray to Allah and take war to them—JIHAD!"

He stayed rail thin. His dark eyes and a mercurial mind could see every detail in an instant. Even as he trained, more Iraqis died of malnutrition and lack of medications—enraging him to new heights. Why did the Americans not end the embargo and give his people back their lives?

He proved himself to Bin Laden, dealing death cards worldwide to those who opposed Allah's will. It was now time to convince the world that the United States would bow to the will of Allah's hand servants.

He was what Father had wanted, the Sword of Gabriel.

But his mother's words still nagged him. *What have you become, Jabril?*

He stared at the dark bullet hole in Rashid's forehead and rapidly shook his head, trying to straighten the jumble of his thoughts. The Qur'an was correct: the infidels must be expunged from the earth. *Mother, don't you know? It is all for you!*

He was interrupted by the guard. "Colonel, are you all right?" His tone was tentative, carefully watching Jabril's smoking gun.

Jabril coughed, holstered the gun, gripped his hands into fists, and focused on the guard's surgically masked face. "Yes. Yes, I am…fine." His words were almost a whisper.

He gripped his hands into fists. "Of course! I am only tired of incompetence. Get this body out of here. This fool has failed, and the rest of the crew is in danger. I must tell them. We must close down the lab. Move all the staff into the dining room. I will talk with them there."

As the guard dragged Rashid's lifeless form to the incinerator, Jabril knew what he must do. His mother would just have to see it the way Allah did.

I must fulfill my destiny. I am the angel of God. I will drink from the cup and join Allah. Allahu akbar, Allahu akbar.

Alone, he made his way back to the quarantine freezer, tears drying on his cheeks.

CHAPTER 15

Jonesey had "procured" an olive-green Humvee and already had his flak jacket on when he picked up Rocca and Jack. The HMMWV they had was an early model with canvas doors, and the noise level inside was like being in a machine shop. Rocca sat in the front passenger seat and shouted as he fastened his own flak jacket. "I'm not exactly sure where El Fahd went. Maybe the guards at the airport gate have an idea."

Jack yelled from the back seat, "Way ahead of you. The guard said that particular black limo usually hangs a right at the light ahead. Then comes the fun stuff: armed guards, Dobermans, concertina fencing."

"Wonder what's so important? "

"Remember Desert Storm, how everyone was so paranoid about nerve agents?"

"Yeah, what a joke." Rocca had been pretty pissed when he found out wearing the protective garb and gas mask had been unnecessary.

"We did find traces. But what we kept quiet was the evidence of biological agents. They had an advanced lab that was capable of making some really bad juju."

"Yeah, yeah, anthrax. No big secret, everyone knew about that. Hell, I even got a sore arm from the vaccine."

"Anthrax was only the tip of the iceberg. You've heard of Ebola and smallpox?"

Rocca felt his scalp tingle. "They were messin' with those?"

Jonesey drove the Humvee like a Porsche. He turned right, running the red light. The tires squealed. They hung on and stopped talking. Jonesey punched the accelerator. Ahead was a wire gate that looked like Check Point Charlie before the fall of the Berlin Wall. One sentry saw the Humvee and signaled the others. The guards stopped and faced the oncoming Humvee, Dobermans and guns ready. The sound of an approaching helicopter overhead added to Rocca's feeling of being literally over their heads—kimchi so deep waders would be no use.

Jack screamed over the din, "Okay, Jonesey, we're locked and loaded. Go in hard and fast. I have a feeling that chopper is not a tour guide. I'll bet it's here to pick up the Ebola King—El Fahd himself."

Rocca braced himself and reflexively ducked down as the Humvee rammed through the gate. Automatic rifle fire bounced off the armored metal and bulletproof glass. When he sat up, he noted guards shouldering rocket launchers. "These guys mean business. Jonesey, I hope you've got nitrous to speed this thing up or we're toast."

Up ahead, the road curved around a small hill. Behind them, the soldiers were ready to fire the rockets any second. *If we can make that first curve, maybe we can avoid a tailpipe full of kaboom.*

Jonesey punched the accelerator, but they moved no faster.

A puff of smoke released from one of the rocket launchers. The smoke trail pointed right at their tail pipe.

Rocca grabbed the door and roof handle and tensed.

Jonesey squinted into the rearview and wrenched the steering wheel right then left and skittered around the long left curve.

The rocket smoke passed to their right, so close Rocca could have touched it. A second later it exploded in the jungle. Rocca relaxed his grip on the handle. "Jesus."

The lab was a hundred yards dead ahead. It was a one-story gray building with camouflage netting draped over most of the roof. The netting also covered a helicopter. The smell and haze of gunpowder and smoke filled the air. Men threw the netting off the chopper and the rotors started moving. A dark figure emerged from the roof door and headed toward the helo. He was saluted by another man, probably the pilot. They got in the chopper. The dark man seemed to look right at Rocca.

Rocca aimed his gun. "That's him in the chopper on the roof."

Jack leaned over and pushed Rocca's gun barrel down. "I need him alive. The intel we can get from him in five minutes would be worth more than everything we've had from all our snoops in Iraq for the last ten years."

"Way I heard it, you didn't have many snoops."

Jack gave a flat smile. "No shit."

Between the Humvee's engine and the chopper starting, the noise was deafening.

"So where's the back-up?" Rocca yelled.

Jack shrugged. "Guess it's us three for now."

Rocca readied to jump out of the truck. "That's better than two!"

During Desert Storm he and Jack alone had annihilated a squad of Iraqi Special Forces. But that was in darkness with better weapons. Broad daylight gate crashing—a tad different.

Jonesey stopped the truck.

Minutes earlier Jabril had found the vials Rashid had pointed out.

Now...which one?

Jorge told him to look for the one with a blue dot. But there were two with blue dots sitting on the upper shelf. There were several other vials on the lower shelf, but he did not inspect them. He had found what he wanted.

He opened both vials and held them up to the light, peering at them as if looking long enough would unlock the future. If he inhaled the contents of the wrong one, would he become the sword of destruction? Would he deliver the crippling blow to destroy the infidels once and for all? Or would he gain nothing?

Once again his mother's memory crowded his mind. *You must forgive, be tolerant, and love, Jabril.*

How can I love the infidels who destroyed my life, my family, and my country?

The noise of the chopper arriving made up his mind.

He tilted his head back and poured the meager contents of both vials into his nostrils—one for the left, one for the right. When he could feel the liquid oozing into his nose he sniffed, deep and long, willing himself not to cough and holding his breath to maximize penetration of both vials.

It was done. In a matter of days the symptoms would begin: the sore throat and runny nose, then the infectious cough. Once the cough started he would travel through five international airports: LAX, Dallas, Atlanta, and then to the final two—La Guardia and London, Heathrow. There he would be most infectious and would stay the longest, maximizing exposure. At that point he would be very close to heaven.

At the last airport, Muhammad would welcome him to his rightful place. Even after death, his rotting corpse would continue to spread the infection. Yes, there would be some casualties in other countries. But the Westerners would suffer the most. Their oil companies would be at the mercy of Allah.

He stoppered and replaced the vials. The guards had gathered all the staff in the cafeteria, waiting for him to make his announcement. He must be convincing so they would not panic. After all, they would be lucky: they would die quickly. He strode down the hall.

Gunfire sounded outside. He broke into a run.

The staff waited shoulder to shoulder in the cramped cafeteria, murmuring to each other and glancing nervously at the armed guards that surrounded them. Jabril would speak to them using the intercom from behind a glass partition, in the room the cook usually used. The guards wore masks and gloves: necessary to make the staff think he needed protection from them.

The chief guard reported that all were assembled. Jabril whispered a message to him and then stood tall and spoke into the microphone.

"I have spent the last hour making sure of what I was told. Do you remember Jorge? He was sent here to evaluate the infection containment effectiveness of this facility and found it woefully lacking. His attempts to improve things were met with roadblocks by Rashid. That is why Jorge was recalled and I was sent.

"Unfortunately, you have all been exposed to the deadliest viruses on the planet. There is no cure."

After he said the word *exposed,* many staff started talking, screaming, and crying. Several ran at the guards, trying to get by. Others ran forward and beat on the glass in front of Jabril.

The loud report of a gun silenced the crowd. Jabril held the smoking .357 over his head and looked at them with a deep sadness.

He was good at selling false emotions, very good.

"You have made the ultimate sacrifice for Allah and your country. Your families will be rewarded, but not as much as you will be in heaven." He tilted his head up, gazed at the heavens, and sighed. "I hope one day I, too, can make the same sacrifice. May Allah be with you."

He left the room. The guards began shooting.

When he reached the stairs, he began to run.

Halfway up the stairs, the sound of their machine guns melded into the chugging of the chopper. He walked briskly out the door onto the roof.

Running is for subordinates, not leaders.

He returned Mustafa's salute and walked with him under the speeding rotors to the door of the helicopter.

Mustafa screamed over the din, "Our man at the marina reports that the Americans are coming."

Stepping into the chopper, something caught his attention out of the corner of his eye, and he froze. An American Humvee had just stormed the front gate. His gaze was drawn to the man in the passenger seat.

The guard at the airport!

Their eyes locked and Jabril felt a prickle of apprehension. Then he laughed, signaled the remaining sergeant to open fire on the Americans, and climbed into the chopper. *Fools! You cannot keep me from fulfilling my destiny.*

Their helicopter lifted off and moved forward. Jabril opened his cell phone and hit *Send*.

The roof and the front of the lab exploded, tumbling the American Humvee on its side.

CHAPTER 16

Jabril felt a gentle shove from the explosion as the helicopter climbed away from the scene. He smiled at the conflagration consuming the laboratory. *My plan is working. The Americans cannot—*

Something *thwacked* the bottom of the chopper. The engine stuttered. They were losing altitude. Mustafa grabbed at his thigh with one hand, his pant leg darkening underneath. A bullet must have pierced him. Jabril glanced back at the Humvee. That cursed airport guard was shooting at them.

Mustafa had survived CIA torture, but a bullet in the thigh… He was already bleeding profusely. The chopper began to fall like a dead bird. Jabril tensed his body, ready for the crash.

Mustafa took his bloody hand off his thigh and regained control of the chopper.

Soon they were out of rifle range. Jabril took a deep breath and exhaled slowly, relaxing into his seat.

The helicopter jerked left, then dove to the treetops. Jabril's seat-belt kept him from flying out the open door.

Mustafa was jerking the joystick left and right, pumping on the foot pedals, and glancing behind them. Jabril torqued his head around. To their rear left, another chopper followed.

A bullet glanced off the overhead.

On the ground, the explosion of the lab had tipped the Humvee on its side. Bullets pinged off the floorboards. From behind the cover of the

Humvee, Rocca raised a fist at the second chopper pursuing El Fahd. "It's about fucking time!"

"Glad you got one with an armored undercarriage, Jonesey," Jack said, hunching next to Rocca, flinching at more bullet *twangs*.

Jack glanced over at Jonesey, who was lying next to them on the ground.

Jonesey stared, sightless and speechless, a jagged piece of metal jutting from his neck.

"Ah shit, Jonesey. I was just getting to like you." Jack closed Jonesey's eyes. "Jonesey's gone."

Rocca glanced at Jack. "Where the fuck you been? He's been dead since the explosion." He squinted. "You've been hit."

Jack felt at his right temple. His hand came away blood-smeared. "Doesn't feel like a bullet. More like I got hit by a baseball bat."

"Probably a head bonk on the door jamb. Not as bad as a baseball bat, unless of course you're a little wuss as I always suspected. Are you a wuss, or should I call the medic?"

Jack moved each body part slowly, taking inventory. "Yeah, I'm a wuss. But for now all I got is a bad headache, not quite as bad as that Margaritaville hangover in Pensacola, but it's steady. Must have blanked out the last few. What the hell have you been doing?"

"Let's see. First I went over and politely asked those guards to stop shooting. While I was there, I got a few Cuban cigars we could smoke. Then I came back over here to present you with the Jakarta Medal of Honor. Don't ya love a good cigar after battle?"

Rocca pulled out a cigar, lit it and puffed a few times.

Gunfire had almost ceased since the reinforcements arrived; the jungle seeming to devour the remaining guards.

A crashing, metal-on-metal sound made Rocca jump and bite into his cigar. From the distant tree tops, in the direction of Jabril's helicopter, a dark cloud of smoke billowed.

"I hope they got that son of a bitch. Sorry, Jack, I know you wanted him alive, but there was something big going on here, and he was the top player. Cut off the head of the snake and it all falls apart. Anyway, fucker killed Jonesey."

Jack stood up and peered at the jungle. "If he's the head cobra, we got to make sure."

"Come on, Jack! Sit back and enjoy the 'gar, man. You don't survive a chopper crash. Those fuckers explode almost before they hit the ground." But Rocca was already shouldering his rifle and grabbing the canteen under the seat.

Rocca threw Jack a rifle, and they started into the jungle.

After only minutes of slogging into the bush, Rocca felt like he was taking a hot bath wearing a wet suit. One canteen wasn't nearly enough.

Jabril hadn't seen the missile hit, only felt the jolt. No explosion. It must have misfired yet still passed through something critical. The chopper had tilted to the right and lost altitude.

They didn't have much altitude to lose.

Mustafa fought for control. Pumping the foot controls while he had a thigh wound had left a dark puddle of blood under his seat. His motions had become slow and deliberate. He frowned with effort, then calmly looked at Jabril and shook his head, his face a pasty white.

For the first time, Jabril began to fear he would not fulfill his destiny. He should say the Shahadah, but his sins prevented him.

Mustafa turned off the fuel pump and pulled the joy stick to his left thigh. Then his head nodded forward.

Jabril thanked Allah for a valiant pilot. The jungle filled the windshield and he held onto the door frame and seat.

Twenty feet from the jungle floor did not seem like a long way to fall. Yet ten thousand moving parts separated by a thin film of oil in an uncontrolled twirling decent were a death trap.

Metal screeched so loud he wanted to cover his ears. He closed his eyes and prayed. Then all movement stopped. He opened his eyes. Black smoke rose from the seat beside him. Green leaves from an unknown plant waved through the broken windshield, flapping against Mustafa's unmoving head.

Jabril raised his face to heaven and quickly unbuckled his seat belt and jumped out, saying, "Allahu akbar, Allahu akbar."

Then he reached back in and grabbed water, a map, and the portable radio. He pulled the pin on a grenade, threw it into the wrecked chopper, and ran into the jungle.

The explosion threw him to the ground, and he dropped the supplies.

The detonation should make it appear as if the chopper had exploded from the impact. All traces of the occupants should be obliterated, too.

He pushed himself up, gathered his supplies, and began an easy jog. He would soon radio in Plan B. He could make it to the other rendezvous by nightfall, though this would mean another delay.

Curse the infidels.

Rocca and Jack had been running toward the smoke when the sudden blast of an explosion hit them like a wall. Rocca picked himself up off the ground and shook his head, momentarily stunned and deafened.

When he regained his wits, he looked for Jack and saw him pinned under a large tree. "Come on, Jack, this is no time for fartin' around."

Jack smiled up at Rocca. "Yeah, well, if you had a tree fall on you, you would be passing gas too. Speaking of gas, that helo must have had a load. Help me out and we'll go check on El Fahd."

Rocca started to walk toward the explosion. "You got yourself under there; you get yourself out."

Jack was already wriggling to get out. He pushed off with his left foot and screamed.

"Fuckin-A, that hurts. Rock, I think I broke my ankle."

"Then I'll baby you just this once." Rocca came back and grabbed Jack under the armpits and gently pulled him out from the tree and rubble. He frowned at Jack's ankle. "I'm no doctor, but when your foot goes that way instead of this way, I think you got problems."

Jack grimaced and leaned against a tree. "I'll sit here and wait for you. If he's not dead, kill him. Forget bringing him back alive."

"Did you not feel that explosion? Or maybe you thought that tree fell on you because of a freak earthquake. It must've blown anyone in that helo to a million pieces. There's no way he lived through that."

Jack winced and reached around to his flank. "Hey, Rock." He raised his palm like a kid with the answer in school. His face was gray, his palm bloody.

Rocca grabbed the handheld and called for help.

Jack passed out and slipped off the tree, rolling on his side, revealing an ugly oozing puncture wound on his flank.

"Son of a bitch." Rocca applied pressure to the wound as rivulets of red streaked the green leaves with Jack's blood.

—

Jabril seethed but stayed huddled for hours under the bridge at the Cisadane River west of Jakarta. He tried to prostrate himself for evening prayer, but there was no adequate place. No one passed by. Night fell. The quiet, dark waters were interrupted by a fast boat skimming to a halt below the bridge. It picked up Jabril, then followed the river north to the Java Sea. From there it was a quick shot west to the Sunda Straits.

Ahead lay Anak Krakatau, a smoldering relic of the greatest volcanic eruption ever seen by man. Above, a meteor etched the sky, the bright tail a temporary wonder in the midst of an infinite beauty more stunning than Van Gogh could ever capture. Jabril had loved studying art with his mother. That seemed a lifetime ago.

Jabril could barely keep his eyes open. He shivered. His head and muscles ached. He smiled at the heavens. "Al-hamdu lillah."

His path to ultimate glory had begun—the infection had started.

Praise be to God.

CHAPTER 17

Rachel had a lot of catching up to do. The sergeant filled her in about the attacks on the Twin Towers and the Pentagon. As she was escorted to a jet at Buckley Air Force Base in Denver, she mused, *Could this all be a trick to get me back to work? Nah. Too crazy.*

Scott was probably dead, ergo the Feds would recruit her to continue his research. Though he had never confided in her, she had a high enough clearance to know their projects fit together like gunpowder and bullet—in fact exactly like that. She made the powder, he the bullets. She'd convinced herself that her project could be used for the betterment of the world and his could only be used to destroy it.

At least, that's what she'd hinted at in an argument with him two days before she left on the trip. She had tried to convince him to get out of the Army and join with her to make things better instead of fighting fire with fire.

He'd said, "Rachel, you're foolish to think that the other side will just give up and not take over the world if given a chance."

Now it looked like he was right.

She should be sad he was gone. He was always so gung-ho Army, play by the rules, live by the code, yah-da, yah-da, yah-da. Boring. In a way, she felt relieved.

Alex's smiling face surfaced. *Shit! Shit! Shit!*

That was wrong, just plain wrong.

The more she thought about it, the angrier she got. *Maybe we will fight fire with fire. And boy, do I have some hot shit to smoke those terrorists with! An eye for an eye. Right, Granny Lane?*

Her grandmother's Bible reading must have stuck after all. She said to the ceiling, "They do *not* know who they're messin' with!"

Sergeant Prescott's eyes locked on hers. "You got that right. Americans are ready to kick ass. We got the perfect president, a real cowboy. Those ragheads should have read their history books, or at least talked to the Japs. Hiroshima was nothing compared to what we can do now. When we get through nuking their country, all that sand will be nothing but a big piece of glass. Hell, maybe we'll sculpt a big glass monument, you know, a warning to anyone who fucks with the USA Maybe the president with his middle finger raised. That would be a kick. What do you think?"

Rachel's eyes were wide. She'd reflexively nodded in agreement. *Do I really agree with him?*

Part of her was revolted at the inhumanity. But a guttural feeling agreed with everything he said, wanting to laugh at the idea of the monument.

Her heart ached. But was it for Scott, or because she wanted to punish herself for already wanting another man?

The words *someone will pay* kept repeating in her mind.

After a few minutes the whir of the plane and the events of the day began to catch up to her. As she dozed off, she thought, *What am I going to do with that Pinot and the dress?*

Doc had to focus on every step as he climbed further down the elevator shaft. Finally the air freshened and he noticed the black marks on the wall. He opened the control room door.

M.C. beamed. "You okay, Doc? Smells like hydrogen sulfide. Nasty stuff."

Doc's eyes were watering, and he coughed a few times. "Yeah, I'll attest to that, though I *am* feeling much better now. Never got to the admin office. No sat phone."

"I bet after this, the head honchos won't argue with me about a back-up cable antenna. It works for subs and sure as hell will work here if we drape it in the trees." He dogged down the door cover. "Get over to the lab. Jesse called; Alex is worse. She thinks he's infected, and she needs your help drawing blood. You'd think being an Indian, she wouldn't have any problems with the red stuff."

"She almost fainted last time I was showing her how to draw blood." He frowned. "It's odd. Alex was looking great the last time I saw him. He'll be pissed about the sat phone."

"Maybe the levels of gas in the shaft will clear. If so, I'm going up. Contact me on the sound-powered phones if you can't get me on the intercom. You remember how to use it now, right?"

"Now that my brain is less foggy. If Alex is bad I might need other things from topside, so wait to go up the shaft until after you hear from me."

"Aye-aye, Doc." M.C. turned his attention to the monitors.

Doc started down the hall, then quickly turned around and poked his head back through the doorway. "On second thought, there might be a cave-in up there. Why don't you wait for me to go up with you?"

M.C. looked up from the monitors and tilted his head back and forth as if weighing each possibility. "If we've had a cave-in, it could take us a while to get that sat phone back. You go take care of Alex. Maybe I'll start working on another way to communicate. If he's infected, La Riva will put us all under quarantine, and we'll all be here a long time, cave-in or not."

"Yeah, I hear you. Talk to you soon."

Doc wheeled away and walked briskly down the darkened hallway. If Alex was infected, another quake would be good, a really big one that buried them forever. Down here in their sequestered, better-than-top-secret lab, they'd modified the DNA of the worst viruses the world had ever seen: Ebola, yellow fever, plague, polio, smallpox, and, recently, prions, the very building blocks of DNA. Prions could turn infectious with a slight tweak, making a calm person a raging lunatic. If Alex had a virus, he'd probably already spread it to them all. Doc thought of the last phrase from a song his mother used to sing, a lesson he'd somehow never learned: *That's what you get for jumping on the bed.* Adventure and risk was his life.

When he reached Jesse, she was in gloves, gown, and mask and had placed Alex back in the isolation room.

Alex was arguing with her over the intercom. "Jesse, it's because I haven't eaten in six hours. Whenever that happens, I get hypoglycemic and tired. I'm not infected. How could I be? We have the best procedures in the world for preventing that."

He glanced at Doc entering the room. "Tell her, Doc. I'm not sick. I'm having sugar problems. Right?"

"We don't really know what happened to you. There may have been a breach in the lab integrity due to the quake we had last week. The elevator is not working, and the elevator shaft has partially filled with noxious gases. M.C. and I think that volcanic vents have been opened by the quake. Wait for a minute while I talk to Jesse."

"How about that satellite phone? Did you get it? I gotta talk to Lora."

"I nearly suffocated trying to get that phone. I couldn't go any further. Now, please, let me talk with Jesse. I'll be in to examine you in a minute." Doc faced Jesse and switched off the intercom. "Fill me in."

She relayed the events of the past hour. "And then, in the last ten minutes, he perked up and seemed his old self again. Do you think he's infected?" Jesse's dark eyes peering over the surgical mask expressed as much as the tone of her voice: it was more than mere concern for a co-worker. The unsaid question was, *Do you think I'm infected?*

"I don't know for sure. Alex has other medical issues. This could be an anxiety attack or a hypoglycemic attack. He's one of the very few non-diabetic people in the world who has a bona fide problem with hypoglycemia. I probably shouldn't tell you this, but maybe it will help you stop worrying so much. Alex had numerous low blood sugar attacks when he was a child. They actually sent him to the hospital. It's a really rare disorder. The treatment is to eat regular, small meals or risk passing out. When you plugged him into the dextrose in the IV, you probably brought him out of it. How did you do that, anyway? I thought you hated the sight of blood."

Jesse blushed. "I didn't even think about it. But when I went to draw blood for viral titers... I called M.C. and he said you would be here shortly. So I decided to wait."

Alex stood when Doc entered. Doc frowned, then stood on his tiptoes, inspecting the top of Alex's head. "Alex, have you got different shoes on?"

"Nope, just the same old Reeboks. Why?"

But Alex knew the answer. He felt better than he had in the last two days, maybe even the last year. Whatever had happened to him, it had made him feel indestructible. Even though he felt so damn guilty about Lora.

"I don't know. It seems like you're…taller. Although when I examined you this morning, you weren't standing." He finished his exam, then rubbed his index finger on his temple and stared into space.

"So," Alex said, "what's the verdict? Am I going to die in a few days or what? I have to tell you, I feel better than I have in months. Maybe, all I needed was that IV."

"You seem fit. If you were infected with any of our viruses, I would expect you to be getting worse, not better. Safest bet is to watch you in quarantine until morning. We'll get some blood and get you a good meal, and I'll have Jesse read you a bedtime story. Get some rest. I'll be back after breakfast tomorrow. If you feel funny or have any problems, let me know. M.C. is working on communication. We should be able to get you in touch with Lora in the morning."

Doc turned away and headed for the door.

Alex took a deep breath and exhaled slowly. If he was okay, maybe Lora was okay. But he knew that was all wrong and that…he wasn't that upset about her. Had he ever really loved her? Guilt overwhelmed him. He had committed to Lora. They were doing so well. And now he knew. She was not for him. If she were gone, he would be sad, but also happy he could do what he must without hurting her.

He thought of Rachel and there was no sadness, only happiness and warmth.

And there was something else. Another presence lurked, a dark one. When he concentrated on it there was nothing. But if he let his mind float he kept hearing that stupid thing from *Jaws*. It would have been laughable were it not so creepy: *Da-dum. Da-dum.* A rolling started in his head like a wave from a tsunami: full of trees, houses, fish, and parts of people.

He lurched, glad Doc was walking the other way and not watching. He shook his head hard and tightened his abdominal muscles like he was trying to prevent a 4G dive from making him faint. Another long, slow breath through his nose steadied him. "Okay, Doc, I'll be here. Can Jesse come in, or does she have to stay in the other room?"

Doc never even turned to look at Alex as he opened the door to leave. "We'll see how you do in the next few hours. I'll be talking with her. Right now, I need to go help M.C."

After shedding the protective gear, Doc had to go through the decontamination room. He thoroughly soaped his entire body, scrubbed under fingernails and toenails, power-rinsed in a shower that stung as it took off the top layer of his skin, and finally spread his arms and legs for a total-body UV light exposure for three minutes. He then toweled off what wasn't dry and donned sterile blue paper pants with a belted tunic.

Reamed, steamed, and dry-cleaned, he felt naked and crinkly.

He told Jesse to closely observe Alex, trying to convince her dark, serious eyes with his reassuring gaze. "I don't think there's any real problem. He looks too good."

Doc walked out, his pants rustling. Jesse shook her head at the closing door. "Right." This was turning out to be much more than a simple theft.

CHAPTER 18

On her flight back, Rachel dreamed. She was watching the video with Sergeant Prescott again, reliving the total disbelief as the Twin Towers went up in flames and, a few minutes later, collapsed. It was surreal… slow motion.

Immediately before the second plane hit, she noted something odd. She paused and rewound the image, blowing it up to see it better. There it was, on the nose of the plane: a wolf with Alex Smith's eyes. It was looking right at her. As the sides of the building engulfed the plane, the picture switched to that of the Pentagon. The camera panned, then honed in on a close-up of the destruction, clearly showing Scott inside his destroyed office. The focus on his mangled body moved up, stopping at his sad eyes looking right at her through the fire that consumed him.

Rachel woke with a start. The jet was taxiing on the runway after landing. *I need to get back to my own bed.* It must have been the videos they had shown her earlier in the flight. But her dreams had never been quite so vivid.

Why was Alex a wolf?

She did love wolves. In fact, they were her favorite animal. But more than that—the image of Alex's face on nose of the plane was arousing.

Though she was sad about Scott, the image of his mangled and burned body brought not grief, but the desire to burn those who'd caused that horror.

Deplaning, she caught Sergeant Prescott's eye.

He murmured, "I'm sorry if I came on a little strong up there. But when we showed you the videos, it hit me again. I guess I got a little carried away."

She stopped on the stairs and faced him, making sure she caught his eye. "You don't have to apologize." Her words were calm yet cold. "I'm sure a lot of Americans feel the same way. It's like an abscess—when the pus starts flowing, it feels better. Only problem is, it's still festering in me. You get me back to my lab and I'll create a piece of hell those vermin will never survive."

Arriving back at Main Lab, she was confronted with frustratingly slow new procedures: a metal detector, empting her pockets, taking off her shoes. A dog sniffed everyone and everything. After Fido sniffed her rear, she felt a little violated but safer.

Jerry Klaus was waiting for her in his office, sitting behind his large oak desk. He was a large, balding, middle-aged man, pear-shaped from too many hours on the computer and too much of his favorite brain food—donuts. He wore a yellow polo shirt, tan chinos and white Nike high tops.

He seemed concerned through his black, square-framed glasses. "You had us worried. The Feds thought that maybe you'd gone over to the other side. This place has been Paranoid Central the last two weeks. We assured them that we have always screened our personnel well, and that, contrary to the rest of the world, we have always been concerned about the possibility of bio-terrorism."

She wondered if he was saying such bullshit because someone was listening. His words sounded sincere, but when he took off his glasses to rub his temples, he glanced at her, and his eyes betrayed him.

He really thought I might defect to the other side—the money side.

"Sorry, Jerry. I needed…Hell, I *deserved* some uninterrupted time without ten people calling me every hour about their pissy little problems. You remember the last time I took a vacation. I spent more time here than I did with Scott." She paused. "You really think I would sell out? Jesus."

Jerry averted his eyes, seeming ashamed. "I am sorry about Scott." *Now* there was genuine concern in his voice. "We sent flowers to his funeral.

It was last week, you know. I thought we could get you back in time. But you…you were hard to find. Though once I got Harry on it, he connected the dots and figured you'd be in Colorado, chasing wild animals."

He paused and refitted his ugly glasses, all the nicey-nice gone. "I hope you got your fill. There'll be no vacations for a long time. The contract we had with the Feds just doubled. And your little viruses got pushed to the top of the priority list." He stood. "What I'm saying is: sorry about Scott, glad your back, get to work."

"Thanks for your concern, glad to be back, and I'm on it." She was eager to get started, and desperate to think about something besides Scott. She turned, barely catching Jerry's goodbye wave, and walked fast and strong to her lab.

Harry, her assistant, was waiting. "Hey, Rache. Good to see you. Sorry about Scott." Harry had a weasel face—small, squinty eyes and a sparse, Johnny Depp goatee. He was in blue scrubs. Though barely in his twenties, his mind was electron-quick, and work was his life. The impatience in his voice proved that today was no exception.

"Thanks, Harry. Good to be back. Guess I need to send something to Scott's sister. I kinda missed the funeral. Still can't believe it all. The Pentagon was so vulnerable."

Her voice cracked and she glanced away.

When she looked back, Harry was mouthing the word *sorry*. He smiled: tentative, but kind.

"Uh, well," he started a bit hesitantly. "Do what you gotta do with Scott's sister. But we should get to work. The big boys have been breathing down my neck for the last week. They must think bad breath makes me work faster."

"Right." She took a deep breath, squeezed her eyes shut, then opened them and wiped her nose with the back of her hand. "Have you heard anything from Alex Smith? I mean, how's the project doing in the Amazon?"

Where did that come from?

Harry's eyebrows went up. "Oh, so now it's Alex-boy, huh? That was quick." He herded her into the changing room. "Now that Lora's out of the way, I guess you can move in on Mr. Smith all you want."

She stopped so suddenly that he nearly walked up her back. "What do you mean Lora's out of the way?" She glared at him. A minute ago she was glad he was pushing her back to work. Now, it would be heaven to see him quiver as she slapped him and walked out the door.

"What? Jerry didn't have the decency to tell you? Those fuckers killed Lora in the Twin Towers, or at least that's what we think. She was making a presentation on the same floor where the initial plane crashed and no one's heard from her since. We haven't been able to get in touch with Alex yet, either. They had an earthquake in Brazil that shut down their communications. Jerry's sending a plane to investigate."

Harry sounded nonchalant but Rachel knew better: he was about to explode. He'd learned calm control as a black belt in karate. And since he also had a thing for Lora, his fuse must be getting very short.

"Hey you, I'm sorry." She touched his arm. "I'm not sure where that came from. Had a weird dream in the plane, maybe that's it. I had no idea about Lora. I know you cared for her. You want to talk about it?"

Harry looked at the floor. "Thanks…but I'd really like to get to work. Maybe we can get back at the idiots who think Islam is going to be the only religion for the world. You know I'm not much on religion, but I even went to church the last two Sundays with my brother. He's a staunch, born-again Baptist. I thought I needed some religion to soften my heart, maybe see a way to forgive those fuckers. I mean, I had it bad. I profiled everyone on the subway, ready to tear the heart out of anyone who looked…Muslim. If they'd have pulled out a prayer mat I'd have smothered them with it."

He continued studying the floor. "So I went to my brother's church thinking it would make me more tolerant. The minister quoted the Bible, you know 'an eye for an eye,' and rebuked the Muslims for always being against us Christians. Felt worse after those two 'church' Sundays than I did before I went." He shook his head. "Work is my ticket, not religion. Work'll get me back on track, and might get back at them, too. So let's get started."

Rachel eyed him.

What has happened to the world?

In the changing room, she put on the protective gear. *Feels good to get back in the routine.* Her mind was rested, and she had a renewed purpose. "Okay Harry, let's give 'em something that'll make 'em cough up a bloody lung."

The smell of rubber gloves and the paper suit crackling against her skin brought her mind into focus. Viruses—she had always loved them, especially the way they replicated. They infiltrated the host cell, remained hidden, and spliced into the host DNA, converting the cell to making DNA that was useless to the host, but essential to the virus.

Viruses like Ebola, Marburg, or smallpox remained hidden from the immune system long enough to interfere with vital cells, resulting in death of the organism. Others did not totally destroy the organism; the immune system could find them and get rid of them. The result was an annoyance, like the common cold or chicken pox. Then there were the in-betweeners: they hit specific body systems. For example the Borna viruses attacked specific brain cells and caused psychiatric disease.

But if viruses could insert their DNA and cause disease, why couldn't they also get rid of genetic disorders or diseases by changing the organism's DNA for the better? They could and had. It was the ultimate silver bullet of medicine. Someone was already trying to eliminate the gene for arthritis by causing a permanent, virus-carried mutation. No more need for Motrin or joint replacements!

Rachel had been trying to find a way to use the smallpox, Ebola and Marburg viruses to alter the genes that caused skin and blood diseases, and the Borna virus to alter psychiatric-related genes. Finding the right genetic sequence could potentially cure depression, schizophrenia, leukemia, and a host of other illnesses. The research was what La Riva was famous for.

But in actuality, the medical uses were a cover. La Riva had been hired by the Feds to secretly create viral contagions. In other words, biological warfare. It had also been Scott's pet project at the Pentagon, though his was purely warfare, and she had kept to peacetime uses.

But now Rachel was no longer concerned with the peacetime uses of their work. She would complement and expand Scott's work, ignoring the small voice of reason that was tickling the back of her mind.

Another niggling thought kept surfacing—Alex Smith.

We have to tell him about Lora. He loved her so much. I'll talk to Jerry. Convince him to send one of us down there with the Feds. Maybe me.

They worked quietly for several minutes.

"By the way," Harry said, "have you seen the articles about Iraq possibly having biological labs that were destroyed during Desert Storm?

"Yeah, I scanned a few before I left. They didn't really find that much, except a little anthrax." She concentrated on the data the computer was spewing out.

"One good thing after the Pentagon attack: many previously classified references about bioterrorism were opened. Something interesting popped up. One of their prominent virologists, Rashid Hammed, has disappeared."

"I remember him." She looked up from the screen. "He wrote several articles about Borna viruses and the possibility of treating depression using genetic viral translocation. I wrote him to see if he had any ideas about other influences of Borna on psychiatric diseases. I don't think I ever got a response. Why are you bringing him up?"

Harry's small, dark eyes twinkled. "He wrote some other articles that were never published, but were confiscated after Desert Storm." He tapped his finger on the table.

"Okay, Harry. What the hell did these 'other articles' have to say? Or do I have to guess?"

Harry was playing his usual game: find a new article and try to stump her with one question after the other. Usually she had read it too, and after acting dumb for a question or two, she would hammer him with the conclusion. But now Harry held all the cards.

"Dr. Hammed was working on some very unusual viruses." He paused. "I'll give you a hint. Their initials are M., E., and S."

"You have got to be shitting me!" Rachel erupted. "Marburg, Ebola and smallpox?"

"The same."

She gaped at Harry. These were the same viruses that she and Harry had been working on for the last year. And the lab in South America was putting on the finishing touches of a viral merger that should be a very effective bio-weapon.

Rachel slapped her hand on the table, startling Harry. "I gotta talk to Jesse and Alex. We need a vaccine ASAP."

"What are the chances the Iraqis actually developed these things without Dr. Hammed? After all, we should have heard something else about his work by now. "

"We can't assume that merely because he's no longer publishing, he's no longer working. Viral labs are not that difficult to start up, or hide. It's also possible someone he trained continued his work, in secret."

She walked to the decontamination room. "I'll tell Jerry about this and get things going with Alex and Jesse. You keep working. The development of a vaccine needs to at least parallel our work here. Alex and Jesse would be crucial to that project."

She moved faster as her thoughts were bombarded with all the possibilities. In the decon room, she was in such a hurry she ripped her gloves off, the rubber snapping back and leaving a small welt on her hand. She quickly washed her hands, cursing the slight pain and the possibility that she might have been contaminated. She scrubbed hard for five minutes, then hurried to find Jerry.

He wasn't in his office. His secretary said he'd left a few minutes earlier.

She stood in the hallway, stymied. A plan had formed in her mind about Jesse and Alex, but she really wanted to talk with Jerry about it first. Maybe her friends in the communications department could help until she could find Jerry. She called them, told them her thoughts, and they agreed to meet in the lounge down the hall.

There was coffee in the lounge. She poured a cup and sat at a corner table, running through options. Several large windows overlooked Alexandria. Skyscrapers jutted into the skyline, incredible feats of engineering, beautiful despite interrupting the trees and the natural order. But now their mirrored walls reflected a new order of the world. Each was a vulnerable concentration of people, a big target for kamikaze pilots.

I'll never enter another tall building like that without wondering: Will this be the next one? At the very least I'll damn sure know where the stair exit is.

Jerry entered the lounge. His height was intimidating enough, but standing over her table, he was a formidable giant. Him trying to look stern with those comical birth-control glasses almost made her laugh. Especially since she knew he was milquetoast.

He glanced around the room, nervously. "I heard you were looking for me and you want to go help Alex and Jesse at Amazon Lab. I want you back at your workstation. There are a lot of—" he looked around again and cleared his throat— "important reasons we must complete your research. I need you working with Harry right now. Alex and Jesse can work just fine on their own."

"Alex doesn't have the faintest idea that Lora is probably dead. And, by the way—" She put acid into her voice. "—why didn't you tell me about Lora while I was in your office? You know I'm a good friend."

He backed off a pace.

"Alex should be here for her funeral," she said. "I don't want him to be in the same position I was." She blinked a few times and took a deep breath. "Would have been nice to be there." She squeezed her eyes tightly once, pushing back tears. "And we need to get someone down there working on a vaccine. If the terrorists have what we think they do, they'll probably use it on a civilian population. Harry can continue the work up here while I go help Jesse work on a vaccine. That'll free Alex to return and resolve Lora's death. I'll only be gone a few weeks. It's the best way to split up our limited resources."

Jerry glanced around yet again. It could only mean he was worried someone was watching or listening. He sat down. "We have preliminary work on a vaccine that we shared with the Pentagon, and—"

She frowned at him. "You know we haven't done any—"

He put his index finger to his lips, shushing her. "It looks very promising. But travel now is potentially very dangerous and time consuming. Two weeks ago, you could travel almost anywhere in the world with little or no worry or waiting. I heard that one of the consultants coming in from Ohio took two hours just to get through pre-boarding inspections. And that was a domestic flight. The Feds have asked us to limit our travel."

He gave her a very strange look, shaking his head and mouthing something she couldn't quite make out.

"Sounds pretty crazy. But about—"

He held out a palm, pointed to the walls, cupped a hand to his ear, and finally put a finger to his lips.

She frowned. Someone was definitely bugging the room.

She recovered quickly, smiling and nodding. "You know, this coffee isn't exactly what I need to get the brain cells pumping. The coffee shop across the street has great espresso. We should catch up more. Chat about Lora. You could have a mocha latte. How 'bout it?"

He closed his eyes and sighed.

"I was a little short with you when you came back to work. Maybe I do owe you a little more time to get up to speed. Let me tell Shirley." He buzzed his secretary on the intercom, and they were off.

CHAPTER 19

The streets of D.C. were crowded with the usual hubbub, making Rachel wish for the Rocky Mountains. Horns honked, a distant siren wailed, joggers dodged businessmen talking into cell phones. Outside the café, a street bum lounged in a too-thin coat with a hunting hat over his ears, his face grease-smudged. He avoided eye contact but held out his hand as Rachel and Jerry walked by.

Jerry gave him a ten. "Hey, buddy. Why don't you take this down the street to the soup kitchen? Maybe they have a better coat, too."

Rachel smiled. *Always a sucker for charity.*

The bleary-eyed bum began shuffling slowly away as Jerry and Rachel continued into the coffee shop. They did not see the bum do an about-face or notice the quickness in his movements and how his gaze now sparkled with excitement. He looked across the street at a parked car, and ran a hand across the bill of his hat like a first-base coach. He leaned against the light pole outside the café, stuffing the ten-dollar bill into his pocket. He murmured a few words to himself, resumed his dull gaze, and waited.

Jerry ordered a grandé mocha latte, and, after Rachel picked up her double espresso, steered her to a back table away from the door. A sad, puppy-dog look overtook his face when he sat.

"What?" she said.

"I am so sorry about Scott and Lora. It's been so crazy the last two weeks. These guys in our office—they say they are Feds but I'm not so sure—came in and took over our security. Initially they thought we might be connected with terrorist activities. But when they saw the medical nature of our work, they settled down. Though their head security guy still has doubts. They installed bugs in the offices and the lounge. I convinced them to stay out of the lab. How can you brainstorm when you're worried about Big Brother listening? Anyway, they say we're at war now, so I guess we need to treat it that way."

He looked into his drink, took a sip, then eyed the entrance of the store as if looking for someone.

"Somebody else coming?" Had someone from security followed them? He shook his head.

"Let's cut to the chase. Have we even started making a vaccine?"

"No. But the Feds who hired us for the," he paused and raised his eyebrows, "*non-medical work* will press for that soon. Your idea about getting something going at Amazon Lab is great. Unfortunately, no one is answering our calls there. We had reports of an earthquake, but they should have at least called on the sat phone by now. These guys in our office think it was no earthquake, but terrorists. Terrorists are everywhere, you know. Probably hiding in your apartment closet even as we speak." He cracked a weak smile. "Anyway, these guys don't want us handling it. They're sending their own team, probably tomorrow. Since they're not the non-medical Feds that contracted us, the shit-fan will start splattering soon."

"Maybe I could go with them and cover up."

He squinted at the front door again and didn't reply for a beat too long. "No dice. We already tried that. They have their 'special team' going in." He made quote marks in the air.

"Surely someone in communications can get a link going? Marge and Henry are the best."

"Marge has her own problems. Her brother was pinned under a beam in the Twin Towers for six hours before he was rescued. When they found him, he was ranting about people screaming and their flesh crackling and sizzling. For days all he could smell was burning flesh. Can you imagine? Marge went to be with him for a few days and came back seeing red. She's one of the main people in our church standing up and quoting the Old Testament about 'an eye for an eye' and all that. I have to admit, even I got my Beretta out and oiled it with thoughts of blowing away the next bearded man with a turban."

He craned his neck to look out the front window. The bum had come back. "And Henry? He had fear of flying before. Now he can't even see an airplane on TV without getting nervous. He's in therapy. Probably what I need."

He tipped the latte cup, taking a big swig.

Rachel swirled the espresso in her mouth, then swallowed. "Alex and Jesse are our best for vaccine work. You're up to your eyeballs here. If they shut us down, the vaccine work will stop."

He massaged his forehead with thumb and forefinger, staring into his cup.

She clamped her jaw in determination. "I have to get down there before these assholes in the office. I can keep a lid on the mission and help Jesse and Alex."

Jerry noisily slurped the remains of his drink and then studied inside the shop and outside the window. The din inside made Rachel wonder if he'd heard her last remark.

She was about to ask again when he sighed. "I say go for it, Rache." He gave her a card with a name and phone number on it. "This is someone who can help if I become…indisposed."

The card read *Sam Houston 555-4357*. She stuck it in her coat pocket.

Jerry stood. "I gotta get back." He gave her a hard look. "Take a little extra time and finish your coffee. We need to split up."

He abruptly walked out.

She stared at his rather generous backside. *Split up?* She stood to follow him.

Then it happened: the bum and another suited man flanked Jerry and herded him into a parked car.

Without thinking, she pivoted around and walked out the back door. In the alley, the cool overcast day amplified the sour-sweet odors of restaurant garbage and old coffee grounds.

Rachel ran.

It had been one week since the terrorist attacks that shook the very foundation of the U.S. security system. Senator George Cardwell from the grand state of Mississippi sat in his office pondering the debacle.

The makers of the Constitution fucked up, and I'm going to fix their mistake.

As a member of a very elite and secret group of wealthy, powerful businessmen, he had called several meetings over the last week to fashion a bill to put before the president and put an end to the bleeding hearts whose high-and-mighty search-and-seizure laws had hog-tied the government's security arms. He'd also convinced the president into starting some of the measures immediately.

Cardwell's own private security force rewarded him within days.

Turned up a goddamned viral lab right in the middle of D.C. Right on our own fucking doorstep! And they have an operation in South America. No telling what they're doing down there. I'll find out who the Muslim mole is if I have to work over every employee. First the boss—Klaus. German name. Probably a goddamn Nazi mole in cahoots with those ragheads.

In a way, the Twin Towers attack was a good thing. At least now they could get rid of all the foreigners ruining the country.

"Senator," his aide said, "don't forget your meeting with Mr. Rucksman at ten this morning."

"Right. Could you get me another cup of this latte before then?" he said to the closing door.

Very efficient. Didn't seem to mind that I was not too courteous. What the heck was his name, anyway? He looked it up on his employee list. *Charles. Good, strong Christian name. Great idea—hiring only Christians. Maybe not so politically correct, but I make the rules. Besides, who would find out? And if they did, Mississippi would love it. So let them eat cake.*

He smiled. "I got mine, with lots of icing," he murmured, to no one in particular.

Rachel once again looked behind her as she wandered through another back street, taking a circuitous route to her apartment. No one had followed her. She knew she probably shouldn't go back to her apartment, but even though most of her necessities she carried in her purse, including a new cell phone, she needed a few things if she was going to be on the lam.

Across the road from her apartment she hid behind a large trash bin, watching while she called Henry's cell. Her nose crinkled at the smell.

Henry answered on the first ring. "H…hello."

"Henry, this is Rachel. Are you all right?"

"Oh, hi, Julia. I'm about to go to an important meeting. What is it, honey?"

Rachel pursed her lips and almost swore. *They already got to him.* "Henry, something fishy is going on, and I need your help fast."

She could hear Henry asking his secretary to leave for a moment while he talked to his wife about a family emergency. "Julia, are you still there?"

"Okay, Henry, I get it. Your office is bugged. I'll talk quietly, and you keep the phone plastered to your ear so no sound leaks out." She was taking no chances. Some of the newer electronics could pick up a pin drop in an auditorium of teenagers.

"A few minutes ago, Jerry was picked up by some goons outside the coffee shop. They looked like they were from the FBI or CIA. They had help from some undercover guy that looked like a bum working the street. What the hell is going on?"

"Honey, you know after the terrorist thing that the government is now involved in all areas of our company. I've got a meeting about that in a few minutes, and I can't miss it. Why don't you ask Sam to come over and help? He's been great with the plumbing before."

She decided to play along. "Thanks, Henry. Maybe you could give me his number."

"Honey, if you can't find his number, check the directory in Alexandria. Those pipes shouldn't have leaked. Maybe we can get a refund. I gotta go now. Call you later." He hung up.

A few seconds later she got an encrypted text message: *Sam 555-4357. Hope he knows how to delete that from his phone.*

She watched her apartment for a few more minutes. It was now or never.

She quickly went inside and grabbed her backpack, still packed with all her Colorado gear, her camera, and a stash of cash from inside her computer case. As she started out the door, the phone rang. As a matter of habit she reached for it, then snatched her hand back.

Henry's voice spoke to the answering machine. "Hi, Rachel. If you get this message, we need you to come back to work. There are some guys here who say Jerry is some kinda Nazi mole and they need your help to get into Jerry's computer."

She didn't hear the rest. All she heard was the staccato beating of her heart as she ran out the door.

No way Jerry's a Nazi. He's too kind, too generous, too much of a pushover.

Who would think that La Riva was a front for terrorism? Were they stupid? Come on! Doesn't anyone in the FBI talk to the CIA?

Gotta get to Amazon Lab. Damage control time.

Minutes later, she received a text message: *take taxi w/ 7 on psngr dor. drvr big, bald w/ srfbrd tat on hd. Fly.* Caller ID was blocked.

While she waited outside for the taxi, she put her hands in her coat pockets and felt the card.

The card from Jerry.

She pulled out the card. *Sam 555-4357.* Funny. It was the same name and number Henry had given her. Who was Sam? Whoever he was, she hoped he could get her out of this mess. She dialed the number.

A low, gravelly voice answered, "This is Sam. Leave a message. I might get back to you."

The taxi arrived.

She left a brief message for Sam and name-dropped Jerry. Whoever this guy Sam was, she hoped he was good.

The beat-up yellow cab had a scratch on the passenger side that resembled the number seven. The driver was so big he had to hunch over to fit into the driver's seat, making it hard to see the surfboard tattooed on his tanned, bald cranium.

Getting in, she asked him where he got his tan.

"In the sun."

Other efforts at conversation were met with only grunts, so she gave up.

They traveled in circuitous routes through Virginia. Once, he insisted they switch to another cab, blue-colored. Another time, he drove into a parking garage and waited for ten minutes before driving on again. Still nothing resembling conversation.

Suddenly, the driver turned around and shocked her by giving her a few lucid instructions. He politely asked her to get out, and drove off.

The cab disappeared. Walls of trees butted up to the roadway; the blue sky had faded to gray.

Welcome to the Twilight Zone.

She started walking in the direction the driver had told her. After a mile she found the moped he'd said would be there, then drove ten miles along the back roads. Just as she'd convinced herself she should have turned right instead of left at the previous intersection, she came to the road lined with overhanging trees mentioned by the cabby. The trees draped the dirt road and initially obscured her contact. But at a fork in the road, as the driver had told her, was a small, round man waiting beside a mailbox.

When she got closer she noted his oily black hair and frowning, mustached face. He spoke in a hoarse voice. "Plans have changed. Flights are being watched too carefully. Take the moped down to the end of this road, hang a left, and follow it to the water. It's a ways, but keep going and you'll find Marcia waiting with a boat."

"A boat? For Christ's sake, I don't want to get there next week, I want to get there yesterday."

The greasy, round man shrugged and walked away, disappearing behind several trees. There was a sound of a car door opening, then slamming closed, and then a battered VW Bug drove out from behind the trees and down the road she'd come. She could have sworn the man waved at her.

The twilight faded and the dirt road she must travel began to vanish inside a dark tunnel.

A melody played in her mind: *do do do do, do do do do…* Rod Sterling's voice said *Welcome—*

"Fuck!" she said, staring at the moped. But the moped did not respond.

What the hell have I gotten myself into? Backtrack, get to the airport, take a flight. Much easier than all this mumbo jumbo. I could use the fake ID I used going to the Rockies.

"Hell with it. This thing better have plenty of gas." She hopped on the moped, started it, and gunned it into the black hole ahead. She twisted the accelerator handle and sped off. Very soon there would be no light, only the moped's small beam, a dirt road, a wall of black trees, and dark, lonely space.

Ten miles later, the road turned muddy and she began to slip sideways. She slowed and stopped at the sight ahead. She turned the key off and the motor died. An abandoned house stood in front of her, with a dock that was probably built in the '50s. It had intermittent rotten and missing planks looking like a giant piano board. At the end, lighter-colored, new planks led to a boat. A powerful engine growled in idle. Even in the near darkness she could make out a large, turquoise cigarette boat.

She threw her leg over and let the moped fall. Barely visible at the helm of the boat was a tall, blond woman. Four fifty-gallon drums occupied each side of the boat's deck like huge cannons facing forward. They left little room for passengers.

Rachel shook her head. *Too weird. But I have to help Jerry. Nazi mole? Not only stupid but a half century late. Our government agencies. Dumb and dumber.*

She stepped onto the dock, testing each step as she walked to the boat. Then she laughed. *No wonder they got us with those kamikazes. The CIA probably knew what was going on before the Twin Towers were hit but didn't want the FBI to get involved because they might take credit. Until it was too late. And now they're arresting anyone who looks suspicious so they don't get blamed. Well, I'm not getting arrested, and I'm going to get the bad guys without any Fee-Bees or Chia pets.* She could feel her face turn stony.

At Rachel's laugh, the blond woman turned around and studied Rachel. She must have thought it odd that Rachel laughed then looked so stern, because she unzipped her coat and started to pull out a pistol. Then she stuffed the pistol back in and smiled. "Hey, Rache! What the heck were you laughing about? This is going to be no picnic running the Chesapeake at night."

Rachel squinted at the woman and smiled, too. "When he said 'Marcia,' I had no idea he meant you! I was laughing at how screwed up the Feds are and how glad I am that we're avoiding them."

She'd known Marcia since college days, and only recently hooked up with her again at Marcia's wedding.

"Yeah, well, I got my training from the Coast Guard, so I can't knock the government too much. We better get going. We've got a long way to go and not much time to get there."

Marcia helped Rachel aboard and threw off the ropes. Within minutes they were quietly motoring out of the small creek.

The controls of the boat looked complicated. The purr of the large engine vibrated Rachel's bones. "Nice boat. Quiet, but it looks like it could really get up and go."

"Thanks. We love it. Has a lot of extra muffling because of where we dock, in this tiny Annapolis creek. Rich people don't mind if we run and gun way out in the Chesapeake, but they'll call the marine patrol if you make their dog bark."

They cleared the last buoy and picked up speed, though they were still able to talk over the muffled engines.

"So, with all this gas, I guess must be going to Cuba, huh?" Rachel pointed at the drums.

"Not quite. Most of these are empty. We only fill them for our really long races up to Martha's Vineyard. But really, it's better if you don't know where we're going, in case we get stopped. Hopefully we won't have to worry about that at night, but we shouldn't take any chances. Our story is that we're going to meet the guys for an early start on the race to New York tomorrow. If they check, they'll see that the boat is registered for the race, and Mike and Joe are registered in a hotel in Virginia Beach. That should get us out of Chesapeake Bay without too many problems."

So we're going somewhere south, thought Rachel. *Then what?*

The huge engines burst into a skull-vibrating roar. Now out of the speed-control zone, Marcia had pushed the throttle. They rocketed forward.

They couldn't talk now, but Marcia seemed to have everything under control. Rachel gave Marcia the okay sign with her hand, and leaned back against the seat.

Alex Smith popped into her head. *What* was *it about him? He always seemed so vulnerable, like he'd missed out on something. I know he'll take Lora's death hard.*

Maybe I can help him take it better.

So that's why you're in such a hurry to get down there. Nothing to do with any…physical attraction.

Right.

What about Scott?

He's gone.

A star-studded sky opened up over the Chesapeake. She felt like a speck in the vast universe as they cruised across the water at breakneck speed. She tilted her head back, letting the clean air flow through her hair and clear her head. Salty spray peppered her lips, and the night enveloped her, twilight completely gone.

CHAPTER 20

Jabril kept reminding himself to be patient. He would have his day. But would he succumb to the virus first? Hours ago he had arrived in the private airport in Bandar, Lampung, after an uneventful but wet ride through the Sunda Straits west of Jakarta. From there he had flown to Manila, where he stayed inside the private plane to avoid prying security cameras. His commercial flight was not scheduled to leave for LAX for several more hours. Fatigue gnawed at him between sweats and chills. He took two paracetamol tablets and tried to sleep. A nightmare of a hyena eating a wolf awoke him. He felt better, got up and started on his disguise, though it was cramped in the small bathroom.

No one should suspect a graying Jewish jeweler with a long, braided beard and who walks with a limp.

The flight to LAX would cross the International Date Line; he would depart and arrive in the late morning of the nineteenth. He could have rested and flown the next day, but he didn't want to risk any delays. The incubation time of the virus was three days, and he wanted to be in L.A. when it bloomed to the infectious phase. He had also wanted to get away from Jakarta and that cursed guard, as quickly as possible. Soon he would arrive at LAX, coughing on everyone he could for four hours before he started his journey across the United States and on to heaven.

Father will be proud. And mother—you will understand once I'm seated next to the Prophet at the right hand of Allah. Of course you will, for the

Qur'an says, "good women are obedient," and, "Men are in charge of women, because Allah hath made the one of them to excel the other."

Mine is not a proud revenge. That is forbidden. It is jihad, ridding the earth of those who do not worship the One True God, the God of Abraham, the One Muhammad died for, the One my people have been killed for.

"Whoso fighteth in the way of Allah, be he slain or be he victorious, on him we shall bestow a vast reward." Ahhh, the glorious Qur'an. The infidel's war may have killed two million Iraqis, but my sword will kill fifty times that.

Allah's will be done.

Doc reexamined Alex and pronounced him normal. He also allowed Jesse to spend the night in the room with Alex. She seemed so concerned he thought it would reassure her and allow Alex to get some sleep. If Alex's attack had been a seizure due to fatigue, sleep would help.

By 2:00 a.m., Doc decided he'd done enough, so he pushed thoughts of Alex out of his mind, turned over and slept like a dead man.

Jesse was overjoyed that Doc had allowed her to go in the room without protective garb. She stood by Alex's cot watching him. He lay supine, breathing peacefully. She bent and gave him a one-armed squeeze. He groaned and sighed. She had to keep working on him, distracting him. He was a good guy. A shame, really.

The air was electric, the instant before a lightning strike.

We're like two magnets, too close to pull apart. Been a good girl so far, only teasing. You had Lora. But where is Lora now?

The government had to change. She leaned over and kissed his lips, long and passionately.

Doc awakened at 5:00a.m. in a pool of sweat. He jumped out of bed and was out the door in less than five minutes. The hallway was dark but the air seemed cooler. M.C. must have fixed the A/C. Maybe he'd got the elevator fixed, too.

He found Jesse sleeping in a cot next to Alex. The room was also cool, another good sign the A/C was working. Doc's bag and his laptop rested on the metal counter next to Alex. He shook Alex's shoulder gently. "Hey, sleepy head, wake up."

Jesse woke. "You're here a little early, aren't you?"

"Did Alex do anything unusual last night?"

"No. Just slept all night."

"Did he seem taller, more muscular?"

"What?"

"Never mind. It was a dream."

"Alex was in your dream?"

"He had the face of Fang, then changed to a wolf and came after me and M.C."

"Weird."

"Yeah, tell me about it." He frowned at her. "How are you doing?"

She sat up and ran her fingers easily through her hair, wishing it was a snarly mess. "Never felt better. In fact, I think I might sleep on this cot from now on."

"Your cheeks are sure red."

Jesse glanced away at his implication. "I thought about jumping his bones, but I wanted you to give the go ahead. You know, what with all these bugs we're screwing around with, I didn't want to get the new virus du jour, especially if it's like AIDS. Oh yeah, I also thought it might be nice to have him break up with Lora before I make him start screaming for mercy."

Doc blushed. "What I was getting at was, do you feel like you have a fever?"

"It's a little hot in here."

"Let me take your temperature." Before she could object, he grabbed a thermometer from his bag and stuck it under her tongue.

Alex stirred and murmured, "What's for breakfast? I'm starved." He glanced at Jesse and sat up. "Oh, shit, Jesse. Did I give you something?"

Doc took the thermometer out and peered at it. "No fever. Could you wait outside for a moment, Jesse?"

Jesse's eyes moved over Alex. "No problem, Doc. But let me know if you need any help with close examinations of important organs." She ran her fingertips over Alex's thigh, then walked out with an exaggerated hip swing.

Alex eyed her as she left. She was a piece of work. A sexy one, too. He remembered Lora, closed his eyes and let out a breath. He should feel more sadness, but it just wasn't there. Rachel was there, though. And something told him she needed him. He looked at the door Jesse had closed. Forget Jesse. He had to get to Rachel.

"Doc, is this going to take long? I'm starved. Feel like I haven't eaten in a week."

"We'll be done in a minute."

Doc did a very detailed examination, accessed his laptop, and compared his results to the last two weeks. "Same height as always. No signs of infection."

"Doc, are you okay? You seem a bit preoccupied."

"Alex, your immune system has conquered again. Whatever it was, you're over it. But if you feel funny, let me know."

He typed on the laptop as Alex got dressed. "Hey, have you had any weird dreams lately?"

Alex felt like he'd been caught with his hand in the cookie jar. "What do you mean *weird*? Seriously, aren't all dreams weird?"

"Anything out of the usual weirdness. Anything that might pertain to us or to the lab."

"I did have a dream that some big-ass 747 ran into a Hilton Hotel or some kind of high-rise. I was inside the airplane trying to stop some terrorist guys from crashing it. But then it crashed and the whole damn hotel collapsed. That's when I woke up. That was yesterday. I think I was in this cramped quarantine room for too long, and my subconscious was wanting to crash out."

"You're probably right." Doc stared off into space.

"Uh, Doc? Is it okay to go eat now?"

"Yeah. I'll see you in a few minutes."

Alex was gone in an instant, slamming the door behind him. No more damn questions. He was ravenous. He jogged toward the kitchen, his steps echoing in the tiled hallway.

He caught up with Jesse as she was entering the kitchen. It wasn't as small as the break room, but still Spartan, with a two-burner gas stove, microwave, small toaster oven, metal table, and four metal chairs. At least the tile was a mellow light green rather than the utilitarian off-white in the rest of the lab.

M.C. was inside, finishing his grits and eggs. He glanced up after sipping his coffee. "How's it going? After yesterday I thought you two might be in quarantine for the rest of the week. You feelin' okay?"

"Never better," Jesse said.

Alex got milk out of the refrigerator. "Yeah, me too. I'm up for a pile of pancakes with a big side of eggs and sausage. How about you, Jesse?"

"I'll take the works. And some OJ while you're in the fridge."

She looked at M.C. as she poured her juice. "How soon until we get the elevator fixed? Alex still needs to check on Lora."

Alex did a sideways glance at her. *What was with her deal with Lora?*

"Workin' on it," M.C. said. "Hopefully we should have the sat phone in our hands by noon." M.C. stood to leave. "But, before I do anything else, I need to talk to Doc about the gases in the shaft. Is he coming up soon, or should I go down there?"

"He should be up here in a few." Alex poured several dollops of pancake dough on the hot griddle. "Why don't you call him on the intercom?"

"I want to see the whites of his eyes when I tell him. He sometimes leaves out details if I don't question his body language." M.C. frowned. "Maybe I'll meet him halfway. We're already behind eight hours. After all, the sooner we get done—"

"The sooner I get to go fishing!" Alex finished.

"Something like that." M.C. dropped his paper plate in the garbage and left.

M.C. was almost to the lab when he heard Doc's footsteps echoing in the hallway before he saw him. "Mornin'." He looked back at the closed kitchen door. I just saw Alex and Jesse. They seem okay."

"Yeah, I hope. We still have blood tests to run. Walk with me. We can talk over breakfast."

M.C. put a palm on Doc's chest. "Why don't we go back to the lab instead?"

Doc started to say something, then caught M.C.'s look. He turned around and they headed back to the lab.

M.C. flicked on the lights in the lab. It seemed a cold white box without Alex and Jesse working. He closed the door as Doc pulled up a couple of chairs from the lab tables.

Doc sat down and studied him. "You haven't been this serious since you lost a buddy in Desert Storm. What gives?"

M.C. flopped down in the metal chair so hard it scooted on the floor. He rolled his head on his neck. "Been a long night. "First, the good news.

I managed to bypass some circuits and get the elevator working. The gases in the shaft have dissipated to non-toxic levels. Also the surveillance cameras were out of commission. I got them working and got a good look around the perimeter and in the admin office."

"And?"

"And it doesn't look like an earthquake. The way the admin office is messed up and by the looks of the outside doorway, I'd say we had visitors." He punched his palm with his fist, a loud smacking sound. "And they used C4."

"An explosion? We have a good relationship with the locals. Nobody except Main Lab and DoD knows we even exist here."

M.C. shrugged and looked at Doc for a long time.

Doc rubbed his mouth with his hand. "Son of a bitch. You think someone from DoD is trying to get rid of the lab?"

"The thought had crossed my mind. No tracks, no foul." M.C. paused and gripped his fist with his other hand. "Or the other side discovered that we have weapons they can't defend against."

"What do you mean the other side? The Russians? The Chinese? Who?"

"Come on, Doc. Those gases must have affected you more than I thought. Who the heck did we *not* finish off in the last war?"

Doc stood up and started pacing, doing laps in the small room. He stopped and looked at M.C. "The Iraqis? We decimated their intelligence and army at Desert Storm. They've been holding on by their rotting gums since the trade embargo. They wouldn't have enough resources to muster intelligence in South America, much less find out what we were doing here."

"That's what the Democrats and liberals want you to think. I was there. I saw how powerful the Republican Guards were. Their intelligence ability was every bit as good as ours. They have people planted all over the world. South America would be a cinch. If thousands of Nazi war criminals found haven there, why not Iraqis? They probably have half their intelligence officers living at the Copacabana eating barbecue and sipping on batidas with some Nazi gas chamber lunatic. There's a new joke: two guys walk into a bar, one wears a turban, the other an iron cross. What do they talk about? Killing Americans. Fuckin' oil money can buy almost anything, including a mole in the DoD. How do you think the Army gets its oil so cheap?"

Doc plopped down and his chair chattered backwards six inches. "If you're right, why haven't they come down to get us?"

"I don't think they know about the elevator shaft, or maybe the entrance was disguised by the explosion."

"Probably won't stop them long. They have to be wondering about the lack of bodies."

"I'll bet they're waiting for reinforcements, maybe some front end loaders to clear away the debris. We probably have a day or so. Unless they find our surveillance cameras, though they're hidden pretty well. Tonight I'll climb up the shaft, make a quick repair of the cable lines, grab the sat phone, and get back down here."

He scrubbed his bald head with his palms, then looked at Doc. "I'll send encrypted info to D.C. via cable, let 'em know we're okay but say we had an earthquake and that the elevator and sat phone are down. That way any moles won't be alarmed. Then I'll use the sat phone to check out the boys in D.C.—I have some contacts I trust who can snoop around, maybe get us help."

"I think you should get the others involved. Alex can go up the ladder a lot quicker than you, and Jesse is great at electronic stuff."

"They're not combatants. Telling them about terrorist suspicions might spook them, throw off their concentration. We can't afford any distractions. Completing the mission has to come first. "

"Might be motivation, get them moving even faster."

"Can't risk it."

"Okay, if you think your knees can take that ladder, let's get moving." Doc started to get up.

M.C. put a hand on his chest, holding him down gently. "Is Alex a hundred percent? I don't want him making mistakes. We need to get this done quickly and accurately."

"Like I said, I don't have the blood tests back but, looking him over, all systems are go."

M.C. removed his hand. "Okay, let me go first. I'll tell them that the gas levels are still too dangerous to use the elevator."

Outside the kitchen, M.C. reached for the door and Doc whispered to the back of M.C.'s head, "I hope they buy it."

They strolled into the lounge. Alex and Jesse were sitting at the table, finishing breakfast and chatting about getting the viruses completed.

Alex looked up, "Hey, Doc. You want some eggs?"

"Maybe just some coffee, thanks." Doc yawned and blinked a few times and went straight to the coffee, avoiding eye contact with Alex or Jesse. He stood beside the coffee pot and handed a cup to M.C.

M.C. sat down across from Alex and Jesse, holding his cup in two hands, elbows on the table, looking right at Alex. "I'm real sorry, but there's still high levels of dangerous gases in the elevator shaft. We'll have to wait for that sat phone a bit longer."

Alex looked at Jesse, then at Doc. "That's okay. Can't have Doc gettin' sick on us." We got some work to do, anyhow." Jesse and Alex stood in unison. "Let me know when you get the phone," Alex said, and he and Jesse started walking to the door. Jesse caught Doc's eye with a look that said, *That was bullshit*, and walked out, banging the door shut.

That night, M.C. went up the ladder in the elevator shaft. The smell of rotten eggs still tainted the air, but the haze was gone. His small flashlight played through the darkness. The 9mm Berretta stuck inside the back of his pants rubbed on the small of his back. He grunted with each step from knee pain. Soon his necked ached from constantly looking up, scanning every corner with the flashlight, hoping for no surprises.

At the top of the shaft, there was a metal door flush with the wall. He lifted the horizontal spring-loaded latch, opened the door and crawled into a midget-sized closet, three feet wide by four feet long by four feet high. He closed the metal door behind him, pivoted on painful knees, edged forward on his hands and knees, and opened the outside door.

First he had to squeeze the door back enough to get out. A desk lay sideways against it. That explained why no one had come down the shaft yet. The desk hid this closet entrance. He held the flashlight under the Berretta and started moving forward. The flashlight beam confirmed the views he'd seen from the surveillance camera: torn-out walls, rubble everywhere, tables and chairs and desks in jagged pieces. He picked his way through the rubble to the communications cable outside the east wall. A six-foot piece of cable was gone, not torn out but cut neatly. A hint of burning gunpowder hung in the air. This was no earthquake.

He moved slowly and deliberately, avoiding any noise. It was difficult picking his way through the wreckage. He only used the flashlight for brief intervals, and then only pointed it at the ground, stopping every few minutes to listen. Hearing nothing, he continued to work.

He patched the cable and reset the satellite dish so they could have Internet access.

He was halfway back to the elevator shaft when he noticed lights playing through the building and voices breaking the quiet night.

He quickly wedged his way back inside the closet to the shaft.

Quietly shutting the closet door, he was about to open the metal door down to the shaft when voices echoed within the admin office. Much too close.

He pivoted on his knees back around to face the door and pulled out the pistol.

His breathing became shallow, inaudible.

The voices stopped. No movement. No sounds.

The sweat from his face dripped onto the floor. His knees screamed hot pain. If he didn't move soon he'd fall over.

The voices returned, very close now. A foreign male voice yelled right outside the closet. "Over here!"

The door to the closet opened.

CHAPTER 21

The boat carried Rachel for an hour and a half, so quickly that Rachel's cheeks tingled from the needles of spray. Marcia pulled back on the throttle to meander through the boat-infested Chesapeake channel to the Atlantic. Marcia checked her GPS and fathometer and told Rachel they were right on course. Once they cleared Virginia Beach they would not have far to go.

Rachel sat on the center console seat, feeling calm yet excited. Her hair whipped in the wind. While the motor was quiet she said, "It's really good to see you again. And thanks for this."

Marcia's white teeth was all Rachel saw of her smile. "I still owe you for getting me through college. And for that wonderful wedding album."

"Glad I could help, on both accounts." Rachel had worked hours on the bound photo album of the wedding. The surprise on Marcia's face had made it worth every minute. "I hope Mike doesn't mind our taking his boat."

"Not a chance. Mike and I have done other work for Sam. The pay's good, and our racing hobby is a perfect cover for running people up and down the coast. This is a cakewalk compared to some jobs we've done. And I get to drive this great boat faster than hell." She laughed and pushed the throttle forward.

They flew off a wave and the motor roared. Virginia Beach was behind them, ahead a light chop. At sixty knots, the sleek boat barely touched the troughs of the waves.

After ninety minutes, Marcia glanced at the GPS and gradually pulled back on the throttle. They had arrived at their destination off Nags Head, North Carolina.

The boat heaved in the waves and Rachel could hear distant surf. Lights from the shore rocked up and down. Rachel swung the boat around, back toward Virginia Beach. "Time for you to swim, Rache."

"What?"

Marcia pointed her finger to the boat cabin. "Sorry. This is as close as I get. There's a wet suit in the closet. Once you've changed, put your clothes in the dry bag and take them with you. You'll need them on the other side of the island. It's only a hundred yards, but a bit of a current. I'll drop you up-current as close to shore as I can. You'll have to walk about two hundred yards to the road. Sam will be waiting in a black van beside the road closest to the ocean. I'll give you a GPS with the coordinates of the van."

"So this is it, huh? No dock?"

"Sorry."

"Hey, it was a great ride." Rachel braced herself for a swell on the way to the cabin. She changed quickly and stuffed her clothes, pocket purse, hair brush, and shoes into the small dry bag, folded over the top and clicked the hasp closed. *This Sam Houston must be connected to more than Jerry and Henry to arrange all this.*

She came up out of the small cabin. The boat was now very close to the breakers. It lurched unexpectedly, tossing her against the gunnel, her hip hitting hard.

"Shit!" She yelped, holding back the full scream.

Marcia grabbed her under her arm, helping her up. "Sorry, Rache. The breakers are a little bigger than the weatherman called for. It smells like a storm is coming."

Rachel touched her right hip and winced. "Fucking weathermen! Wouldn't it be great to be wrong half the time and still keep your job. Glad I'm swimming and not running." She pivoted her legs over the side. "And thanks, girlfriend. We'll do dinner when I get back."

After she hit the water, she bobbed up and waved at Marcia.

Marcia waved back and reversed her engines. The powerful boat moved north. Within minutes the engine sound was gone.

Lightning lit the sky in the distance. Thunder reverberated, adding to the crash of distant waves on the beach.

Rachel was a strong swimmer, but the knife-like pain in her hip hindered her stroke. And the dry bag with her clothes pulled on her like a sea anchor. When she brought her head out of the water, the breakers didn't sound any closer.

In college, a hundred yards would have taken her a few minutes. Now it seemed like she was treading water. The undertow of amassing waves was tugging her the wrong way.

Kicking hard, gritting through the pain, she burst forward, caught the next wave, and managed to bodysurf almost to shore. Crawling onto the sand to escape the undertow, she pushed up and immediately fell down from the pain in her hip.

"Shit!" she swore in a prolonged whisper. She forced herself to stand, then gingerly limped to shore.

First, get off the wet suit. She decided to skip dressing. Her bra and underwear would look more like a swimsuit if she were seen, and she'd save time. Quickly putting on her shoes and orienting herself with the help of the GPS unit, she silently thanked Marcia again, then headed toward the highway.

This early in the morning, there was no traffic and few lights. On this barrier island, the tallest plants were sea oats. She stuck out like a lone tree on the prairie.

Finally she saw what looked like a dark VW van. Stealth was impossible, as exposed as she was. So, as the rain started falling, she acted like a drunken collegiate, half limping, half skipping toward the van, singing, "I'm singing in the rain, just singing in the rain…"

As she passed, she peered into the van through the open passenger window. A small, nondescript man said, "Get in, Rachel. And please, get some clothes on. It's freezing. What kind of shit are you trying to pull?"

She got in and he threw her a towel. His coal-black eyes reflected and magnified the available light—two black mirrors watching every move. He was a small man, his sitting height about six inches lower than Alex's. He wore blue jeans and a long-sleeved shirt with *Sam's Surf Shop* in red letters on the front. He pulled on a sky-blue *Tar Heels* ball cap and started the van.

"Although," he said looking at her before she wrapped the towel around her, "I agree with your disguise. It goes well with the island. But you better get dressed. I don't need any diversions tonight if we're going to make it to the Amazon Lab before daybreak."

He pulled the van onto the road.

Rachel squirmed into her jeans and pulled on her blouse. "I take it you're Sam Houston."

"If I'm not, you're going to have a hell of a time getting to South America. By the way, what exactly are you trying to do, besides getting us killed by the Feds?"

"I think you know exactly what I am trying to do." She spoke fast, not allowing for any answers. "But, to clear the air, I need to go to our lab in the Amazon. Since the earthquake we've had no communication. We really don't want to leave it up to the Brazilian government to check on things since we have some sensitive projects that require special consideration. Jerry thought I should go down there. Unfortunately the Feds have gone a little ballistic after September 11 and think we're part of the problem. My job is to convince them otherwise. Jerry gave me your card a minute before the Feds hauled him away." She took a breath. "Marcia was a nice touch, by the way."

She tied her shoes, pulled out the brush, and unsnarled her hair.

Sam glanced at her. "You carried a brush?"

"Hey, a girl has to look presentable."

He turned the van onto a tree-lined dirt road. "Okay, your story checks with Jerry's."

"Why did you ask if you already knew?"

"One can never be too sure with strange women on the beach wearing only underwear." He smiled at her. "But, seriously, at Amazon Lab, how were you planning to dig down to them if they're covered in earthquake rubble? Or have you got a dehydrated front-end loader in that dry bag?"

She scratched her lower lip and squinted at him with confusion. "Guess I was counting on your help with that. I'm more of a scientist, planning on helping with their lab work."

He maneuvered the van around several wheel-sized potholes, and gunned it through a small stream.

At a straight section of road, he glanced at her. "I can help with your problem. After all, Jerry vouched for you." A corner of his mouth ticked up.

He stopped the van in a paved clearing near a small Lear Jet thirty yards away. "We're here."

He jumped out of the van and jogged toward the jet.

She limped after him. "I thought they were monitoring flights, so we couldn't fly."

"Around D.C., that's true. Down here they're not quite so crazy, especially since I fly from here to Peru quite often to surf. Lima is a good jumping off spot for Punta Rocas or Kon Tiki. The waves are crazy bad there. I have a few buddies who stick there most of the year. But the big crashers aren't there yet, so they should be up for a little adventure elsewhere."

"So you really do surf? I thought it was only a disguise for the beach."

"It keeps me in shape. When the sport took off in the '80s, I already had a shop and a line of boards started. It pays for trips like this one."

He knocked on the door of the jet.

A young black man with dreadlocks to his shoulders opened the door. "Hey brah, how's it hangin'?" He pulled Sam into the plane. They clasped hands and slapped each other on the shoulder, disregarding Rachel.

Finally the man eyed Rachel. "Who's your mama?"

"Ron, Rachel Ann Lane. She'll be going with us. On the other side of the Divide we'll need her. After that, we might get a little white-water rafting in the Andes while we wait for the big waves to start."

"Hey Rachel, glad to meet ya." Ron's voice was a smooth, sing-songey baritone. His eyes were an unusual beige color, with mirth in them that Rachel immediately liked. Despite the cool night, he sported a tank top, shorts, and flip-flops.

"Glad to meet you, too."

Sam was already seated in the cockpit and starting the engine. "Okay, let's go. Ron, get her strapped in and get your butt up here. We gotta fly this baby before that storm smashes us. We may have outrun it flying in, but it is not far behind."

"Ron, don't listen to him. I can strap myself in. Go on up there and do your thing. I'm a big girl."

But Ron made sure she knew all about the safety features, lights and restrooms before he left.

After he left, she felt drained, and the hip pain returned. "Hey Ron, sorry to bother you again, but are there any pain meds on board? I bruised my hip pretty bad and it's starting to throb."

He unbuckled and came back. "No prob. You want Percodan? Vicodin?" His grin seemed a bit too wide.

"Good old Motrin would do me just fine."

"That's good, 'cause all we got is Motrin and Tylenol on board. Anything stronger and we might have to spend time in a Peruvian prison—not my bag."

He gave her the bottle of Motrin, some water, and went back to the cockpit.

As they took off, Rachel eased her seat back. In fifteen minutes the Motrin kicked in and she fell asleep. The calm confidence of her new friends coupled with the gentle vibration and loud hum of the jet made her feel more secure than she had since she left her last base camp in the Rockies.

Several hours later she awoke crying out. "Ow!" The armrest had attacked her hip. The hum of the jet was now a very loud whine.

"Sorry about that," yelled Sam. "We hit a pocket of disturbance clearing the Andes. That should be the worst of it. Are you okay? I noticed you limping a bit when we got out of the van. Do you need to see a doctor?"

"Only a bruise."

She rubbed her hip, hoping she was right. If the lab had suffered a lot of earthquake damage, she would need all her physical strength. The hip would just have to mend fast. She didn't have time for it.

She yelled at Sam, "What comes after Lima?"

"We'll take a puddle jumper to Amazon Lab. I'm told the trail from the river to the lab is pretty good. You think you can walk that far?"

She shifted her hip. "No problem."

He glanced back. "Do you have a passport?"

"Of course."

"We'll need to make some changes to it. There are some people looking for you."

"Don't worry. I've got a fake one. I had to use it recently, so I think it'll be okay." She was glad she'd grabbed it before she left her apartment.

"Just the same, let Ron look over the fake passport. The last several days our guys have been hassled over piddling stuff. Even though we've had a lot of experience getting people through customs."

Ron unbuckled from the copilot seat and walked back to her as she got her fake passport out. He studied it. "Pretty good, except the plastic laminate is not right."

She grabbed the passport and looked at it again. "What the heck do you mean, *not right*? It's only plastic."

"They might not have noticed it in U.S. airports before the terrorist attack. But since then they notice everything. Let me tweak it a little."

"I can't believe they can tell the difference."

Ron pulled out his passport and detailed how acceptable passports had a very clean edge, nothing turned up, the laminate without any bent areas or crinkles. Looking at the two she acquiesced, handing him her fake.

He went to the back of the plane. There was a slight whirring noise and the smell of burning plastic. A few minutes later he walked back to her. The plane bucked and he grabbed the back of the seat in front of her, then handed the passport to her.

She could immediately tell the difference. "Pretty obvious when you know what to look for. Sorry I gave you such a hard time."

"No prob. Here to help." He bowed at the waist.

"But how did you get a passport-making machine?"

Ron nodded his head at Sam. "He gets a lot of stuff. I just go along. Oh yeah, forgot to tell you, if you want a shower before we get there, we have one in the back. It's pretty small, but it should do. There are towels, soap, and shampoo. We have about forty-five minutes until we arrive."

"Sam must do pretty well with surf boards." She climbed out of her seat and started back toward the shower.

"You have no idea." Ron murmured.

Getting undressed in the tight quarters of the small bathroom, she briefly inspected her right hip and gasped at the bruise that had already spread down her upper thigh. Touching the area, she felt a silver-dollar-sized balloon full of liquid. It was tender, but not nearly as bad as it had been last night.

The hot shower felt good, though she knew ice on the hip would be better. She dressed, brushed her hair, and gargled with the mouthwash sample she found behind the mirror. Walking out, she felt like she could tackle whatever lay ahead.

"Hey, do you have any ice?"

Ron got up and pulled out a cold pack from the above-seat compartment, twisted and squeezed it, and gave it to her. "We go through a lot of these, so if you need more, help yourself."

Placing the cold pack between her hip and the armrest, she leaned against it and hoped for an instant cure. She could hear Sam talking to the Lima airport, getting landing instructions.

He finished and spoke over the intercom. "Ladies and gentlemen, we are making our approach to the Lima International Airport. To the left is a spectacular view of the Peruvian Andes, with peaks six thousand feet higher than Mt. Whitney, and the Cotahuasi Canyon, twice as deep as the Grand Canyon. If you look closely, you can see the cloud cover to the east where the greatest river basin of the world begins. The Amazon River supports the largest rain forest in the world, emptying twenty percent of the entire world's fresh water into the Atlantic Ocean, more than fifty times the volume of the Nile. It has a thousand tributaries, seventeen of which are over a thousand miles long. When we get there, I hope you like bugs and birds, because there are two-point-five million species of insects and over one-fifth of the world's species of birds. Don't forget your machete to chop through the seventy-five thousand species of trees and one hundred fifty thousand species of other plants. And that's in only one square kilometer. You'll also need your snake repellent for the anaconda, the largest snake in the world. I could go on and on, but we are about to land. Fasten your seat belts."

Ron turned around and shrugged. "He loves that speech."

Rachel couldn't help but grin. Quite a pair.

She glanced out the window at snow-capped peaks and bottomless canyons. No wonder Alex and Jesse liked coming down here.

"Sam, you wouldn't happen to have a camera, would you? Preferably with a telephoto lens?"

"Yeah, I have an old Pentax k1000 with a sliding macro a hundred-and-fifty millimeter lens. It's not great, but works for most of our shots."

"While I'm here, maybe I could get some shots of the Amazon. And maybe once we get done, we could take some time up in the Andes. What do you think?"

Sam looked at Ron, and the two of them laughed.

"What the hell are you two giggling about? Did I put my bra on backwards?"

"No, no." Sam said. "I mean, I don't know about your bra, but we like your attitude, that's all. Not too many people can think about doing hobbies when they're running from the CIA and are about to enter an earthquake zone. You might be going to a federal prison, but you're thinking about a photo stop in the Andes instead. We're just happy you're along. You'll fit right in."

Sam looked at Ron. They both grinned and then broke out laughing again.

Rachel frowned. "What do you mean go to a federal prison? All I'm doing is trying to help some friends and save our company."

Sam held up his hands. "The five-hour flight has me a little punchy. While you were sleeping Ron and I were considering what our chances would be if the CIA or Marines catch us aiding and abetting a person of interest—that would be you—get out of the country."

Her blank look was followed by silence.

Sam gave the controls to Ron and asked her, "You really haven't got a clue as to what happened to your boss or why, do you?"

"I'm not sure what you're talking about. I thought that once they questioned him and found out they'd made a mistake, everything would get back to normal."

Sam got up and walked back, sitting beside her. "Let me explain. There is a senator on the Hill who has been waiting for the right time to increase the power of the CIA, FBI, and all the other security boys. In the past they couldn't listen in on your phone because of certain laws. Now those laws are about to be changed in the name of fighting terrorism. When you ran from them, you became a person of interest.

"The new rules about wire-tapping and capturing suspects of terrorism have not been instituted yet, but the senator has a private security firm. Private firms can already invade your privacy as much as they want.

"Since your company's involvement in bio-warfare research has been hidden by the government, the senator has no idea your company and everyone who works there aren't terrorists. He will tap your phones, search your apartments, and download your computer files. They'll know every little secret you have, down to where you got your last pair of Nikes. And, if you're not cooperative enough, they'll take you to a CIA secret prison and torture you until you tell them what they want or die in the process. And if you die, they'll spin it so everyone thinks you were a terrorist. They don't really care about the Constitution of the United States. *We the people* refers only to them, not anyone else.

"So. You, me, and Ron will never get to the Andes, let alone Brazil, unless we get through the next two hours of customs at Lima without someone discovering who you really are."

Mouth agape and eyes wide, she slumped back in her chair.

Then she frowned and sat forward. "Oh, that. Yeah, I knew all that. Sure, it's totally obvious. The CIA will pull my thumbnails out so they can find out that I work on viruses. Hell, they already know that! That sergeant who picked me up, what's his name, Prescott, he knew I was working on the same stuff as Scott. So why would they want to torture me? I mean, after all I have rights. I'm a U.S. citizen. Aaaannnd," her voice wavered and her eyes welled with tears, "I lost my fiancée in one of the attacks, for Christ's sake."

"Hey, now. It's okay." Sam's tone was soft. "I'm on your side. I'm only trying to tell you where we stand. We just experienced the first attack on the continental U.S. since the Civil War, and the whole country is looking for vengeance. Some people who run the government have thrown away the rulebook and are getting cheers for it. I knew Scott and a lot of others who died, and it makes me mad, too. But it's a fact of life that some of the freedoms that the makers of the Constitution worked so hard to get have been taken away. Let's hope it doesn't result in a police state. Anyway, I am here to help you. You just need to know the downside before we get knee deep in the Amazon. Are you with me?"

Rachel dried her tears and nodded; forcing a determined look on her face. "Yeah, I'm with you. Thanks. What do you need me to do to keep us safe and get us where we want to be?"

Sam looked her over, then called out to Ron, "Tell them you need to circle once more." Then he said to Rachel, "You need to be in something a little more revealing, to throw off the guards. It'll be around sixty degrees in Lima, but the airport should be warmer. Let me get you an outfit one of the girls left last time. You're going to play the part of a brainless bimbo here to watch us surf. The airport officials are used to seeing that, so it'll seem natural."

"Whatever you think."

He rummaged through one of the closets by the bathroom and returned with a spaghetti-strapped, lemon-yellow tank top, sky-blue boy shorts, and gray platform shoes. He also tossed her a black thong swim bottom.

"You need to lose the bra. You might consider doing something a little more bimboish with your hair, too. We'll pack your stuff in our dry bags."

She laughed and held up the thong. "You guys do live well, don't you?" She traipsed off to the bathroom, dangling the thong off her thumb, held out like a hitchhiker's.

When she returned, Sam was seated beside Ron again. He turned to see her and stared. And she knew why. Small, erect nipples showed through her tank top, and, as she twirled around, the short shorts revealed the curve of her butt at the tops of her shapely thighs. Her hair was teased in several different directions. A touch of rouge and wrap-around Arnette sunglasses topped off her transformation. Only someone who knew her would see through the disguise, and then only after close scrutiny.

"Wow!" he said. "Now that's a disguise that should throw off the customs officers. Their little heads will be so active their brains will disconnect."

She took off her glasses, revealing dark eyeliner, mascara, and brown contact lenses. "Hang ten, baby!" She gave a little giggle. "If you're going to go for a disguise, might as well go all the way. The fake passport says I have brown eyes, so I used the contacts I had when I went through DIA. I found the sunglasses and the makeup in the bathroom. When do we land?"

Sam looked at his watch. "Probably in about ten minutes. How do the shoes fit?"

"They'll do, but I won't be doing any hiking. How long do I have to keep this act up, anyhow? I can't wait to get back in my Nikes. Do you really think the CIA will know where I bought 'em? Why would they care?"

Sam shrugged. "They care. Probably even interviewed the sales clerk."

She sat down and adjusted the straps on her shoes. Better make this good.

Sam spoke over his shoulder as he walked back to the cockpit. "I figure we should get through customs in about an hour, maybe less, since it's only 4:00 a.m. Although, when the other guys came down a few days ago, customs took forever. They even inspected their shoes, and they were wearing flip-flops, for Christ's sake."

He strapped himself in. Ron flipped a few switches and pulled a lever. The landing gear lowered and the wing flaps changed angles. The jet slowed and they descended.

CHAPTER 22

Fifteen minutes later they were walking onto a sunny tarmac. Rachel was a little chilly in her outfit but warmed quickly on reaching the protection of the customs alcove. She decided to ham it up a little, tussling Ron's dreadlocks and keeping a running conversation with him.

"So, Ronny boy, tell me, how do you dry out this hair if you're surfing all the time? Doesn't it hold a lot of water? And don't you get tired of fixing it up in these locks all the time? It must take forever."

Ron talked in a lilting, Jamaican cadence as he walked, glancing back at her. "Dreads symbolize da patience and da beliefs of da Rastas, mon. Peace and kindness." His voice became normal. "I'm not totally devoted to all the Rasta beliefs, like Haile Selaisse being the savior, but I like the hair thing. Besides, it gives me a little something to talk about with the girls."

He winked at her and put his arm around her shoulders, giving her a squeeze.

It wasn't hard for her to play along with the ruse. He was very gentle, with captivating eyes and a melodic, mesmerizing voice, which kept her at ease, though her undercurrent of concern about what would happen at customs was barely contained.

The lady at the one customs desk was heavy in the middle but had a bright smile and jovial attitude, which helped Rachel loosen up. The lady inspected her face and started to look down, but stopped abruptly and went back to her face and offered her bright teeth again. Next came the baggage claim room, only three small ramps where the luggage came in from the planes, and two large tables. Two guards stood with holstered handguns. They had no problems looking at her from the neck down.

A Pakistani family was in front of them. They went through a full body search, even the children. The contents of their luggage were strewn all over the search tables, falling onto the filthy floor.

This was not going to be fun. She wanted to help the Pakistani family or at least punch the stupid guards.

If they went through her pocket purse with that much care, they would find her other ID and she would be toast.

While she waited, she stood with one hip out, occasionally scratching one thigh with a finger. One of the guards kept eyeing her legs, then he motioned with his arm for her to come over to him. She caught his eye and turned on a big smile, walking with exaggerated hip sway.

While still glancing at her legs he opened her purse and dumped the contents of her purse onto the table. There was a loud knock on the customs table and he turned dark eyes to the table, now suspicious.

A pocket knife of her grandfather's had made the knocking sound against the Formica top. The fake ID was right next to the pocket knife. The guard reached down and picked up the pocket knife, folded out the blade and squinted at her. While keeping her gaze, he cupped one hand and flexed it in "come here" motion toward the other guard. Rough hands grabbed each of her arms. She tensed and glanced sideways at Sam. He shook his head. The inspector eyed her up and down, a bit too carefully, she thought.

Sam placed three bills on the table. Without looking at Sam, the inspector plucked the bills from the table, folded the blade closed, and pocketed the knife. He turned and walked back to the gate.

The guards released her.

She started to go after the pig who took her grandfather's knife, the knife she had cleaned her first fish with, her grandfather helping her with his gentle hands.

Sam put an arm out, blocking her path. "Put your stuff back in your purse, and let's get out of here."

"That was my grandfather's knife. I'm getting it back before we leave."

He whispered, "Is it worth going to Peruvian jail and getting raped by four of those goons?"

She closed her eyes and clenched her jaw. The contents of her purse, including the blaringly real ID, took only a few seconds to replace in her pocket purse.

She glared at the inspector and took a step towards him. Ron put an arm around her. "Come on, Rachel. You don't want any of this. Trust me."

Walking behind Sam, he ushered her out of the airport toward a waiting VW van with a mural stenciled on the side—a thong-clad Brazilian woman pointing through the words *Sam's Surf Shop* toward a chiseled, blond American surfer riding a wave.

Rachel shook her head and did a one-eighty. This would not do. She had to get that knife back.

Ron hugged her arms against her sides. "It's not happening, Rachel. The knife is gone."

She struggled. He held on. "Tell you what. Next time I come through here, I'll see what I can do about getting it back."

She relaxed. After another several seconds he released his hold.

She flicked off a tear with one finger. "You'd better."

"I will."

She closed her eyes and rolled her head around on her neck. When she opened her eyes she peered at the mural for a few seconds before hopping into the back seat. "You guys do have an image to uphold, don't you?"

Sam started the van and glanced back at her. "Marketing is important, even in Peru." He pulled out onto the road. "A little cash does a lot more down here than in the States. By Peru standards, we pay the hired help very good money. But by U.S. standards, wages are dirt cheap, so I pay a paltry sum. So I capitalize a little. They also capitalize, and we live in harmony. Without my business, a lot of little Peru kids would be going hungry."

"Your cash didn't do anything for my pocket knife."

"I'm sorry for that. But it did take the guy's mind off the rest of your purse's contents. Including your real ID "

She pursed her lips and studied the floor.

"Anyway, that's the way it is in Lima, Peru. The other plane is waiting down the road. It's not well-heated. We have coats, but you'll need warmer clothes for the ride over the Andes. You can change in the back of the van."

"I take it that's what the curtains are for," she said, closing the curtains, including the one between the back and front seats of the van.

"Well," he murmured softly to Ron, "that's one option."

She popped her head through the slit in the curtains. "I heard that. My momma didn't raise no slut. Get your minds out of the gutter and tell me why the hell we didn't stay on the jet all the way to the lab. It would have been a lot easier."

She closed the curtains so fast she almost pulled them off the rails.

"Jeez, I was joking, trying to lighten you up a bit. We're taking off from a private airport that doesn't ask questions. We have an amphib that can take off on dirt here and land in water in the Amazon River close to your lab. There are no airstrips where we're going. Lear jets don't take off again after landing in a river."

She pulled the curtains back, now fully clothed, but with her hair still spiked. "How long will it be before we get there?" she said, fitting on her Nikes.

"I'd say late afternoon, depending." He looked at Ron, who nodded his head.

She looked first at Ron, then Sam. "What the hell do you mean by 'depending'?"

"Well," Ron said, "we were thinking it might be better if you stayed here in Lima. We have a nice house close to the beach. You'd be comfortable. If we need you, we can contact you by radio. The jungle can get pretty hairy. And there are still guerrilla fighters down there that enjoy women in the wrong way."

"Trying to make up for that curtains optional crack, right? Well, I appreciate the thought, but I need to get the lab back up and running, and I have information they need that I can't really tell you over the radio. In case you forgot, I am also a virologist, and I have skills that will help them. So I'm going." She glared at Sam through the rearview mirror.

He raised an eyebrow at her and looked away. "Okaaay. So, tell me, do you know how to shoot a rifle? And what about rappelling? I understand they have one hell of an elevator shaft. If the elevator is not working, we may need to rappel down to rescue the other scientists."

A dirt airstrip came into view.

"I grew up shooting, but haven't fired a rifle or pistol in about ten years. I hate hunting, though I know my way around a rifle. And I rappelled just last week, by myself, with no male help!" She caught his eyes in the mirror again. "What about you? How are you at shooting while having shaking chill from malaria? Have you had your vaccinations for yellow fever and typhoid?"

His monotone answer was muffled by the sliding stop of the van on the gravel. "Yeah, we had our shots, and we got some doxy."

Beside the airstrip was a small plane that looked like a four-seated crop duster, with wheels below the aluminum pontoons. When the dust from the van cleared, rust and dents covered the plane's body. This would fly them over the Andes?

Two men were bent over, inspecting the underside of the engine. At the sound of Sam driving up, they ducked around the engine and walked over. One was straight from a Harley Davidson ad, sporting blue jeans and a white crew-necked tee shirt. He was missing the leather coat but he had the leather boots and a tawny Fu Manchu mustache and wavy red hair combed back from a freckled forehead. A skull and crossbones was tattooed on his bulging freckled right biceps. He held a wrench in his left hand and a greasy rag in his right. He said in a gravelly voice to Sam, "This fucker's a piece of junk. Tell me you're not going to fly it today. I've been working on this since last night and it's still not right."

"And a hearty hello to you, too, Jimbo," said Sam.

Jimbo's blue eyes sparkled as he squinted into the morning sun. "Listen, if I'm going with you, to hell with the formalities. I'm going to need more time on this engine unless you plan on parachuting instead of landing."

The other man looked like a native Andean: short and slightly built with black shoulder-length hair, Roman nose, and dark eyes that danced as he spoke. His accent was barely noticeable, his enunciation precise and law-yerlike. "James, please stop your mussitations. This plane is in excellent mechanical condition. Don't let the body fool you. I have flown it for two years without so much as a sputter. We need to change the oil and make a few more tweaks, and we'll be ready." Looking at the newcomers, he said, "Hi, Sam. Sorry about James. He hasn't had his coffee yet."

"He's always the pessimist, I know. How's the family, José?" Sam shook both men's hands and hugged José.

Turning to Rachel, Sam said, "Rachel, this is Jimbo O'Connor and José Phillipe. Jimbo runs the surf shop here, and José helped us get things started five years ago. I called them after Henry gave me the heads-up yesterday. They'll be helping us get you to the Amazon Lab. Guys, this is Rachel Lane."

Jimbo grunted a hello and José bowed. "Welcome to my country. I hope you had a pleasant journey."

Rachel was charmed by the well-mannered José. "At least the company has improved now that I've met you. Is this thing really going to get us over the Andes, all the way to Amazon Lab?"

"This is my baby. I know her like the palm of my hand. She will fly to your Amazon Lab, though we must stop once and refuel in Iquitos."

"I'm bringing my parachute." Jimbo put one hand on his crotch, "And a cup." He glared at José. "And I'll mussitate all I want. You and your fancy words." He made a flourish of wiping his hands on the greasy rag.

José put an arm around Rachel's shoulder and directed her to the east. "You are good luck, Rachel. The normal fog is gone today. You can see our beautiful mountains quite well, and we will have grand flying weather."

To the east, dry plains met rugged foothills, brown and stark, and were framed by the majestic, snow-capped Andes. The crystal-clear air shrank the distance, making the snow on the peaks appear so close that Rachel shivered. A wind-whipped dust devil moved across the plains, blurring the view for an instant. Above the little twister, a gull floated on the sea breeze, higher and higher, until it was a speck in the azure sky.

Sam walked to the plane. "Let's get moving."

CHAPTER 23

The flight over the Andes was as smooth as José had predicted, the plane mostly purring like a well-tuned Corvette. Once, it sputtered for a few seconds and Jimbo cringed, grabbing his crotch and head. Rachel chuckled when Sam explained that Jimbo thought his family jewels held his mojo. At the height of their flight, she was glad for the extra coat and hot coffee from Sam's thermos. But after the stop in Iquitos and then more descent into the Amazon valley, she shed the extra clothes, soon wishing she had the shorts she left behind. The heat became oppressive.

The plane had been bucking a headwind, so the flight took longer than expected. It was twilight when they arrived. They had a smooth water landing. Before deplaning, everyone but Rachel pulled out a handgun and either stuck it in a shoulder holster or in the small of their back. Sam gave Rachel a Berretta 9mm handgun. "Just in case."

In the fading light, Sam led. Rachel slapped insects and trudged up the same helter-skelter stone path that Alex had been up two weeks ago. So much green. She could understand now how the Amazon forests generated fifty percent of the world's oxygen.

"What is that odd bird song?" Rachel asked. "It sounds like a jerky flautist."

"A musician wren, I believe," Sam said. "They are supposed to bring good luck."

They crested the hill and the sight dashed Rachel's hope of good luck. The security gate and fence were mangled and the building was nothing but smoldering rubble.

Sam stopped at the wrecked fence and put an arm out in front of Rachel. "We should wait 'til morning. We could use the light and I might call for reinforcements."

Rachel took out a flashlight. "We all have guns. You stay here with the damn mosquitoes, take a bath in DEET, I don't give a shit. I'm going down to the lab."

"Come on, Rachel. This does not look like an earthquake."

"Even more reason to move ahead. You implied you were good with a gun. So let's go."

"Right. Just take it slow and follow my lead."

They rummaged around the wreckage, looking for the elevator.

Jimbo mumbled, "I don't like this."

"Do not worry, my little chicken, there are no monsters here." José stuck his thumbs under his armpits and proceeded to flap his bent arms like chicken wings. Then he stopped. "Hold on. Sam, come over here. I think this is something."

Rachel got to José first. "This is the door to the elevator shaft. Let me." She had José and Jimbo pull back on the leaning desk and she opened the door and shone her flashlight inside. A familiar figure pointed a gun at her.

She sunk to a knee quickly. "M.C., it's Rachel. Don't shoot. "

M.C. let the gun drop to his side. "You're lucky I heard your voice before you opened the door." He crawled out on his hands and knees. She and Jimbo had to almost lift him up to standing.

"Are you okay, M.C.?" she asked.

"Just bad knees."

She hugged him. "Man, am I glad to see you. I thought you all might be dead, or at the very least buried from the earthquake…or whatever this was."

He stuck the gun in the small of his back. "Rachel, you're the last person I expected to see. We're not dead, but we have had a few missteps since the…uh, earthquake."

He glanced at the others. "Who are all these guys? Are they cleared?"

"They may not be cleared, but they risked their lives getting me here. After the September 11 attacks, things have been very strange. The Feds even took Jerry in for questioning, if you can believe that. They think he's some kind of Nazi."

"September 11 attacks?"

Sam walked behind Rachel and held his hand out to M.C.

"We'll fill you in about that stuff later. I'm Sam Houston. The guy with the dreads is Ron, and these are Jimbo and José."

They all shook hands, Ron adding a high five.

Sam said, "I think I know a friend of yours from the old boomer world. Does John Harter ring a bell?"

M.C. rubbed his pate with one hand. "Harter? Yeah, I knew him. We shared a few beers when I was stationed in Reykjavik. How'd you know him?"

"His son had a little problem with a big wave once in Hawaii. I helped him out and met his father in the hospital. What a great guy. Tells me you play a mean game of gin rummy."

"Oh yeah, good old boomer days. Weeks of boredom cutting holes in the ocean with a submarine filled with nuclear missiles. Where would I have been without gin rummy in the chief's mess?"

He paused and peered into the darkness. "I'm sure you all know that this was no earthquake. We should get out of the open, down to the lab. You can catch us up on this September 11 attack. We've had no com for a week."

They followed M.C. down the shaft, now lit by several flashlights wandering the walls. Sam came last, making sure there was enough debris heaped up to conceal the closet door. The only sound was the distant hum of the lab machinery. A misstep from José prompted a growl from Jimbo.

Once they were down, M.C. limped as he led them down the hall.

Doc had stationed himself behind the first door coming from the elevator hall. He woke with a start to the sound of footsteps. He almost fell off the chair, nearly dropping a .45 he'd retrieved earlier from the wall safe. Too many footsteps. M.C. had been gone way too long. This must be the terrorists.

He faced the closed door: wide stance, gun raised, safety off. The gun was shaking so much he didn't know if he could hit the door, much less shoot another person. He was a doctor, not a soldier. Last time he'd even fired one of these things was five years ago.

M.C.'s voice said, "Doc, it's me. With friends."

Doc lowered the gun, thumbed the safety on, and opened the door. "Good thing you said something." He wiped the sweat off his forehead.

"Rachel," he said. "What the heck are you doing here?"

Rachel stepped forward and kissed Doc on the cheek. "Long story. I'll tell you in the kitchen."

Doc gave her a quizzical look. She stared him down. "Okay, so who are these other guys?"

"In the kitchen." She turned and walked that way.

It took a few minutes for everyone to make it to the kitchen. Introductions were made, though Doc took a second to respond to Ron's high five.

M.C. made coffee and once everyone was settled, said, "Okay, Rachel. The floor's all yours."

Rachel walked to the coffee pot, looked at Doc and told the story of the September 11 attacks. Doc and M.C. looked at each other, wide eyed.

"Jesus," Doc said. "How many dead?"

Sam said, "Still counting. Over two thousand in the Twin Towers, a couple hundred in the planes, and a little over a hundred at the Pentagon. More firefighters killed than any other disaster, I think they said."

"And Muslim extremists did this?" M.C. eyed the elevator. "Maybe they're up there, too?"

Rachael said, "Whoever bombed you topside will find the elevator shaft soon, so let's get to work. Where are Jesse and Alex?" She slapped her palm on her forehead. "Damn. I forgot about Lora."

"Lora?" Doc said.

Rachel shook her head. "She was at ground zero for the Twin Towers. No one's heard from her."

"Damn," Doc said. "Alex has been having strange feelings about her. I thought it was just déjà vu."

M.C. caught her gaze, "What about Scott?"

She studied the ground and her voice got quiet. "He was killed in the Pentagon attack. I didn't find out about it until a few days ago. And the bastards that did it are going to pay."

Doc's eyes widened. He'd known Rachel a year and respected her as a virologist. When she made up her mind to do something, completion was guaranteed. So her last comment made him cold.

Revenge. A simple word that caused wars and destroyed people.

He spoke gently. "I'm sorry about Scott. But I think it would be better if you let *me* tell Alex about Lora. You've had enough strain…and Alex is not himself."

Her gaze softened, tears forming. "Okay, Doc. Whatever you say. It's been a rough twenty-four hours."

M.C. cleared his throat. "Before anyone talks to Alex or Jesse, hear me out. First, we still have a mission to complete. Whoever bombed this place must know what we're doing. I agree with Rachel: they'll be coming soon."

He paused a beat and glanced around the room. "Second, Jesse and Alex don't know about the bombing topside or that the elevator shaft is safe. They think we're cut off for another couple of days. I want to keep it that way. Jesse had some ties with Muslims in grad school, so she will likely be very upset. Alex and her are pretty tight, and Alex is already on a tightrope about Lora. They need to work nonstop, no interruptions.

"Third, they're asleep right now; they've had a rough few days and needed a few hours. I suggest Rachel and Doc get started in the lab."

"Charlie Mike, always complete the mission. Huh, M.C.?" said Sam.

"Well, somebody's got to get their priorities right. From the sounds of it, you guys might get sidetracked going after bad guys." M.C. started getting up. "Let me get the elevator started. While Doc and Rachel do their thing, we'll go set up a few surprises for any visitors."

"Speaking of mission," Rachel said. "The Iraqis have been researching the same viral weapons. We have to develop a vaccine, and pronto. Probably even more important than finishing our bio-weapon. I've done some preliminary work back at Main Lab and can access that if you have Internet access."

"We should," M.C. said. "I patched the cable and reset the satellite dish."

"Great. While Doc works on viral pairings, I'll get started on the vaccine. By the way, how effective were the new enzymes we sent down with Alex?"

"They helped a lot, but we've had mutations we haven't seen before. So be real careful with those babies."

M.C. and the others left, their receding footsteps echoing.

"Hurry back!" Rachel shouted. "Be careful!" Her shout bounced around the hallway. *If they don't come back, I'm screwed.*

No answer.

Doc shifted in his seat, his pants squeaking. "Rachel, come on, let's get going. M.C. can handle himself. He even has help."

—

M.C. entered the elevator, biting his lower lip and gripping his hands. Part of him wanted to go back up the ladder in the shaft. Once the elevator door opened topside they would be sitting ducks. But someone could have watched them enter the closet and be planted there as well. Besides, his knees couldn't take the ladder again.

The door to the elevator closed. The other four men looked like they were patiently waiting at a bus stop. The whir of the motor reminded him of the sound of submarine engines lulling him to sleep when he was a young sailor.

But there would be no sleep tonight.

CHAPTER 24

Jabril had waited too long in the Manila airport. He fumed, but his anger could only help keep him vigilant for so long.

An airport security guard approached, and Jabril blinked back fatigue. This was the third time he'd seen the guard, and this time he was definitely studying Jabril closely.

The departures billboard flashed. The flight to LAX was boarding.

Jabril pointed to the billboard and using hand gestures and broken English, tried to communicate that he would be leaving soon. The guard nodded and walked on, querying an Asian who'd been standing outside the restrooms for a little too long.

Once on the flight, Jabril stored his briefcase and overnight bag at his feet. He was asleep even before takeoff.

He dreamed of his mother again.

She is healthy and smiling. He is a young boy. She kicks the soccer ball, and he runs as fast as the wind. Looking down, he sees hooves pounding the ground, the legs of a black Arabian horse. Faster. Faster still. He thinks he's riding the horse until he kicks at the ball and sees the ball bounce off his hoof. The ball sails through the goal. Mother jumps up and down, clapping at his success. She runs to him and kisses his cheek and pats his hairy chest. He hugs her with his arms, feeling aroused, and then ashamed.

He realizes he is a centaur, torso muscled and glistening with man-sweat, his lower body that of a powerful, sleek horse. He aches to prove how fast he has become. Proudly he struts, his animal urges and energy brimming over. Pawing at the earth, he bursts into a run.

He races through a familiar Afghanistan mountain pass following another centaur—his grandfather. They are with a herd of his kind, all galloping faster and faster, until soon they are flying, somehow having sprouted wings. The winged centaurs were like Al-Buraq—sleek and shimmering in the warm sunlight.

Flying higher and higher, the mist of clouds wets his cheeks. There are snow-capped peaks below him. Ribbons of silvery rivers flash in the sun. He finally flutters into a white radiating cave in the sky. Changing back to a man, he walks to the side of Muhammad, who embraces him, kissing each cheek twice, beckoning him to sit at his side.

His mother is also there, but something is wrong. She has a head full of snakes and is standing naked, leaning over the chair he is to sit in. She has a large cactus thorn in one hand and beckons him to sit in the chair below her. As he sits, she sticks the thorn into her other hand. Two black drops drip down. One misses him, but one warm, wet drop hits him square on the forehead. And then he is falling...falling without control into flames burning his back and legs.

Please, Allah, he begs, take away the pain. It is too great.

He awakened and must have cried out, because a young boy stared at him from two seats ahead. The boy gazed at him with soft, brown eyes, as if trying to ease his pain. Jabril smiled at the boy. His face disappeared behind his mother's shawl as she pulled him to her.

The fever seemed to have passed, and he no longer felt the urge to cough. The low rumble of the plane's engines drowned other sounds; the air conditioning was cool on his beaded forehead. With his hands he squeezed each thigh and glanced down to make sure he had no hooves. Everything was as it should be.

The dreams had come before, after he had left Iraq for school. *It's the stress. You're overtired. Take a sedative tonight and there will be no dreams. Then only a few more days.*

Trying to think of something else, his eyes focused on the rise and fall of each buttock of the black stewardess as she walked up the aisle. Almost immediately he became energized, no longer tired. He watched the shift of her hips, the sheen of her pants, perhaps a bit thinner fabric and tighter than regulations allowed. He wet his lips and touched his tongue to his teeth. He was so hard he ached.

Hmm. Perhaps he would not be sleeping tonight.

He pushed the call button. She turned toward him. She was beautiful: full lips, white teeth, rust-colored eyes, and nipples that tented her white blouse. As she walked, the swaying and bouncing of her breasts made him dizzy. A soft guttural groan escaped before he could squelch it. He quickly looked away. Hopefully she had not seen him ogling her or heard him moan.

Coming up beside him, she reached across his face to turn off the call button, her breasts only inches from his nose. He closed his eyes and turned his head to the side.

"Can I help you, sir?" Her voice was silk. He opened his eyes, and she stood above him with a pleasant smile, looking at him with those warm, caring eyes.

He must have her. Yet how could he seduce this young black woman while keeping his disguise as an elderly Jewish jeweler?

"I have forgotten my medicine for my arthritis. Do you have any Tylenol or Advil?" His voice had exactly the right timber for an aging man, with a slight Mid-Eastern accent.

"Of course, sir. I'll be back in a minute."

She walked up the aisle again, her hips moving more quickly.

He loosened the top button of his shirt and opened the air conditioning blower. He flexed and un-flexed his wrist and elbow. The muscles were engorged with blood, as if he had been pumping weights. He felt so incredible that he wanted to scream a challenge to the world. Who needed the Qur'an, Muhammad, God? He could conquer anyone, anything, anytime.

But not now. The woman sauntered back down the aisle, clutching water in one hand, steadying herself on the seat backs with the other.

She reached his side and handed him the water and pills. "Here you are, sir."

"Oh, thank you. Your husband is certainly a lucky man to have someone as kind as you." He said it gently, like an uncle.

Her smiled widened but her eyes studied him. "I hope to be engaged soon. We've been dating for a while."

"Forgive me for being perhaps a bit too forward. Do you believe in fate?"

She glanced at the passengers behind him and lowered the volume of her voice. "I guess so."

"As fate would have it, I am a jeweler and I have an assortment of engagement rings. I am prepared to offer these to you for a substantial discount."

"Wow…I guess this is fate." The tone told him she was losing interest. "We were looking at rings only last week. And they are so expensive. But—you know—work calls." She turned to leave.

He gently took her hand.

She twisted her head back toward him, frowning.

He let go. "Forgive me again. I will be staying at the midtown Radisson Hotel in Los Angeles. Perhaps you could come by tonight and look at a few samples over coffee."

"Maybe…" Her look became thoughtful." "Yes, maybe that could work. I have a layover and a flight out in the morning. Do you have a card? If I can't make it tonight, maybe I can call you and set up a meeting later."

"Regrettably, my cards are in my other bag. But you may call the Radisson and ask for Jabril Aswan. Of course, the front desk will need to know your name. They know I am a private person. I am particular about my guests."

His eyes were soft, warm; his touch gentle. Merely a kind old man offering to help.

"Kara, my name is Kara Ward. And I might just call you tonight."

"I will look forward to it. But do try to call before 8:00 p.m. If I drink coffee much later than that I am up all night. I am not so young anymore." He bowed his head briefly.

She turned and walked away. He watched every move: Her hips, the space between her legs closing and opening in a smooth easy tempo like a waltz. What a wonderful night this would be.

When he got off at LAX, he smiled at her at the door. She whispered, "I can't wait to see those rings."

He nodded. "It will be my pleasure."

His cab ride to the Radisson was a blur, weaving around thoughts of the evening ahead. Calling a cousin in L.A., he arranged to meet him that afternoon after the cousin first stopped at the bank and retrieved the jewels from a safety deposit box. If she wanted diamonds and rings, he would have them.

Perhaps he would tell her his plan. She seemed so accommodating. His mother would have liked her: One of the Africans downtrodden by white Americans. She would understand the need to wipe the infidels off the face of the earth.

At 7:00 p.m., his phone rang. "Hello, this is Jabril Aswan."

There was a pause. He strained to listen, hoping.

"Mr. Aswan, is it still okay if I come over? I had a few drinks to unwind. If that offends you, I won't come."

Her speech sounded slurred. The chemical he had in mind would act even quicker with alcohol.

"No, my dear. I had a little wine myself tonight. Please come. I have something special to show you. Third floor, number 315." He was such a good uncle.

"Okay, I'll be there in about twenty minutes."

"That will be fine."

He waited to hear her lovely voice again, but she'd hung up.

Twenty minutes was too long. His body was poised like a bow drawn to its limit. Pacing slowly at first, his tempo increased until he was running in circles in the small room. The sweat ran down his temples and he felt his beard coming unglued. No! He stopped and rolled his shoulders and flexed his fingers. He must get control of himself.

He checked himself in the mirror and touched up the makeup and false beard. He noticed his own beard had grown a centimeter. His eyebrows seemed bushier and his eyes seemed to have an auburn tint. Smiling at his reflection, his teeth seemed whiter, canines larger. He shook his head and looked again. All was normal except the beard growth. Perhaps he was more in need of sleep than he thought.

He walked to counter and the jewels he had set aside for her in a black onyx bowl. Perhaps he should pray. He stuck his finger in the middle, slowly stirring them. Reflections of the jewels sent tiny spotlights dancing on the ceiling and walls. It reminded him of his dream, the lighted cave in the sky. He felt weightless.

He jerked his head down to check his legs, then let out a slow breath. *Human, not animal.*

A knock on the door was like a shot under his feet. He instantly stood, smoothed his coat, took a deep breath, and willed a slow walk to the door. Opening it, she was there, a vision he wanted to imprint forever.

Her copper eyes entranced him. Half-lowered lids made her seem like she was already in bed, ready. A yellow cotton top fit tightly across her torso and breasts; the color contrasted with her smooth, ebony skin, magnifying every luxurious curve. One thin strap had alluringly fallen down on her arm, leaving a shapely and bare shoulder. Her short skirt was truly breathtaking, revealing almost the full length of her smooth, brown thighs.

"Hello, Mr. Aswan. I hope this is not an inconvenience."

Was she purring to him? Her voice was so smooth and low and—

From behind her, a huge black man rushed by and plowed into Jabril, toppling him like a pile of sticks.

The man struck Jabril's head with a small, snakelike object.

Kara closed the door and walked over to him, just has he was losing consciousness. "Don't kill the guy, Benny."

Her words were not slurred at all.

Benny checked the second swing of his blackjack, looking at the now-unconscious man under his knee. "Okay, Baby, where's the stuff? Grab it and let's get out of here." Benny stood, satisfied that his victim was out cold.

The jewels shimmered and overflowed in a black bowl on the low mahogany coffee table. "Jesus. This guy has some fine shit here. Maybe we should take a few and leave the rest. We take all this, and we'll have some serious heat on us."

"Fuck that! I been waitin' all my life for a big haul. We're goin' to Jamaica, girl!" He grabbed the heavy bowl in one enormous hand and emptied the contents into a black cotton bag she'd brought. He pulled the pursed end tight and stuffed the bag in his pocket, then jiggled the pocket, laughing at the sound of so many jewels.

Kara looked at him, her eyes wide, her mouth open, yet it was not happiness in her eyes or lust in her mouth Benny saw. And he realized it was not him she was looking at.

A low growl filled the room, seeming to emanate from the floor.

Too late, Benny turned, swinging the blackjack.

Kara could not believe what she saw. The old man was now standing. His beard had fallen off, and his eyes glowed red. His body had grown, limbs swollen, arms nearly bursting his white shirt.

With one muscular arm he deflected the blackjack like a Ping-Pong ball, and with the other hand grabbed Benny's thick throat and raised him so his thrashing legs only touched air.

The growling voice said, "I am Jabril, servant of Allah. Who are you to defy me?"

With a thrust of his arm he tossed the three-hundred-fifty-pound Benny like a rag doll against the far wall. Benny did not move.

The monster turned his attention to Kara. His eyes roamed over her body, finishing with her breasts, licking his lips.

His voice was an echo from hell. "You will be mine tonight. It is my destiny."

Kara wanted to run but her body would not respond. The monster took a step towards her, but before he could take two steps, his eyes dulled and his step faltered. A rose-colored spot blossomed, darkening his white shirt in his lower abdomen. Grabbing at the wound with his hands, his eyes seemed to pop out like fried eggs on the griddle, and his arms flailed around, trying to grab at Benny.

Benny held a knife that skewered Jabril from flank through navel, like a piece of meat on a grill. "You messed with the wrong black man tonight, suckah. I'm gonna bleed you like a pig."

Benny looked at Kara. "Get outta here, baby. Let me take care of this thing and I'll be right down. Meet you at the usual place."

Kara was rooted to the ground. What the hell had just happened?

"Move, Kara!"

Benny pulled out the knife, and Jabril's body fell forward.

Seeing the body fall broke the spell. She opened the door and ran. She ran like the night her father came home drunk, leaving her mother a crumpled mass from his fists. She ran knowing her world had changed and she was never going back.

A scream echoed behind her, a low, male roar that ended abruptly. But she didn't stop running.

Back in the room, Jabril awakened and stood. The big black man started turning around with the knife ready. Jabril grabbed that arm and
squeezed. The flesh and muscle felt like soft bread dough against the
hard bone. Jabril jerked his hand ninety degrees and the bone snapped.
The man screamed but was cut short as Jabril clamped his other hand
around his trachea and crushed it.

Jabril tilted his head from side to side, studying the twisting agony of
the big man. Curious but of no real concern. He let go of the man's arm
and touched his own left flank where the knife had passed through. The
blood was clotted and dry, the wound almost healed. Animal strength
surged through him. Instinct had replaced conscious thought.

He pulled the black bag from the man's pocket. "Thou shall not steal."
His voice was a low rumble.

He tossed the bag onto the table. The precious gems rattled on impact.

The huge black man's quivering ended. The only sound was the click
and whir of the air conditioner turning on.

CHAPTER 25

Kyle Rucksman of the NSA had waited in the hallway outside the senator's office twenty minutes and was starting to pace when the door opened and a young man came out to escort him into the office.

"Hello, Mr. Rucksman. I'm Jonathan. Senator Cardwell apologizes for the wait. A last-minute problem came up related to the September 11 events, and he has been detained. But he just called and wants you to wait in his office. He should arrive in a few moments. Would you like a latte or coffee? We have our own machine with excellent Colombian coffee."

"Thank you, Jonathan, but water will do." Rucksman hoped there was enough edge to his voice. This was bullshit.

Jonathan returned in less than thirty seconds with a cold bottle of water, then left, softly closing the door behind him. Rucksman was now alone in the office of one of the most powerful senators in Congress. Cardwell's ties to every aspect of the government were evidenced by the pictures, plaques, and memorabilia scattered about the office.

Rucksman focused on the present as he perused Cardwell's past trophies of power. The president needed him as an ally; God help him if he got on his bad side. That was why Rucksman was here, to take the heat for the president.

Directly behind Cardwell's leather chair loomed a stuffed grizzly bear, its head touching the eight-foot ceiling. When visitors sat and conversed with the senator, they must also face the menace of the bear, reminding them who they were up against.

The door opened, and Cardwell and a small entourage bustled into the room.

"Sorry for the tardiness, Kyle. Couldn't be helped. I'll need your opinion on some recent developments, so I am glad you're here. You know Fred and Robby from my security service. How's the NSA these days? Seems to me they lost some of their prestige with the September 11 fiasco."

Cardwell sat. His face had a perfect tan and his expression an undisguised leer, uncanny in its resemblance to the grizzly's smile. He motioned for Rucksman and the others to sit.

The private security gurus smirked at Rucksman, confident they knew more than the NSA. They'd developed their own secret firm after leaving the Agency several years ago. Rucksman had to admit they were good, Robby the dumb-but-quick gun and Fred the slower thinker. But their methods flirted with the edge of legality: wiretaps, surveillance, and chemical coercion. In fact, he was sure they were well past the edge now. The hawks would approve of almost anything in order to avenge the September 11 terrorist attacks.

Cardwell said, "We were having a discussion with Jerry Klaus. Did you know his company, La Riva Labs, is working on a very unusual combination of viruses? He tells me he has authorization from the government at very high levels. I'm not sure if I believe him, though Fred assures me Jerry is telling the truth. And Fred can be very persuasive. But still something bothers me. I don't understand why they need a lab in South America. What do you think?"

Leaning back, Cardwell tented his fingers, a hint of a smile twitching his mouth.

Rucksman wanted to punch those fingers right into the man's smile, mangling the hand and the mouth in one blow. Cardwell was absolutely sure of his superiority and that he already knew what Rucksman would say. What an ass.

"Senator, La Riva Labs has been authorized to research and develop viral DNA applications for medical treatments. They need the lab in Brazil to easily acquire monkeys to study the viruses. Getting those types of studies done in the U.S. would be impossible with the DNA and animal rights activists threatening to shut down half of our existing animal research. We recently asked them to develop vaccines to defend against any bioterrorist attacks using the viruses they've been researching."

Cardwell gazed at Rucksman like he was a manikin wearing a suit he wanted to purchase, detached but greedy. "Okay, let's say I buy that. Why would their top virologist disappear when they need her the most?"

"Possibly because you kidnapped her boss at the coffee shop. You probably scared the shit out of her. You boys have been busy the last week…but you might check the Constitution, though, especially the newer parts about government illegal search and seizure."

"Ah, yes. Search and seizure. Doesn't really apply to private security firms. And as far as government searches go, perhaps you've been out of touch." Cardwell's leer somehow got uglier. His tone reminded Rucksman of one particular college professor answering a stupid question from a freshman. "There is a bill, soon to be before Congress, that allows patriots to remove the scum from our midst much quicker than before those September 11 terrorist attacks. Soon none of the ragheads will be able to escape our grasp. We will be able to extinguish any terrorists before they can even finish their plans. The best defense *is* a good offense, and our offense just got a whole new team, and all Heisman Trophy winners."

"Well, you better take your offensive goons off Jerry Klaus and Rachel Lane. We have things under control with their lab, and we need their help. If the other side has viral warfare, La Riva Lab will be crucial in defending against it. We don't want to piss them off." Rucksman stood. "If you will excuse me, Senator, I have a long day ahead of me."

"Kyle, I am sorry to have detained you." Cardwell's voice was buttery. "We'll absolutely turn off our search for Rachel Lane." Then the hard edge came back. "For now. But if it turns out you do not have control of this situation, the oversight committee will not take this conversation lightly. We have it all on tape."

"Of course, Senator. I expected nothing less." Rucksman strode away, but stopped and faced the senator before opening the door. "Please, let Jerry Klaus go. He's a good man, and has served this country well. We don't need another McCarthy episode. You do remember what happened to McCarthy, don't you, Senator? Speaking of tapes, we have a few of our own."

He held Cardwell's gaze long enough to make sure the message was understood. Then he walked out, letting the door close behind him. If he could have cheered he would have. He kept it to a smile and one fist clenched in defiance as he walked to the elevator.

Senator Cardwell seethed. *What the hell did he mean, tapes of their own? I've done nothing wrong. I'm a patriot.*

He had tried to get the new bill named "The Cardwell Act," but Senator James from Wisconsin wanted it to be more non-partisan: "The people need to feel like we're doing something patriotic by enacting this new law." Right now it was termed "The Anti-Terrorism Act of 2001" and it needed to be wed to the "Public Security and Cyber Enhancement Act." The drafters of both bills agreed the final version should have a catchy name, something with "Patriotic" and "USA" or "Axis of Evil" in there. Then all they had to do was come up with appropriate words to make an acronym, a requirement of anything coming out of Washington D.C.

As long as it passed, he really didn't care what it was called. They had to end the ridiculous, antiquated, 1986 wire-tap requirements imposed by the Church committee on the Electronic Communications and Privacy Act. Now that the terrorists were infiltrating the very marrow of this great country, good men had to be able to strike quickly.

He thought about Rucksman's comments for ten more seconds and then dismissed them as an idle threat.

He addressed Fred and Robby. "I want you to find Rachel Lane. And as for Jerry Klaus, let him go for now, but keep all the taps on his phones. And make sure we don't lose him. There's something going on here that Rucksman didn't tell us. I want to know exactly what it is."

Robby could hardly contain himself. He would show those morons at NSA. They would regret passing him over for assistant director. What they saw in Rucksman was beyond him. Too into rules and constitutional rights. Once this was over, Mr. Kyle Rucksman would be out and Robby would be in, probably the new director of the NSA. Rucksman would be mopping floors in the museum around the Constitution he held so dear. Senator Cardwell would make sure of that.

Fred, however, was fully contained, as calm as a pool of water waiting for the first raindrop to fall from a thunderstorm. He saw a different raindrop than Robby. He usually did, because he thought before he acted. "We'll get right on it, Senator. Let's go, Robby."

"Damn right we'll get on it." Robby said. Once I get that bitch, Lane, we'll find out some answers, you can be sure of it. I could get some answers out of Klaus if you give me an hour."

Fred closed his eyes and shook his head.

"No, let Klaus go back to work. Perhaps he will lead us to someone. Find Rachel Lane, though. She might be valuable. But be discreet." Cardwell frowned, wondering again about Rucksman's comment on tapes. "If the NSA is watching them, they're probably also watching us."

"Whatever you say, Senator." Fred motioned for Robby to follow, leaving Cardwell frowning below his grizzly companion.

CHAPTER 26

Doc and Rachel worked on the vaccine for a few hours before they both decided they needed Alex and Jesse. They were the experts. Rachel had been aching to see Alex, so she tagged along with Doc for "support." Part of her didn't want to go, her feelings about Alex and Lora and Scott were so jumbled. But she had to face it head on.

Just as Doc was starting to knock, the door suddenly opened.

Alex stood before him, wide awake and fully dressed, his hair tousled, blue scrubs wrinkled. "Hey, Doc. I was on my way to get Jesse. Man, did I need that sleep. We were going to get started early, but I guess—" He craned his neck and looked around Doc. "Rachel, what are you doing here? I thought you were in Canada."

"Hi. Alex," Rachel said, almost a whisper. She had trouble meeting his eyes.

"Okay, what's wrong?" Alex pursed his lips.

"Alex," Rachel said, "why don't you sit down on the bed? I need to talk to you about something."

"It's about Lora, isn't it?" blurted Alex. "She's dead, isn't she?" He plopped down on the bed. "I feel empty in the spot where she used to be."

Rachel drew up the lone metal chair and sat facing Alex. "We don't know for sure." Then Rachel told him the story about the terrorist attacks including Lora's last known whereabouts.

Her voice cracked when she told him about Scott.

"Shit, Rachel. I'm sorry about Scott. He was a great guy, even if he was working for the government. But…Lora. She was on the same floor as the plane crash. It feels like she's dead. I miss her, but—" He glanced at Rachael. "—subconsciously I've known it for a week now. And I must have already worked through it, because I haven't cried for her once." He looked off to his left. "Like a candle went out two weeks ago and I already had the funeral and have moved on."

He looked back at Rachel. "I'm not surprised you're here. I had the strangest dream last night, about you. You were riding on top of a huge bald eagle, waving a gleaming scimitar and flying over snow-covered peaks, hollering *yippee ki-yay motherfu—* Well, you get my drift."

Doc frowned. "You sure are having the dreams lately. How about that one with the 747 flying into the Hilton?"

"Oh yeah, guess that was about the Twin Towers thing huh?"

"Are you kidding me?" Rachel's face sagged. "You actually dreamed about that?"

"Yeah, I know. Kinda creepy." Alex looked down and to his right, and shifted his body sideways to Rachel. "I just feel…different."

"Alex has been having all kinds of premonitions lately." Doc eyed Alex, then Rachel. "I have a theory. Alex, do you remember that mutt Jesse and I picked up on our coffee run to Manaus?"

"Fang?" Alex said. "He was a mean ass dog, man. Bit through the goddamn wire fence."

"He was not mean! And his name was Whitey, not Fang!" Jesse's voice echoed in the hallway outside Alex's open door like a specter from beyond, causing Doc and the others to jump. She walked into Alex's room, glaring at him.

"Jesus, Jesse, you scared the shit out of me," Alex said. "You need to warn us before you materialize like Houdini."

"Hi, Jesse," Rachel said. "We were just telling Alex about things that have happened in the last few weeks. And he was telling us about his dreams that seemed to have predicted each occurrence."

"Rachel, what are you doing here?" Rachel thought Jesse's tone defensive, and her look suspicious.

"And what is this about White Fang?" Jesse stood her full, imposing height barely two feet from Rachel. "He was just an abused dog who got some screwy virus and died. He never hurt anyone, really. He just nipped me because he was scared and sick."

Doc held up a hand. "We know you loved that dog; I was just talking about a theory that involves him and his infection. But right now that can wait. Why don't we get back to the main lab and put a few hours in? By then M.C. and the others will be back and I can explain it all. Rachel can fill you in about the last two weeks while we're working."

Jesse took a step back and lowered her head. "Sorry, I loved that poor dog. Tell me, what exactly happened the last few weeks, and why you're here."

Rachel told the story for the third time, but omitted anything about Scott, not wanting to get tearful again.

"Yeah," Alex said. "So Lora is probably dead. But what she didn't tell you is that Scott is definitely dead. He died in the Pentagon attack."

"Oh, Christ. I'm so sorry, Rachel. You must be devastated. And here I was getting all huffy about a dog! What a bitch I am. Guess I need coffee more than I thought. And, Lora? What the hell are the chances that two members of our group would have someone killed in a terrorist attack?"

Alex said, "Probably the same chance that an asteroid killed all the dinosaurs."

"The scary thing is that we might have never been here if it weren't for that asteroid," Rachel said.

An unsettling quiet set in. They glanced at each other, then the floor.

"Who do they think did this?" Jesse asked.

Doc glanced at Rachel, then sighed. "They think they were Muslims from Al Qaeda working for Bin Laden."

Jesse kept her gaze on the floor and scraped her bottom lip a few times with her upper teeth.

Alex fidgeted and kept glancing at each person. Rachel noticed a sheen of sweat on his forehead. He blurted, "I know one thing. No offense, Jesse, but those Muslim bastards should pay."

Jesse remained silent.

Alex jumped off the bed and walked outside the room, then back in. "Maybe I've accepted Lora's death, but that doesn't mean what those bastards did was right. And it wasn't just Lora. What did you say, two thousand dead? And the Pentagon and Scott, and now everyone running around scared shitless to even take a flight in the good ol' USA?" He slapped a palm against the wall. "They have to pay. And we have all the technology right here."

Rachel jumped up, careening the chair backward into Doc. But she didn't care. She wanted to give Alex a high five. "You're damn right we have the tools. That's one of the reasons I came down here. I want to help the CIA, or whoever it is that hired Jerry, to create these little babies so we have something to use against those terrorists. Let's face it. 'Nuke 'em 'til they glow' doesn't cut it anymore with NATO. But if we could develop a disease that could wipe out those bad boys and make it look like a new outbreak of a local disease, then that would be like a surgical knife taking out the cancer…"

For a long moment Jesse continued gazing studiously at the floor. Then she said, "We've started something using the yellow fever, smallpox, and Ebola strains. We haven't quite got it finished, but it has promise. M.C. also started looking at the Borna viruses, thinking that maybe we could develop some kind of psychiatric disease that would disable our enemy's minds enough so they couldn't fight. We've also got some ideas for vaccines. If we develop those quickly, we could potentially vaccinate key members of any underground resistance movement. Another thing we started working on was spreading the disease via a vector, say, a mosquito. If the disease got out of hand, we could drop pesticide, killing the vector and rapidly halting the spread of the disease."

Doc could not believe how calm Jesse appeared. He wondered if she'd keep it inside and later blow up.

"I figured in three to four weeks we'd have something." Alex said. "But with you here, Rachel, things might really progress. You have a lot more expertise in vaccines than we do. And you've had more experience with vectors. In our backyard here, we have an abundance of tropical vectors. But if we're talking about the Middle East, we may need desert-living vectors, like sand flies, cockroaches, fleas or ticks. We have experimented with bunyaviruses like Crimean-Congo hemorrhagic fever and with hemorrhagic fever with renal syndrome. There are also West Nile isolates in our stores. If we could get the DNA from the Marburg virus and one of the above to intertwine their DNA, we could have a potential winner."

"That might be too much," Rachel said. "What about all the innocent people that would be killed with those bad boys?"

Alex slammed the side of his fist against the wall. "They didn't care about innocent casualties. Why should we? It's like what the Nazis did to my…" He looked away and smacked his fist in his palm. "Maybe we should get rid of the entire Middle East. They bombed this, they bombed that, they killed women and children and then said it was okay with Allah because it's jihad. Let's show them our own jihad! Yeehaw, you motherfuckers!" He pointed his finger at no one in particular with each "they" and ended with his fist in the air. His eyes were wide and wild. Sweat trickled down his neck. His scrubs were dark from the sweat on his chest. His whole body seeming to vibrate with energy.

For a moment, the only sound was Alex's heavy breathing. Rachel had been as wired as he was, but this was over the edge. She looked sideways at Doc and he glanced at her. She sat down and took a deep breath.

"Hey, Alex," she said in a low soft voice. "It's okay, buddy, I'm with you. But take it down a notch. We're supposed to be the good guys, right? Set an example for the rest of the world. That's the reason we never really attacked another country before they attacked us. When we do attack we make sure it is a strategic strike against the military, the fighters, not the innocents."

Alex stared at her, the whites of his eyes as wide as she had ever seen anyone. Had he taken a drug? "How the hell are we supposed to get at them if they're all living with the quote-unquote *innocents*, huh?" He was yelling at her, and she wanted to get behind the chair.

"My uncle was in Vietnam and he said they'd go into a village and the women or the kids would kill you with a bomb, or lead you into a trap that would kill your whole platoon."

He stared at her. She didn't know what to say.

"Don't you see?" His voice had dropped an octave, but the volume hurt her ears. "You can't know who's good or who's bad. Sometimes you just have to level the whole field and start over.

"You have to do what my uncle did, napalm the whole damn village if you think Charlie is there.

"And if the napalm doesn't do it…" He twisted his hands back and forth like he was twisting someone's neck. "Exterminate every last one of them."

He glared at Rachel with eyes she could not look at, crazy, lunatic eyes.

"You have to kill them all. Dead. D-E-A-D!"

Jesse had been watching Alex and her eyes took on a funny gleam, her mouth parted, and she moved a step closer to him.

Rachel scooted the chair back. Doc moved in between her and Alex.

Something had snapped in Alex. His arm muscles pumped, sweat dripped from his brow, jaw clenched, legs flexed like a cat ready to pounce.

Jesse stood beside him, breathing rapidly, staring at him as if he were a god. She strutted her breasts and clenched her fists.

Alex locked eyes with her and neither of them moved.

"Hey, Alex." Doc said.

Alex and Jesse looked at him like he was their next meal and he froze.

Rachel slowly got up and moved next to Doc and whispered, "I hope you have something to calm them down."

Doc sidled in front of Rachel.

Then, careful to keep eye contact with Alex, he spoke smoother than Bill Clinton. "Hey, Alex, how about some coffee and breakfast, maybe some French toast? What do you say? We could talk about fly fishing in Patagonia. You're still going there after we're done here, right?"

At the mention of food and fly fishing, Alex visibly relaxed. Jesse mirrored his reaction, her eyes becoming semi-glazed.

"Hiya, Doc," Alex said. "Guess I got a little carried away. I'll have that French toast. But I think I'll hold off on the coffee."

He wiped his brow and rolled his head around, stretching and relaxing his neck muscles. He reached over and gave Jesse a hug with his right arm. "Hey, Jesse, let's chill out and have a little chow, okay?"

Jesse nodded and answered haltingly, coming out of her trance. "I do feel…hungry."

The two clasped hands and walked toward the door like grade-school kids going to lunch without a care in the world.

CHAPTER 27

Rachel almost fell to the ground, her legs were so weak.

Doc helped her to the chair as the door closed. "Rachel, I hope you can come up with a vaccine pretty quick because I've revised my previous stupid-ass theory. I now believe those two are *definitely* infected with the same virus that got that damn dog. I'm not sure how, but if it's airborne, we may all be headed for Alex's madness."

Rachel just shook her head. "Did you see his arms? It was like he'd been pumping iron. And his face. God, it was like he turned into some kind of animal."

"I know. I felt like a rabbit cornered by two big cats. Jesse would be a tough one to avoid if she started pouncing. I'm surprised I didn't roll over and start twitching."

Rachel chuckled. "Is it only me, or did it seem like Jesse was Alex's babe? I mean, wow! He sure got over Lora fast."

Her voice trailed off, the chuckle gone, and she gazed at the floor. *Why am I disappointed that Alex is so attached to Jesse?* Then she remembered her dream in the Rockies, Alex's touch, his kiss, his...

She wanted to punch Jesse.

"I need to get back to the main lab and see if I can figure this out. You coming?" Doc said.

She sat staring into space for a second, then stood up. "Sure. Right behind you."

—

The lab still looked the same when they arrived. No eight-foot Frankenstein monster strapped to a table with lightning sending voltage into their cranium. She busied herself where she'd left off, studying viral protein capsules on the Internet. Doc disappeared.

He returned with some vials and sat next to her. "Jesse's always had the hots for Alex. You know that. But I think she's just trying to comfort him after Lora's death."

"You're joking, right? A hell of a lot more than comforting going on there, Doc. It was like that movie *Invasion of the Body Snatchers*. The two of them were locked on the same wavelength. And we were mere outside interference."

"I don't know about that, but I do think they're infected by the same virus. And I have a confession. I forgot about it until we started talking about the dog. I drew blood from the dog before he died."

He held a vial the size of his finger like a priest holding up the sacred wine. "Neither Jesse nor Alex knows this, but we have a culture of that virus." He gave her the vial. "With this you can make a vaccine in half the time."

She took the vial and held it at arm's length like looking too closely might infect her. She quickly placed it in another plastic container and screwed down the lid.

"I'm going to need help with the monkeys," she said. "When do you think M.C. will be back?"

"He may be gone for another hour. Can you get by without him until then?"

"Yeah. I'll start working out which part of the virus is most antigenic. We can only do prelim stuff here, though."

"I know. But that's what we have right now. Once we get back in D.C., we can finish it pretty quickly."

She started to leave the room, then stopped. "How am I going to get back into the U.S. without getting picked up by the Feds? Don't you think we should notify La Riva that we're here and everyone's okay? I mean, I'm not keen on a life in prison. This war on terrorism seems to have taken away our freedoms or at least mine, anyway." She shook her head. "Doc, have you ever thought how strange it is that too much love and too much religion seem to start a lot of wars?"

"Of course. They start 'em then work like hell to stop 'em. God and love. I wouldn't have a job without them."

Rachel smiled slyly at him. "My grandmother was Scotch-Irish and raised Catholic, but made her money in a whorehouse in Denver before she settled down and married a Swede who had no religion. So I guess that's why I don't understand religions fighting over what's right and what's wrong. You know the origin of the word 'infidel' is Christian, not Muslim, right? During the reformation, the infidels were any non-believers. The Catholics thought the Protestants, the Episcopalians, and any followers of Henry VIII were infidels. And if you were deemed an infidel, you were ridiculed, or placed in stocks, or burned at the stake. Alex is right. It's like the Nazis or the KKK. If you don't believe in what we do, then you're a threat and must be eliminated. It never ends."

She wiped tears off her cheeks. "And love? Is there any hope for humans, Doc? Are we always going to wipe out people that don't conform to our beliefs? It's just so much bullshit." She stood up and walked to the window and looked into the Class IV lab.

Doc went to her and put a hand on her shoulder. "Rachel, you and I are not like the Nazis or the KKK. Sometimes a few people get carried away, but that doesn't mean the whole human race is bad. What about love? Don't you think love and respect for human dignity will always win out against those idiots?"

"Love, love, love. That's all we need, huh? What about Alex? He'd loved Lora so much he forgot about her in two weeks. He loves Jesse now and they're off to destroy the world, rip the head off terrorists, and spit in their bleeding necks." She turned and faced Doc. "I don't know if I can do this anymore." She pushed his arm away and walked back and sat staring at the computer. She thought, *And I want to be right there with Alex, killing them all.*

"Come on, Rachel. This is not like you." He walked over to her and rubbed one arm with his other hand. "Alex's state is likely due to the viral infection. We need your help. If we can develop a vaccine, maybe we can prevent others from being infected. We also need to manufacture antiviral medication to see if we can rid Alex of the disease. You are one of the best at both of those tasks."

She stared at the computer.

He clapped his hands. Rachel jumped. "Snap out of it!" he yelled. "Let's stick to the facts and get busy fixing things here and now. Science and facts—remember? That's really all we have control over. We are scientists. Can't fix the problems of the world, but we can do this one little thing." Doc's tone was now matter of fact, business as usual.

Rachel blinked a few times, wiped her cheeks with the back of her hand, and shrugged her shoulders. "Yes. You're right. Sorry about the pessimism. Beginning to sound like my Aunt Marjorie." She peered at him. "Never saw you clap or yell like that."

He smiled. "Yes, well, I was a soldier once."

"Guess it worked. Anyway, maybe I'm just jealous of Jesse. And a bit guilty with Scott, hoping...you know?"

"Oh, puh-leeze." Doc rolled his eyes. "Why does Alex get all the women?" Then he added with a distinctive New York accent. "What am I, chopped livuh?"

"Doc, uh, I thought you had a girl? Did I miss something? I mean, you are a little older than Alex, but you're...a very good-looking man."

He grinned widely. "Yes, my Julie would probably do more than twist my head off and spit in the stump. Get busy."

Rachel chuckled. Doc put a hand on her shoulder. "You okay now?"

"Sure. You better go get those two lovebirds and M.C. We have some work to do."

Doc started out the door, then turned back to her. "Oh, don't forget about those new antiviral meds I brought down. With your modifications, they'll help get Alex and Jesse back to normal."

He left and Rachel grinned. Doc knew how to motivate.

She started back to work, a woman with a mission. If she worked quickly, perhaps she could not only help Alex and Jesse, but prevent major loss of life or at least a lot of craziness. The particular virus they had seemed to do two major things: increase strength and muscle mass, and make the person wacky.

What she really needed was computerized robotics to perform DNA analysis and combinatorial chemical reactions. Then she could produce a chemotherapeutic agent that could kill the virus without harming the host. At Main Lab in D.C., this would be a piece of cake.

But here? Possible, but time consuming.

The theory was simple. Develop a chemical that attacked a particular aspect of the viral life cycle, usually somewhere in the replication stages, and make sure the chemical was not too toxic to the host organisms, i.e., humans.

What she wanted was a drug like acyclovir, the first effective, selective, and very successful antiviral drug with almost no toxicity. Herpes sufferers worldwide used tons of it, especially those with HIV.

Her hero, Gertrude Elion, had discovered how to use DNA and nucleic acid metabolism to design new anticancer drugs in the early 1940s. She'd helped develop acyclovir, then figured out that acyclovir could be used as an antiviral drug. She went on to develop drugs to help AIDS, prevent kidney transplant rejection, treat gout. Forty-five patents and never even a PhD. Couldn't even get a job as a scientist in the '40s because she was a woman, but finally got the Nobel Prize in 1988, forty-seven years after she first started research.

Well, I'm not shooting for a Nobel Prize, merely a little drug to save the world.

Smiling, Rachel said out loud: "And I certainly don't have forty-seven years." Her voice echoed off the sterile white walls, and she quickened her pace.

Hope one of Doc's antiviral meds works.

—

Doc stopped by his room and got a file and tucked it under his arm as his footsteps echoed in the hallway to the kitchen. It was time to share the contents. At the kitchen the skillet was on low, a yellow-streaked egg-milk mixture in a bowl on the countertop next to a stack of sliced bread. The coffee machine was making a steaming, crackling noise as the pot finished a few final drips.

Alex and Jesse weren't there. Maybe they were in the bathroom throwing cold water on their face to cool off after their angry outburst.

He filled a cup from the cabinet, sipped it, and sighed. Now *that* was coffee. He was about to call M.C. on the intercom when Alex and Jesse walked in.

"Don't bother calling M.C." Alex said. "He'll be here shortly." Then he casually dunked a piece of bread into the French toast mixture.

"Yeah, he should be here any minute now," Jesse said, pouring some coffee.

Doc traded looks with each of them. "So are you two going to open up a Tarot card and palm-reading shop when you get back to the States?"

Alex looked sheepish. "Sorry, Doc. You remember my premonition about Lora and the episodes when I was a kid?"

"Yeah." Doc stared into his coffee.

"That ability is back. In spades. A minute ago, on the way to the bathroom, I saw M.C. coming down in the elevator like I could reach out and touch him. It was so real I asked Jesse about it. She said she was seeing the same thing. We decided to go check it out. Sure enough, when we went to the elevator, it was working—and starting to come down. So we came back to finish breakfast for everyone."

Footsteps echoed in the hall.

M.C., Sam, and the other three walked in.

"Son of a b—" Doc whispered under his breath.

"If that's breakfast," M.C. said. "I could sure use some. I feel like my stomach hasn't seen food in so long it's about to eat my liver."

M.C. introduced Sam's crew to Jesse and Alex, then gave a report on the elevator being fixed, noting that it would move more slowly until he got some other parts.

Doc and Alex locked eyes when M.C. finished his report. Then Alex helped Jesse hand out plates of French toast and eggs.

"Where's Rachel?" Sam said as he took a plate of food and cup of coffee from Jesse.

"She's getting started on a vaccine and antiviral meds." Doc said. "Seemed anxious to get going, so I let her." He forked his food around the plate but didn't eat, looking at the file beside his plate.

M.C. swallowed two hasty bites and looked at Doc. "You okay?"

"Sure. Yeah." He looked at Alex. "Just thinking about all I have to do." He crossed his arms. "Rachel could use some help and I need you pretty quick."

"We'll go help in a few minutes," Jesse said. "First some fuel to get the little gray cells pumping on all cylinders."

Alex caught Doc's eye. "We better get moving, Jesse. I feel like we may not have much time." And then he looked at her and thought, loud and clear, *And it's not because Doc's in a hurry.*

CHAPTER 28

Doc pushed his untouched plate away, took a drink of coffee, picked up the file and stood up. "Before Alex and Jesse leave I have something to share I think is pretty important."

He opened the file. "I've carefully recorded a number of unusual recent events, and a pattern has emerged. It's pretty weird, but hear me out.

"First, there was the change in the abused dog Jesse picked up outside Manaus weeks ago."

Alex interrupted. "Yeah, Fang. He was creepy and totally nuts."

"His name was Whitey!" Jesse sounded hurt.

"Right." Alex stared at the floor.

"Wait a minute," Sam said. "I thought your crew never left the compound."

"You like the coffee?" asked Alex.

"Best I've ever had," said Sam.

"Yeah, we all got pretty addicted to it," Alex said, "and love to grind the fresh beans. But they're only sold in one local store. Though La Riva wanted complete isolation, Doc insists on an occasional psyche break away from here every few weeks."

"The last trip to get coffee, Doc took me." Jesse said. "When we got into town I saw a skinny, flea-bitten blonde Lab being kicked around outside a local bar. A man would lure the poor thing within inches of a piece of chicken and then suddenly kick him, sending the dog rolling across the dusty street. At first the dog would only groan and slink back.

But then he started snarling and snapping at the man. The man cursed in Portuguese and pulled out a shotgun."

"And that's when," Doc pointed at Jesse and chuckled. "Jesse inserted her large frame and even larger vocal tirade that made the man step back a pace and lower his gun. She whipped around, grabbed the mutt by the scruff of its neck, tossed it into the cage of the Explorer, slammed down the tailgate, and the dog was ours.

"On the trip back, the damn canine was constantly baring its fangs, growling and lashing out at the wire cage. Jesse had to sedate the crazed mutt with a dart gun before we could transfer it to another cage."

"I loved that dog." Jesse said. "Named him White Fang. Poor Whitey."

Doc leaned on his hands and gave Jesse a look of admiration. "You worked so hard with him, too." He waited for Jesse to look at him. "But he still bared his teeth if anyone else so much as looked at him."

Sam yawned. "So you had a problem mutt. What's the big deal?"

Doc held up a hand. "Bear with me. One day Jesse took Fang…uh, Whitey, for a walk. She had put him on a leash and was on the way out when he lunged, breaking open a cage that held a lab monkey. Whitey met monkey. In the brawl, the monkey buried his fangs in the dog's shoulder.

"Over the next week, Whitey became increasingly agitated and actually bit through part of the wire fence. He also required two pounds of food a day.

"Then he turned on Jesse two mornings in a row, snapping and howling. He sounded like the Hound of the Baskerville. I agree with Alex. The dog was creepy and nuts. I convinced Jesse to put him down.

"Autopsy revealed an enlarged head and paws, unusually long claws, hypertrophy of all muscle groups, complete healing of the mange, and thickening of body hair. I've done hundreds of autopsies on Labradors, and I've never seen canine teeth that large. Also, the dog had gained nearly twenty pounds in three weeks.

"Not only that, but the brain had purulence and petechiae…what I mean is, a thin layer of puss and small pinpoint blood-blisters over the temporal lobes."

Jimbo looked queasy. "Hey Doc, I'm eatin' here. Could you lay off the pus and gore?"

Jesse blurted, "You mean Whitey had some type of encephalitis?"

"That's what I thought, too," Doc looked at Jesse, then at Jimbo, "Sorry, but this is necessary for all of us to understand and contribute. I'll try to tone it down.

"I didn't sacrifice the monkey. I wanted to see if it developed any signs of the dog's disease. So far the monkey is healthy."

"Good thinking, Doc." Alex said. "We're going to need that little guy if we want a vaccine."

"Yes, but there's more," continued Doc. "We're working with retroviruses, like HIV, and using monkey tissues as cultures."

Jesse raised her eyebrows and shook her head. "You're not thinking about the polio vaccine theory of HIV, are you?"

"Exactly."

"Wait a minute, "Alex blurted, spraying out a piece of French toast. "I thought they disproved that theory."

Sam made a *T* with his hands. "Time out. What theory are you talking about? I thought HIV was started in Africa from gay guys."

Doc sat down and leaned back in his chair as if lecturing a student. "There are two theories. One is that chimp hunters in the 1950s got infected with Simian Immune Virus, or SIV, then infected travelers once urbanization hit Africa. The other is that the original oral polio vaccine, developed and tested in Africa, used SIV-infected monkey tissue cultures, and when the first vaccines were administered in Africa, some of those infected white cells were injected and started the HIV epidemic."

José precisely dabbed each corner of his mouth with a napkin. "I didn't think we could get a virus from an animal."

Alex had started pacing again, then stopped and said, "Once it gets into humans, SIV evolves. It actually gets into our DNA and changes our immune systems. But usually that evolution takes years, sometimes decades."

Sam got another cup of coffee. "So viruses can change human DNA?"

Doc had been anxiously watching Alex pace. When he stopped, Doc quickly scanned the rest of them, hoping no one had caught it, the final implication Doc was building to. Sam held his gaze, glanced at Alex, then back at Doc, raising his eyebrows.

"Yes," Jesse said. "People with inherited diseases can be cured by viruses. The virus inserts DNA codes that replace the defective inherited genes."

José stood quickly, rattling the table and looked at Doc, with alarm. "If humans can get this virus from monkeys and you guys were exposed to the monkey that bit Fang, then you must be infected."

"Nah," Alex said. "The monkey was quarantined and it's not sick at all. Fang probably had some preexisting disease. And there's never been a report of a viral infection causing so much muscle hypertrophy in such a short time. Besides, all our blood tests have been normal. Right, Doc?"

Doc glanced at the floor, then at José. "Please, sit. There's more."

José eased down, but continued to look nervously at Doc. Sam had cocked his head and his black eyes glittered.

"Before I came down here this time," Doc said, "I knew I had metastatic prostate cancer. This was going to be my last tour."

Rachel gasped and her eyes got wet.

"Why didn't you tell us?" Jesse said.

"M.C. knew. But I didn't want anyone else to worry."

Jesse started to say something else, but Doc cut her off.

"Besides, after a few weeks, the bone pain went away. I rechecked a PSA and it was normal. There have been reported spontaneous cures in all kinds of cancer. I thought maybe it was the new drug I had started. But then I started rethinking things over the last two days."

"You think the viruses cured your cancer?" asked Sam, his hands splayed on the table.

"It seems so. But there's more to it than that.

"I've been doing a lot of creative thinking recently, experiments with different Amazonian herbs and plants that we've discovered. The entire procedure—chemical compositions, breakdown properties, even final products—flash in my brain like a movie I've already seen. Sometimes I wake up at night with formulas and ideas. I've been writing them all down and have filled up four notebooks in two weeks. I thought maybe the prostate cancer had changed something in my brain, or we got a good batch of coffee. Until today." He looked at Alex.

"But Doc," Alex said, "You always have great ideas. You're a smart guy."

"Thanks, Alex. But this is mountains above anything I've ever done, and hundreds of times faster. Now, let me finish."

Doc took a deep breath in and sighed as he held Alex's gaze. "I believe you and Jesse have been infected, too. That's why your sixth sense is so keen. We may all be infected, either through small errors we've made in containment, or through that tremor or explosion we had affecting the containment systems. Or some unknown reason."

Sam and his three friends stood up quickly and started backing off from the rest of the group. M.C. also stood, but looked very calm and unconvinced. "I don't feel any different. How come I didn't get the genius virus or the crystal-ball infection?"

"Sam," Doc said. "If you're thinking about leaving so you won't get infected, you're too late. If we're infected, so are all of you. In fact, the animals and other critters outside our compound may have gotten infected and are going to be showing the effects soon. Remember what it did to White Fang, and think of the monsters that might be waiting for you up there if a leopard or anaconda gets the infection."

M.C. walked to a small panel in the wall above the coffeepot. Opening it, he took out a couple of fuses and pushed another button and pocketed the fuses. "No one is going anywhere. I locked the elevator shaft door and disabled the elevator. We're here until we come up with some answers."

Silence. The tension was like a piano wire stretched across everyone's neck.

"Okay, okay," Sam said. "Look, I'm with you. But that was some scary shit you just laid on us. Is there a light in your garage of horrors, or should I expect to foam at the mouth while that monkey eats my brains?"

"First of all, the dog did not foam at the mouth. His strength improved and he exhibited problems with his learned behavioral responses. He was used to being abused and fighting back, so I think he was only doing what he had been taught to do by the school of hard knocks. The light in the garage is that the monkey, the original vector, has shown no signs of disease. I am hoping that primates are not as susceptible to the negative effects of the disease. It may even be that this virus will be a boon to the human race, making us all smarter and able to see into the future a little."

"Doc," Jesse said, "you keep mentioning *this virus* like it is only one. We've been working on a bunch. Which one is it, and how do we know that there aren't several others waiting to infect us? Also, we've been so careful in our isolation and cleansing procedures, it seems impossible that we could be infected. And if you thought Alex was still infected, why did you let him out of isolation? And another thing—"

Doc held up a hand "I have a few answers, but I also have a lot of the same questions. First—"

A low rumble shook the room, toppling plates off the counter and M.C. stumbled and caught himself on the table. Dust filtered down from fissures in the ceiling, and a fog so thick it was hard for Doc to see anyone else. He gagged at the strong smell of rotten eggs, and knew this was going to be much worse than the elevator shaft.

CHAPTER 29

Kara ran outside the front of the Radisson, hung a hard left on Figueroa Street, ran a block, dodging a man and his black Great Dane, then cut left on Expedition Boulevard, around the nose of a building that housed a Starbucks. She slowed and turned around, panting hard. The guy and the Great Dane were waiting at the light. No one was following her. She turned around again and angled toward the Starbucks. There were teenage girls walking out, carrying shopping bags, a bald guy sitting with a Danish peering at his laptop, a few others in line, and the sound of a cappuccino steamer huffing. She stood inside and caught her breath, watching through the window.

That nice old jeweler—fuck that, he was a crazy-assed monster. Thankfully he was nowhere in sight. She had to find a phone. She had to tell Joe about Big Benny so he could go check on him. How could that old geezer toss Benny against the wall like he was a piece of meat? Benny was big—real big, and he had cut that jeweler good. Yet the scream she'd heard sounded like Benny's. But, hell, who could tell when you were running for your life? Joe would find out. Joe was good. She wished she had called him earlier, but Benny didn't want to split up the loot.

She bought a regular mocha and asked the girl if she could borrow the phone in back. The girl looked at her. Kara flipped out her airline ID. "I have to check in, you know, in case of something like the Twin Towers thing." That got her.

Kara found the phone under a yellow sweater in the employees room and dialed. The other end picked up.

"Joe, is that you?"

A deep, digitally-altered male voice replied, "Kara, I told you never to call this number unless it was an emergency."

"This would be classified as a real nine-one-one call."

"You have two minutes. If I hang up, switch phones and call back in five minutes. Now talk!"

She told him what happened in less than a minute. "You gotta go check on Big Ben. I think he got hurt."

"I will. That Radisson is right across from the USC campus, right?"

"Yeah."

"Okay. If no one is following you, go home. I'll call you later." The eerie voice switched off.

Kara looked at the phone like it was haunted, and slowly hung it up. She stepped into the hallway and headed for the door. A big man was shrugging in sideways through front door. She held her breath. He turned and had wide shoulders. But he was as white as a full moon. She breathed easier and walked outside, turning right first and studying the way she'd come. She turned around and started walking, then threw the rest of her mocha into a garbage can and ran.

Joe had lived in the Marks Tower DMT as a freshman not so many years ago at USC. It was an eight-story building with the roof a perfect observatory for the Radisson across Figueroa Street. Joe lived about five block away in a run-down, two-story building. It wasn't far from the Staples Center. He'd even gotten an autograph from Kobe Bryant last year. Joe moved with quiet efficiency collecting two pair of black tennis shoes, black pants, two white shirts, and of course his tools. Of medium height and build and without distinguishing facial features, he was able to blend in with any crowd of African-Americans in L.A. His close-cropped hair was habit from military days. Smooth facial skin belied the scars on his back and abdomen from times he would rather forget. But the training they had given him had paid off. He knew how to become invisible, and how to find anyone, anywhere.

He was always prepared for this type of thing. It's what he did. Kara was family, so that made it important enough to carry a few extra items.

"Kara, Kara, Kara." He said to himself. "What the hell have you gotten yourself into this time?"

He'd thought she was finally on the straight and narrow after she got the job as a flight attendant. Now it seemed the job was only a ruse to make another mark. Big Ben...? What did she see in him? And if this mark was strong enough to throw Benny around, then Joe would have to watch his step. Maybe take along a little extra help.

He picked up the phone. "Chauncey, I got a job. Can you meet me in fifteen?"

"Sure, bro. Where at?" The reply was pure Louisiana drawl.

Joe gave him directions, hung up, collected his bag of tricks, and walked out, setting the alarm and the special security system he had personally designed. He knew that after he left, several green lights would blink. With special glasses you could see the infrared laser beams crisscrossing the halls and rooms, with many extra lines around the computer room. The computer itself would be slowly sinking into the floor, replaced by another computer that slid over from the wall. Ruses. That was his game. And he was good at it.

Kara's grand plans, on the other hand, never quite turned out. Rescuing her was getting old. He hurried down the stairs.

He met Chauncey at the Marks Tower and they took the stairs all the way to the roof. Deactivating the roof alarm and picking the lock was as easy as it had been when he was a freshman there. It was 8:15 p.m., an hour after Kara had called him. They set up on the roof, mostly hidden behind one of the A/C units, and changed into white shirts, black pants and black tennis shoes, the perfect waiter's uniform for later. Joe looked through the telescope while Chauncy directed the parabolic sound amplifier toward Room 315.

The room was dark at first. Then a light went on and Joe saw a very thin, Arabic-looking man enter and close the door behind him. He wore a dark sports coat with a tear in one upper sleeve. Kara had said the guy had been thin at first, then turned into a huge guy. Joe figured it was the thin man's partner. He looked around for the partner. Nobody else. Maybe he split. If so, this would be a piece of cake.

The rooms on the floor below were conference rooms and were empty. In fact, most of the rooms in the hotel were empty. A lot of people were staying home after the September 11 attack.

The room to the left of 315 was dark, and inspection with the infrared revealed no occupants. A white man occupied 313, but the four other rooms to the right—311, 309, 307, and 305—were all vacant. Then came the elevator shaft. The geezer in 313 was so old he should be in a grave and so deaf the TV volume hurt Chauncy's ears over the mike. Rooms 413 and 415 were a suite full of a French family and their screaming and running rug rats. Franco-American relations would be strained if the old guy below them wasn't so deaf. Perfect neighbors.

Then Mr. Aswan did what all very private people do. He called room service. Their cue.

Chauncey focused the sound amplifier and jotted down the order while Joe packed up. They slipped back downstairs and were across the street in under two minutes. They went in the back entrance, got into the service elevator, and took it to Mr. Aswan's floor. Joe picked the electronic lock to 305, the first room on the left. They went in and waited—room dark, door cracked.

In five minutes the elevator dinged and the waiter rolled the cart out and started down the hall toward 315. They overcame the waiter, put the unconscious man in Room 305, and rolled the supper tray to 315.

So far, simple.

Joe did last-minute snooping under the door with a pencil-sized fiber optic scope while Chauncey put an electronically amplified stethoscope on the door.

Everything was easy if you had the right equipment and the right people. Chauncey was excellent. Black as midnight, wiry and small, he was the ultimate night operator and could fit into many places others could not. His quick mind had absorbed the intricacies of electronic surveillance. He was one of the best pupils Joe'd ever had. And the Louisiana drawl—what a bonus. No one suspected the backward-sounding black man of being smart enough to outwit them.

They had had many, many marks, with as many takes. Tonight should be no different.

Joe knocked on the door and called, "Room service."

Jabril was ravenous after killing the black man.

He'd stuffed the body in a large suitcase, carried it downstairs, and hidden it under small crawl space under the hotel's open parking garage. It would eventually be found after the smell ripened: another of the hundreds of unsolved murders in L.A. each year. After that, his strength and speed seemed to wane, to the point he was winded walking back up the stairs. But his senses seemed ultra-sensitive. He wanted to go next door and crush the loud TV into its owners head. But first he must clean up.

He wasn't worried about the girl talking to the police. She had committed the crime, not him. He was merely protecting himself and his jewelry. And the only blood was his.

Back in his room, he called room service for a prime rib dinner. There would be penance for going off his strict Muslim diet. But, after sacrificing his life, what more could Allah ask?

And, at the moment, Jabril felt as though he would never need Allah or prayers again.

After showering, he dressed, replaced his beard, and touched up his disguise. There was a knock on the door. "Room service."

Walking toward the door, he felt a prickling at the nape of his neck and the blood begin to engorge his muscles.

CHAPTER 30

Rocca had accompanied Jack to the USNS *Mercy*, which had been constantly cruising close to the northern coast of Australia over the last week after the terrorists attacks. Despite Rocca's jesting with Jack, he was worried about his friend. The wound on Jack's left flank required two hours of surgery. The doc who sewed him up told Rocca that an artery was lacerated, and if Rocca hadn't applied pressure, Jack would have bled to death. His other injury, the broken leg, was easily set by a Navy orthopedist on temporary assignment from San Diego Naval Hospital. The general surgeon in charge was pleased, but because Jack had lost so much blood and had such extensive surgery close to his kidney, he put Jack on the first flight to Naval Hospital, San Diego, via the Royal Australian Air Force Base in Perth.

Rocca wanted to go with Jack, but instead caught another flight to Pearl, then to the USS Chosin CG 65, a command ship steaming outside Pearl Harbor, in order to debrief them on his incident with Jabril El Fahd. He crossed the International Date Line and landed the day before he took off, and, even though he got about five hours' sleep, he still felt groggy.

The helicopter landed on what looked like a gray postage stamp marked with a large X, astern of the many bristling antennae and radar array antennae and spheres. Rocca was thankful the seas were calm that day, though walking from the chopper to the open hangar door, he stumbled.

He walked down one hallway, down stairs—what the Navy called a ladder—then down another hallway, where the petty officer deposited him in his cabin. There were three straight-backed metal chairs, a tiny bathroom, a fold-out desk on one wall, and a rack on the other—a bed to Army guys like him. Pretty much everything was gray, except the olive green bedspread on the rack. Rocca sat on the rack and started to lay down when there was a knock on the door. He wearily stood and let in Navy Commander Alexander and a civilian NSA geek, Howard Saxon. It was 16:00 hours on September 18 when they sat in the uncomfortable chairs.

"We need to find El Fahd ASAP," Rocca said, blinking hard to bring him back to full alertness. "He had some kind of biological weapons in that lab."

Saxon scratched his chest and shrugged. "Big deal. You said in your report El Fahd was blown up in the helicopter crash. Case closed."

"You need to read between the lines, Howie. I said he was *presumed* dead. I also said there were grenade fragments found in one of the seats at the crash scene and in a tree twenty yards away. My report was only supposed to give the facts. It's not hard to take those facts and conclude that El Fahd blew the chopper to cover his escape."

Rocca was right about El Fahd being alive, he knew it in his gut. Now to convince this geek to use some of their fancy NSA surveillance to find El Fahd before the terrorist released the bad juju he had in that lab.

Alexander said, "Let's say we buy your theory about El Fahd. How are we going to find this guy now? He could be anywhere."

"My bet is that he is going to the States to spread a biological agent. Sort of a West Coast Twin Towers, only with microscopic bullets that may do way more damage. My gut says L.A. Don't you NSA guys have some kind of facial recognition software? You have video cams in airports around the world. Why don't you crank up those puppies and search the airports around Indonesia, Vietnam, and the Philippines?"

Saxon eyed Rocca like a piece of bad hamburger, then abruptly stood. "Could you excuse me and the commander for a moment, Mr. Rocca?" Saxon said.

"Sure."

Rocco's response bounced off the already-closing door.

Damn spook. About as polite as Howard Stern. Even had the same first name.

Rocco propped up his feet on the fold out desk, tipped his chair back, and rested his head against the wall—the *bulkhead* the commander would probably interject. He closed his eyes and all sounds disappeared.

The door opened; Rocca jumped; the chair slammed down on all four legs; and Rocca sat forward, wide awake.

Commander Alexander stared at him. Saxon was not there. "We agree with your assessment, Rock, and are taking steps to locate El Fahd. Make yourself comfortable on the rack behind you. I'll be back in a few hours. Would you like something to drink or eat?"

At least the Navy has manners, Rocca thought, and he liked it that the commander called him Rock. "No thanks on the meal. Already ate. I'll take you up on the bed, though. If you get any maybes, wake me up and I can eyeball them for you. Got a real good look at him at the airport. Never forget his eyes."

"The software is only good if the disguise is not substantial. We'll give you a call if we need you." The commander closed the door behind him.

Rocca slipped off his boots and lay down on the bed. Finally they were taking him seriously. Stark fluorescent lights reflected off gray walls. Gentle swaying and the distant hum of nuclear-powered engines reminded him that this was a ship of war. He was asleep before he could even think of setting his watch alarm.

He was into a good dream, catching rainbow trout on a dry fly, when the door latch clicked. The door opened and Howard Saxon peered in. Rocca watched him with slitted eyes, feeling a bit like a cobra in the grass.

Alarm registered on Saxon's face when he noticed Rocca's stealthy gaze.

Rocca sat up. Was Saxon planning on sending him back to Pearl? He shook his head and widened his eyelids, forcing himself to attention.

Saxon rubbed his forehead with the tips of two fingers. He would not meet Rocca's gaze, and one hand grasped the other elbow. "Okay, I guess we need your help. Let's go."

CHAPTER 31

As they walked through the maze of hallways and down even more ladders, Rocca was glad to hear the resignation in the geek's voice. It had only been about an hour since Rocca had dozed.

Saxon's voice seemed more meek and contrite as they walked, "The NSA computers can sort through sixty million faces in one minute. The only photo we had of El Fahd was over two years old, until Jakarta International Airport released one taken two weeks ago. There was your photo as well, but it was not digital, and once scanned into the computer was not quite what we'd hoped for.

"We had installed state-of-the-art, digital cameras in the Jakarta airport about five days after the September 11 event. Unfortunately, neither the Border Patrol nor the airline computers were connected to the cameras yet. It took us two days to convince Jakarta airport security to release the disc. Seconds later we had all the data. If only human decisions were that fast."

Rocca rubbed his palms together. "Great. This should be easy."

Saxon's mouth puckered on one side, as if he'd eaten a lemon. "The hardware is great, but the software is not that sophisticated yet. It uses only six points of reference to develop a Local Feature Analysis algorithm: distance between the eyes, width of nose, depth of eye sockets, cheekbones, jaw line and chin. If El Fahd's wearing big glasses, a beard, and puttied up his cheekbones, then we're out of luck. If he only wears a beard and glasses that don't distort his eye width, not so bad."

They climbed down another ladder, and he resumed at the bottom: "We've narrowed it down to six probable suspects and about twenty other possibles. I hope you can help sort them out."

Now deep in the bowels of the ship, they entered a room crammed with large gray rectangular and square machines, desks, a clear plastic board in the middle with grease pencil writing on it, and computers. He hated computers. Alexander sat next to a nineteen-inch computer monitor filled by an Asian man's face. Rocca sat in the chair Saxon directed him to, next to Alexander. The chair was so cold he shivered. Most of the workers in the room wore sweaters or light jackets. One woman even had on earmuffs. "Do you have a jacket? This is like Antarctica compared to the jungle I'm used to."

Alexander got up and grabbed a sweater from behind the entry door, where several others hung. He handed it to Rocca.

Rocca pulled on the sweater, barely making it over his chest. "That should do."

He studied each of the first six faces—no matches. The third guy had the right features, but his skin was pockmarked and his eyes were wrong.

So much for computers.

The next ten images: full black beards, coke-bottle glasses, and goatees got in the way. Number eleven wore wire-rimmed glasses and had a graying, braided beard. Rocca was about to move on when something about the eyes seemed familiar—like the guy thought he was better than the rest of the world.

He put his index finger on the screen. "I think that's the son of a bitch."

"Look at the rest, then we'll come back to him." Saxon's voice had changed from meek to excited. He licked his lips as if the photo were a flavor of Baskin-Robbins he was waiting for.

Rocca snorted softly. *That'd teach the geek to not trust us ground pounders.* "Is there any way you could take away the beard and glasses on this guy?"

"No sweat. We need to use different software, though. Why don't you see if anyone else is a possible, and then we can revamp all the possibilities at once?"

Rocca looked at the rest and on a whim picked one of the last three, with very thick glasses and a full beard.

He pushed back from the computer table like he was done with dinner. *Okay, Howie. Let's see what you can do now.*

Saxon had Rocca get up while he sat in front of the computer. He saved the two possible faces to a file, then loaded another software package. Recapturing the two faces, he typed in a few commands. The glasses and the beards disappeared.

Rocca stared at the first image.

Eyes are perfect. The jawline…not quite right.

"Do the other guy," he said, now curious.

Saxon adjusted the other suspect.

Rocca shook his head. "Nah, the first is much closer. But his jaw's not right."

Saxon replaced the other photo. "Since he had a beard, the computer gave us the most likely jaw line underneath. But it was a very full beard. What do you think his jaw looked like?"

"Straighter, with more of a distinct angle."

Saxon revamped the jaw.

Rocca snapped his fingers, pointed at the screen, and stood. "That's him, Howie. Definitely. Let's go get him."

Saxon looked away and rubbed his forehead with two fingers. Commander Alexander put his hand on Rocca's shoulder and forced him to sit. "There's a slight problem finding this particular guy. In fact, we suspected he was the one from the get-go, because of his evasiveness. He was scheduled to be on a flight from Singapore to Bangkok, but he never got off the flight in Bangkok. We are checking other airports and may have an answer in the next hour."

A young enlisted sailor walked in the room, catching the commander's eye and giving him the thumbs-up sign.

Rocca noticed the exchange and was instantly on his feet. "Okay, let's go."

Saxon and Alexander looked at each other, then back at Rocca. Saxon's smile was flat and his tone like a first-grade teacher spelling out a geography lesson, and he looked at the computer screen. "We have our own guys for this type of thing. We can locate him and have him interrogated before we could even have you on a plane."

Rocca rubbed his clenched fist against his upper lip and his gaze stayed on Saxon, hard, daring him to look him in the eyes. "Wait a minute. This guy nearly killed my partner. I want to take him down."

"Come on, Rock. You know the drill. We'll handle it from here. Take it down a notch," Commander Alexander put a hand on Rocca's shoulder again, like he was his father.

Rocca shrugged off the placating hand and folded his arms but kept the hard eyes on Saxon, who continued to study the computer. "Okay, I got it. How about sending me back to San Diego? I could at least see Jack."

He took off the sweater and started to leave, then turned back to the commander. "Just for giggles, could you at least tell me where this guy is right now?"

That little weenie Saxon chimed in, his tone almost musical. "Look, Rock, let us handle this." Rocca leaned into Saxon, wanting to slap him for calling him Rock. Placating bastard.

Saxon stepped back. "Hey, you've done a great job here. Exactly what we needed. It's been a hard week for you. Take a vacation." He paused and looked Rocca straight in the eye for the first time. "Go fly fishing in Colorado." He stepped back another pace, and got a wicked gleam in his eyes. "Maybe around Longmont."

Rock heard the message: *NSA can screw up your life big time. Hell they even knew he fly fished and his sister lived in Longmont. Computers are everywhere, and who has the best hackers?*

He squeezed his temples with thumb and forefinger. *I'm not exactly squeaky clean, either.*

He glared at Saxon again. *Fucker.* "Got it, Howie."

Walking up to the mezzanine deck, Rocca looked out at the cobalt blue water. Dolphins played in the wake of the ship, and silvery flying fish skipped from wave to wave like a flat rock thrown across a lake.

This wasn't over yet. He *knew* El Fahd was going to the States, and his gut told him it was to L.A.

And San Diego wasn't that far from L.A.

CHAPTER 32

Another long flight sitting in a seat too small for sleep. All Rocca wanted to do was stay on the ground for a year.

A block outside the San Diego airport, Rocco called a buddy who worked for the FBI in L.A. to see if he had any leads on El Fahd.

His buddy's voice was a flat monotone of false sorrow. "Wish I could help, but you know how it is." His friend hung up and Rocca slammed the phone into the receiver so hard it broke the earpiece. He took a deep breath, blew it out. Forget L.A. He went directly to Jack's bedside at the Naval Hospital, hoping not to wake him. He arrived at 0730 hours, September 19.

"Hey, Rock! How's it hangin'?" Jack wriggled up in the bed, not quite able to sit up, a pained look on his haggard face.

"Jack. You're lookin' pretty good," he lied. "How's the leg?"

Jack lifted his casted leg a few inches off the mattress. "I'll save the dancing for tomorrow." His grin was a boot-camp fake, like he wanted to please the sergeant but if he did another push-up he would vomit. "Feels one hell of a lot better than it did with that tree on it."

"Great." Rocca paused, wondering if he should bother Jack, but then decided it might take his mind off the pain. "You remember that creep, El Fahd?"

"Have they found him yet?"

"So you didn't think he was blown into little pieces, either. It looks like he fragged the chopper and hit the road. Probably in L.A. as we speak." Rocca looked at the floor.

"They're not going to let you take him down, are they?"

Rocca pursed his lips and looked back at Jack. "Nah, and I guess I can see their point. They probably already have the guy. Anyway, I'm due vacation time. My sis lives in Colorado. She's always begging me to come see her and go fishing with her husband Ronny. He's a guide. Guess I'll take her up on a visit. You know, Jack, the last time I was fishing was with you off the stern of that amphib in Desert Storm."

Jack smiled. "Yeah, you caught that big-ass shark and had to shoot it. Kind of pissed off the skipper."

"Pissed-off big time. He had Giorgio and me at a brace in his office for twenty minutes screaming at us."

"Yeah. Giorgio. He was a great battalion commander. I heard he was killed in the desert."

"Took a headshot from an escaped prisoner putting rounds in tents. What a waste."

Rocca looked outside and saluted and stood silent—respect for a fallen comrade.

After a minute, Jack said, "Thanks, Rock."

"For what?"

"For saving my life. You stuck with me instead of going after El Fahd. I know you wanted that guy, bad. But you stayed with me. The doc said I owe you my life." Jack stuck out his hand.

Rocca grabbed it instinctively in an arm-wrestling grip but quickly eased off when Jack grimaced. "Forget it. I thought he was in a million pieces, so I didn't really have anyone to chase." He pulled the covers over Jack's cast. "Anyway, I came to say goodbye. I'll be heading out for Colorado. You heal up quick, partner. Maybe we can do some fishing after you're well. Give me a ring when you're out of this cutter hotel."

Jack nodded and gave a thumbs-up as Rocca walked out the door.

Rocca's flight to Denver was smooth, unlike his thoughts about El Fahd. *Should have nailed that prick the first time.* He gripped his hands into fists so hard his knuckles turned white. He wanted to hit the seat in front of him at the thought of not being allowed to help with his capture.

The pilot announced, "To your left you can make out the Mohave Desert and one of the greatest engineering feats of all time, the Hoover

Dam below Lake Mead. Downstream the Colorado River has so much water harvested that by the time it gets to Mexico, it's a muddy trickle."

Rocca relaxed his fists, looked out the window, sighed and ordered another beer.

Piss on 'em.

Hours earlier, after Rocca left the ship's operations room, Saxon reviewed the intel on El Fahd. After finding the terrorist in Manila International Airport, they lost him for hours. Then, at 11:00 a.m. L.A. time, they got another hit on one of the cameras at LAX, and Saxon called in CIFA.

After the September 11 attack a special counterintelligence force had been started under DoD, later to be called Counterintelligence Field Activity, or CIFA. It was made up of the most elite members of the intelligence community, including military, CIA, FBI, and local law enforcement agencies.

The new team in L.A. had followed El Fahd from LAX to the midtown Radisson hotel. Rather than pick him up right away, the leader of the team decided to find out about his local contacts and snare the lot. They set up in the hotel room across the hall from El Fahd.

Historically, the CIA and the FBI shared little intelligence information. Information was power, and power meant funding. The best secrets got the most money: anything on al-Qaeda was a jackpot. Trying to figure out what secrets to share in this new era slowed every decision down to the pace of a snail on ice.

Tony Finelli—many called him Tony the Tiger, which he rather enjoyed—was in charge of the CIA part of the team in L.A. Built like the center for the Raiders, he almost bulged out of his green fatigues. His energy level did not allow for the inaction he had been forced into. Sitting in Room 314 at the Radisson, he spoke into the handheld radio, his face red with anger. "This operation being compromised by fucking Fee-Bee pencilnecks who can't make a decision. I'm going—"

One of his men, looking into the eyepiece of a fiber optic scope snaking under their door, waved a hand at him.

"Wait one sec," Tony said.

He squinted one eye and fit the other onto the scope. He whispered into the radio. "Two black guys just arrived in waiter outfits and… Shit! They've got surveillance equipment. Did you order these guys in here?"

—

Joe called out "Room service!" once more, holding a finger over the peephole. He noticed Chauncey frowning and tilting his head slightly, like he had heard something.

Then Joe heard it, too. It was not coming from Mr. Aswan's room. It was the sound of a door opening behind them.

Three barely perceptible but very distinct clicks followed.

Joe and Chancey turned in unison. Three dark holes were aimed at their heads, CIA-issue Berettas, now with the safety's clicked off. They were ready to make the third eye of Buddha in Chauncey's and Joe's foreheads.

The door to El Fahd's room exploded outward, and the rest was a blur of motion and gunshots.

Tony held one of the Berettas and got a glimpse of a dark-haired man bursting out of El Fahd's room, pushing everything and everyone in front of him with a briefcase. The dinner cart and the two black men floundered backwards into Tony and his two men.

Tony and his men fired reflexively. Bullets flew everywhere.

Incredibly, the man from El Fahd's room managed to keep the dinner cart moving against them. That was a lot of mass to be shoving around.

The two black men tumbled into the agents; the agents fell backward against Tony; they all fell in a heap into Tony's room.

The door to Tony's room slammed shut.

Jabril had sensed a presence outside the door. Finding the peephole blocked confirmed his suspicion. He ran to the back of the room and looked out the windows—no ledge and six stories up. The front door was the only possible exit. He grabbed his briefcase, then went to the front door and ripped it open, barreling against the dinner cart and the two black men. When shots came from the open door across the hall, Jabril crouched even lower, and, using the briefcase as a shield, he forced the cart, men and all, into the room across the hall. He slammed the door shut and ran.

Ten feet from the stairwell, he heard the door open and men swearing behind him. A gunshot glanced off the stairway door's frame.

He lunged through the door.

Training took over. Instead of down, he ran up. He was up two flights before he heard the door open below him. Moving to the outside of the stairwell, he silently crept up the remaining steps until he reached the top floor, where he found a locked door.

He heard receding footsteps going down, then fade out. He pushed against the door with all his strength. The door was too solid.

He took out his special pocket knife and used the modified lock-picking tool. After ten long seconds he heard footsteps ascending the stairs.

He took a deep breath and concentrated. The lock clicked open.

Through the door and onto the roof. He looked around, calculating how long he had. *Two minutes maximum.*

Then he heard a new sound and saw the helicopter's dark shape and running lights about a mile away. *Thirty seconds.*

Tony had asked for the chopper a half hour ago. *If those fucking admin weenies had only made up their minds a little sooner!* Bounding up the stairs two at a time he heard the roof door close four flights up.

Gotcha!

Jabril ran toward the edge of the roof, his legs moving as fast as the centaur of his dreams. Two more steps and he planted his foot on the side of the roof.

He leapt for the next roof, thirty feet away.

Tony arrived on the roof to the deafening sound of the hovering chopper and was temporarily blinded by the halogen spotlight. The din of the chopper completely obliterated any other sound.

A small herd of alley cats lived on the adjacent rooftop and had, only seconds before, let out a collective low growl at Jabril brushing by them. Then the helicopter searchlight punctured their world of darkness and they scattered like ants, skulking off to find another dark corner.

Saxon received the call about an hour later—El Fahd had escaped. Saxon stewed as the other agent told him about the administrative fiasco that had bungled the mission. Then he thought about Rocca and his use of

"Howie." He thought about how a private citizen would have no administrative bureaucracy to slow things down and bungle a simple capture. Rocca would have another edge: revenge sharpened the wits, quickened the pace. And since he was outside the usual channels, no one could prove any direct involvement with the CIA—only a private citizen doing his good deed. A win-win all the way around.

Saxon called the San Diego hospital and asked to speak to Jack.

CHAPTER 33

When the dust cleared deep underground at Amazon Lab, Alex initially felt helpless seeing Doc pinned under a huge beam that had caved in from the ceiling. The beam must have supported a lot of weight because it was massive—eight inches deep, two feet wide and a good twenty feet long—and one end had completely broken off, the other still attached so it lay at an angle, Doc under the grounded end. Doc's face was gray, his eyes glazed, and when he exhaled pink froth drooled from his lips.

Alex peered through the dust cloud for M.C., found him blinking and brushing off dust, and ran to him. "M.C., there's a heavy beam lying on Doc's chest and pink foam on his lips."

M.C. hurried over with Alex, and frowned at Doc. "A broken rib probably punctured a lung. We have to get him to sick bay, pronto."

Without even thinking, Alex squatted under the beam, braced his shoulder under it, and lifted it off Doc.

M.C. stood watching, eyes wide.

"Now would be a good time to pull Doc out," Alex said, his words squeezed out with the strain. It was like doing squats in high school weight lifting class, though he was not maxed out. He could do a few reps if he had to.

M.C. pulled Doc out by his armpits.

Alex tossed the beam off his shoulder and it sounded like a tree crashing on cement. He looked around for anyone else who needed help.

Sam and his crew stared at him. Sam's head was tilted and he squinted at Alex as if he was trying to figure out what had just happened.

Alex shrugged. He wanted to laugh he felt so good. He was not going to apologize for his new strength. "Hey, guys. Could you help M.C. with Doc? I gotta find Jesse."

He began walking out of the room. Jesse had always hated the thought of being buried alive. She would have tried for the elevator.

"Alex." M.C. called. "Where're you going? I need your help."

"I gotta find Jesse. She probably went up the elevator shaft, knowing her and her fear of being buried alive."

M.C. started lifting Doc, and Doc's head flopped like a rag doll. M.C. put him back on the floor. "Help me here, would you?"

Alex ripped off one of the kitchen cabinet doors and handed it to Sam. "Help him. I gotta go."

Sam started helping M.C. scoot the cabinet door under Doc's head and neck.

Alex started out of the room again.

"Wait," M.C. said. "Didn't you hear what Doc said about what could be up there?"

Alex partly turned his head to look at M.C. "Right. DNA Boogie monsters." He smiled. "I think I can handle them."

"Something else. There's toxic hydrogen sulfide gas in the shaft. You could hold your breath, but..." He glanced at the huge beam on the ground, then back at Alex. "The fumes almost got Doc after the first tremor." He paused. "And those were not earthquakes."

"What?"

Sam had found some duct tape and was winding it around the cabinet and over Doc's forehead.

M.C. stood put his hands on his hips. "I didn't tell you and Jesse before because I didn't want to alarm you. It was a bomb—probably more than one—terrorists trying to get rid of our lab."

"Shit." He took a step toward the elevator.

"Wait! You'll need the keys to the elevator shaft." M.C. began patting his pockets. "Also, I set a few booby traps. Don't open the main desk drawers or any windows." He shook his head. "Jesse must have got the keys. I hope." He caught Alex's eyes once more. "Keep your head down up there, or someone might shoot it off."

—

Jesse was already sixty feet up the elevator shaft when she heard the metal hatch bang open below, echoing.

Alex shouted up the shaft, "Jesse, come down. There's toxic gases in the shaft, and bad guys are waiting topside."

She ignored him, continuing her climb. The smell was lessening the higher she went. No way was she being buried alive if another quake happened.

As he ran down the stairs of the building next to the Radisson, Jabril was anxious at having come so close to capture, but confident that the new powers Allah had bestowed him allowed him to escape the infidels.

Once outside, he called his L.A. contact on his cell phone. "They found me. I'm on the run. Tell Khan I the plan changes to 'Next Day.'" He hung up.

Never leave yourself without a way out. That was a prime dictum he had been taught early on in his Afghan camp.

To that end, a car had already been placed a block away. He found it and was on I-110 in minutes. The tan Honda Accord would blend in like a piece of sand on the beach. It seemed every American owned an Accord. Even so, if anyone got suspicious, the modified engine would make him uncatchable.

For now, he would motor five miles per hour over the speed limit to avoid attention, exactly as he had been trained. *Fit in. Be invisible.* He set the cruise control and unfolded the map from his briefcase.

Many of Jabril's superiors were still in the Afghan mountains. One was not: Albert George Khan, the creator of the Next Day plan.

Khan had been in college in Colorado Springs when he answered Sheik Abdullah Assam's plea to help rid Islam of the Israelis and their American benefactors, joining Al Qaeda and fighting in Afghanistan for two years. Then he returned to the U.S. to join a sleeper cell. He finished his degree at Colorado College in the late '80s and got a job in Cañon City at the correctional facility. He was a natural prison guard, ruthless when necessary but able to interrogate as gently as a mother. And, by living in a rural area nearby, he was able to keep to himself.

While there, he placed a few other sleeper cells. The closest was in Cheyenne Mountain nuclear bunker, NORAD. The bunker had over a thousand residents focused on tracking threats to the U.S. from the outside.

On the morning of the September 11 attack, Khan had watched the workers scurry into the mountain minutes before the huge three-foot-thick, twenty-five-ton blast doors closed.

Across the country, the same kind of activity was seen by other sleeper cells at Fort Meade, Maryland; Raven Rock near Waynesboro, Pennsylvania; Berryville, Virginia; Omaha, Nebraska; and Shreveport, Louisiana.

The locations were all sites of "secret" U.S. underground havens where the government could run the country should there be a massive nuclear war.

An idea had formed in Khan's head. He laughed at its simplicity.

That evening he had communicated with the other cell leaders. It was like a house fire: when the building starts burning, the first thing you do is go to a safe place.

What safer place than Cheyenne Mountain, buried beneath seventeen hundred feet of granite in a self-contained city that even had a restaurant? Unless, of course, the water was toxic. The other cell leaders all loved the idea and agreed to use it to supplement the original El Husam plan, in which Jabril would have to spread the virus by himself. Khan had tried to convince them of this plan as the original, but Jabril had had the ear of the leaders and wanted to do it all by himself.

Now Jabril would have help, lots of it.

"Next Day," as the plan was called, took shape but was known only to a sparse few. When Khan got Jabril's call and found out the El Husam plan was defunct, all the key elements were in place for Next Day.

But first, Khan must wait for Jabril to make it through to the safe house.

CHAPTER 34

Jesse opened the elevator shaft closet door to the ground floor administrative building and was confronted by chaos.

There was no roof. Jigsaw pieces of the roof along with the cinder block and cement walls were strewn about. That and smoke and small fires made it nearly impossible to navigate. The waning tropical twilight cast an alien pall. Running back into the elevator shaft held promise.

Then she saw open sky.

She gingerly stepped out of the smoldering rubble, and the smoky haze dissipated to wonderful, cool air. She gulped it in. The indigo sky was scattered with bountiful stars, brighter than anything she'd seen.

She sat on a rock and gaped at the heavens, calm and relaxed. M.C. might be mad that she'd taken his keys, but she didn't care. She hoped Alex would show up soon, though she was feeling so good that she really didn't care if he made it at all. She was above ground and alive.

There was a faint coughing sound and something stung her neck. She grabbed at it and pulled out a small solid cylinder. A dart-gun syringe. She rubbed her fingers against her thumb. They were already numb.

Her thoughts fizzled and she slid to the ground, unconscious.

Alex scrambled out of the upper elevator shaft hatch and crawled on hands and knees into the camped closet. The outside door was ajar about six inches.

He wanted to call out Jesse's name, but instead, remembering M.C.'s warning about possible waiting terrorists, he peered outside.

Jesse's limp body was being carried off by two men clad in jungle camouflage. They carried her toward a flatbed truck. Eight other men—actually, Alex decided, they must be soldiers from their dress, guns, and coordinated movements—melted into the bush, probably waiting to see if someone else blundered out from the previous front of the building.

Without thinking, as if by some new instinct, he moved quickly through the detritus of the explosion to the back wall that was still partially standing and, using it as cover, faded into the jungle as soundless as a moth.

The soldier, hiding about two hundred yards away on a slight rise behind a Mimosa tree, was elated at the sight on his infrared scope—another outline was moving inside the smoldering building. Capturing one of the virologists was great. Two: fantastic!

Then the infrared silhouette dissolved. One second: there. The next: nothing.

He radioed the other lookout who was fifty yards to his right to see if he had a better view. Perhaps their quarry had stepped behind an obstruction. After ten seconds of radio chatter, the other lookout decided to circle around the perimeter to solve the mystery.

Alex saw the other lookout coming, his rifle held in front, but his attention more on the exploded building site, so he never saw what was coming. His head was severed from his body. The only sound was a very soft, muffled thud of his cranium hitting the jungle floor.

Alex caught the soldier's lifeless body, quietly laying it to the ground. He sniffed the air, raising his nose and moving his head from side to side, trying to catch every odor. The blood, mixed with the scent of the soldier's urine, tainted the air strongly with death. He focused further, on the sweat and mosquito repellent of another soldier, thirty yards ahead.

Alex's skin was cool to touch, so cool that it would not show up on any infrared detection device. His breathing was slow, his heart rate barely perceptible. He wiped the blade of the knife on the dead soldier's pants and moved quickly to his next prey.

No thoughts. No emotions. Just stealth.

—

Jesse awakened from the drug's effect with one wrist handcuffed to a ring on middle right side of the flatbed truck. There were benches on either side, wooden slats for walls, but no back or roof. She cautiously peeked at her captors. One was standing looking over the cab, the other sitting on the left bench, facing the rear. Both were relaxed, as if they did not expect anything out of her. She did feel strange, but the drug's anesthetic effect was almost gone.

The man who'd been sitting came toward her and said something to her in a foreign language sounding like guttural Chinese. She remained limp.

The other man said something that she assumed was obscene from the way they chuckled afterwards. They started to go back to their posts.

She immediately kicked the bench sitter off the back end of the truck.

The other man reacted quickly, hitting her squarely on the forehead with the butt of his gun, knocking her down.

He prodded her with the barrel of his gun. The only movement was her dead weight jostling back and forth from the bumpy ride.

The soldier knocked on the back window of the truck cab and motioned for it to stop.

Turning around, he was met by Jesse's roundhouse fist on the side of his temple, dropping him like a rock.

She quickly searched his pockets for the keys to the handcuffs.

The driver stopped the truck, jumped out, and ran to the back, aiming his .45 while searching with his flashlight. His partner was unconscious, handcuffed to the truck.

Footsteps sounded behind him.

Whirling around, his beam poked at the jungle, stopping in the direction of approaching footsteps, his rifle raised. The jungle parted.

The soldier Jesse had kicked off the back limped through.

The driver yelled at him. He put his hands out, palms up.

They argued more, and Jesse used their loud voices to hide her escape. She moved quietly and quickly away from the truck. The moon cast an eerie light, allowing her to slip through the bush at a fast, noiseless sprint, astonished she could accomplish this feat. She was Indian, true, but she'd never been able see in the dark or run this fast. Pretty cool, though.

Within minutes she was back at the scene of her abduction.

She sensed Alex nearby. The noise of the returning truck was getting closer.

She hazarded a whisper. "Alex, are you there?"

"Right behind you. We gotta warn the others."

He grabbed her hand and began gently pulling her toward the lab rubble.

"Okay, yeah, I'm fine, thanks for asking. Drugged, butt-stroked with a rifle, handcuffed, and now I can see in the dark like it was daylight."

"Yeah, me too. We'll talk later."

He pulled her more firmly as the headlights from the approaching truck glanced off the trees next to them.

Moving swiftly, ducking behind remaining walls, and side stepping burning papers, Alex and Jesse stayed in the shadows and reached the elevator shaft closet.

Jesse went in first. Alex grabbed a long tree branch laying on a desk, then eased back inside the closet, keeping the end of the tree branch near a drawer M.C. had said housed a booby trap. Voices and footsteps were coming closer.

He crammed the end of the branch into the drawer handle and pulled.

The explosion slammed the closet door closed and rocked him backward. He banged his head against the wall of the closet.

Stunned and deafened, he felt his way to the inside elevator shaft door.

It was pitch black in the shaft, but he could see and feel each rung clearly, though they had a faint green hue. He crawled out the bottom shaft hatch and Jesse stood smiling. "Pretty cool seeing in the dark, huh?"

Gunshots sounded—not from above, but from the hallway behind Jesse.

They looked at each other. Neither one had a gun.

Alex led. He could feel Jesse right behind him. He knew that would happen. No words were necessary between them now. They came to a split in the hallways. The shots came from the left: the lab. They split up. Alex moved directly toward the lab, Jesse to the right, around through the lounge.

From the lab, Sam, the surfer guy, shouted, "M.C., are you okay?" No answer from M.C.

Alex moved faster.

He rounded the last corner and glanced around the doorway. The smell of gunpowder was strong. Two men lay on the floor, one in camouflage.

The other wore khaki pants and olive shirt and had a mass of black hair and a bloody face. Sam was crouched behind a cabinet, his back to Alex, firing intermittent single shots with a handgun over the top.

The room was still dusty with plaster and pieces of walls on the floor. There were a few bullet holes in the glass partition to the Class IV room. Shots were coming down the darkened hallway that lead to the lounge. "Sam, its Alex. I'm behind you. I am going in to find M.C. Don't shoot me."

Sam spoke to Alex but didn't move from facing the hallway ahead. "They came in about ten minutes after you and Jesse left. Probably expecting scientists, not armed men, so their guns weren't ready. We got a couple, but there are more. Let me go in with—"

Alex was already halfway across the room, moving like a cat. "Don't shoot me."

He disappeared around the corner.

Sam shook his head. Alex was not very smart for a scientist.

There was no shot, only a muffled scream.

Sam moved forward, using the remaining cabinets for cover. Hearing male and female voices in the hallway, he decided to throw away caution and storm the next room.

When he got there all he could do was stare.

Jesse had Jimbo and Ron, one under each arm, carrying them out the door like sacks of grapefruit. Alex was tying up two soldiers with some of their own clothes: shirts for their arms behind their backs, pants for their legs, and tee shirts stuffed in their mouths. Both soldiers looked at Alex with wide eyes—more than anxiety. Fear.

Alex's shirt was torn and there was a bleeding wound on his back, a back that rippled with muscles larger than any steroid-pumped soldier Sam had ever seen. Alex easily grappled the limp body of M.C. under one arm.

"Sam, we'll take care of Ron and Jimbo. Stand guard here."

Sam stared into eyes he'd only seen once before: a jaguar at night in the jungle. The vermilion glow was unnerving by itself. But Alex's deep, hoarse voice made the hairs rise on the back of his neck.

He carried M.C. out the door.

Sam closed his mouth, shook his head and rubbed his eyes with his fists.

One of the captured soldiers whimpered and Sam glanced at him, noticing a swollen right eye and welts over his chest and throat. The other soldier's jaw muscles rippled as he bit down on the tee shirt. His eyes looked like fried eggs, not moving from their gaze at the door Alex had gone through. Both men had a distinct Asian look.

Sam squatted beside them and took out their gags. "Who sent you?"

The soldiers spoke in feverish, unintelligible gibberish, with an occasional English word thrown in. Their language was unusual, like Japanese with a European twist. Familiar, but not. He stood. During their last surfing trip, Sam had been surprised that Ron knew Chinese and Korean. Maybe he would know the soldiers' language.

The soldiers both eyed the door and repeated a word: "Moonstew. Moonstew."

Sam shook his head, stuffed the shirts back into their mouths, made sure they were secure, and went to get Ron.

Alex almost bumped into him coming back in the door, wearing a different shirt. No red eyes. No weight lifter physique. Just Alex. What the hell we going on with him?

"I need to report this ASAP. Do you have a sat phone?"

Alex tilted his head and eyed Sam with suspicion. "Are you with the CIA or Spec Ops or something?"

"Look I don't mean to be rude, but I have to report this. Here's the short version. You ever see the movie *Mission Impossible*?"

"You mean with Tom Cruise?"

"Yeah, good old Tommy. In the movie he stole a list—the non-official cover list. My name would be on it."

So what does that mean, exactly, 'non-official cover?'"

"We are not officially covered by diplomatic status or other government titles. Our cover is usually as businessmen, like my surf board industry. It allows us more freedoms, but more risk. Like John Paul Jones said, 'He who will not risk, cannot win.'"

Alex frowned and smiled at the same time—his crock-of-shit face. "I heard the CIA axed most of their agents when the USSR died."

"That's true. The leadership sucked and communication was piss-poor. The low point was when private businesses and then terrorist groups started using high-tech stuff that was better than ours."

"So why are you still working for them?"

"Working with secrets is like using cocaine: Once you've had a taste, the big bosses know they've got you for life. Plus, there's such a thing as loyalty. Jerry Klaus and I go back a long way. As it turned out, the CIA needed the lab down here investigated about the same time Rachel wanted to come down. So things kind of worked out for all of us. Now, the sat phone?"

Alex wasn't budging. "What about the goons that got Jerry back in the states? Rachel said they were Feds. Why did you guys take Jerry like that?"

Sam shook his head and sat heavily and sighed in frustration, but looking resigned to make Alex believe he could be trusted. "That was not us. Those guys work for a very powerful senator named Cardwell. He recruited several dissatisfied Cold-War-era NSA and CIA agents and started his own security force. The business sector was way ahead of us in high tech capabilities, and that was a big enticement, especially to those NSA geeks. NSA was worse off than the CIA. They had so many e-mail systems it took over thirty *Send* commands to get a message out to the entire agency. CIA didn't recruit enough in-country agents in Russia, East Germany, the Middle East or India. There was a lot of frustration when Washington learned from CNN and not us about the Fall of the Wall in '89, the Iraq attack on Kuwait in '90, Gorbachev's coup in '91, India's nuclear test bomb in '98, the bombing of the U.S. embassies in East Africa in '98, and the first attack on the World Trade Center in '94.

"I could go on, but you get it. The highest security agency in the world wanted to do it the way it had always worked, and didn't want to change. So a lot of dissatisfied agents started rogue groups, like Senator Cardwell's. Unfortunately, they are pretty good at getting information. Information is power, and Senator Cardwell is hoping to get enough of both to become the next president. The boys that work for him are getting paid better, doing lots of high-tech stuff, and doing it their way. It's a marriage made in spook heaven."

Sam stood up and started pacing, now glaring at Alex, his patience obviously wearing thin.

"Cardwell got a whiff that La Riva was doing biological warfare research, and after the terrorist attack on September 11 he was empowered to investigate, big time. Though I think he'll be forced to let Jerry go. NSA's been doing new, improved, high-tech snooping into the good senator's life. He's been a very naughty boy. If his constituents find out, he'll be history."

Sam stopped pacing and looked at Alex, the frustrated glare softening into a pleading look accompanied by holding his arms out, palms up. "So, Alex my boy, you think you can trust me enough now to allow me to use the sat phone?"

Alex puckered his mouth sideways and shrugged. "Yeah. All that would be hard to make up, and Rachel trusts you, so I guess you're okay. It's in the drawer right next to your leg."

Sam slapped his hands together. "Now we're talkin." He pulled out the phone, turned on the power, and waited while the phone located the satellites.

Alex's sideways pucker turned flat and he squinted one eye. "It puzzles me, though, how you can train people in the NSA or CIA to lie, steal, cheat, and even murder, and then expect them to do the right thing at the right time for the right side."

Sam scratched his forehead and rolled his head on his neck, seeming to think of the right response. "When you're in the field, sometimes the lines between right and wrong, good guys and bad guys, get blurred or even erased. If the bad guys have enough money or the good guys treat you like crap too many times, you say *fuck it* and go over, like Aldrich Ames. Only problem is, guys like him screw it up for the entire organization by supplying the other side with info about our good guys doing the right thing."

"You didn't really answer my question. How do you get the good guys to do the right thing if you trained them to do all that bad shit?"

The sat phone beeped and Sam tapped his finger on his chest. "You gotta have it inside, man. Right here in your heart." He dialed a number and waited for the delayed relay.

"Do you have it in your heart, Sam?"

"I guess you can be the judge of that over the next few hours. The real question is, do *you* have it in your heart? 'Cause after the stuff I've seen you do, if you don't, I'll have to use some of that bad shit they taught me and take you out."

Sam raised his eyebrows and one open palm out as if to place a punctuation on his question: *Did Alex have it in his heart?*

Alex vaguely remembered wanting to save Jesse, running through the night, a knife flashing moonlight in his eyes, blood dripping from his hand. He sat down hard on one of the metal chairs, feeling as if perhaps he didn't have it in his heart.

Sam held up his index finger, apparently connected on his call and walked away, talking low with his back to Alex.

Jesse came into the room. "Alex, you look sick. Are you okay?"

"Jesse. You were up there. I gotta know." He glanced at Sam to make sure he was not listening. "Did I kill anybody?"

She went down on one knee in front of Alex, cupped a hand to his face, and looked softly into his eyes.

"Alex, they would have tortured and killed me and probably everyone else here. You did what you had to."

Slowly, he felt his gaze harden and his chest tighten. "You're right. They probably wanted information. How did you get away?"

"Must have been my Apache coming out. I threw them off and ran through the pitch-black jungle like it was daylight."

Alex cocked his head. "You don't really think it was your Apache, do you?"

Sam got off the phone. "Hey, Jesse. How are the others doing?"

She stood up, giving Alex's cheek a pat before she turned toward Sam. Her gaze faltered, and she did not look at him. "They're okay?"

"What do you mean, 'okay'?"

"Jimbo's fine except for minor bleeding from a groin gunshot. Ron has a minor concussion from hitting his head." Her voice became very quiet. "José died from a gunshot to the head. I'm so sorry. He was such a gentleman." She wiped her eyes.

"Damn! José's dead? Man, I can't believe it! I've been hittin' the waves with him for five years." Sam looked off into space, gritting his teeth. "I'll have to tell his family soon."

Then he smiled. "Jimbo got it in the nads? I'll bet he's pissed. He loves his nuts. We gotta save those or he'll lose it."

"He's in no danger of losing…it." Jesse said.

Sam's smile grew. "No, I don't mean lose his little head; I mean lose his big head."

He paused. "I'll get Ron so we can interview those two guards. They sound Korean or Chinese, and if they are, we need to get that info back to Washington ASAP."

Jesse looked wary. "Wait a minute. I thought Rachel and M.C. said—"

Alex interrupted, "It's okay, Jesse. Sam is with the good guys. He's trying to help. It wasn't his agency that got Jerry."

Jesse gazed into Alex's eyes, and he passed information without speaking. She sighed and turned to Sam. "If Alex says you're okay, that's good enough for me. Be careful with Ron, though. He may still be woozy after that head bonk."

Sam turned to leave, but hesitated, catching Alex's eye. "I was going to ask if you two would be okay without me here. Pretty stupid, huh? I'll be back in a few."

Alex waited until Sam was gone. He eyed Jesse. "We should get back to the States as soon as possible. I feel it in the pit of my stomach, only it's not like chocolate cake; it's rotten spaghetti. A very bad thing is about to happen, and I think only you and I can stop it."

Jesse nodded. "I feel it too. But what can we do? We need someone to fly us out of here. And then there are those soldiers up above."

"Sam flew in; he can fly us out. But we must have the vaccine and the antiviral drugs. How are Rachel, Doc, and M.C.?"

"They're okay. Doc looked like he had a lung injury, but turned out to be a cut in his mouth, a mild concussion, and a bruised thigh. Nothing else. M.C. whacked his head. No problem there, right? His head's iron. Once Rachel found they were okay, she went back to work. She took Doc with her. If we help her, we could get a workable vaccine in a few days. By then maybe we'll have a way out."

Alex studied her. Even in the low light she looked done in, dark crescents under her eyes and half-closed lids. "Except we only have twenty-four hours, or that bad thing will pop. Now all I have to do is talk Sam into it."

CHAPTER 35

Jabril stewed and fretted, stuck in traffic and wanting to get out of L.A. The powerful blood that had given him such extraordinary skills still thrummed in his arms, his legs, his brain. But L.A. spewed an endless stream of vehicles, six lanes both ways, and most vehicles shiny and new. He wondered how anyone could live in such decadent, busy nothing, on their way to mindless, capitalistic jobs.

Forward movement all but ceased. Likely some minor accident.

He sighed, resigned to waiting, reckoning no one knew he was here. If they had discovered his original plan, they would be watching LAX or other major airports. They could not know about the Next Day plan. In many ways it was better, though he would have preferred to do all the damage himself. Yet he would still be a huge cog and this plan would result in fewer civilian casualties. It would hit mostly the leaders, not the worker bees. The top ranks were to blame for what had happened before—they were the ones who had supported the Israelis, planned the embargo, the starving of millions.

They killed my mother. They will pay. In blood.

In few more days the house built by the infidel leaders would collapse from the inside out.

Rachel had been working for half an hour in the moon suit, uncomfortable and sweating. But she was almost done with the initial chemical structure for the antiviral medication. What she needed was an in-vivo test—a live subject.

"Hey, Doc, didn't you say there was a monkey infected with this virus?"

Doc sat behind the glass partition, not great at the intricate work Rachel was doing, and what she did was pretty much a one-person job. He rubbed ice on his thigh. "Yes. The dog got the virus from the monkey. Did you compare the two viral cultures in the incubator? A's the dog and B's the monkey."

Rachel made a face. *Stupid.* She took out the culture labeled B, then realized they had no facility to test DNA nor electron microscopy.

"Did you send the cultures out?

"I think Jesse did. They may not be back yet."

She went online and, entered one password to get into La Riva's site, then two others to finally get into the DNA and Electron Microscopy tests Jesse had sent out a month ago. The results had only become available last week, so no one here had seen them yet. They confirmed that the A and B cultures matched perfectly.

"They're identical, Doc. But I saw the monkey. He still looks healthy."

"Yeah, we won't be able to tell if the monkey gets better, 'cause he's not sick. We need an in-vitro test on the viral culture. Try a very dilute solution of the medication first, say 1:1,000,000. Then bump it up until it kills the virus. Once we get above 1:10,000 if no kill, then we need to try another med."

Doc paused, thinking. "You know what? We can also check a viral load in the infected monkey now, and then a week after—"

Rachel put a hand up. "I know all that. What I was wondering was why this monkey shows no signs of infection. Alex and Jesse obviously are showing signs, and so did Jesse's dog."

"Sorry, guess I was thinking out loud. It seems to me, like any virus, it won't cause symptoms until the organism's immune system can't fight it off, either because its immunological structure is totally new or the organism's immune system is weakened, perhaps from stress."

Doc got up and started limping around the room. "Bear with me a minute while I brainstorm. The monkey's been leading a pretty peaceful life before and after Fang's attack. Fang, on the other hand, was mentally off balance to begin with and then quite stressed once he was infected. Once we started working with the Borna virus, mental disturbances in the animals were bound to become more common. When combined with other viral DNA the effects on brain chemistry resulted in the rage we saw in that dog."

He stopped pacing and turned to face Rachel who had her full attention on him. "Now let's turn to Alex and Jesse. They have certainly had their share of stress. That coupled with the weird Borna mutant virus they seem to have acquired from Fang would make them a bit crazy."

"How the hell did they get infected?"

"Direct contact with bodily fluids, like HIV." Doc's gaze did not waiver.

Rachel thought about Jesse and Alex together. "What exactly are you saying? Our contamination procedures are flawless, and those two are very careful."

He winced with pain and sat down, looking away from her, as if he didn't want her to see his face. "I puzzled over that one for a long time."

She wanted to climb out of the hot suit, go out and look in his face, find out if he was going to lie to her. Instead she had to listen carefully to the tone of his voice.

"Initially, I thought Alex was infected first. Then I remembered the dog. I think Jesse was infected by that damn dog and didn't show any signs of infection until her stress started, maybe seeing Alex sick or the lab in turmoil with those bombs. There is also the male/female factor." He paused and looked up at her.

Here it comes, Rachel thought. He's going to tell me they had sex.

"I think Alex got a more rapid development of his disease because his immune system may not be as strong as Jesse's. You females live longer than us males for a reason."

Alex and Jesse strode in, laughing at something.

"Hey, Doc, how's the leg?" Alex asked.

Rachel wanted them to go away. She didn't like it that they were so happy with each other. She wanted to query Doc more.

"Doing fine, considering," Doc said, rubbing his thigh. He nodded toward the glass partition. "Rachel's ready to evaluate the effectiveness of an antiviral medication and a new vaccine."

Jesse eyed Rachel in disbelief. "How'd you do that? It usually takes years to manufacture a medication to hit a specific virus."

Rachel was thankful now for the steamy inside of the suit that fogged up the facemask enough so Jesse couldn't see her face. She tried to make her words sound nonchalant through her frustration at these two as lovers. "One genius and Lady Luck. Doc was the genius who not only thought to save a sample of the monkey's blood so we could culture it, but he also brought several meds down. One was an anti-HIV medication, XRV-32. It's a near-perfect match to the compound I found in my analysis of antiviral drugs that would work on…our virus. I'm going to try it in-vitro and then on the monkey."

Alex and Jesse looked at each other as if passing information without speaking.

"The sooner the better," Alex said. "Sam wants to leave in two hours. He's worried there will be another attack on us soon."

Rachel held her hands up like she was being robbed. "No way I can be done in two hours. We'll have to take some of the samples with us, and the monkey."

"That is actually a good thing, Rachel," Doc said, walking to the window and putting a palm on it, like he was trying to put a hand on her shoulder. "We need a proper lab to finish this work faster. Wrap it up in there and let's get packed." He frowned at Alex. "I need to get some blood from you and Jesse and carry those with us, too. It may be that the virus from the monkey is making you exhibit some unusual characteristics."

Alex squinted as if in pain. "More needles. You already got a ton of blood from me."

"Just one tiny needle stick and it will be over," Doc said.

Jesse nodded her head, her eyes drooping. "You can draw my blood, but I need sleep before I can help."

Alex yawned. "Maybe we could spell you and Rachel after we've caught an hour of shut eye."

"Okay," Doc said. "We'll roust you in an hour."

Jesse bared her arm and Doc drew three tubes of blood. He finished and motioned for Alex.

"Not now, Doc. Maybe later." Then he caught Rachel's eye. "Maybe after this is all over, you could join our Amazon team."

Rachel looked at him then away. "I'd love to see some of the places down here, like the Andes and the Amazon rain forest. But I really like having the freedom and safety of the States. If I worked here I'd always be worried about a less friendly dictator taking over or some terrorist trying to use me as a hostage."

"Yeah, I hear you. But we do have a little more freedom in our work than you do in the States. I mean, can you believe all the monkeys we have to work with?"

Jesse tapped Alex on the shoulder. "How about that nap?"

"Sure, Jesse. Right behind you."

He turned to leave then turned back to Rachel. "Anyway, we'd be happy to have you if you change your mind." He gave her a big grin and walked away.

Rachel watched him leave. She wanted to laugh and scream in agony all at the same time.

Maybe I'll prick my finger with this virus so Alex will find me more attractive as a superwoman or mutant or whatever Jesse is.

There was something about Alex. Maybe it was his green eyes, or making jokes, even in danger. He did risk his life to save all of them.

There was that other look: the animal. Scary, but…interesting.

Maybe I can control that with medication—have Mr. Hyde whenever I'm in the mood. Bad boys, bad boy, bad boys.

It was too soon. She was not over Scott. Besides, what about the rule? No coworkers.

Then she remembered her dream when she was camping—hot sex with Alex—God, that was good.

Pretty stupid rule. Don't get too attached to Jesse, Mr. Smith. There's a red dress and a bottle of Pinot waiting at my apartment.

She held that thought and went back to work.

Jesse was tired as she walked with Alex walked toward the sleeping quarters, but what she really wanted was Alex to more than lay down with her. Their footsteps echoed off the walls. Neither spoke.

Finally Alex broke the silence. "I'd like Rachel to come with us to D.C."

Jesse kept walking said nothing.

"She's good," Alex continued, "and we three can complete the antiviral medications and vaccine in a hurry there."

Jesse stopped abruptly, forcing him to stop and look at her. "We need to get out of here tonight, with or without Rachel. And what about Lora? What about our kiss last night?"

She mentally slapped herself. *You are not falling in for this guy. Period.*

Alex twisted his mouth and frowned like he was hurt. "Come on, Jesse! I already told you I'm over Lora. Probably not right, but it's the way I feel. I just think Rachel is damn good at her job. We could use her."

Jesse felt her face fall and started walking, leaving him behind her. *He never said a damn thing about our kiss. Not a damn thing.*

Alex caught up and walked with her in silence again. At her room, she opened the door and looked back at him, tilting her head up, hoping for a kiss.

He gave her a peck on the cheek. "I'm bushed. See you in an hour." He walked away; she closed the door and wanted to cry. But then she gritted her teeth and felt almost happy she didn't have to love him. What she had to do would be easier now.

In his room, Alex called Sam on the in-house phone, hoping for a quick, straightforward conversation so he could get some sleep. But Sam's words were disturbing. "Alex, these guys are North Korean. Ron is sure. I talked to my contact in D.C., and they want us out of here ASAP. How many of them did you see up top?"

Alex thought for a moment. "I think there were ten or twelve. But they are minus a few that I…uh…eliminated."

"Are you kiddin' me, man? Those are North Korean Special Forces, bad-ass mo-fos. So that's what you were talking to Jesse about earlier when I was on the phone. Guess I missed the part about you killing them. Shit! I mean, that's great. It changes our battle plan for the better, especially now that we gotta go back up there. I sure hope they haven't destroyed our plane."

"Yeah, well, I did it, but I'm not proud of it. Don't know what to think, really. I do know one thing: Jesse and I gotta get some rest. Whatever we got really wears us out. Even with some sleep I can't guarantee that I'll be up for killing anybody. Ever. I don't like what's going on with my body."

Alex wanted to kick himself for saying too much. But he was too tired to care.

"Okay," Sam said. Then he paused. "I understand. Get a little shuteye."

Sam hung up and stared at the phone. Alex may be out of control. What Sam hadn't said was that he'd found out what the two soldiers had been babbling about. Alex had changed into something that terrified even the Korean Special Forces. A *moonstew*. A monster.

Alex hung up and forced himself to shower, scrubbing hard. He brushed his teeth just as hard and fell onto the bed. He tried to sleep, but one thought kept hammering him: He was definitely infected and he'd probably already passed it to Jesse. No way was he going to infect Rachel.

Above ground, in the Amazon night, six of the twelve soldiers in the jungle were dead. Their superiors decided to take no more chances. It would be nice to have at least one scientist to squeeze for information, but with the what seemed like obvious military help that had killed their best soldiers it was time to cut their losses—kill all the scientists and destroy the lab. None of the remaining soldiers had any demolitions experience, but a demolition team was being sent. They would arrive at dawn.

For now, the only illumination was faint moonlight on the smoking rubble, like fog rising off castle ruins from an old Dracula movie. And, like the movie, an unusual creature slept under the ruins. Only this one was real.

CHAPTER 36

Senator Cardwell had been busy. First, he had personally apologized to Jerry Klaus for any rough treatment. Then, while Jerry watched, Cardwell chastised the men who had held Jerry hostage. After Klaus was released and gone, Cardwell had apologized to the men and handed them a bonus for their work. He promised them much more would follow, as long as they maintained surveillance of La Riva Lab, and Jerry Klaus.

His main problem now was the Amazon Lab. And Rachel Lane. Somehow she had managed to get through customs without being spotted. In the next few hours Cardwell's men would move in on the Amazon Lab. Once she was captured, Cardwell would revisit Klaus with Rachel in tow, torturing her to loosen his tongue. Once he spilled the information Cardwell knew he had, he would kill them both.

Someone knocked on the door.

"Enter!" He always enjoyed the look of fear people had entering his office with the bear looming above him.

Robby plowed in with two men in fatigues. His grin reminded Cardwell of a boy with a Cracker Jack prize.

"Senator, you are not going to believe this stuff. It's from L.A. We happened to be plugged into the local Agency guys, and…well, just listen."

He started the digital recording on the micro player, a small handheld device that could download audio files from anywhere in the world and reproduce them with crystal clarity.

The first voice was obviously angry, but unfamiliar. "What do you mean he got out of the room? How could El Fahd escape you and five other men?"

"Listen, you fuck." This voice was Tony Finelli's, a deep growl. "I asked you to get the goddamn choppers out of here. Can't hear or see shit with them. I didn't ask you to tell everyone and their neighbor who we were after. Get Bingham on the line!"

The rest of the recording was unintelligible.

Cardwell frowned. "That's it? That's all you've got?"

Robby's jaw muscles flexed and he closed his eyes slowly, and reopened them with and exasperated sigh. "Yes, Senator. Basic SIGINT. Someone must've jammed the rest. But it's all we need. Didn't you hear it?"

"Don't get superior with me. Didn't I hear what?"

"The name, Senator, the name. El Fahd. He's one of bin Laden's best buddies. The pissed-off guy was Tony Finelli, head of the CIA anti-terrorist force in L.A. The background noise was helicopters. By analyzing other background noise, piecing together flight plans of choppers, and tracing Tony's car, we found out exactly where they were—the midtown Radisson. But that ain't all." He paused. Secrets were his treasure and Cardwell knew the pause was pregnant for the value Robby thought this secret held.

"Spare me the drama." Cardwell's tone was acid.

Robby held a hand to his mouth and coughed to disguise a laugh. "I'm sorry, sir. It's just that the CIA and FBI are so damn incompetent. We run circles around them. One of our men in the area spotted a Honda leaving the scene at a high speed. Needless to say, he was the only person following this dude, since the CIA and FBI botched the operation, as usual."

Cardwell understood and extrapolated. If they could capture El Fahd, it would not only put the Cardwell in the spotlight but also show that the CIA and FBI needed bolstering by the private sector. He would win a lot of powerful friends who agreed with all of those things.

"So where is he now—this El Fahd?" asked Cardwell.

"It looks like he's going to Vegas."

"You don't sound happy about that."

"It's Vegas, Senator. The place everyone goes to do things they don't want anyone else to find out about, where even the most famous people can go and not be noticed; where, for forty-eight hours, you can literally fall off the face of the earth." Robby ended with a big sigh, as if he had done all he could.

Cardwell stood and gave Robby his best imitation of the bear glare. "With all the money I spend on your goddamn SAGANT or whatever you call it, I want El Fahd found and brought in. Not when he gets to Vegas, now! Comprendé?"

Robby stood but didn't leave. "It's SIGINT. And there's one small problem."

"Small problems are not my worry. I want to see the whites of El Fahd's eyes in the next twenty-four hours or you'll be history."

Cardwell sat, turning his attention to the paperwork on his desk.

Robby walked out, the two men in tow. Politicians, he thought. They had no idea of how difficult it was to get the information they want. But he was relieved at not having to disclose the "one small problem." After the door closed, he motioned to one of his men. "Tell the agent who followed El Fahd not to worry. I will take care of the problem he gave me. But next time he goes out to eat in L.A., even with his girlfriend, he should have a full tank of gas. You never know when you might have to chase a terrorist."

Robby had security contacts already in Vegas. Success was in the preparation. HUMINT was vital to espionage, another thing the CIA had neglected. But Robby hadn't. All his recruiting had paid off. El Fahd would soon see what good old American ingenuity could do with some appropriate monetary backing.

The accident in L.A. finally cleared and Jabril rolled up his window and sped away. He'd wanted to be further away from the city by now, but some things could not be helped.

He headed north on I-15. Coming up to Baker, fatigue set in, and he could hardly keep his eyes open.

After a few swerves to the middle, he slowed and rolled down the windows. The cool, pre-dawn hour on the Mojave reminded him of home. Driving directly northeast, the rising warmth of the sun, fading smell of the desert night, and the glimmering mirages on the horizon invoked strong memories that crowded out conscious thought.

—

He's with his mother in a microbus carrying supplies from a trip to Damascus through a desert as bleak as a moonscape. Two people are sitting beside the road. The bedraggled blonde woman and child are gaunt, on the edge of exhaustion. His mother stops. The two get in. The little girl perks up and stares quizzically at Jabril, her dark eyes clear and innocent.

The fresh smell of the desert morning stales from the fetid smell of the passengers.

Jabril's mother has one fist-sized loaf of bread and a handful of dried beans. She gives them to the strangers, along with water. The blond woman thanks her and offers a prayer. Though the language is foreign, Jabril knows a prayer when he hears it. The two devour the food and slurp the water. The child's wide, moist eyes mirror Jabril's curiosity.

Light flashes down the road. A group of men have blocked the road with an ancient Mercedes so covered in dust that it has obscured the true color. A glare of sun off the windshield keeps Jabril from seeing the men. His mother looks nervous. Fear spreads through the car. The other mother covers her blond hair and holds her child close.

A bearded man stops them and opens the side door. He yanks the woman and child out before Jabril's mother can even get out of the car. The woman's shawl falls, revealing her blond hair and fair features.

"Aheee!" the bearded man screams, shaking a long Ghurka Khukri knife over his head.

With one savage slice of that ugly knife, the blond women's head cants at an odd angle; the eastern sun winks through the widening crease in her neck; bright blood spurts over the child in her arms. In slow motion her headless body teeters and slumps to the ground.

The child struggles to a sitting position. The bearded man raises his bloody scythe again. A lance of sorrow pierces Jabril's heart.

The knife hangs in the air. Jabril recognizes the man's face—angry, dark eyes, always certain that he is right—his mentor in Afghanistan, a man he once worshiped, who taught him everything about revenge.

The child picks up her mother's limp hand, and looks at Jabril, her mouth open in disbelief, the dark wet orbs pleading: Do something.

The glinting blade drops and severs the child's fragile neck. How can God allow this? Something breaks inside Jabril.

—

Jabril woke, shuddering. The risen Mojave sun slammed pain into eyes. He blinked back tears. His foot must have come off the accelerator. The Honda rolled, snail-slow on the right shoulder of the road. Apparently he had unconsciously, automatically steered there. The rush whine of a car on the road behind him whooshed by. Sickly, sweet-sour odors wafted in. A putrescent and mangled carcass lay on the other side of the two-lane, probably a dog, but the gray and black fur covered in flies could be anything. He stopped the car, sat back in the seat, and wiped his cheeks. Why was he crying?

Covering his nose with his shirttail to filter the smell, he stared out the window. His stomach growled and he could barely keep his eyes open. But he dare not sleep. His mother would come back to haunt him.

Always concerned about the innocents. Sometimes they have to be sacrificed for the good of the jihad.

Don't they?

He blinked hard and clenched his jaw and looked into the rearview mirror. Empty. He turned the steering wheel toward the highway and pushed the accelerator to the floor. The car lurched forward, tires squealing. Warm desert air purged the car of death. His drive would be long, but fatigue and hunger were now a distant memory. Soon he would be in Las Vegas.

Even before daylight, Khan had awakened. He loved the chaos he could create with simple bombs. But now, with a wonderful biological weapon, Jabril, primed and blooming, he was too excited to sleep. Jabril would get his wish to have a place beside his revered Muhammad.

And Khan would be wealthy. The next time they called on him he would be running the show from a beautiful island in Southeast Asia. The women there were much more submissive than these American whores. The weather was warmer, and he would be virtually invisible and far away from this new bug they were unleashing.

Making reservations was so easy now with the Internet. He entered his fake information, and voilà! He had an e-ticket in hand in the name of Vivian Richards, a famous cricket player for West Indies team from the '70s. He hadn't used the name for over a decade, and it was useful for either a male or female disguise. A few more details, get Jabril to the safe house, and he could leave, letting the wonderful events unfold while he was far away on his island, sipping a drink he'd come to love, a Margarita, watching brown beautiful women swim naked in his pool. He looked at his watch. Yes. Plenty of time for that porn site.

Nine hundred and eighty miles away, a bespectacled man surrounded by towering, humming NSA computers was scanning a CRT screen, one of the many he was tasked with watching these days, and noticed something interesting. The name of a passenger on a flight from Syria to Afghanistan in 1989 matched the name on a reservation made two minutes ago on a flight from Colorado Springs to Los Angeles to Manila: Vivian Richards. He notified his superiors, and kept scanning. You never knew.

CHAPTER 37

After a good night's sleep, Rocca and Ronny, his sister's husband, got up early to fish. The cool fall morning was perfect for stalking trout in Rocky Mountain National Park, northwest of Longmont, Colorado. The North Fork of the St. Vrain was new to Rocca, so Ronny had wanted to stay with him. But he needed the solitude and insisted Ronny leave him to it.

Initially, thoughts of El Fahd kept interfering. His cast had been stiff and sloppy, the fly slapping the water and scaring the fish. The sound of the river, the cool breeze, and the warm autumn sun soon did their job. His cast smoothed. The pull of the rod, the sinuous flight of the fly line and placing the dry fly in the perfect drift became his only thoughts.

A hunger pain jogged him to check his watch. Jesus. It was already past two—five hours gone like a bullet.

He waded to the grassy bank and sat. Oh yeah. That felt good. A dull ache pressured behind his eyes. He'd forgotten to drink any water. Ronny had warned him that the cool crisp mountain air and altitude was deceiving. Rocca was used to sweating his ass off in jungle heat for the past year and had thought he was immune. Now he was dehydrated. He drained one bottle of water and half of a second, arched his back, and flexed his knees. Age was catching him by the joints and felt like shit.

The trees swayed in the breeze. Trout dimpled a pool, taking dries. Yeah, he was getting old, but this place made him young again. With his wading boots still in the water he lay back on the bank closed his eyes and took a deep breath. Pine mixed with moss and a faint fish-smell from the last cast lingered on his net. Dew-chilled grass tickled his cheeks.

Why the hell did you go to Jakarta in the first place? Stinky jungle, always needed a shower. Who needs it?

Definitely gettin' old.

The sound of someone walking through the brush brought him back to the present. Ronny.

"Hey, Rock. How's it going?"

"Good. I was getting' a little snack. How about you? Any luck?" Rocca knew Ronny had probably caught five to his one, but he had to ask.

"Not bad. They should start rising to Blue Wings with the clouds moving in, as long as the wind doesn't pick up." He looked up at the darkening western sky. "Let's get back to the truck. I got a secret spot that should be great in the next two hours."

"Okay by me. My legs need stretching."

The fifteen-minute walk and wade through the river and onto the well-worn path back to the truck felt good.

Once in the truck, Ronny grabbed his radiophone. Judy was eight months pregnant, and Ronny had promised to keep in touch. He keyed up the radio while he pulled out onto the road.

"Hey babe, how's it goin'?

The volume knob was maxed out, so the concern in her voice filled the cab.

"Doin' good. Listen Ron, is Rocky there? I need to talk to him."

"Yeah, sure." He turned the volume knob down and handed the radio to Rocca.

"What's up, sis?"

"You got a call here from a guy named Jack. Wants you to call him as soon as you can. Something about a colonel that got away, *again*."

"You said, 'again.' Are you sure he said that?"

"Oh yeah. He made me repeat it, like he didn't trust me to get it right."

"That would be Jack, alright. Thanks, Judy. I guess I'll have to cut the fishin' short. We'll see you in a bit. Oh by the way, Ronny wants to know, how's that little tyke in the oven?"

Judy chuckled, "He's almost done, but he's being patient. Wants to come out just right. See ya in a few. Out."

"Sorry, Ronny. I guess that secret spot will have to wait."

Maybe I'll finally get a chance to get El Fahd. Hopefully he was not in for another letdown.

When they got back to the house, a small, old farmhouse outside the city limits, recently painted white, with rust colored mums framing the front porch, he almost jumped out of his waders and called Jack.

"Hey buddy, listen," Jack began. Rocca thought he sounded very tired. "They don't know I called you, so keep it under your hat. They lost the colonel somewhere in L.A., driving east. But they picked up a suspicious airline reservation from Colorado Springs going all the way to Manila. After hashing it all out, I believe the guy going to Manila is El Fahd's contact in the States. Now that he's arranged things for El Fahd, this guy is done. I think maybe our Colonel will be heading towards Colorado Springs. Birds of a feather. Probably leaving together, or maybe El Fahd is taking over there. Whatever it is, the Springs looks like the place."

"Okay. You're the intel guy." Rocca paused trying to decide why Jack had called him. It wasn't to pass the time. "I could be there in a few hours, if you want me to mop up this mess." He paused. "Unless you want one of your crack CIA teams to take care of it."

"Sarcasm? From you, Rock?" Jack chuckled. "You'll need to get your own help on this one, buddy. If my superiors find out our conversation, I may finish convalescence in Leavenworth."

"My lips are sealed. If all goes well, they will be giving you a medal, or whatever it is that the CIA gives out for good deeds." He paused again. "Hey, how you feelin? You sound a bit punk."

"Fine. Just fine."

"You get healed up I don't want you added as a star on the CIA wall. I'll talk to you when it's all over."

Rocca hung up.

On the other end Jack said to the dial tone, "Good luck, partner. You'll need it."

Hanging up, Jack felt drained as he looked at Saxon and CDR Alexander standing beside him at his hospital bed. They both nodded in approval.

Saxon said, "Don't worry, Jack. We'll be right around the corner from your friend."

Jack looked out the window, feeling like he'd sent Rocca into the lion's den. He murmured under his breath, "That's what I'm afraid of."

Rocca was packed and out the door in twenty minutes, apologizing profusely to his sister and Ron. Once he was on I-25 he made a few calls to prior Army buddies who now had civilian jobs around Colorado Springs. They were happy to help, and planned a rendezvous around 9:00 p.m. at the Broadmoor, one of the swankiest hotels in the Springs, or for that matter, Colorado. *Might as well splurge. Never know.* He smiled. *I'll bill the CIA.*

After two stops and driving in circles for an hour, Jabril finally finished the reconnaissance of Las Vegas. His cousins had the bombs ready, and were prepared for their sacrifice. He had even kneeled with them and prayed, though with his newfound power, wanting help from Allah felt foreign, unnecessary, foolish. The convoluted drive southeast over Arizona Highway 93 to Kingman and to the cutover to 89 and northeast through Prescott and on to Flagstaff had proved he was right. Security had been stepped up somewhat, but this would actually help. And if it failed, there was always the backup plan of another plane in L.A. Anyway, he needed a few more days to make sure he could spread the infection. A new bloom of virus must have hit him. He was sweaty and having a hard time concentrating.

Only a few more hours and I can sleep. Or perhaps if it followed the previous pattern, after the chills would come the power. This thought alone kept him wide awake.

Robby had flown on Senator Cardwell's private Lear Jet into Farmington, NM, and joined the team that had been following El Fahd's Honda all day since spotting it outside Las Vegas. El Fahd had been on back roads since Flagstaff and was now on Highway 64. Robby was ecstatic, but also concerned. For some reason the terrorist had taken an hour to pop out on the other side of Vegas that morning.

They followed him east from Farmington through Bloomfield. Cell phone coverage died in the desert of sage and dry grass and sandstone rocks and rubble. Robby used the sat phone to call Cardwell.

"Is it him?" Cardwell said. He sat in his senate office, in the easy chair by the window. The room was dark except for one small desk light. It gave the bear an interesting grin, a grin that Cardwell hoped he could share.

"Yes, Senator. I'm sure it's our guy. Do you want me to pick him up?"

Cardwell shot one fist in the air. They would soon capture a terrorist that the NSA and CIA had missed. The presidency was in the bag.

"Yes, but *do not kill him*! Once you have him secure, bring him to our little place in Colorado. I want to make sure we have time to question him before the big boys get him. If he has any secrets, I want to have them first."

"Roger that, Senator. We should have him in the next couple of hours."

Robby hung up.

He radioed the other cars. "Move in closer. He should need gas around Dulce. And even if he doesn't, we'll need to find a good place and take him there."

As his companion passed along the word, Robby looked outside. He could imagine John Wayne chasing redskins through the cleft where the road ran between rugged sandstone cliffs and buttes. Robby was just the man for taking El Fahd in this country. *The West. Cowboys and Indians. Man, this should be good.*

After little more than an hour of sleep on his fold-out bunk in his small room, Alex awoke, still drained but with an internal voice that said *time to go*.

As he dressed he suddenly realized something. He hadn't needed an alarm to wake up. Too bad Lora wasn't here to see it.

His heart ached momentarily; he gritted his teeth and finished dressing and walked down the hall to awaken Jesse.

Jesse was opening her door as he walked up. Not a surprise to him.

"Feel any better?" he asked.

"Great. When do we leave?" Her tone was flat and she did not look rested.

"Yeah, I still feel punk, too. But we have to get out of here today. Probably take a day to get there. Maybe Sam knows short cuts."

Halfway down to the main lab, they met Sam and Rachel in the hallway.

Sam said, "We were about to come wake you two. Change of plan. We're leaving in twenty minutes. Rachel's ready with the drugs and vaccines. I talked Doc into letting you leave with us, but only if you wear surgical masks. Doc and M.C. have things under control here, so they are ready to go. Jimbo is going to need a little more medical care in the States, but Ron is a hundred percent, minus a little bruise on his head. We should have reinforcements arriving in the next hour. Then we are all outta here."

"That's great," Alex said. "I was hoping we could leave earlier. Not sure we need the masks, but whatever Doc says. We're both still dead tired and will probably sleep most of the flight anyway. What's the flight plan?"

"Sam thinks we should fly back to Lima," Rachel said, "then hop-skip through Mexico, up to Colorado Springs, instead of going back to D.C. He got a tip that there's a terrorist going there some place near Colorado Springs. Maybe it's the dude you're plugged into, since the guy was driving from L.A."

Alex and Jesse looked at each other.

"That feels right," Alex said. "I feel that this terrorist is going to create a really bad catastrophe, something that will make the Twin Towers incident look like a slap in the face."

Sam nodded. "My contacts agree. They're trying to mobilize a team in Colorado. We might get there after all the smoke and dust has cleared. But we're going. Maybe the two of you can help figure what this guy is planning. If you're that connected way out here, when you get next to him maybe you'll be able to read his mind. You, Jesse and Rachel grab your stuff, but pack light. I'll see how my buddies are doing up topside. Meet at the main lab in ten."

The soldiers above ground had regrouped and decided to try to find the entrance to the lab before daylight. As they cleared the last bits of debris from the elevator shaft door, the sound of helicopters punctured the Amazon night. Leaving their task, the soldiers went to greet their comrades. They needed help to finish this job and were tired, having had no sleep for the last twenty-four hours.

Trampling through the jungle with flashlights, they were easy targets.

The helicopters did not carry their comrades, but instead held U.S. Marine pilots and Navy Seals. Their fifty cals shredded the jungle and strafed the flashlights. Everything went dark.

However, two soldiers, covering the periphery with their lights out, had escaped death. They radioed their true comrades. It was time to leave. But their commander told them to stay put. Their own helicopters were minutes away.

Alex and Jesse packed essentials and arrived back at the main lab wearing surgical masks. One of the Marine helicopter pilots had already landed above and climbed down the elevator shaft. Sam was talking to the pilot. "Thanks for getting here so quickly, Chris. Ron and I need to get a few of these virologists out of here to help out with the terrorist back in C. Springs. My plane is a couple of clicks down river. Can you cover us while we get there?"

"We have a jet already waiting. Don't worry about your plane. We'll take care of it. I'll fly my chopper to the jet. Are you ready?"

"Wow! Red carpet treatment. Feels like the good old days. Rachel Lane should be here in a minute. These two are Alex and Jesse. You already know Ron. Guys, this is Captain Chris Loudette, one of my homeboys."

Exchanging greetings, Chris frowned and nodded at the masked Alex and Jesse. "We should have you in the States soon." He continued eyeing the masks.

"We got the flu last week and don't want to spread it around," Alex said. "You know, us virologists are pretty hyper about that stuff."

"Right."

Rachel arrived with a refrigerated black case, and everyone exchanged greetings.

Alex started to climb into the elevator shaft when Rachel stopped him. "We should try the elevator. M.C. said it's working."

She pressed the up key. It lit up and the elevator door opened.

"Wish I would have known this yesterday," Alex said. "It's a long climb."

"Tell me about it," Chris said.

"Sorry, I didn't know," Sam said as they loaded into the elevator.

Once they reached the ground floor, they squeezed between fallen beams and, with only a few stumbles over rubble, finally stepped into a clearing. Twenty Seals in camouflaged fatigues materialized from the jungle. One saluted the pilot, Chris. After a brief discussion, Chris gave hand signals to the other men, and the entourage of scientists, surfers, and soldiers began walking toward the *whop-whop* of waiting helicopters.

Sweat trickled down the small of Alex's back. The last stars were still visible through humid, smoky cloud above the rubble of the lab. Raising his head slightly, Alex sniffed the air and tweaked his head, listening.

He ducked.

The bullet missed his head but continued into the soldier beside him. He grabbed at his neck. It had probably severed his spinal cord, because he fell instantly about the time the report of the rifle sounded. Alex figured the sniper was two or three hundred yards away.

The sound of approaching helicopters mingled with the reports of a distant sniper to their left. Bullets hissed through banana leaves next to Alex. He grabbed Rachel's hand, motioned for Jesse, and they ran, with Sam and Ron right on their tails. The red carpet had just been rolled up and incinerated to ash.

Alex tried to will the new strength and speed into his tired body. But all he could muster was a slow motion run, heaving for breath under the surgical mask, as more bullets slashed at bushes around him.

CHAPTER 38

The other Seals dispersed into the jungle, disappearing completely from sight.

Chris pushed his neck mike and said, "This is Swamp Rat. Jet and JJ: terminate sniper. Viper and Kilroy: eliminate incoming, then move choppers to Site B. Pick up in fifteen, that is, one five minutes. Everyone else, move with me. Cover package. Now!"

Chris heard on his ear piece."Jet with JJ, Roger."

Two of his men silently ran toward the last sniper shots. The others surrounded the virologists.

Chris pushed on his ear piece with his finger to hear better.

"This is Viper. I'm in the air. Kilroy's taking fire. See you at Site B. Out."

"Merde!" Chris swore under his breath, hoping his friend, code-named Kilroy, would make it. He had underestimated their opponents. All he could do now was protect his package and get the hell out.

Viper felt bad about Kilroy, too, but didn't have time to think about it. He sharply banked his chopper, barely avoiding incoming M-60 fire. "Shit! These guys mean business."

He locked on the incoming helo and fired off a salvo of missiles, exploding his target. "Hell yeah!"

Banking right, he looked around for Kilroy. A mangled Huey lay on the ground, engulfed in fire. Banking left, he radioed, "Kilroy, this is Viper. Where are you?"

No answer.

He repeated. No answer.

He called Chris. "Swamp Rat, this is Viper. No more bad guys. Kilroy is grounded, roasting hot dogs. Be there in five."

"Roger, Viper." Chris wanted to shoot his rifle in joy at getting the bad guys, and turn around and find Kilroy. But he had another priority. He kept moving through the jungle at a fast jog. He heard a grunt behind him and, "Damn!" One of the civilians had fallen.

Chris's radio squawked, telling of Viper making one more pass and another radio query for Kilroy. Nothing. He said he was moving on to the pick-up site. Everyone on the ground knew Kilroy needed help. Someone would be back for him. No one got left behind.

After getting all the civilians back up, and helping out the older guy with the limp, Chris made it to Site B. Viper was waiting and they loaded up uneventfully.

Chris heard Elmo called in saying they had disposed of two snipers, and needed a lift.

"JJ, this is Swamp Rat," Chris said. "We're too heavy. Sit tight. Find Kilroy. Look for the bonfire. Get the rest of the package ready for delivery. Little Hammer will be here oh-eight-hundred."

"Roger that. Out"

The noise of the rotors was deafening, even inside. Chris hurriedly pushed and pulled and got everyone seated and buckled in. He snapped himself in and gave Viper the thumbs. The chopper lifted off and Chris once again felt the exhilaration at completing a mission, and flying out safe. Chris was proud of his pilots. They were green, but handpicked from his own parish in Louisiana. They took orders, no questions asked. Good men.

Then he thought of Kilroy's wife and punched the wall of the helo with his fist. He sure hoped he would not have to tell her he was dead.

Chris envied Viper, flying at night in the quiet, remote jungle—completely undetectable. Except soon in the early dawn light he would be too visible. To compensate, he would fly at treetop level. The close rush of the jungle below was a rush Chris loved as a pilot. It would ensure Viper staying wide-awake. This was what he lived for.

Alex wedged himself into a corner of the chopper, too tired to care about the deafening rotor noise, or the cramped position, or that he'd sensed something not quite right with Jesse. He figured his fatigue had screwed up his telepathy. He was asleep in minutes.

He dreamed of more pleasant times with his father on a picnic in the Snowy Range of Wyoming. Fresh-caught fish were grilling on the open fire. Smelling the campfire, the grilling fish, and feeling the cool mountain breeze on his face was a comfort so deep that he almost missed the wolf staring at him from the trees. He wanted to pull on his father's arm, but the wolf was mesmerizing. It was a look filled with love and hope, but yet there was a permeating sadness.

Suddenly he was the wolf, returned after forty years of near-extinction. A new beginning. He could live in harmony with the earth and other animals, but man was not to be trusted. Man killed out of hate, something that mystified the wolf. But, knowing this, he could survive.

Sam watched Alex breathing peacefully and wished he could sleep. Why hadn't Alex transformed into the monster when the snipers threatened him? Maybe he didn't want anyone else to know? Or was it something he couldn't control? Alex slept, not waking

The chopper jostled hard right, then left. Alex slept on. Maybe he was too exhausted to muster a change. Whatever it was, Sam was glad he didn't have to explain more than a surgical mask to Chris Loudette.

What would he do with Alex and Jesse once they got back to the states? The best thing would be to study them. But if they could help out with the terrorists? Maybe he should keep his mouth shut. No. This was too big. He would make a call at Manaus.

CHAPTER 39

Rocca made the drive to Denver in no time. But the traffic picked up, and there was an accident around Invesco Field. He halted for the accident, and his thoughts wandered. *Too bad they changed the name from Mile High Stadium. "Invesco" doesn't sound like Denver. More like money. Mile High. Now that's Denver. When will people with money realize that some things are more important than their egos? Like history.*

History defines. Money defiles.

Not bad. Have to remember that one.

Finally he started moving again and passed an overturned VW bus, ambulance already moving through the traffic up ahead. A lone cruiser was parked taking up one lane, lights flashing.

The traffic sped up and he cruised on to Colorado Springs. It had been a while since he'd driven this stretch. He was surprised at the steady flow of traffic. As the sun set, a long snaking stream of red taillights paralleled a similar white snake of headlights on the left that led into the distance. End of another workday and going home.

How long had it been since he'd been home, or even had a home? His wife had left for another guy and a more stable life style. Couldn't blame her. His daughter, Samantha, would be six in a month. An image filled his head from another time: a rosy-cheeked smile and innocent hazel eyes.

Would El Fahd prevent him from seeing her again?

—

Jabril turned onto the next road, looking into his rearview mirror, trying to detect a tail. The evening sun glared in the mirror, at first reminding him of the morning not so long ago, with hate and killing in his dream. Then, the scenery got greener, more trees, more grass. It reminded him of how far he was from home. He pressed the accelerator down and the car shot forward on the two-lane highway. There were many miles yet to go.

So tired. So…very…tired.

Robby was ecstatic. The Honda they were following slowed down as the desert gave way to greener grasses and piñon and cedar trees. Dulce was coming. Soon there was an Exxon where Highway 64 jogged from north to east. Then they moved on and Robby's heart sank. Just as it looked like they were out of town, they came around a left turn, down a slight hill and the Honda pulled over on the left side of the road at a very run-down gas station on the corner of the turn. The gas pumps belonged in a museum and the adobe was crumbling, showing the cinder blocks beneath.

He radioed his men. "Jones, pull ahead of him and make sure he doesn't get around you. Lake, you park behind him. I'll wait for you to get in position, then I'll take him from the passenger side. Once I make my move, be ready. No screwups! Remember—this guy is on our top-ten hit list. We have to get him. Are you with me?"

"Ten-four."

"Okay, let's do it. Make your mommas proud."

Robby slowed his car, waiting for Lake to pass him and pull in behind the Honda. Jones parked in front of the Honda and held up a map, as if lost.

Robby drove to the passenger side of the Honda. The driver sat in the car next to the pump. The station attendant came out. Robby could only see her head above the Honda's roof: dark hair, pretty face. A woman. Nice that a place like this still had full service.

Robby stopped and put his Dodge Charger RT in park but kept the engine on.

Two shotgun blasts shattered Lake's windshield, spraying blood over the remaining windows. The station attendant had a shotgun at her shoulder and swung it towards Robby.

"Fuck!" He put it in gear, punched the accelerator, and spun the wheel right to get back on the road.

"Jones!" he screamed into the radio, "Get your ass out of there. It's a setup. Move!"

Robby could see Jones already backing up. The distinctive sound of an AK-47 erupted from inside the adobe station, bursting Jones's windows and pocking the side of his car.

Robby was around the Honda now and rolled down his window and returned fire with his automatic pistol. He hit the shotgun girl. She fell backward, face upturned, dark hair flowing.

Jones sped out of the gas station and onto the highway, tires squealing.

Robby braked and swerved to miss Jones. He fired another burst into the Honda. He didn't give a shit what Cardwell had said about keeping the raghead alive. He was going to pay for Lake.

The *thunk-thunk* of the AK-47 echoed across the back of Robby's car. He swerved onto the highway, darting onto the left side dirt shoulder to avoid an oncoming car, then lurched forward when his wheels gained purchase on the asphalt. He drove up a hill and around a right curve and caught up with Jones.

Jones's car had slowed, one taillight gone, the other blinking in the darkening twilight. The car undulated between the lines of the right lane.

Robby keyed the radio. "Jones, are you hit?"

"Bleedin' bad, man. Took one in the gut and the thigh." His voice was weak and hoarse.

"Pull over. There's no one following us. Now, dammit!"

Pulling to the right side of the road, he waited for Jones to do the same, but instead the other car sped up and careened off the left side of the road, slamming into a deep ditch. The motor initially gunned when the back wheels came off the ground, then choked and misfired to a halt.

Robby opened his door quickly then froze, looking over his left shoulder. The gas station was not far behind, over a hill but not visible. There were no lights. Nothing.

Night had fallen, the air ten degrees cooler. The only sounds were his car idling and the steaming radiator of Jones's car.

He sat back down, keeping an eye on the rearview mirror, thinking about the last few minutes. Had he hit the guy in the Honda? His head had jerked forward, but…

He should make sure. First, backup.

He dialed the phone, got out and walked to check on Jones.

Two men ran out of the adobe service station and worked quickly, quietly, and efficiently, with only the occasional red illumination from their night flashlights. The bodies of Lake, the woman with the shotgun, and the man in the Honda were first undressed completely, then layered onto a tarp in the trunk of an old Buick behind the station. They poured an acrid-smelling solution over each body, paying particular attention to the hands, feet, scalp, and mouth. The bearded man who'd been in the Honda they lay on top, and did not pour the solution on his scalp. The guns received a thorough dousing and were piled in around the bodies.

They pushed the other two gun-riddled cars into the garage and pulled tarps over them. "Closed" and "Gone Fishin'" signs were posted in the front window. They sprayed the pumps with cleanser and wiped them down. Then they raked dirt over the blood-caked ground, making sure to direct the beams of white flashlights at the ground to inspect their work. In twenty minutes it was finished and they dead-bolted all the doors. One man slipped into the Buick and gently closed the doors. The Buick's big motor purred and the car moved off into the night. The other man followed in an old Datsun pickup. They drove southwest to Road 537, then south until they spied a dirt road leading west. In a few minutes they were deep inside the Jicarilla Apache Nation Reservation.

With their dark skin they were easily taken for Apaches. After the terrorist attack on September 11 they'd spread the word that they felt persecuted by the whites in the area and were going to move back to Pakistan. Closing the station was only natural.

The Buick high centered on the two-track a few times, but they were able to push it through with the pickup. They stopped in a deep arroyo, wiped the Buick inside and out with a bleach solution and covered it with rocks, dirt and finally sagebrush. Then they both climbed into the Datsun pickup and pulled off into the night, back east toward Road 537, then south to Highway 550. By morning they would be in Mexico. The percolating sound of the Datsun harmonized with the occasional groaning of old springs as it eased over the rutted dirt road.

On a nearby hill, a coyote watched the truck leave and raised his nose in a lonely howl.

Robby could not get through to Cardwell, which pissed him off. He thought he'd run over to Jones's car, but the night was about as black as he'd ever seen. And it was getting cold fast. He used his flashlight and picked his way carefully to Jones's car, all the while worried that someone from the service station would see him. Jones sat in his own blood, stiff and cold and dead. No big loss. Robby'd never really liked the guy. He casually closed the door and ran through possibilities of men to replace Jones. *Gotta be Smith. Jason Smith. Cardwell would love it. First Jones, now Smith. Perfect.*

He failed again on his call for reinforcements and started fuming—not only pissed at that failure, but that those assholes in the service station had made a fool out of him. He would make them pay.

Finally he reached someone. Then he turned on the car and the heater and waited. He tried to sleep, but the longer he waited the more pissed he got, and the more awake.

Only a solitary pickup passed by all night, and didn't even slow.

Reinforcements finally arrived at dawn in a dark blue Crown Victoria, just as Robby nodded off. He blinked awake and said, "About fucking time. Come on." He led them in his car.

It was like nothing had happened at the service station—all locked up with two covered cars in the windowed garage. Already feeling like his men doubted him, he was about to break into the garage when a dusty green Jeep Cherokee pulled up. "Rio Arriba Sheriff" was painted on the side, the driver's window rolled down.

Robby walked over and spoke through the open window.

"Howdy, Sheriff. We work for Senator Cardwell, and need to get that car in the garage. One of my men needs it towed to Farmington to get it fixed."

The door to the Cherokee swung open, and the middle-aged American Indian sheriff slowly stepped out. He stood for a few seconds observing the men and the cars and the service station. His raven hair touched his ears and he had high cheekbones and puffy cheeks that were acne-scarred. His inspection of the scene was methodical without any signs he cared about anything Robby had said.

Finally he addressed Robby. "Don't think I caught your name. Mine's Sheriff Na-Hash-Chid. My mother was Navajo. Most people call me Nahash." His voice was calm and quiet, but carried well. He stayed glued to the spot, standing stock-still, not walking to Robby, but offering his hand and looking Robby straight in the eye.

Robby squinted at the sheriff and was forced to take a step forward and shake his hand. The grip was firm, and Robby felt the sheriff was reading his mind through his eyes and handshake. This guy was no bumpkin. Robby decided to level with him.

"I'm Robert Fowler, chief security adviser for Senator Cardwell. Most people call me Robby. Let me start again. We had a problem at this station last night. We were following an Iraqi terrorist suspect, and when he pulled in here we were ambushed. I lost two men and I barely escaped with my life. You can see the bullet holes in the back of my car there." He pointed to his car parked in front of the sheriff.

The sheriff ambled over to the car, stuck his finger in a few of the bullet holes in the trunk, glanced at the ground around the pumps, walked to the garage and looked in at the cars with tarps over them, and ended up gazing at the "Gone Fishin'" sign in the window.

Sheriff Na-Hash-Chid did not like this white man who thought he could first lie to him, then bowl him over with his importance. But something had happened here. He squatted down on his haunches and picked up some dirt, letting it sift through his hand, thinking—

Why would someone rake the ground at the pumps?

Maybe to make a shabby gas station look neater.

Why would you put up a 'Gone Fishin' sign if you didn't fish?

Maybe to fit in.

Why would you cover the cars in the garage with tarps?

And that was the one question he couldn't come up with a good answer for, except—

To hide something.

He finally broke the tension. "Okay, Robert Fowler. I've heard of Senator Cardwell. Why don't you show me your dead men?"

"One is in his car east of here. The other I think is in one of those cars in the garage. And Sheriff—we need to hurry. It is a matter of national defense."

Over the next few minutes Robby related the whole story, and began to feel like the sheriff was on his side, finally. A search warrant was issued, and within the hour the garage contents inspected. Robby was excited when he saw the blood on the headrest of the Honda, so excited he excused himself to call Senator Cardwell.

Cardwell had been pacing in his office, ready to call in someone else to help Robby when the phone rang. He snatched it up like it was filled with gold. "What the hell is happening?"

"Senator, it's Robby. In the firefight last night—I believe I killed El Fahd."

"What do you mean 'you believe'? And I thought I made myself perfectly clear when I told you not to kill him." Cardwell wanted to sound angry, but knew it came out almost celebratory.

"Sir, it couldn't be helped. It was either him or me. Anyway, the car he was driving has blood all over the headrest. I'm sure I got a head shot last night."

"Do you have a body?"

"Not yet, sir. But I feel that is only a formality at this point. We are pursuing that with the local sheriff. I'll let you know as soon as we have any further developments."

"You do that."

The senator hung up before Robby could hear him cheer into the phone, "We got him! Thanks to *my* security team he will kill no Americans. Let that be a lesson to the namby-pambies who don't want us bugging the phones."

He would celebrate with an extra Scotch tonight.

Robby hung up and walked to the sheriff, sweating and frustrated with the slowness of the investigation. The sun was already getting hot and it had only been up a few hours. "My man wasn't in those cars. I gotta find him, not to mention the people who killed him. The man in the Honda was a known terrorist, and the people who did this need to be questioned as soon as possible."

Nahash blinked slowly, knowing he was doing all he could and part of him wanting to slow it down to piss off Robert Fowler. Should have a

"Junior" or "the Third" tacked on to that very important-sounding name. "I already put out an APB on their Buick. But if they changed cars, or went to Mexico…" He shrugged.

Nahash's radio squawked loudly from inside his Cherokee. He'd left the volume on high so he could hear any calls. "Sheriff, this is Joseph, we got a call you want to take ASAP."

The sheriff ran back to the truck and keyed the mike

"This is Nahash. What do you have, Joey?"

Joey put on a local coyote hunter, George Davis Johnson, who relayed how he'd seen some lights last night over around Coyote Ridge, down in the Sage Arroyo. Nahash kept remembering that George's Indian name was Dog of Many Tricks, and everyone called him Many Tricks. It was hard to believe him at times, but Nahash had a feeling he was telling the truth.

The senator's whipping boy was listening quite intently and seemed to overhear. As soon as Nahash was off the radio, Robby said, "Why don't you ride along with me and my men? We'll take you over, identify the bodies and be done with this whole thing."

"No can do, Robert. This is my jurisdiction. We use my men. You can ride with us. But leave the rest of your men here."

"Come on, Sheriff. I need my men. They are all experts, prior CIA and FBI. I can't go into a potential firefight without them."

Nahash tried to keep from smiling. Robert Fowler the Third just didn't get it. "I don't need any more dead experts in my jurisdiction, especially white ones. If you want to go, you go my way. Otherwise, we call the real FBI and CIA and get them here, probably sometime tomorrow."

Sheriff Na-Hash-Chid was true to his namesake, stubborn as a badger. Good reason for that, he thought. A lifetime of idiotic cowboys and Indians. Then there were the Feds: a whole step down from stupid. These "former Feds" were in deep dumbshit, up to their eyeballs. It was good to show them the way. Children needed leading.

CHAPTER 40

I-25 wound through the old and new buildings of Colorado Springs like a python through a tree. Rocca was pumped, ready for action as he finally turned onto Tejon Street, passed several aging burrito take-outs, and reached the Broadmoor by eight. The outside was typical southwestern style with beige stucco walls, terracotta tiled roof and three arches out front. There was a middle tower that looked like a lighthouse. A concierge waited to help Rocca, but he waived him off. He could carry one small backpack. When he walked into the lobby, a burly man with a pony tail, jeans, and a black baseball cap put down the newspaper he was reading and strode over.

"Hey, Rock! How's it hangin'?" The man had a Van Dyke beard and hazel eyes and weighed about thirty pounds more than Rock remembered him from ten years ago in a hot field of sand and bullets.

"Lonny. Jesus. Good to see you."

"Yeah, I know, the hair came first, then the weight. But I been liftin' again."

The two grabbed hands in an arm wrestling grip. Rocca held the grip easily and nodded at the purple brim and initials *CR* on Lonny's ball cap. "Why would you wear the hat of losers?"

Lonny's jaw muscles flexed and his grip hardened for several seconds, then finally loosened his grip. "Okay, Rock, you still got it. You wait, though. The Rockies are up and coming." He shook his hand a few times wincing. "But, before you get checked in, I got something you'll want to hear. Let's step outside and get some fresh air."

Once out in the driveway of the plush hotel, Lonny lowered his voice, "I got a friend working security for a Senator Cardwell. He says they probably got El Fahd down in New Mexico."

Rocca looked at Lonny, doubtful. "Yeah, well, I'm not so sure you can believe anything you hear from someone working for Cardwell. All those guys care about is gadgets and money."

"What about Fred Harriman? Would you believe him?"

Rocca's eyebrows raised. "Fred's working for Cardwell? No way." Fred had helped Jack get Rocca out of some tight jams in Desert Storm, slow and methodical, but always accurate. His daughter was about the same age as Rocca's and bonded well with her at their unit's homecoming Chuck E. Cheese family party.

Lonny's voice fell to a whisper. "Fred's doing a little inside work for the CIA."

"Son of a bitch. Okay, yeah, I believe Fred. But you said 'probably.' Do they have him or not? We've already missed this guy twice."

Lonny looked at his shoes and adjusted his cap. "I haven't been able to raise Fred for the last hour. But last thing he said, it was a done deal."

Rocca watched every car enter and leave the hotel driveway for ten seconds. His voice sounded detached, even to him. "You guys can leave if you want. I'm staying overnight at the very least. I need a rest and I've always wanted to stay here."

"Hey, if you're stayin', I'm stayin'. What about a few beers and a nice steak? I've been here before and they have some great grub."

Rocca nodded, feeling that familiar let down return. Rocca wanted to plant a bullet in El Fahd's teeth. He walked toward the entrance. "Sounds good. I'll see you in half an hour at that place next to the lobby."

"The Tavern? Great choice! Prime rib to die for."

Rocca watched Lonny leave and clenched his fists. *Damn, I wanted that fucking Colonel.*

Once Alex and his friends landed in the private airstrip at Manaus, it was an easy trip back to the states. Having diplomatic immunity, the CIA's jets avoided customs hoopla, so without interruptions everyone slept on the long trip.

When they landed, Alex felt more rested than he had in weeks. He noticed Sam was already up, and had made coffee. What a good little CIA host.

"This beats Delta!" Alex said cheerily through his mask as Sam walked over and gave him a hot cup.

"Anything beats Delta." Sam added a cube of sugar to his own coffee, stirring slowly.

"Yeah, though seems like yesterday they were the best. Goes to show you, can't rest on your laurels."

"Or maybe you need to embrace change before it leaves you behind." Sam blew on his coffee. His eyes over his coffee cup seemed to smile.

"You're not talking about Delta now, are you?"

"Alex, you might be the military's best hope for the future soldier. And believe me; once everyone finds out about what you can do, they will embrace you."

The coffee had initially tasted pretty good, but now Alex felt bile rise in the back of his throat. "More likely keep me caged up and poke me with needles."

Alex looked outside the window as the plane taxied to a halt. "So, Sam, is that why we're in San Antonio instead of Colorado Springs?"

Sam's response was barely audible, "Something like that."

The plane had stopped well out from the normal deplaning area. Camouflaged military vehicles surrounded the plane, emptying out soldiers with machine guns, who established a perimeter around the plane and trucks. They allowed two large, white panel trucks inside the perimeter. They backed up to the plane's stairs and their rear doors opened.

One man came out clad in a moon suit Alex was all too familiar with. He carried two rectangular boxes, each smaller than a loaf of bread, and a white plastic bag, about the size of a kitchen garbage bag stuffed pretty tight. He waddled up the deplaning stairs. The door to the plane opened and the man stepped in with his box and bag. His faceplate steamed on the side with each breath.

"Sorry, Alex." Sam's voice was sad but resolved. "Orders. Too many people afraid you might be contagious. We're all going into quarantine. You and Jesse are going to a special unit at Wilford Hall."

Alex puckered his mouth, and shook his head. "I knew it. More needles. Should have stayed in the jungle."

Jesse and the others were yawning and stretching and one by one locked eyes on Alex and Sam.

"Look," Sam said. "You gotta admit that what you and Jesse did back there was pretty incredible. If a virus did that to you, we *have* to know. And if Doc was right about it improving his mind, we have to know that, too. And if it takes another course—maybe deadly—you don't want it spreading, right?"

Alex hung his head and lowered his gaze and shook his head.

Sam continued. "They were initially going to isolate us all in the Amazon, but then the Koreans came and there was too much danger. We're much safer in the U.S. And, we make pretty good guinea pigs. Better than monkeys, right?" He smiled and cocked his head as if trying to inject a little happiness into a bad situation.

"They can't do this to us. We're American citizens." Rachel said, standing and slapping both palms on the back of the seat.

Sam pointed out the window. "Yeah, but some of those rights went out the window after the September 11 terrorist attack. You might consider us casualties of war." He gestured an open palm to the spaceman at the door and fanned his arm back toward the windows. "As you can see, we have no choice. So please, put on some gloves, a mask, and gown, and lets follow the guy in the white suit."

The white suited man held out the two boxes and the white plastic bag. They all donned the blue gloves, white masks and yellow paper coveralls and trailed out of the plane, the scientists and Sam's crew into one panel van, the Seal crew into the other. Once seated in the truck and on their way, Jesse asked, "What about the terrorist you were worried about around L.A.? What are you going to do about that?"

"His name is Colonel Jabril el Fahd, and we believe he's been eliminated."

Jesse's eyes over her mask looked shocked. "It doesn't feel like that. How was he eliminated? What happened?"

"Don't worry about that. We have pretty good information."

"So you don't need me or Alex anymore to tell you where he is?"

Alex interjected, "Oh, they need us, Jesse, only not for that." He gave Jesse a half-smile while he thought, *Man, what I would give to be fishin' in Patagonia, or for that matter, go back to being a simple country virologist.*

Khan was awakened by the phone call in the wee hours of the morning and was angry about the incident at Dulce. If the Americans knew enough to follow Jabril, what else did they know? Did they know about Next Day? It was too secret. The plan could still work. He would merely move the timetable up a few days.

First he called Las Vegas and ordered the four cell members to get their scuba gear and other equipment ready for immediate action, then worked his way down the other sites, contacting the cells, adjusting plans.

Other secret cell members had already begun their part in Washington, D.C.; Shreveport, LA; Fort Meade, MD; Omaha, NE; Waynesboro, PA; Rome, NY; Berryville, VA; and of course Colorado Springs and New York City. The infection they had already contracted would soon be spread at each site.

When the next fire started, all the important American leaders would go to their safest place.

That's what happened after the September 11 attack. The leadership of America had been afraid, and scurried to their safe houses in all those different cities. It would be the same after the disaster to come. This time their safe houses would be a huge broth for festering disease. And, in two weeks, the rampant infection would leave the leadership of the U.S. government and their military in total disarray.

Al-Qaeda would have the cure, and only those willing to serve Allah would get it. Al-Qaeda would rule the western world, Israel would quickly succumb, and Islam would become the only religion. Or so the plan went.

Khan didn't care, as long as he got his money.

Jerry Klaus came to Wilford Hall to personally supervise the tests run on Alex and the others. He wanted to make sure about the results, but also about his people. He did not want them mistreated.

After lunch he looked over the results on blood Doc had drawn in Brazil, and then went to tell Alex. He spoke through the intercom to an impatient Alex in the quarantine room.

"The good news is that none of the tests run on you or Jesse show any signs of infection. White blood cell count, sed rate, and all other metabolic panels are normal. Titers of all the viruses we've been studying are negative. However, you've been infected with another virus. It looks like you had a touch of the flu in the last month or so. Your flu test and antibody levels are pretty conclusive. Maybe that would explain the fever and fainting episodes."

"That's funny. The flu. Guess I wasn't lying to that pilot dude. Anyway, that's great news. When can I get out of this…prison?"

"Pretty soon. But there's this matter of you being a Jekyll and Hyde. Apparently Rachel thinks your muscles grew, your eyes changed colors, and you acted strangely. Pretty far-fetched stuff. Have you noticed anything unusual?"

"Well…uh…nothing like that, only a little déjà vu stuff. It's like I told Doc. I had some similar spells when I was a kid. It was like I could see into the future. I know it sounds weird, but my mom sure thought it was the real thing. She thought I got it from her sister. I usually only have the feelings about people I'm really close to. Anyhow, I think I felt really bad about the time Lora was dying in the Twin Tower."

"What about Jesse?" Jerry said. "How does she fit in with her intuition about things? The others say she acted weird too."

"Jesse? Heck, she's always had a sixth sense about people and stuff. She's got that Indian blood coursing through her brain cells. I think she would have been a great fortune teller. "

"Yeah, Jesse is a swami alright." Jerry was pensive. "Okay. I guess we'll leave it like that. I'll let you know later today about release."

Alex looked dejected. "Okay, I'll be waiting."

Then he added, "How are the others doing?"

"Everyone else is fine. You don't need to worry. I'll have them come see you soon."

It took Sheriff Nahash and his men the better part of the morning to locate the car. From Coyote Ridge most of the arroyos looked the same, especially to the hung-over Many Tricks Johnson. Once he sobered up he narrowed it down to three areas. Two wild-goose chases later, they finally found the car under a pile of sagebrush and dirt.

The ground around the car had lots of coyote prints, and there were two burrowed-out areas under the trunk. A faint sour odor hinted at what was to come.

When they opened the trunk of the big Buick, the stench cloaked the air and infused every pore.

"Jesus, what the hell happened to them? How could they be so rotten in only sixteen hours?" Robby pulled his shirt tail out and held it over his nose.

Sheriff Nahash was puzzled as well. It looked as if the skin had melted. The scalp from one head was sliding off the skull in pieces. The only thing that was intact was one guy's face on the very top of the body heap. The face was obviously Arabic with a very dark beard and even had a turban wrapped around the head. Everything else oozed. The bodies stuck together, with colors that reminded Nahash of an over-cooked peach pie. The hands were the worst, with bone already visible in some areas. He barely noticed the guns lying in a pile beside bodies covered in a slimy soup.

"Probably the heat. But I've never seen it this bad before."

He called the medical examiner, who said he'd be there in a half-hour. He was finishing up his morning clinic over at the reservation.

"Close it up, Billy," Nahash said to his deputy. "We're going to have to wait around here a while, and the less I have to smell of this the better."

Robby thought of something and put up his hand. "Wait a sec." His words were muffled under his shirt-covered face.

He pulled out his camera, snapped a few pictures of the Arab face on top, and then gave the okay sign.

The trunk thudded closed, but Robby kept his nose covered. "Man, I hope your M.E. hasn't eaten for a while. If I had to go mucking through that shit I'd definitely lose it. That is nasty!"

He walked up the hill out of the arroyo, let his shirt fall, and took a few big sniffs of clean air. Then he called Senator Cardwell. "I think this is our guy. It matches all the descriptions. I got some digital shots and will send them back as soon as I get back to the laptop. What now, sir?"

"Get back here as soon as possible." Cardwell sounded elated. "I want you to be here when we flush this down the CIA's throat. And you still need to find out what the hell La Riva Lab is up to."

"I'll be on the first plane out."

Robby was anxious to leave this dusty, hot, lonely country, and get back to civilization. He handed his business card to the sheriff.

"Can you drop me and my men back at our cars? That way I'll be out of your hair this afternoon."

Taking the card from Robby, Nahash instructed one of his men to take him back to Dulce.

Robby added, "But, Sheriff, please call me if you have any other questions."

Nahash nodded, watched Robby get into the car. *Typical. The Feds come in, shoot up the place, leave several bodies, then take off while we clean it all up.*

As the car drove away, the sheriff looked at the card, then scraped the edge of it against his cheek, back and forth across his day-old beard stubble. The scratchy sound seemed to improve his thinking. Robert Fowler—not the Third.

He loosened his grip and the card slipped out of his fingers.

A puff of hot desert wind picked up the card, making it dance like a feather. It stuck like an ornament in a tall clump of sagebrush.

Sheriff Nahash walked away.

CHAPTER 41

The food at the Broadmoor was excellent, and Rocca topped it off with two local microbrews and a piece of Dutch apple pie and vanilla ice cream. The next morning he woke later than he wanted, but after carousing with his friends until 4:00 a.m., getting up at noon didn't seem that bad. After a three-mile run in the warm autumn sun, he was ready for anything.

Before he showered he called Lonny. "So what's going on with our man? Is he dead or what?"

"Yep, definitely dead. Cardwell called Robby back to D.C. I'll be hitting the road shortly. The boss has some things for me to do, so I'll see you later. Let me know if anything else comes up. Good seeing you again."

"Feeling's mutual. I'm gonna head over to Salida and see about fishing the Arkansas for a few days, then head back to Loveland."

"Hey Rock, almost forgot. Got another call this morning."

"Yeah?"

"I know you were tight with Jack. Someone called from San Diego Hospital saying he's got some kind of infection."

"An infection? Well how bad is it? I mean is he going to die or just cough up his lung?"

"He sounded okay, but you know Jack."

"Yeah, he'd be telling jokes at his own funeral if he could. Okay, thanks Lonny. I'll give him a call. Talk to you later."

Rocca called San Diego Naval Hospital, but Jack was gone to the lab and x-ray. He'd be back in about an hour.

How bad could it be anyway? Last time I talked to him he seemed okay. Maybe a little tired, but who wouldn't be after what he went through.

He decided to go for a swim while he waited. Coming out of his room he bumped into a stunning redhead. As it turned out, she was also going to the pool. For the next two hours he forgot about Jack.

Jabril slept without dreams when he finally crawled into the bed at 10:00 a.m. The small house was adequate and very isolated, so he could rest for a few days before the final push. He would call Khan after he slept a few hours. He was too tired to deal with him now.

For the first time in over a week, Rachel felt safe. Though it was little bit hotter in San Antonio than she liked, she was back at work, and no federal agents were on her tail.

Working with the infectious disease specialists at Brooke Army Hospital and Wilford Hall Medical Center had really accelerated development of a vaccine. Wilford Hall had one of the most advanced immunology departments due to the incredible number of organ transplants they did every year. With their help she would finish the major work on the vaccine and antiviral medications in about a week.

And their advanced lab had confirmed that Alex had no infection.

She thought back on the last twenty-four hours in the Amazon Lab and it seemed like a dream. Maybe it was a hallucination like everyone thought. But she could have sworn she saw Alex…

Yet those underground gases had been very strong.

And as for Doc's story about the dog, his cancer and Alex mutating? Nobody was buying it. Doc had been visiting the chief psychiatrist for the last two hours. Doc had been on chemo; the cancer had finally responded; he felt better, relieved, got lots of energy. Case closed.

After lunch she was asked to go to the chief shrink's office for a tête-a-tête with Jerry, who'd flown down to make sure they were all okay. The office was nice for being military: thick carpet, walnut desk, matching bookcases. A picture of Sigmund Freud hung on one wall, the Three Stooges on another.

Jerry and his BC glasses had stuffed himself behind the large oak desk. "I'm going to let Alex out of quarantine tonight. None of the tests show any sign of infection. Except that he may have had the flu."

"Okay, so what does that have to do with me?"

"You two are needed in another project. Our federal friends uncovered a top-secret lab in Jakarta, and found viral cultures similar to the work we have been doing."

"Jakarta? Talk about across the globe. They'll probably have that back here in say, a week, right?" She glanced at the picture of the Moe poking Harry in the eyes with his fingers.

That would be the Feds.

"No, they already have it in the States. But due to the dangerous nature of the viruses they don't want to move them again. They want you two in Colorado Springs as soon as possible."

"Colorado Springs?"

Jerry shrugged. "Apparently they have a Class IV lab there specifically for bioterrorism evaluation. I got an address and a phone number, but that's about it."

"Okay…uh…do you think I could stop in Denver and pick up some of my things? I left them there before I went to the mountains." She had no intentions of going to Denver, but if Alex was along she wanted some extra time with him.

"Sure. No problem. Since you guys need a little time to unwind, why don't you drive. I'll tell them you were needed on another project for a few more days. I have a some strings I can pull. But be there ready to work in two days."

Rachel looked suspicious. "That was way too easy. Is there something else?"

"No. Like I said, you guys have been working pretty hard for the last week and been through a lot. A break would do you good. The country won't implode in a few days."

"Great! Thanks, Jerry. A little breather will be wonderful. Maybe I can show Alex some of the mountains along the way."

She looked at Freud's picture. *Hmmm.*

"Oh yeah, that reminds me. Jesse wanted to go home to visit a sick relative. Maybe you could drop her off. I think she lives somewhere around Farmington, New Mexico."

"Jesse? Do you think the two of them can be trusted together?" She paused. "What I meant to say was, if you think this was all a hallucination, and I don't have to worry about the two werewolves having me for supper, then I'll be glad to have her with us."

"Glad to hear you can joke about it, now. Hallucinations, no matter if they are from LSD or toxic gases can be quite frightening. But, I assure you, they both look very normal and all tests have been negative."

"So you guys didn't really want us all to be infected and study us like rats, like Sam said." She gave Jerry a suspicious look.

"I can't believe you would think I was even capable of that. Sam must have been given bad information. Anyway, you have a safe trip. We'll be in touch."

Jerry left.

Rachel waited a few seconds and punched her hand in the air and yelled, "Oh yeah!"

Alex for two days. Move over Jesse.

Then she glanced at Sigmund Freud's picture and asked him, "Should I pinch myself to make sure I'm not dreaming?" Then she eyed the Three Stooges and gave Sigmund her best imitation of Curly, "Nyak, nyak, nyak!"

True to his word Jerry had a rental Jeep Cherokee dropped off outside her room before supper. She and Jesse were packed when Jerry called at 8:00 p.m. and gave the word—Alex was cleared. They could leave anytime.

Alex was anxious to get out of town quickly, so they left at o'dark-thirty the next morning, with Alex driving the first leg.

He merged onto I-10 and Jesse said, "Just take me to Albuquerque and drop me off there. I have a cousin in Bernalillo. She can pick me up."

"No way!" Rachel said. "We're taking you all the way. It can't be that far from Albuquerque to Farmington."

"First, it's not exactly in Farmington." Second, it *is* a long drive." She paused. It was closer to Albuquerque than Farmington. But the less they knew the better. "And third, I've already arranged it with my cousin. She's left this morning. Besides, there's someone near Albuquerque I need to see." Jesse's voice got real low at the end, like there was something sad about the friend.

Rachel's eyebrows pinched up in the middle and she looked like she wanted more explanation.

"Look, you two," Alex said. "We have a long ride together. This is no way to start it. Rachel, if Jesse wants her cousin to take her, let her.

After all, this is a family illness, and she probably wants to catch up on things."

"Alex is right. My cousins in that area are all children of my Aunt Jessibella. We're pretty close. I'd like to spend some time with them, find out what's what before I go to her, you know, deathbed."

"Jessibella," Rachel's tone softened. "That sounds pretty close to Jessibelle. Were you named after her?"

Jesse gazed out the window. "Yeah," her voice was barely audible. "She and my mom were not only sisters, but best friends. They went through a lot before I was even born. Those were tough days on the rez."

For a full minute the only sound was the rhythmic *slap, slap* of the wheels on the cement joints of I-10.

Alex huffed in frustration at waiting for a decision. "Okay then. It's settled. We'll drop Jesse off at Albuquerque, and Rachel and I will cruise up I-25 to C. Springs. If we drive straight through, we should be there by eleven or twelve tonight."

"That would be great." Jesse said.

Alex changed the subject. "We got sandwiches for breakfast, but how about some Tex Mex for lunch. What about El Paso? Any suggestions, Jesse?"

"Lot of chain restaurants in El Paso. If you can wait another half-hour there's better food in Las Cruces. One of my cousins went to college there. Pretty good restaurants."

"Sounds good to me. How about some tunes?" Alex pulled out a small wallet of CD's, grabbed one and slid it into the player. Dire Straits filled the Jeep. He sang along at the top of his lungs to the line, "Money for *nothin'* and your chicks for *free*."

The two women looked at each other and laughed.

Outside, the rolling Texas hill country gradually gave way to the high desert and sage. Inside, Alex rocked on.

The redhead had been nice, but, after a little small talk and a beer at the pool, Rocca said adios. He didn't need any more women in his life. So it looked like an early supper: another steak, beer and no company, except his thoughts.

In the Army he'd been one of a select few, highly trained and skilled at his job, with something these highly-paid contractors didn't have:

camaraderie. He missed that. Jack was one of those comrades, and he'd saved Rocca's life—more than once.

A passing blonde caught his eye, tagging along behind a fat, short, bald guy. She was tall, built better than the redhead, and her eyes said she would love to tag along with Rocca. He gave her a wan smile and shook his head.

No nightcap tonight.

He finished his meal and called for the check.

Back in his room he tried Jack. They said he was still in x-ray but should be back soon. The bed was comfy and the next thing he knew it was 0100 hours and there was a blinking message light on his phone.

He rubbed his eyes, wondering why he hadn't heard the phone. He dialed voice mail. A smooth female voice, Lieutenant Rose at Naval Hospital, San Diego, asked him to call her about Mr. Jack Dillon.

He punched the number and miraculously got through. The front desk connected him to the nurse's station. A gravelly older woman's voice came on the line, sounding bored when he asked for Lieutenant Rose.

"Lieutenant Rose is busy with a patient right now. Could she call you back?"

"No, I'll hold, unless someone else can tell me about Jack Dillon or connect me to his room."

A brief pause on the other end of the line. A sigh. "I'll get Lieutenant Rose." She put him on hold.

One minute became three, then five. He listened, for the third time, to the recording about the new projects completed at the hospital.

One more cycle and—

A familiar young woman's voice purred, "Mr. Rocca, this is Lieutenant Rose. How are you tonight, sir?"

"Fine. Perfect. What about Jack Dillon? What's going on with him?"

"May I ask, are you family?"

"I'm a good friend. We go back a long way and we recently went through a major ordeal together. How's he doing? I've been trying to call his room but they say he's been having some tests. What gives?" He didn't want an enemy in this woman, but he knew his voice had a slight edge.

"I am sorry to bother you, sir, but do you know how we can get in touch with his family? He didn't fill out that part on his intake form. He left your name as his only contact point."

"His parents died and he's not married. He had a sister in Alabama, but that was years ago. Can't you tell me what's going on? I mean, we are very close—like brothers. Doesn't that count as family?"

"I am sorry, sir. But if you're not immediate family we can't give out any information. According to the Privacy Act, I can't tell you anything over the phone. It would be illegal."

Rocca snapped. "Yeah, I've heard of the fucking Privacy Act. It's the one that allows insurance companies to know anything they want about you, but doesn't allow your best friend to know jack shit! Let me talk to your supervisor!"

"Sir, profanity is not necessary. I am the night supervisor. There is no one above me except the Nurse of the Day, Commander Jonah. Would you like to talk to him?"

She's so nice it's like trying to whip Mary Magdalene.

"Yeah, I guess so. I'm sorry. I only want to find out what's going on with my friend."

"Commander Jonah will call you back within the hour. He is tied up with some other difficult hospital matters right now. Is there anything else I can do for you?"

God, if she gets any nicer.

"How about the guys that were looking after him? Are they still there? Can I talk to one of them?"

There was some screaming in the background. "Sir, I will have someone call you back. We have another problem right now. I'm sorry to hang up, but I have to go."

A dial tone buzzed in his ear.

He beat the bed with the phone. "Fuck! Fuck! Fuck!"

Then he calmly hung up the phone, dialed room service, and asked for a bottle of Chevas Regal to be brought up. One sure way to cure this bullshit.

CHAPTER 42

Rachel drove once they reached Fort Stockton, and it was her turn for music. White Snake played. I-10 bypassed El Paso, and soon the "Welcome to New Mexico, Land of Enchantment" sign greeted them. Ten minutes later *Kittens Got Claws* finished. There was the *whoo* of the wind and the hum of the motor. Then Las Cruces.

They exited on Motel Drive, not exactly a cool name, and found Nellie's Café a few minutes later. Though it was past the lunch rush and on a weekday, they still had to wait thirty minutes for seats. The locals clearly loved Nellie's: this busy and they didn't even serve booze. Alex and Rachel went back to the Jeep for beer while Jesse waited for the table.

The beers in the cooler were cold and tasted good. They sat against the hood, drinking. Rachel eyed Alex, who seemed to be quietly drinking his beer and not talking much. "How's it going with…you know…Lora's death?"

"Don't beat around the bush. Ask me the toughest question you can think of."

"Sorry. I thought you were—"

"Over her?" He drank another swig of beer and eyed her over the long neck.

Rachel lowered her eyes and felt her cheeks burn. "I'll shut up and drink."

Alex's hard gaze cracked into a smile. "Fun to see you squirm."

"You!" Rachel wanted to pour the beer on him but instead smacked him on his bicep with her fist.

"Okay, okay. Man, that hurt. You been workin' out."

He rubbed his upper arm and took a sip of beer. "I'm fine about Lora. I just want to get the guys that did it, that's all. What about you and Scott?"

Yesterday she might have cried. Might have. Today? "You know," She blinked a few times. No tears. "I'm not quite fine. But Scott and I... It's like Scott was a different life, one I never truly wanted. Maybe I knew it all along. Scott was too military, too gung-ho, straight-and-narrow. Didn't even like camping."

What she didn't say was: *Scott was on the rebound from you, Alex—adventurous, antiestablishment, out there.* Remembering the scene in the lab and Alex becoming more muscled, more virile, more... Her cheeks warmed. She needed a lot more beer.

She watched him gaze into the restaurant, loved his tousled blond hair and innocent face. Why wasn't he looking at her? "So...you and Jesse are pretty tight, huh?" she said.

"So...if I give the wrong answer, you'll hit me on the head with that beer bottle, huh?"

Beer spurted from Rachel's lips and she started laughing, louder and louder, until she held her side. Part of her realized this was too much. But the other part that had been too sad and serious for too long didn't care.

Alex caught her gaze, a hint of slyness in his eye. "I wasn't the one who broke it off, remember?"

She reached out to hug him.

Jesse's voice called out, an edge to her voice. "You want to finish up? Table's ready."

Just getting started, bitch. Rachel lowered her arms. *Bitch? Where did that come from?*

Jesse's voice had been hard, hadn't it? She could have been just jealous about Alex, but Jesse had been rubbing her the wrong way since Alex had been going to the Amazon. Yet it was more than that, especially the last two days. It wasn't just about Alex, either. There was something else she couldn't put her finger on.

They ate lunch. Jesse loose and easy and even joking about the old geezer in the table next to them. "With that long beard and dirty clothes he's probably still prospecting for the Organ Mountain lost silver." Everyone chuckled. The green chili was excellent. Rachel relaxed. It was good to sit and laugh with friends.

Jesse drove, though she wanted to dump Alex and Rachel in the middle of the desert. Jesus. When Rachel turned around and rested her chin on the seat back, gazing at Alex like some high school crush, Jesse wanted to backhand her. She pushed on the accelerator. Move on and get out of this car.

Two nights ago she'd kissed Alex and wanted more. But she knew there could be no more. She had to concentrate on important matters ahead. There was her aunt, yes, but more importantly she had to finish the deception of the last three years, and finally kick the government in the balls.

She watched the highway, trying to avoid seeing Rachel eye Alex. A dust devil moved randomly on the left side of the car. It dodged sagebrush and cactus and ended its short life enveloping the Jeep. Dust coated the windows, but only for a few seconds. Speed and wind cleared it up. She accelerated even more.

They reached Bernalillo, a collection of cottonwoods and small houses north of Albuquerque. Jesse pulled the car to the side of the road at the exit ramp and stopped. No one was waiting as she had hoped. She needed a few minutes. Alex and Rachel protested, but she got out and grabbed her pack from the trunk. "My cousin's always a little late. If I survived what we went through, I can certainly wait a few minutes in this sleepy town. I have a cell phone. You guys get going. You have a lot of ground to cover yet."

She shooed them away. They waved and drove off.

Finally. Jesse dialed Jabril on her cell phone. His voice was as smooth and loving as the first time.

"Is this who I think it is?"

"Of course. The bell of the ball. Where are you?" she asked.

Rocca was sitting on the hotel bed when he took his first swig on the bottle of Chevas. The phone rang.

"Rock, is that you?"

"Fred?"

How had Fred found him?

"Yeah. I blasted over to the hospital when I heard."

"Heard what? What's going on with Jack?

"Rock, Jack's dead. He died of a clot in his lung from his broken leg."

Rocca swirled the bottle of Chevas, staring at the amber liquid, ready to hurl the bottle at the wall.

"Rock, you there?"

"Yeah, I'm here, goddamn it. Gimme a sec."

He put the phone on the bed, took a deep pull on the bottle, wiped his mouth, and sat the bottle on the table without a sound.

His eyes felt like stone; his jaw hurt he clamped down so hard, but his mind was dead calm. Only his arm moved to pick up the phone. His body and head were as still as a sphinx's, relaxed and ready.

"Fred, I want to see the guy you got…this El Fahd fucker. I want to see his face. His *face*! And if it is *not* him, I want to be the guy who finds him. I want in!"

"Rock, I can't."

Rocca waited, crunching his molars and flexing his jaw muscles.

Fred owed him. And Jack. That's the way they had ended things ten years ago.

"Okay, okay. I'll see what I can do. You sit tight. I'll call you back within the hour. And Rock—don't do anything stupid. You're in. Let me make some calls."

"Fuckin'-A I'm in. You make your calls. I'll wait for two hours: a hundred and twenty minutes. If I don't hear from you I'm gonna make some calls of my own."

"Rock, you don't need—"

Rocca hung up, gently. He carefully screwed the top on the Chevas and then took a shower.

After dropping Jesse off, Rachel didn't say much, thinking about Alex and her. At Santa Fe she decided and turned north up Highway 285.

"Where are we going?" Alex sounded concerned.

She glanced at him, hoping he would be okay with this. "Look, I'm worn out. I need something other than computer screens to look at. I need one more good night of sleep before I'll be any good. Jerry said we could take a few days. Besides, I'm not sure I want to do this, anymore."

"But this guy is—"

"What?"

"I don't know. Just a feeling."

"You don't know what he's doing, really. It's only a feeling. Well I have feelings too. And I need to…relax another day. Just one more day." She wanted more than that. She had to find out about her and Alex. Did she love him? She had to find out if she could continue this job. Could she go back to bio-warfare work?

Alex gazed into the distance, she hoped thinking about her. "Okay. But tomorrow we have to get there."

"Thanks." She felt tiredness leave her. "You won't regret it. There's great stuff to see up here. We can see them in a few minutes, get a motel and crash. We'll be in the Springs before 10:00 a.m. tomorrow."

They made it to the Great Sand Dunes National Park at sunset. Approaching from the west, the dunes lay before the Sangre de Cristo Mountains which in turn were a jagged silhouette against a lavender sky, the whole vista reminding her of photos she'd seen of Mars. She parked in the small, deserted parking lot. They clasped hands and half-walked, half-ran up and through several dunes, finally making it to the top of the highest dune. They both breathed hard and sat to watch the sunset. The dunes cast snaking shadows, like a giant ocean had recently left piles of sand to play in. Clouds on the western side of the San Luis valley hovered above the older, gentler San Juan Mountains, and turned a dark yellow as the sun receded. The sun moved behind the mountains and the clouds became burnt orange.

The temperature dropped ten degrees. Alex sat quietly, his arm around her shoulders, warming her. "The sunset reminds me of Wyoming on the river with my dad."

Rachel watched his face. The clouds reflected auburn on his cheeks. His eyes did not move, as if he were looking far beyond the clouds.

"I never thought he would die so young. Probably the cigarettes. Though after what he went through he probably should have died even sooner."

"What do you mean, 'what he went through'?"

He puckered his lips, and slowly exhaled through his nose. "Well, you need…" He looked in her eyes. "My parents were in Auschwitz."

Rachel frowned and shook her head. "Auschwitz. Really?"

"Yeah. They were Polish Jews. Their families all died there. Dad's family was Klauswitz, Mom's Feldstein."

Rachel grabbed his face and kissed him. She broke the kiss and looked into his eyes, wanting to step inside and sweep away his hurt. "I'm so sorry. God, how terrible."

They hugged each other tightly and then lay on their backs and stared at the first stars. One coyote howled. Another yelped.

"What happened to them?" Rachel said, softly.

Alex rubbed her palm slowly and gently with his thumb. "They were some of the few Jewish children still alive at the end of the war. Mom went mute and her hair turned white. They were both skeletons. Someone helped them out and got them to Wyoming."

"Who?"

"A Sandra Smith. Short for Alexandra. Dad was never able to track her down."

"American?"

"Don't think so."

"British?"

"Not sure."

"So that's why you're Alex?"

"Yep. Mom and dad changed their name to Smith, too. They became Baptist because my mom blamed being Jewish for losing her parents and the Baptists had helped her regain her speech and pretty much saved my parents' lives."

Rachel took a deep breath and sighed and gripped his hand tighter.

Alex looked at her. "Are you okay with that? You're the only one I've ever told."

"I'm okay with anything about you."

A coyote howled and an owl hooted, stark and eerie against the silent twilight. Night was settling in, and with it colder air. They stood and followed their tracks back in the waning light. Alex produced a pen flashlight. The small beacon illuminated tiny double tracks of a desert kangaroo rat. They wandered back and forth, eventually intercepting their previous footprints, then picked up their pace. The chill was getting downright freezing when they finally made it back to the car. The heater felt good as Alex drove out of the parking lot.

Down the road a few miles they entered the small town of Moffat. Rachel told Alex about a B&B she'd seen when surfing the net the night before they left San Antonio. Alex turned off the main drag. It wasn't easy in the dark, but they finally found it—Willow Spring Bed and Breakfast Inn. A Colorado state flag flapped on a tall flagpole outside the Inn. Wind chimes on the covered porch gave a musical welcome. The steps to the front porch and door were wood, worn smooth and sunken but solid without creaking, probably the originals. Large, hundred-year-old willow trees grew close to the west side of the inn and blocked most of the ever present wind and shaded those hot summer afternoons. The upper half of the front door was four-paned glass in different thicknesses that gave a warped view of the inside. More original equipment. Alex rang the bell. A man with an easy smile and ear-length blond hair answered. He was barefooted, had an earring on his left ear, and wore faded jeans and a navy-blue tee shirt with GO BRONCOS lettered in orange. He looked like a hippy uncle Rachel had known. His voice was as easy as his smile. He introduced them to his wife, another hippie throwback with a tie-died tee shirt, jeans, and hoop earrings. They were proud of their enclave and gave a brief tour. The Inn had been a hotel in the days when the railroad made Moffat a town. But the town and hotel atrophied after the highways became more important than the railroad. Luckily for the hotel, the '80s brought this new-age couple from Boulder who renovated the old hotel and opened it as a bed and breakfast. They got most of their business from travelers visiting the nearby town of Crestone: an eclectic mix of retired businessmen, lawyers, and doctors, as well as very active artists, photographers and ecologically inventive minds. The host explained that this entire area was said to be a holy center for American Indians and so attracted a number of exotic religious centers and new-age gatherings. The couple bade them a good night, and they carried their luggage upstairs to their room.

Rachel wanted a shower, so while she went down the hall to the bathroom, Alex went back to the Jeep for the small cooler. He picked up a copy of the Crestone Visitor's Guide from a table in the den. Back in the room he sprawled on the bed and perused the pages, and read a few of the highlights out loud to make sure he wasn't seeing things. "The Temple of Consciousness Ashram and Retreat Center, The Shumei International

Institute, Inc., the Crestone Metaphysical Fair, the Permaculture Design Certificate Course, The Crestone Mountain Zen Center."

He paused. "Maybe I'll stick to the Crestone Music Festival and the Buckwheat Zydeco. Better yet, how about the Valley View Hot Springs, where clothing is optional?"

Rachel walked in, brushing her wet hair and her eyebrows went up. "Wanna go?"

"Maybe next trip."

Alex hopped out of bed and grabbed a couple of beers from the cooler, gave one to Rachel and hooked his Walkman to small speakers. Whitesnake filled the room.

He turned around and Rachel lay on the bed, tight jean shorts and braless cotton tee shirt, seductively sipping her beer.

He lay down beside her. "I'm sorry about Scott."

She pushed her index finger onto his lips. "Not tonight. We don't talk about the past tonight. We have here and now. You and me."

She kissed him.

They made love slowly, exploring at first, then, remembering familiar curves, the waves of pleasure increased in tempo. At the top of the final wave they both opened their eyes. They saw peace. They felt complete. Gone were loss, revenge, and hate. The fires that had burned their nerve endings raw were blanketed with the soft snowy curtain, finally…finally climaxing with a weightless fall into a drift of white flakes melting on their cheeks. Their tears were spontaneous, mutual, and unquestioned, joy at the ultimate shared human experience, the reason why songs are sung and poems written.

They lay still. It soaked in. They slowly fell asleep to the last song on the CD, *The Wings of the Storm*.

Outside, a gusty wind pushed ocher-colored clouds from the west. They moved over the valley and covered Crestone Peak to the east, dropping big snowflakes on the fourteener.

A mile north of Moffat, a pickup camper was parked beside the road. A man stepped out and aimed his binoculars at the Willow Spring Inn.

CHAPTER 43

Twenty minutes after Rocca hung up, the phone rang again. He was already dressed and packed. Putting the .45 in his chest holster, he picked up the phone. "Yeah?"

"Rock," It was Fred. "I can e-mail you the picture of the guy they got at the scene."

"No good. I have no computer here. How about I give you the fax of the hotel and you can send it to them?"

"I guess that will have to do. But go down there and be ready for it. I don't want anybody else to see this. Not only is this guy's face top secret, the picture is pretty gruesome."

Rocca retrieved the fax, took it to his room and studied it.

The face was intact, but the body was a hazy goo. *Damn eyes are closed. If I could just see the eyes. Face is about right. But the beard screws things up. Maybe they could shave the face, and then I could look at it again.*

He punched in Fred's number.

"The person you are dialing is away from the phone. If you would like to leave—" He slammed the handset onto the cradle.

Taking a deep breath he dialed again. Slowly, carefully.

Fred picked up immediately. "Rocca, did you get it?"

"Where the fuck were you, Fred? I dialed and got a voice message."

"Chill, would you? I was in the middle of the hospital. Sometimes the cells don't pick up too well in there. Anyway, what do you think?"

"The beard is throwing me off. If I could look into his eyes I could tell right away. But that ain't happenin'. So how about shaving the guy and taking another picture? Maybe I could tell then. What about finger-prints, can't we get them?"

The reception on the phone crackled in and out. Finally, Fred said, clear as a bell, "…so you see how it is?"

"Fred, I missed all that. You faded out. Say again."

"Okay. Whoever killed the guy immersed his hands and the rest of his body in some kind of strong lye, like a commercial drain cleaner. All the prints are gone. We might get DNA, but that could take a while."

"What about shaving the guy? Can you do that and send me another picture?"

There was a pause. Rocca heard Fred's voice talking to someone else in the background.

"What about an artist's rendition of the guy without the beard?" Fred said.

"I've tried those things before. I need to see the real thing."

Rocca heard more muffled discussions in the background.

"Yeah, I think we can do that. The guy should still be on ice. Let me con-tact the medical examiner down in Farmington. It may take a few hours."

Rocca sighed and flopped onto the bed. *Might as well catch a few zs.*

Sheriff Nahash got the call about 8:00 p.m., while he was trying to put a domestic disturbance to bed about fifteen miles south of Dulce, deeper into the Jicarilla Apache reservation. His dispatch deputy, Billy, put it together like this: John Big Horse Macallan had been hitting the bottle all day—most of the week, for that matter. Horse's daughter, Jesse, was coming to visit. That was what usually got Horse going. But then he got the real story. While Horse had been throwing knives at a tree outside, his wife had called him for supper, and he'd thrown a knife in her direction. Nahash knew Horse would never harm his wife, but the knife had hit the front door frame and scared the hell out of their visiting daughter-in-law. She had recently moved down to Albuquerque from Boston. She'd instantly called Billy at dispatch and locked Horse out of the house.

It had taken the sheriff about a half hour to get there, and Big Horse had done what big men can do: he'd busted in the door and grabbed his daughter-in-law. He was outside behind his pickup tying her hands with rope when Nahash's headlights illuminated the scene.

"Kinda early for a roundup, isn't it, Horse?" Nahash was matter of fact in his tone, and slow in his movements. He didn't want to get into any confrontations with this three-hundred pound piece of muscle.

There was sheer, pleading terror in the daughter-in-law's eyes. Big Horse had duct-taped her mouth.

"Damn kids," Horse replied. "Not from around here. They need to keep out of our business." He finished hog-tying her hands and feet and picked her up with one hand under the rope around her waist, gently sitting her in his truck bed, like she was glass.

"Horse, where's Sally and little Sam?"

A loud voice came from the house. "We're in here, Sheriff. We're okay."

Nahash peered through the screened front window. There was Horse's wife, Sally, and his grandson Sam.

"You sure you're okay, Sally?"

"Fine, Sheriff. It's Louisa I'm worried about." And she added to her husband, "Horse, you're scaring the hell out of little Sam. Let Louisa go."

"Nobody locks me out of my own damn house!" Horse bellowed. "Especially not some rich Jewish princess from Boston."

Horse's face was flushed and he was breathing hard. Back in his prime, Horse could have taken on ten men and gone back to his whiskey in no time. But the years and the whiskey had taken their toll—more whiskey since he'd been laid off a month ago from the plant in Farmington.

"Hey, Horse, you've already taught her a lesson. I can take her to the bus stop from here. Why don't you take it easy and get some sleep? Little Sam is pretty scared and you don't want that now, do you?"

The radio in the sheriff's truck blared out, "Chief, we got an urgent call for you concerning the Buick contents from this morning."

Nahash ignored it.

"Sheriff Nahash, there is a *very* important caller on the line and says he has to talk to you, right now. A matter of *national security!*"

Nahash put his open palm out to the big man. "Horse, please sit down there for a minute."

Horse was already starting to sit, back sliding down the driver's door. He looked pale.

Backing up slowly, keeping an eye on Big Horse, Nahash grabbed the handset. "This is Nahash. What's going on, Billy?"

"Chief, you gotta talk to this guy. He's wanting Doc to shave that Arab guy."

Horse's eyes closed. "Billy, I got a situation here that supersedes that request. Tell him I'll call him back in ten minutes."

"I already tried that, Chief. He was not happy and said he would have a Congressional investigation started ASAP if we didn't cooperate."

Big Horse fell over onto his side, head lolling like the neck muscles had stopped working. His tongue hung out.

"Billy, stop! Get an ambulance over here. I think Big Horse is having a heart attack. Tell that guy he can have the president come down here on a personal visit with the Marines for all I care. I'll call him as soon as this mess is over. Out!" *Goddamn Feds think they own us.*

Nahash cleared out the pieces of jerky that had lodged in the back of his throat and Big Horse started breathing on his own. Nahash thanked God he didn't have to do mouth to mouth on the big man. He had rotten teeth and reeked of liquor. He would have probably thrown up. He left Horse lying on his side, cuffed him for insurance, and unbundled Louisa.

The ambulance arrived and to be on the safe side they decided to take Horse to the hospital in Farmington. Watching the ambulance drive away, Nahash used Sally's phone to call Billy, who patched him through to the CIA guy.

"Sheriff, this is Fred Harriman. Listen, I know you have a lot of things going on, but we really need to make sure this guy with the beard is the right guy. If he's not, then we need to keep searching until we find him, or we might have another Twin Towers incident in the next week."

Nahash thought about objecting. There was no permission from next of kin, and, being Muslim, they might not take too kindly to their shaving his facial hair. But he was tired of the games. He wanted this case over.

"Okay, then what?"

"Take another photo of the face without the beard and send it to us ASAP."

The Feds sure like that word ASAP. "Anything else?"

"Well, if you could prop open the eyes with toothpick or something that would help too."

Nahash said nothing. Seconds passed.

"Okay, only the shave. Thanks, Sheriff. We'll send somebody down to pick up the bodies soon and get this whole thing out of your hair. Maybe one of these days I can buy you a beer or take you fishing."

"Sounds good." Nahash hung up. *A beer and fishin'? Well, maybe a Bud. But if he wanted to go fly fishing and catch and release… We don't play with our food.*

He called Billy and made the necessary arrangements for the shave and photos. Billy did not sound happy.

A tug on his sleeve from little Sam brought him back to the present.

In her time, Sally had turned many heads, including his. But life and work had left her worn, stooped and haggard—fifty going on seventy. And now she looked even worse. Disheveled and distraught, she and Louisa were hugging and crying.

He left Sam and walked over and stood by them. They kept sobbing. He went on one knee and put a hand on Sally's shoulder and she looked up. "It'll be okay. You know Horse—he wouldn't have hurt either one of you. He was only, you know. Being Horse."

Sam had followed Nahash, and Sally pulled him in with one arm, pursing her lips. She looked up at Nahash.

"Thanks, Peter. I know you mean well. But this is the last straw. I'm leaving. I'm taking Sam and going to Albuquerque with Louisa."

Nahash didn't let too many people call him by his first name. Sally was an exception.

She'd been through a lot with Horse. Their son kept in touch, or rather, his wife did. Louisa liked family. The daughter had run off with a Pakistani guy to some college and now was a microbiologist working for some big company back East. Big Horse was hurt when they left, not because he missed them, but because they left the Jicarilla Apache ways.

Sally was just hurt.

Nahash looked at Sally and her grandson and the shaken Louisa. Enough was enough. "Can I help you in any way? You need a ride?"

"No," She smiled the way he remembered her from his early days. "Louisa has her car. We'll be packed and gone before Horse gets out. I'll leave him a note. You probably shouldn't tell him anything. He'll pull out his IV and make a mess of the hospital like he did last time."

She kissed Sam's head and her face hardened. "I would like a restraining order. Maybe that will keep him from coming to Albuquerque right away."

"I'll get right on it. And I doubt if that old truck of his will make it more than sixty miles, but I'll alert the Albuquerque police. I understand Jesse is back in the area. Do you want me to notify her?"

"He was looking forward to seeing her, despite all this." She gestured an open palm at the truck. "No, I'll tell her."

Nahash started towards his Jeep Cherokee. "Well, if I don't see you again, I hope all goes well."

She nodded and gave him a wan smile and wrapped one arm around the sobbing Louisa and the other around Sam. She put her cheek on Sam's head and he could see the top of her head. It was streaked in gray.

Before Nahash got in his car, he looked up. The endless black void was peppered with bright stars and a half moon that was so bright he wouldn't need headlights. It connected him back to the earth, a deep feeling in his gut. Everything had a purpose, and it all moved in a circle, back to the beginning.

He got into the car and turned the key, wondering where this particular circle was leading.

CHAPTER 44

After the three-hour drive north, weaving in and out of desert and mountains, Jesse spent the previous night with her cousin in Dulce, the seat of the Jicarilla Apache Nation. It sounded so regal: Apache Nation. But sleeping in a sleeping bag on the floor of a doublewide, surrounded by empty beer cans and half-eaten burritos was anything but majestic. If it hadn't been for her Aunt Bella, Jesse would have never come back.

What's in a name?—Jesse, Bella—different but so close.

Aunt Bella had been there for her on those nights she had run from her drunken father. Jesse didn't want to think of her any other way than a robust, strong, and determined aunt. She had helped her study and get the scholarship to the University of Arizona. At eighteen Jesse had left, returning only twice, both times during college, and both times ending in family disasters.

After the last time, Jessed had gone back to college and met Joshua, who introduced her to jihadist beliefs: it was the perfect solution. She could get back at the government for making her father a drunk, for making her people live on a reservation, and for screwing up her life. It actually felt good to be jailed in Tucson for protesting the Iraq sanctions.

But you had to fall in love with Joshua, didn't you?

Then Joshua had been killed on Christmas vacation. His entire family perished in an Israeli attack on Palestine. She flew to the scene but could only mourn over the crushed piano and one remaining wall that held one picture of Joshua and his mother playing that piano.

That night she'd attended a jihad meeting and met Jabril El Fahd.

He was smart, handsome, and so damn thin she could not believe he was a renowned jihadist. She towered over him. He called her Jessibelle. Made it sound like an angel.

Should have never... You were on the fucking rebound!

She'd never had any terrorist training—only learned to pass information. The information from her work with Alex would allow al-Qaeda to make a vaccine that would protect them from any infection the U.S. tried.

Jesse sat at the kitchen table, hungry but not wanting to eat there. The fruity-sour smell of dirty clothes in corners and half-eaten food all over the place tainted her hunger. There was a cloth couch that she could have slept in last night, but she preferred the floor to bed bugs. At least the sleeping bag had been little used. On one wall hung pictures of her uncle with a trophy elk just above another shot of him standing behind their Chief signing the oil agreements. The government and big oil had kept that money from her people for decades. Now that they had some, at least they could build good schools. But it was not enough to make up for what they had done to her family.

So she would see Aunt Bella and leave and forget this place.

Jabril was waiting.

Across town, all eight streets, she found her aunt's neat ranch house, new white paint on the white siding, with Aunt Bella's favorite marigolds in the window planters. She let herself in—these doors were never locked. There was the same old flowery foldout couch and brown Naugahyde easy chair and a TV that should have been junked long ago, and every corner clean, nothing out of place. Aunt Bella was sitting up in bed, her abdomen protuberant with the excess fluid from the tumor. Jesse knew the doctors had told her she needed chemotherapy, but she preferred to die naturally.

"Hi, Jesse. How are you?" Her voice was soft, her eyes as calm and seemingly all-knowing as ever. It had been eight years and she acted like she'd just seen her yesterday.

"Good, Aunt Bella. And you?" No emotions. Get this over and move on.

"I will be with the Great Spirit soon, but for now I must help you with your problems."

"Problems?" She couldn't know about Jabril.

Her eyes never wavered in their calm resolve. "Your father."

Jesse shrugged and didn't blink, relieved this was not about Jabril. She crossed her arms. "Horse will always be a problem. I don't think you can change him."

"Your mother finally left him yesterday. She is staying in Albuquerque with Louisa. You must go to him and help him to quit drinking. It is killing him and his family."

She pulled her arms in tighter. "I came to see you, not him. I'm glad Mother finally left him. She should have done that years ago."

Bella's dark eyes seemed to shimmer in liquid as they focused on Jesse. "My future is written. But your father's is not. He is special to our people, and you are our best hope. You are a direct descendant of Kohoshi."

Jesse tried not to, but her aunt's eyes beckoned, and once she locked into them there was no escape. There was pain, sadness and hope all mixed in. Jesse wanted to cry. "I'll go see him. Now tell me, what else can I do for you."

Her aunt related Big Horse's recent problems with the police, gave her a list of simple things to gather and people to contact before Bella died. They sat with each other for several minutes before Bella nodded off and Jesse slipped out.

Jesse knew the story, or at least the way her father told it in a drunken jumble of Navajo and Jicarilla myths. Eons ago, the People, led by Kohoshi, chief of the Anasazi, a big man like her father, like her, lived on the plains, the Llaneros band of the Jicarilla, as far back as when rocks began. Game was plentiful. There were no enemies. One evening Kohoshi gazed into the setting sun and saw a bright streak across the northwest sky—a sign that change was coming. That night, Kohoshi dreamed that an enemy was coming. On the plains, this enemy could not be conquered. They were too powerful. Kohoshi dreamed of houses in the sky—caves protected by air. They would live amongst the clouds and not have to fight the coming warriors.

Convincing the tribe to rebuild their homes in the cliffs had not been a simple matter. Many rebelled. In the end, only those willing to make the change had survived. Kohoshi became a legend, and his offspring survived to move back to the foothills and plains: Big Horse and Jesse. Now it was Jesse's turn to change. Would she survive the next big change?

———

Jesse quickly completed the last-minute tasks for her aunt, then headed south to her father's place, further into the reservation and more surrounded by sage and piñon trees, her new rental Honda sticking out like a diamond in dirt. She could feel her back and neck tighten and her stomach twist the closer she got.

Probably drunk off his ass, so what the hell am I worried about? Bella thinks he can save the world because he's a direct descendant of a famous Anasazi chief. Christ! He can't even save himself.

There was new tan paint on half of the frame house, the windows taped off, the few cedars not much larger than eight years ago. The old Ford pick-up, two-tone black and red, was backed up near the shed. Big Horse was putting down a large wooden chest beside a trash can, apparently doing some fall cleaning, something he never did. A huge man for Jicarilla, he still had a presence and strength when he moved.

She got out of the car and he stood from his task, squinted at first, and then his face lit up as she remembered it during birthday celebrations.

"Jessibelle! You've come home." He walked towards her with open arms. She could now see his face was more lined, his gait halting as if in pain, and his shoulders slightly stooped.

She wanted to go to his open arms, but yet she folded her arms and did not move. "I know what you did. Aunt Bella sent me."

He stopped, gazed at the clouds, puckered his mouth and shook his head slowly. "Poor Bella. Even dying she's trying to help me."

It felt the same but different to her. He always apologized, but somehow this felt more sincere.

He looked back at her, his eyes watering. "But you actually came out here to see me. That says something."

She wanted to go to him, put her arms around him, forgive him. But she gripped her elbows and her words came out sharp. "I promised her on her death bed. What else am I supposed to do?"

His smile and head tilt indicated confidence. He pointed to the trashcan. "Look inside."

She took a step forward and looked inside, looked back at him, then back in the trashcan. It was full of empty bourbon bottles and beer cans.

"I love your mother," he said. "I poured good liquor down the sink for her."

She was impressed. All those years she'd never known him to empty out even one bottle of Jim Beam, except down his gullet. Unfolding her arms, she walked to him and stood only a foot from him.

"Dad, I'm proud of you."

They embraced—his arms gentle but strong—like when she was a girl, when he could protect her from anything.

"I missed you, girl." It was a hoarse whisper, his emotions filling each word. "Can you ever forgive me?"

Not supposed to happen this way. We were supposed to have our typical argument, and then I could leave and get on with my business.

Tears dripped off her cheeks onto his shirt. She wanted to leave, get far away, never come back. But he had taught her to ride a bike, showed her the secrets of the rivers, shared the history of their people.

"Yes, Daddy." Her reply was a soft whisper, a tenderness from times lost. "I forgive you. I'm sorry, too."

For the next hour she helped him clean up the house. Then he called the local AA chapter and the Apache doctor for herbs to help him get through withdrawal.

She called her mother and told her the good news.

They sat hugging each other before she left. A bald eagle flew over-head, and she watched it soar effortlessly over the hill.

She smiled up at the warm sun.

I love you, Daddy.

Sam was cold when he awoke in the pickup camper on the dirt road outside Moffat, the sun not yet over the Sangre de Cristo range to the east. He picked up the binoculars again and found the B&B and the Jeep Cherokee.

He lit the burner to start making coffee, and mumbled to himself, "Somebody's got to follow you, Alex. Know what I saw. Don't care what they say about damn geyser gases. Never saw anything like that after weed or acid. You may not be infected, but you know about El Fahd. And I'm gonna follow you until you lead me to him."

He peered through the binoculars again, the trees beside the stairs of the B&B without a movement. "Besides, someone's gotta watch out for Rachel."

CHAPTER 45

Jabril awoke late but was not refreshed. Every muscle ached, each breath wheezed. He could have sworn each cough raked his palate with jagged glass. The sickness was blossoming. Part of him thrilled, but another part wanted the power, the strength, the feeling of ultimately controlling his own destiny.

The view from the window was rolling hills speckled with cedar trees, and in the distance there was a gap indicating the canyon of the Arkansas River.

Time to move. But where is Jessibelle? I must have her here to turn me in.

Once again he reviewed the plan. His comrades had gathered their gear and would carry out their part: the assault on the reservoirs. First, along the Colorado River, dams would have surprises floated into the water intake of the turbines. Tiny marbles, disintegrating spheres would release chemicals that would corrode and destroy the turbines in twenty-four hours.

Second, one day after the marbles were released, the reservoirs would be blown up. The comrades involved would likely die in the process, but they were prepared for the sacrifice. Allah would reward them. Millions would be left without water or electric power for years, not crippled, but wounded.

But the main, most immediate result of the plan would be to drive the military and political powers to react to the new threat on their country, presumably the same reaction as after September 11: they would hide.

This time the consequences of running for their safe houses and nuclear bomb shelters would lead to infection from contagious members of their staff—sleeper cells that had been planted years ago, now ready for action. The results of the contagion would wipe out the top leaders and their ability to respond to military threats. This was more than crippling. It would allow al-Qaeda to take control. The U.S. would experience turnabout for its past imperialistic acts. They would feel the frustration of losing control of their government to another who believed their way of life was better.

Only this time it would be true. Islam *was* better.

Jabril was one of the most important cogs in this wheel of destruction. Upon capture, they would take him to one of the main underground centers of the U.S. military, Cheyenne Mountain, where Khan's spies had seen numerous top military and political leaders come after the Great Event. It was the only place for hundreds of miles that was protected where they could interrogate him. There he would infect all who questioned him. After he died they would die. His sacrifice would kill many of what he was sure were top generals in their armies and political leaders.

Simple, honorable, heroic.

But he needed Jesse to turn him in to the right authorities. They would believe her when she told them how she had been helping and now was having second thoughts. If they looked into her history, they would believe every word.

His cell phone chirped, and he looked at the screen. *Finally.* "Yes. Where are you?"

"I am still with my father. Something has come up. I don't know if I can come."

Jabril gripped the phone and wanted to beat it against the wall. "You must get here today!" Yet there had been something in her voice, something sad and vulnerable. He changed his tack. "Your family? I understand. But I am going downhill fast, Jessibelle. I need your help now."

There was a long pause. "It's complicated. I need more time with my family."

"Of course, Jessibelle. But, please, first come and do this one small thing for me. It will take mere hours. Then I will personally arrange your return to your family." That was the way to handle her. Focus on her family.

"How will you do that in the middle of the mountain?"

"I have people helping me in many places. You know I keep my promises."

There was a longer pause. He started to speak when she said, "Okay. I'll leave within the hour. Be ready."

"I am always ready for you, my Jessibelle." He hung up and unconsciously licked his lips.

Always.

The mere thought of her body and he was hard and his muscles pulsed and fatigue faded. If he didn't die of the infection, he could kill the entire army with his two hands. He would enjoy Jessibelle first.

The M.E. at Farmington was not happy at having to shave the face of a cadaver, and at such a late hour. But after it was done, he discovered a rather large mole on the left jawline that the beard had hidden. He took a few pictures, loaded them into the computer and faxed them to the number he'd been given.

Rocca's phone rang at 2:00 a.m. The fax was in from Farmington.

He was still wide awake and had just finished fifty pushups. He went down to the hotel office and collected the sealed envelope from the thin and balding desk clerk. Rocca pulled out his knife, a switchblade he'd kept from Tijuana days, flicked it open and slit open the envelope. The clerk's eyes got wide and he left. Rocca pulled out enough to see the edge of photos then pushed them back in and returned to his room.

He shut the door, sat on the bed and pulled out the photos. The dead man was *not* El Fahd! The beard had changed the whole contour of the face. And the mole—it was the clincher.

He was on the phone with Fred in thirty seconds. "It's not him, Fred."

"Yeah, we kinda figured, with the mole and everything. I'll be leaving on a military jet in fifteen minutes. Meet me at Peterson Air Force Base in, say, five hours. They'll have you cleared at the gate by then. We have no idea where this guy could be, but we have another man who may have a lead on El Fahd. I should have a report soon from him."

"Who's your man?"

"Sam Houston. You don't know him, but he's very reliable, and very good."

"Sam Houston…Sam Houston. I've heard that name somewhere. Oh, yeah. I remember now. He was the governor of Texas who loved Indians, hated Mexicans, and really wanted to be a Yankee, right?"

"Okay, Rock. Good to hear you got your sense of humor back. We'll see you soon." Fred hung up.

Rocca replied to the empty phone line, "Yeah, I got a great sense of humor I'm gonna share with a certain Colonel Jabril El Fahd."

Alex was happier than he'd been in a long time. When he awakened, Rachel was still sleeping, her hair mussed and her face catching the morning light as it filtered through the curtains.

A beautiful face. A wonderful woman. Maybe there's hope for me after all. Goodbye, Lora.

He took his clothes and went down the hall to the shower. When he peeked back in the room fifteen minutes later, she stirred slightly, one eye opening only enough to see him. She murmured sleepily, "Get back in this bed now, mister. We have plenty of time."

If only I could. But there's no time. Something is about to happen.

"Sorry, Rache. We gotta go. Our hosts have breakfast all laid out for us. Could you please get ready because I'd like to be gone in the next hour."

She sat up, pouting, the sheet and blanket pulled up around her. "What do you mean we have to go? Breakfast can wait. We don't have to be there for another day."

"Tomorrow?" he said.

"Jerry said we had until tomorrow. You're okay with that, right? I wanted to show you some more of Colorado." She rubbed one eye like a child.

"Sorry, but the little green men in my brain keep saying, *Danger Will Robinson, Danger!* That guy we thought was gone, you know the bad guy I was talking about? He's back in my head, and I feel he is very close. We gotta get going."

She yawned deeply, stretched her arms overhead, dropping the cover, and revealing her full breasts. "If you really think so."

Walking over to her, he reached around her waist and took her mouth into his, savoring the kiss for a moment. Then tightening his grip around her waist he lifted her up until she was standing and gently slapped her butt.

"I love you, too. But let's save some for tonight."

Then kissing her again briefly, he was firm, "I'm serious. Something very bad is about to happen, and I gotta be there before it goes down. I'll see you at breakfast." He let her go and walked to the door.

She threw a pillow. He closed the door before it got to him.

"Crap!" she said to the door.

Padding naked across the room she looked in the wall mirror and smiled. "He said he loves me!"

Jabril could feel something. He had been sitting on the front porch, watching a rattlesnake slither across the red earth into the shadow of a cedar when he felt it. A tickle in the back of his mind made him look over his shoulder.

Nothing.

It was a little like when he was driving into Las Vegas. He thought someone was tailing him then, so he had changed cars and called compatriots to leave the city before him in the same color of Honda Accord with his look-a-like in the front seat. Jabril had waited and did some reconnaissance of the Hoover Dam before driving east.

But this feeling was different—stronger, almost like someone was reading his mind.

Sitting absolutely still, he tried to meditate. Emptying his mind, he could see a shape of the watcher, a form. Then he coughed and the pain shattered the image. But not before he had seen.

A mere man. And an infidel.

He reflected for a moment.

Nothing to worry about. I'm too strong.

Even so, perhaps I should call Jesse.

He dialed her number. "What is it?" Was there impatience in her voice?

"You must hurry. I've had a vision of a man watching me." Although he knew it was more than a vision. He seemed connected to this infidel like some mental telepathy. And he was sure the infidel could see him as well.

"What does he look like—this man in your vision? Does he have blond hair?"

"Yes, an infidel, and he looks and feels like a playful little boy."

"I *know* him. His name is Alex Smith, and he may be more trouble than you think."

"Meet me at the alternative house. It has some extra precautions." The prior owners had built the house in preparation for a nuclear bomb back in the '70s. Perhaps the reinforced walls would block the infidel from seeing Jabril.

"Okay. I'll see you there." Jesse closed the cell phone, and remembered her joking and flirting with Alex at Amazon Lab. Such a boy. But he had changed. Perhaps he could save her from Jabril.

While packing she noted the thermos bottle in her suitcase. She'd stolen it from the lab. It contained the virus and beginnings of the vaccine.

Maybe you should send the vaccine to Jerry. It would stop this whole mess. Then again, maybe Jabril will understand and stop this whole thing. It's about family. And he knows about family.

Yet Jabril hated Americans so much, he might not give in. Only yesterday she had felt that same hate. But now…

She had to convince him, and it would have to be in person.

On the dresser was a photo of Aunt Bella hugging several students back when she had been healthy.

Aunt Bella might help. Though Jesse had not planned on seeing her again, she finished packing and drove there.

Arriving at the small house, Aunt Bella's daughter, Rose, let her in. She was four years younger than Jesse, a shy, plump girl, and her face was downcast. Without words she showed Jesse into Bella's small bedroom.

Her aunt lay in her bed, covers neatly pulled around her body, eyes closed, visibly jaundiced, her breathing barely discernible. How could she have worsened so quickly? Jesse felt tears well up as she bent over bed.

"Aunt Bella, I… You are so sick. I came to say good-bye, but maybe I should stay."

Bella's eyes fluttered open. She lifted her head and started to push up, but fell back. She breathed hard and looked at Jesse, the whites of her eyes as orange as the marigolds she loved. "You have come to ask me something."

Jesse took a deep breath in, wishing Aunt Bella had not been so clairvoyant. Jesse did not want to ask her, but knew not doing so would torture her aunt in a time she needed peace. She had lived to help others. Perhaps her last memory could be of helping her favorite niece. Jesse let out the breath and began.

Her aunt listened intently with her eyes closed as Jesse described her dilemma—to change the world, or to save her family. She felt weights lift off her; she felt guilty at how much she had lied; she felt hope that her aunt would have the answer.

When she finished, her aunt's eyes snapped open as if she knew exactly what to say. She looked at Jesse for a long moment. "You…know…the answer. Listen to your heart."

She stared off into the distance and began singing: faint, melodious and pure Apache, starting high, and ending low, over and over.

The Death Song.

Her daughter had come to stand at the bedside. Aunt Bella stopped singing. Then she stopped breathing. Her daughter started crying.

Jesse turned and walked out the door, tears welling in her eyes for her aunt, her people, her family, and…her soul.

CHAPTER 46

At the Hoover Dam, a man and woman waited on a jet ski, Danielle sitting behind Craig. Each had a backpack on their back, and each concerned about the dark clouds massing from the north over the mouth of the dam. They had joined a splinter group of the Muslim Brotherhood, the Converts, many years ago. Tired of the drugs and the loose society of southern California, they had flown to Peshawar, Pakistan, then made it across the northern border to Afghanistan and fought side by side with Al Qaeda. Having blue eyes and blond hair, they had infiltrated the Russian camps easily. It was only natural that Bin Laden had chosen them to be his moles in Nevada, waiting for the time he would need them. The time was now, and they were on their way.

It would have been so much easier if they could have done this from the road that went just above the reservoir's main wall. But after the Great Event, the road had been closed. Now they had to use the jet ski. Ahead lay the final channel of the massive reservoir, narrower than Lake Meade, and if someone was watching closely they would be sitting ducks, so they had to make this look good.

The plan was simple: ride a jet ski to the three-hundred-foot limit line, fake a wipe-out, and, in the process, toss their backpacks over the buoy line that kept anyone from getting too close to the dam. The backpacks were made of a woven rice material that would melt in the water, releasing the miniature submarines inside. The submarines would self-destruct within the four intake towers, where they would release many marble-sized chemical packets.

The plan began to come apart a few minutes after they got into the final channel. The dark clouds had moved in quickly and the thunderstorm started to churn up the water, making the water so choppy that they had an unplanned wipeout—further away from the fence than planned. They threw the backpacks anyway. One backpack hit the buoy line and bounced back on their side. The other one made it over the buoy line. They climbed back onto the jet ski. The storm intensified. Danielle had one arm around Craig, and with her other hand used a remote control and guided the tiny submarine toward the penstock intakes. Huge waves tumbled the jet ski sideways. They both fell off, and Danielle lost the remote. The safety cord pulled out the key, and the jet ski stopped and righted itself. They crawled back on and made for the Kingman Wash boat ramp.

They had just beached the jet ski and were walking up the sand to their truck and jet ski trailer when lightning exploded only feet behind them, crashing them forward onto their faces. Head-sized concrete pieces of the boat ramp landed all around them.

But no concrete boulders touched them. Allahu akbar.

The stage was set. Within twenty-four hours the caustic chemicals inside the submarines would destroy the turbine rotors. At least, if the submarine had gone where Danielle had aimed it. It did not matter, because Allah had saved them from the lightning. On one of the tours tomorrow they would get into the bowels of the reservoir, and cause an explosion that would make everyone inside the guts of the dam to evacuate, so no one would detect the corrosion until the spinning rotors had spun so fast they detached like flying missiles and destroyed the housing and most of the machinery. Repair would take years, and by then America would be theirs.

They reached their truck seconds before the storm released a torrent of rain, seldom seen in this desert land. The local Navajos would likely be thankful. This much water in one day gave life for months in the desert.

Craig kissed Danielle. She held it, feeling his joy. Then Craig started the truck and backed up to load the jet ski. Soon they would be in their motel. And in two days they would be on their way to heaven, martyrs for Allah.

Similarly, other jihadists had been placed at key reservoirs: Lake Powell above Glen Canyon Dam, Lake Mohave and Davis Dam, Lake Havasu and Parker Dam, and the Imperial and Laguna Dams near Yuma. The whole of the Colorado River would soon return to nature, destroying water distribution and hydroelectric power to millions in southern California, Nevada, Utah, New Mexico, and Arizona. And the greatest joy in the hearts of all the jihadist was that the most important seats of infidel impurity and depravity would be suffer the most: Las Vegas and L.A.

The only thing Rocca cared about was getting El Fahd, and getting him today. He sat inside the terminal outbuilding where the sergeant had escorted him to await Fred. Driving through the front gate and making it to the terminal, he had passed retired jets and bombers on display beside the roads, displaying the firepower of the military. With all this power, they could not get to Jabril. It would be up to Rocca. When Fred finally showed up, it was after seven hours, not five. And Rocca was pacing.

"What the hell kept you? I thought you guys had faster jets than civilians."

"Hi, Rock. Good to see you, too. It took slightly more than a few minutes to pull the strings necessary to get you approved. Some admiral working with the NSA in San Diego remembered an incident with you concerning guns and a shark on his amphib a few years ago. He thinks you're a loose cannon and he wasn't happy that we even asked. But, lucky for you, there were a number of others who remembered your valor in Desert Storm. And your ID of El Fahd, combined with Jack's death, clinched it."

"Sorry, Fred. Thanks for going to bat for me."

"No problem. I owe you from the desert, anyhow."

Fred looked at the ground and nodded. "We need to watch our six, though. You know how politicians and the Company can be."

Rocca nodded. "Yeah, they never take the blame for anything. I hear ya, pardner, loud and clear. So where do we go from here?"

Fred outlined a plan to catch up with Sam Houston, then use Alex Smith and his "connection" to find El Fahd. "The only problem is, we haven't heard from Sam for the last several hours. Let me try again."

Fred called Sam on speaker, but got, "I'm sorry, your Cingular customer is not available. If you would like to leave a message…"

He sighed. "Damn cell phones!" Then he left a message.

Rocca smiled at him. "Now you know how I felt when you were in the hospital."

"Yeah, you get used to things being so easy that when they don't work it really messes things up."

Rocca chuckled, "Cell phones and computers—give me a land line and paper file anytime. "So where was he last? Maybe we can head towards him and—"

Fred's cell phone chirped. He flipped it open and put it on speaker. "Sam, it's been a while. Where are you?"

Sam's clear voice was intermittently distorted with static. "I'm on Highway…five, going nor…turned toward Sali…"

"You're breaking up, Sam. It sounds like you're going towards Salida. If that's correct, we'll drive up Highway 50 and meet you at the Royal Gorge Visitor's Center in Cañon City. Is that okay?"

"Ten-four. Visitor's Center. Out."

Rocca was already grabbing his gear. "Scenic Cañon City. So let's go."

The drive southwest through Fort Carson on Highway 115 was pleasant in the autumn afternoon. Western clouds with wind-whipped edges blurred the view of the fourteeners of the Sangre De Cristo range. Within an hour, a gray-and-black billowing quilt covered the peaks. A storm was brewing. It was always difficult to tell how soon or how far it would push down the eastern slope. Mother Nature was hard to predict in the mountains, and usually just plain hard.

Weeks ago, Jorge had taken one blue-dotted vial from Rashid's lab, made several copy cultures, and shipped them via Federal Express to Khan. Khan had held onto them until recently, when he had sent them to D.C., Virginia, Pennsylvania, Omaha, Colorado Springs, Rome, New York, and several other cities and small towns, all near strategic bomb-proof bunkers that were meant to protect members of Congress, the president's cabinet, CIA, NSA, and all major military and civilian commands necessary to run the country in the event of World War III.

The chosen ones at each location had received their packages with excited anticipation. They'd infected themselves at Khan's directive days ago, knowing they would die but wanting the end result of this sacrifice more than their own lives. It was their calling, their duty, and they prayed for several hours that day. Soon they would be infectious.

One was a clerk at Offutt Air Force Base. He had lived in Omaha for twelve years, managing to pass all the necessary Civil Service exams and security checks. He was one of the "necessary personnel" who had been in the deep bunker with Senator Cardwell during the days after the September 11 attack. One of the main runners, he took coffee, papers, and anything else needed throughout the bunker. He would be there the next time as well, in about three days. Only this time he would be delivering something else. His nose had started running this morning, but nothing that would keep him from work. No one would know he was sick until it was too late. To ensure the infection spread rapidly, he planned to disable the special ventilation system for about eight hours. People would get warm and need cool drinks. If anyone asked why he was coughing and blowing his nose, he would say he had allergies. As he coughed and sneezed and ran cool drinks to all, he would be contaminating them all with his saliva.

The more people he infected, the better. He would start today, rubbing any nasal drainage onto papers, inject it into bottles of water and soft drinks, and do whatever it took to infect as many as possible, especially the ones in power.

He opened the door to Colonel Craighill's office, not scheduled to return for an hour, placed an infected file on his desk and sneezed on the computer keyboard.

CHAPTER 47

They were on their way to Poncha Springs, driving north through the San Luis Valley. If it wouldn't have been for Rachel, Alex would have missed it all.

"Alex, aren't they magnificent?"

"What? Those coyotes? I don't know if you would call them—"

"No, sweetie. Look around. Better yet, stop the car."

"I can't stop. Don't you understand? I need to hurry!"

"Please? I want you to get out and actually look. This has got to be one of the coolest spots in the world, and I want you to see it."

Alex could see he was fighting a losing battle. "Okay." He pulled over at one of the unlabeled dirt side roads that ran off into hills. As he got out, a truck with a camper passed them and seemed to get the same idea, pulling off a quarter mile up the road.

Rachel was right. The valley was surrounded by mountain ranges: the Sawatch, Sangre De Cristo, San Juan, Mosquito and Front Range. Together they included almost all of the fifty-four mountains over fourteen thousand feet in Colorado. Turning around in a circle was like being in Shangri La, the fertile, irrigated farms of the San Luis Valley surrounded by snow-capped mountains.

Alex's hurry-up agenda shut down. He just looked. He thought of a song he'd sung many times in grade school, just one of those songs they made you memorize and sing but that he had never really thought of, never felt the words, until now.

O beautiful for spacious skies,
For amber waves of grain,
For purple mountain majesties
Above the fruited plain!
America! America!
God shed his grace on thee.
And crown thy good with brotherhood,
From sea to shining sea!

"Alex, is there something wrong? You've been so serious this morning; I was hoping this would cheer you up." She wondered, *Did he regret last night?*

Alex gazed at the western mountains catching the soft light of the morning. The cool north wind on his cheeks was a reminder that winter was not far away in the high country. *God shed his grace on thee.* Did God shed grace on the terrorists who'd killed thousands? Was God somehow responsible for the unusual changes Alex had experienced?

And crown thy good with brotherhood, From sea to shining sea. Alex did not feel any brotherhood towards this hateful man that haunted his mind. All he wanted to do was kill him.

He looked at Rachel. *I do love you, Rachel.*

This is truly a beautiful spot…the mountains and…

But I gotta go.

Don't move. Stay here. Make it last before…hate…death.

He felt warm tears run down his cheeks.

Rachel touched the tears on his cheek and kissed him. "Hey, Alex. I love you."

"I know, baby. Let's go."

He brushed the tears from his eyes and got back in the car.

Gotta do this. She's gotta live.

Sam acted like a tourist. He passed Alex and Rachel's Jeep, then stopped in a vehicle pullover about a quarter of a mile ahead. He took out his camera and took some pictures while he waited. He needed the stretch.

Man, what a view. And in your own country. Didn't have to go to South America, or Switzerland. Enjoy a little piece of home. Nice.

He turned his head aside as their Jeep passed.

He hopped in the truck and followed the Jeep. Soon they were over the pass and down the canyon lined with autumn yellow trees and the occasional log cabin nestled into the canyon walls. They turned right onto Highway 50. The road through Salida passed diners, motels, 7-Elevens, a Pizza Hut and then finally curved right and out into more open farm land, and the Arkansas River was on his left. He wanted to stop, find a kayak rental, and go for it, all the way to the Royal Gorge. The tease of the river continued, turn after turn after turn.

Rachel worried about what Alex said as they started the winding road down the Arkansas River canyon. Neither one of them had said much since they'd pulled over on the other side of the pass. Sure, he had said he loved her, but had not repeated it after she had said it, only *I know, baby.* Was he just mouthing the words to make her happy? He seemed so preoccupied.

"Are you okay, Alex? I mean, if you don't really love me that's okay. I just thought…"

Alex glanced at her, his eyebrows raised. "Yes. I love you. Absolutely. Back there with those mountains and you and…" His voice got a hitch in it and he looked back at the road. Then he glanced at her again. "That was truly a cool thing. And it made me realize how much I really do love you. I've just got a shit load of stuff going through my head right now."

Rachel smiled at him. "So you *do* love me. That was not a one-nighter?"

"Of course I love you. And I can't wait for a repeat performance of last night. It was better than chocolate, or even fly fishing in Patagonia." He winked at her.

She threw her arms around his neck and hugged him.

He swerved to the edge of the road, gravel flying from the shoulder into the river. "Okay, okay. Now let me drive this thing or we are gonna get real wet."

The yellow Jeep Cherokee was like a bee buzzing back and forth down the canyon. The tea-colored river snaked beside them, carrying precious water to the plains and adding grit from the mountains.

Alex was worried now. The mental connection with the evil man seemed to be fading. How would he find him?

—

Jabril drove two miles over the speed limit until he arrived. The house was surprisingly rustic in appearance, outer walls of rust-colored stucco blended in with the surroundings. The only road to the house was not part of the county system, so it was dirt and gravel, and very neglected. But that had also turned out to be a benefit. The dust that rose behind any car gave it away miles before it reached the house.

Inside, pains had been taken to maximize the view of the surrounding grandeur. Windows were placed for strategic views of the Arkansas River and the Royal Gorge Bridge. One room had a panoramic view of the countryside, simple but effective for detecting visitors from a distance. The house also had a series of security defense systems installed to prevent any electronic eavesdropping, including, at the insistence of the Russians, extra thick, concrete-reinforced walls and a special microwave jammer. Until now, Jabril had thought it a waste of money. But now, experiencing the intrusiveness of mental eavesdropping, he was convinced that the extra systems were worth every dollar. At least he hoped it would stop this Alex from finding him.

He turned on the jammer and went to the master bedroom. There was a king-sized bed, an old phone sitting on a blonde oak bedside table, a pine rocking chair and a telescope facing out the large picture window. There was a car coming up the distant road, a dust trail behind it. He put an eye to the scope and could not only pick out the make of the car, but also the driver.

Jessibelle.

Jackson Pate was finishing his patrol of the secure zone of buoys at the mouth of Hoover Dam. The powerful twin Yamaha 80s allowed the seventeen-foot Boston Whaler to cruise at forty knots full out. He was going to make a quick run, but then saw something on this, the safe and non-secure side of the buoys. Probably more nasty litter from the damn tourists. He throttled back and came off plane and slowly cruised towards the object. Some kind of brown rucksack. Using the boat hook he tried to snag it, but the hook melted through the slimy appearing fabric. Then he caught something, a shiny bottle or can.

It was too big to be a can or bottle.

He called his boss.

CHAPTER 48

Jesse made the trip from New Mexico in record time, unfortunately, speeding fifteen miles over the speed limit the whole way. *Where were the cops when you needed them?*

She made one wrong turn, then found the correct single-lane dirt road. She rolled the windows up before too much dust blew in. The multi-level stucco house was picturesque against the bright blue sky and white puffs of clouds and beige and red earth dotted with sage and dark green junipers and red rock outcroppings. Maybe she could start building a place like this for her family outside Dulce.

Jabril was standing on the wooden plank front porch, eyes bright and smiling. She got out and felt stiffness in her neck and dread in her heart. He hugged her, squeezing tighter than she wanted, and kissed her, drilling his tongue way too deeply. She tried to act like his long-lost love, but her feelings about her family and Alex were tugging too hard.

"What is wrong?" He broke off the kiss and his dark eyes bored into her.

"My family is having trouble. I want to help them." It was true, making it easier to look him in the eye.

He looked up at the sky, his eyes critical of the clouds. "Your family has always had trouble. I thought you gave up on them. Besides, what I have planned will help them. You will assist in bringing Islam to the west and in ending U.S. domination over Native Americans."

She cocked her head and squinted at him. "What do you mean? I thought you were merely going to spread a little disease and then offer up the vaccine. Aren't you going to leave for Chicago soon?"

He looked back at her, but did not hold her gaze. His black tee shirt had a patch of sweat in the middle of his chest and he kept clenching and unclenching his right hand. "I was being tailed in L.A., so I had to change plans. But I was never going to spread a *little* disease."

"That's what you said."

"Yes, that is what I told you. Now things are different."

He told her about the bombs at reservoirs throughout the country, and the plans to infect the shelters for all the United States leaders and military infrastructure.

"There are several reservoirs on the South Platte River not far from here. Tomorrow you will set bombs at each and return here. You will then turn me in to the authorities, telling them you have had pangs of remorse, and it will begin."

Her mouth dropped partly open, and she lost focus. Did he know? Had he guessed she had real pangs of remorse? And what the hell was he talking about, bombing reservoirs? She pictured the Hoover Dam's monstrous destruction: A rumble deep inside, followed by cracks in the walls, dripping water, one crack spider-webbing, then enlarging. Huge pieces of the dam wall spewed, then gushed a green-brown wall of water and chunks of cement, taking everything in its path: trees and cars and houses.

Her mind multiplied this seven times down all the reservoirs on the Colorado River. Add one year and it would all be desert again.

It will be the end of the western United States for decades. I only wanted to make them wake up. Not this. This is…inhuman.

Then she realized that would only be the beginning. The entire government and military leadership would either perish or be too ill to function. The USA would be forever gone.

She started to shake. How wrong could she have been. Not this. Never this.

She recalled their college lovemaking days, his tenderness. He was not inhuman. She could convince him this was wrong. She had to. She forced in a slow breath and eased it out, trying to calm the panic to run. Run now and get help.

"Don't you think this is a bit drastic?" she said. There was only the tiniest quiver in her voice. She gritted her teeth. "I mean, giving everyone a little bit of disease that could be cured with your medicines is one thing. But completely destroying the lives of millions is another. Don't you remember your mother?"

His eyes flashed and sweat beaded his forehead. He partially raised his right hand and balled a fist. "Of course I remember my mother! Why do you think I am doing this? To hurt the infidels who bombed and starved my country murdered her."

"Do you really think it was the U.S. that killed your mother? What about Saddam Hussein? It seems to me he took most of the money that was supposed to go to the people and squandered it on himself and his royal family. Isn't that what we found out from your cousins last year?"

She stopped. *Went too far.*

Now both fists were clenched and he took a step toward her, so close she felt his heat and smelled sour sweat. Spittle clung to the sides of his mouth and his lips parted over his eye teeth. "Saddam Hussein saved me from being a cattle salesman. I am one of the chosen to make this jihad. And you make light of it?"

He grabbed her shoulders and shoved her backwards towards the bed. He was out of control. She had to do something.

She slapped him in the face and turned around to leave.

He grabbed her left upper arm with a vicelike grip that was strong—too strong. He'd always been strong, but this was much more. He spun her around like a toy, clenching her left arm and, with his other hand, grabbed her chin like her mother used to do to make her look at her. A faint red glow rimmed his large black pupils.

He released her arm and tore at her shirt, several buttons popping off. His eyes, those terrible, awful eyes, hungrily scanned her breasts.

"You will be mine now. Then you will obey me."

She was too stunned to move. He had changed: taller by several inches, thicker arms, his voice deep and robotic. Something was definitely wrong.

She had to change her tactic, make him believe she wanted him. Tenderly she put her hands on his face. "I'm sorry, my angel." He had always loved being referred to as an angel. "Of course I'm yours. Let me go shower and change. I'm so dirty and confused from my trip. I know you want me clean."

His grip on her face loosened. "Mother will be happy you will be clean. Not like those other whores."

He released her. "Very well. Do not make me wait too long."

She lowered her eyelids and ran the tip of her tongue over her upper lip. "I'll be right back." She glanced at the king sized bed in the room behind them. "Why don't you get into the bed. The sheets will feel wonderful." If she could get him undressed that might buy her more time.

Closing the door to the bathroom, she turned on the shower and quickly pulled out her cell phone from her pants pocket. It was difficult to dial, her hands were shaking so much.

Alex answered. "Hello, Jesse. What's…" and then the line was filled with static. His tone had been matter of fact, perhaps expecting some social call from her home.

"Alex! Are you there?"

"Jesse. Hi. You sound worried." More static.

"Alex. Thank God. But I haven't go much time, so stop talking and listen." She related Jabril's plans for the bombings and infections. "He's turned into some kind of monster. Get me out of here!"

"Jesse, I couldn't quite get…"

Jabril banged on the door, rattling the hinges. Jesse jumped and almost dropped the phone.

"Let me in," Jabril said, his voice sounding low and almost robotic.

She put a hand over the phone and took a shaky breath in. "Darling," She spoke loudly into the shower. "I have only just begun. Please give me some time. I feel so dirty. Please another five minutes. I will make it worth the wait." His steps moved away from the door.

Looking around, she spotted a window, just at her shoulder height, but only a twelve inches tall.

I'd never fit. But maybe…

She opened it and held the phone outside it in hopes of getting better reception. She quickly repeated her story to Alex, cupping her hand over the receiver to keep Jabril from hearing.

Outside the door Jabril went back and sat on the bed, then got up and paced. He stopped in front of the door and listened.

Jesse stuck her head almost out of the window. "Alex, hurry. I need—"

The door to the bathroom burst open, slamming the knob through the ceramic wall. Splinters flew from the latch. Jabril bulled into the room, pinning her between him and the back wall. His clothes were still on, yet his shirt was wet, his body so hot he must have a fever. He ground his hips into her and swiped his hand at the phone but she pulled it into her chest with both hands.

His breath was warm and foul on her nose and cheek. "Who are you calling?"

His voice had a monotone deep timber. No voice she had ever heard. It sent chills up her spine.

"My mother."

Jabril continued to breathe hard but said nothing. He backed away and frowned. Again she noted the crimson ring of his irises. He put a hand on her hands. "Let me see the phone."

She pulled the phone in tighter. "If I do, you're going to throw it away. I have to warn her. If we blow up all those reservoirs, my mother and my entire family will suffer, possibly die. I do love them. Especially my mother. My father finally quit drinking. We have a chance to be a family, and your hate and revenge may hurt them all. Can't you see that?"

Jabril felt the frailness of his own mother in his arms the day she died. He hated the infidels, yet he wanted to cry. He coughed and it felt like knives in his chest. His nose was running and he wanted to vomit. He backed off and plopped down on the closed toilet seat, arms hanging, mouth parted, feeling suddenly drained and unsure of what to do next. Surely Jessibelle had a right to call her mother. He closed his eyes and put his head in his hands. *What am I, a hate machine that dispenses revenge? Revenge for whom? Mother? Father? My people? Or just myself? Someone should pay for this life of hate.*

He saw his mother, helping children in the hospital—kind, compassionate, loving.

I could have been a doctor. She would have wanted that. That would have been good, right, pleasing to Allah.

Then he saw her wheezing and fighting for her last breath and felt her hand squeezing his before she died. Father had been right. Becoming a mere doctor was not Jabril's fate. *Allah wants more, Jabril. You can help* more *than a few. You can change the* whole world. *You are the avenging angel, Gabriel. You have a greater duty than to save a few innocent people.*

The voice of his teachers in Afghanistan reverberated: *Complete the mission—save the world from infidels. Jihad!*

He opened his eyes. A cool breeze from the open window ruffled the print on the shower curtain—teepees, elk, and mountain lions. He shivered, coughed and wiped his runny nose. Her cell phone was sitting on the windowsill. She obviously did not care if he looked at it now.

Where is she? He hurried out of the bathroom, leaving the cell phone.

Jesse was sitting on the bed, head in her hands, sobbing uncontrollably. When she heard him, she looked up briefly. Her beautiful hair was tangled, her eyes red and swollen from tears.

How long had she been crying? He put his hands out to her, trying to make his voice soothing. "Jessibelle, I am sorry. Allah has called me to the jihad. I must fulfill my destiny."

At his words, Jesse stood, eyes wide, body rigid, looking like she would attack him. "*Your* destiny! What about *my* destiny? My *mother's* destiny? My *people's*? You're as bad as the Arian Nation, or…Goddamn Hitler, Mr. Save-the-World from the infidels. You think *your* cause is so much better and you try to rape me? Are *we* not people too? Or just because we are black, or Jewish, or Baptist should we be wiped off the face of the earth?"

His sickness was worsening. There was not time for this. "You know this is not true. Islam will take in all the infidels who want to convert. They will find peace with us. I thought you agreed with me that the United States should suffer for what they have done to your people."

"Suffer yes, but only enough to change their policies. If you do this, there will be nothing left at all for my people."

He took a step towards her. This had gone on long enough.

She stood her ground and faced him, her palms raised as if fending him off, her eyes shimming in tears. "Jabril, please listen to me. All you seem to have is hate. But surely you can still see that murdering thousands, if not millions of people, is morally wrong. The U.S. has done some awful things, but in the end we respect the human being—the basic rights of life, liberty and the pursuit of happiness. Look at the Constitution. It doesn't start with 'Only Muslims, or Only Catholics, or Only Caucasians'. It starts with *We the people.* And you are one of them. You can live here and worship Allah and not be killed for it. Can't you see that? Please. Do not do this."

He took another step closer, held his palms out and took a deep breath in. This would be his last try to resolve her fears. "Jessibelle, you have said some truths. But Muhammad teaches that the belief in Allah is the primary way to save the world from destruction."

He hardened his voice. "The United States has outlived its ideals, its Declaration of Independence, and its Constitution. They only want to make more money. Other countries cannot be free as long as the U.S. controls their purse strings and their resources. All they want from my people is oil. A truly enlightened society does not need money, but only belief in Allah and giving to all. That is what I am after. Don't *you* see?"

Her shoulder sagged for a few seconds, then she straightened. "So who is going to control your *truly enlightened society*? Saddam Hussein? He kills anyone who opposes him. He acts like he believes in Islam to gain political power. He used the oil-for-food money for himself, purchasing as little food as possible, causing most of the deaths during the embargo. Don't you read anything but the Koran? Or maybe you would prefer to have Osama Bin Laden in control? If you decided you wanted to help some poor black Jewish woman in Louisiana, do you think he would allow that? He'd probably bomb your house. Or in your case, since you are one of his great colonels, he would cut off your head in a public ceremony, then set fire to your thousand-acre estate in Taos."

He coughed and grabbed her hand and yanked her to him. "You know nothing of Osama Bin Laden or Saddam Hussein! They are great men to whom I owe my life."

She shook with sobs. "What life? You will be dead soon. You've got that virus and will die within the next week. Now that I am here, I will die too. So what the hell. Rape me and get it over with. I'm already fucked."

Jesse knew nothing could dissuade Jabril. She wished she had never met him. She eyed the doorway.

The ringing of her cell phone in the bathroom startled her.

Jabril shoved her onto the bed and strode to the bathroom. "I will get it. I wish to talk to your mother, to…"

She couldn't let him answer it. She pushed off the bed and tried to side-step around him.

So, Jabril thought, *she does not want me to see the phone after all. A liar. Just like all the other whores.* He grabbed her arm and flung her to the floor. Her head bounced off the wall, and she did not move. He made two steps to the bathroom sill, grabbed the phone and opened the little clamshell.

There was static, then a man's voice. "Jesse, is that you? I got your message about the bombs, but it was still garbled. Please let me know where this is going to happen. Jesse? Where are you?"

Jabril closed the phone. Even as Jesse crawled away, he advanced on her, a slow determined walk, his leg and arm muscles suddenly engorged.

He heaved her off the floor by her hips, her tennis shoes stuttering on the wood, her breath catching in her throat. He threw her onto the bed. "You betrayed me. I thought you were different. But you are like all the other whores. So I will treat you like one."

Jesse felt as if this were a dream. Her head hurt where it had hit the floor. But she realized what was about to happen. Part of her started to stay in that dream, like the nights her father had lost it with her and her mother. Just let it happen and it will be over soon. Then he tore off her bra. She slapped him as hard as she could. He slapped her back with a hand like a rock. She blinked trying to stay conscious, then relaxed, once again hoping it would all be over quickly.

He ripped off her shirt, dropped his pants to the floor and eyed her naked body. His eyes glowed red. Every muscle in his arms stretched like a weight lifter's over his completely soaked black tee shirt. Rivulets of sweat poured off his face. He coughed hard, wincing with each spasm, then crawled atop her.

On his second thrust he screamed with release, a shriek that abruptly ended with another sound: a crack and tiny ring of the bedside phone that Jesse smashed onto his temple.

He fell onto the bed, blood oozing from the corner of his eye, dazed and moaning. Jesse pulled on her jeans, stuck her cell phone in a pocket, quickly donned a coat, and ran.

Minutes later, Jabril awoke. His head pounded and his vision was blurry. He shook his head and looked around. She was gone. The handset from the phone was lying on the bed, beeping. He grabbed it and beat it against the oak nightstand. It shattered. He tossed the broken fragment, took a deep breath and let it out, then calmly got dressed and ran out the door.

CHAPTER 49

Alex pulled over and stopped at the antique-looking gas pumps at the Cañon City service station. He was tired, hungry, and his back ached. They'd come through a thunderstorm and sleet still clung to the wiper blades. About thirty miles east of Salida he'd completely lost the mental homing signal on the man he was tracking. He couldn't wait to get out and stretch, hoping the open spaces out of the canyon would allow a reconnect with the man. He had just started to get out when his cell phone rang.

It was Jesse.

He stayed in the Jeep and listened intently, getting bits and pieces in the static. There was a man's voice, a loud crash, she whispered, "Alex, hurry!" and the connection ended. He hit *Redial*.

On the screen, the tiny phone connection-pending dial kept circling. Finally, *Unable to connect* lit the screen.

Rachel was leaning across the seat. "Who was that?"

"Jesse. She's in trouble." He looked at Rachel, remembering her tiff with Jesse. She would never let him go back for Jesse alone. He thought about last night. He thought about this morning and her doubts about his love.

"What happened?" she said.

"She's having relative problems. We may have to go back and pick her up. You go to the bathroom and get us some sandwiches. I'll fill the tank and tell you all about it when you get back."

She started to say something, then nodded and went inside. Alex called Jerry to tell him what Jesse said about the bombs and viruses. Jerry got very excited, but wanted Alex to get details from Jesse and then call him right back.

He called Jesse.

The tiny dial on the screen circled again but this time he heard ringing. The connection clicked on but no one said anything. Maybe she could hear him if he spoke. "Jesse, is that you? I got your message about the bombs, but it was still garbled." No response. He glanced at the phone screen and it still said *Connected*. "Please let me know where this is going to happen. Jesse? Where are you?" The other end terminated the call.

Jabril came back into his head with a suddenness that made him unsteady. There was hate, anger, and something else—Jesse was running from him.

Rachel walked back with the sandwiches and started to open the door, then must have seen his face and noticed he hadn't pumped any gas. "What's wrong?"

His eyes were closed and he could hear nothing. He realized he'd screwed up. The person he'd been talking to on the phone was not Jesse. A hot sharpness behind his eyes told him that he must have been speaking to the terrorist Sam had said was dead: Jabril El Fahd. *Should've made sure it was Jesse, waited for her to answer. Damn.*

"Alex." She put a hand on his shoulder and he opened his eyes and jerked his head up at her.

He could not let Rachel go with him. He massaged his temples with fingers and thumb. "Sorry. I got a terrible headache. Must be all the driving down that canyon. I also really need to go to the bathroom. When I come back I'll tell you all about it. You fill up. I'll be right back."

Rachel put the gas nozzle into the tank and turned on the pump. She watched Alex walk inside, get the key and walk around back to the bathrooms. What the hell was going on?

She took a deep breath of the cool air and decided to wait and let Alex tell her.

The station was old but quaint, with tall, antique soda-fountain-style gas pumps. She wished she had her camera. The gas pumped in slowly, and she surveyed the Wells Fargo bank across the road and wondered if she had enough money saved to make the cabin left to her in the Sierras livable, take in grand views with Alex, raise a few rug rats, forget DNA and viruses and—the automatic stop clicked. Putting the handle back on the pump, she decided she could use a little pick-me-up. She meandered into the store and looked for some chocolate.

M&Ms with peanuts. Oh yeah. Add a Diet Coke and I can drive for hours. Maybe the peanuts and chocolate make the Diet Coke pointless. But it works for me. DC current with a chocolate and peanut generator— vroom, vroom!

She finished making her purchases, started to walk out, then saw the tin of Excedrin on the counter. Might help Alex's headache. She paid for those and walked back to the Jeep, and planted her butt on the hood of the car, munching candy and sipping DC. Engorging her lungs with the cool fall air, she closed her eyes. The memory of making love to Alex last night gave her complete peace.

Finally she opened her eyes and glanced at the corner of the gas station with the toilets. *We didn't eat that much. Maybe he had a nervous stomach. Hope his headache is not too bad.*

A minute later she started to pace.

A white pickup truck with camper rolled over the old-time rubber rope, dinging a bell inside the shop. Not that anyone would come running to pump gas now. But maybe they kept it just to know a customer might be coming in. She looked again at the back corner of the gas station, then quickly ran to the restroom and yelled at the door. "Alex, are you okay?"

No answer.

She pounded on the door and shouted even louder. "Alex, come on! I thought you were in a hurry."

Nada.

She twisted on the doorknob. The door opened. The key was on the floor with a cherry-flavored roll of ChapStick neatly sitting on top like a little red rocket.

Where did he go? And what the hell is with the ChapStick?

Then she looked up. On the mirror was a note printed in cherry ChapStick.

Sorry Rachel. Don't want you to get hurt. See you in C. Springs.

He'd signed it with a big *A* inside a Valentine heart, with the front and back of an arrow on either side of the heart.

"Goddamn you!" Rachel screamed, hitting the metal mirror with her flattened hands, angrily smearing the note.

A male voice behind her asked, "Is everything all right, Rachel?"

Startled, she whipped around. The glare from the afternoon sun reflected off the picture windows of the store next door, outlining a familiar figure. Shielding her eyes with her hand, she got a view of the man's face: dark eyes, weathered tan, ball cap.

"Sam? Is that you?"

Sam moved to the side, out of the glare. "Yeah, it's me. Where's Alex?"

Rachel took a step out of the bathroom, shaking her head, feeling confused.

"I don't know. I thought he was here."

Sam peered into the bathroom, key on the floor, the mirror smeared with pink grease.

Rachel quickly pocketed the Chap Stick while Sam continued looking around the bathroom. "Sam, what the hell are you doing here? When we left you in Texas, I thought you were going to California to surf."

Sam looked behind the door, then picked up the key and shut the door. "I didn't buy the hallucination story about Alex at Amazon Lab. I know what I saw and I remembered Alex saying he wanted to go after El Fahd. We though he was dead, but then I got word that El Fahd escaped, so I decided to follow Alex. He seems to have a homing beacon on El Fahd."

Rachel started back to the Jeep, breathing slowly through her nose to keep from crying. Sam walked right beside her, his shoulder almost touching hers.

"Rachel, where are you going? Talk to me! Where is Alex?"

"I told you. I don't know." She pushed him away.

Then ran.

Sam was quick, but not quick enough to catch her before she slammed the door of the Jeep and locked it.

She opened the center console and picked out the cell phone. *Thank God he didn't take it. Now I can find Jesse. And where Jesse is, Alex will go.*

Reaching to turn the ignition key, she found none. She looked on the floor, felt under the seat. *Nothing.*

There was a tapping sound on the window. Sam smiled and pointed to the keys sitting on the hood, where she'd left them.

"Open the door, Rachel." He exaggerated his lip movement so she had no trouble understanding.

Butting her head back against the headrest and simultaneously beating her palms on the steering wheel, she screamed, "Fuck!"

Then she reached under the steering wheel and started fumbling with the wires.

Staring at the multicolored wires, she hesitated. She pulled a pocket knife out of her pocket, looked at the wires again, and put the pocket knife back. She was a scientist, not a car thief.

She opened the door. "I gotta find Alex. Get in and help or get out of my way. "

"Anything for a damsel in distress."

CHAPTER 50

Senator Cardwell should have felt great: he was sitting under his bear with Robby by his side to tell the tale of how they had caught the terrorist Jabril El Fahd and watch Kyle Rucksman turn green. But something was wrong. He looked at his watch again. Rucksman was an hour late. He wanted to sneer at Rucksman, laugh at the incompetent CIA when he told him about capturing El Fahd. The country was well on its way to winning this war on terror, due to him and his laws. President Randolph B. Cardwell—had a nice ring to it.

"Robby, find Rucksman. I want this concluded before my dinner date. I have a party planned with friends."

Kyle Rucksman walked in the open door. Robby sat back down.

"Well it's about time." Cardwell stood and glared like the bear.

"Senator." Rucksman nodded at Cardwell, though his gaze held no respect. "We have identified the man Robby here thought was El Fahd."

"What do you mean, 'thought'? You told me it was him." Cardwell squinted sideways at Robby.

Robby looked like he'd been accused of cheating at cards. "It had to be him. We followed him from Los Angeles, and he had the same face as on the poster."

Rucksman shook his head but kept a straight face. "Not El Fahd, we're certain of it. El Fahd had no facial marks. When we shaved this man's beard, there was a mole, big as life. Someone who had actually seen El Fahd before has ID'd this man as an imposter."

Cardwell stared like a deer in headlights.

He'd make a good meal for that bear, Rucksman thought, keeping his face bland. "Have a good night, Senator."

Rucksman did a one-eighty and left the room. As he closed the door he coughed to disguise his laugh.

Rocca had seen twenty people go in and out of the Wendy's outside his room at the hole-in-the wall motel where he and Fred had been waiting for the call. Across the street was a pawn shop. Down the road was the Royal Gorge Visitor's Center. There were a few trees, some with leaves turning yellow, but mostly there was asphalt and cement. Not really a pretty part of town. They were just around the bend of Highway 50, east of the Cañon City prison, a.k.a. the Colorado Territorial Correction Facility.

Rocca left the window and paced across the beige, threadbare carpet. *This guy Sam Houston better call soon.* Eventually he stopped pacing and started doing push-ups. On number forty the phone rang.

Fred, who'd been watching a John Wayne flick on the tiny color TV, answered it. "Yeah, where are you? I know the spot, I'll be there in a minute. And, Sam, don't let her out of your sight."

Rocca stood up, slightly breathless. "What's going on?"

"I'll explain on the way."

Once inside the POS rental Ford Taurus, Fred drove like he owned the road, both sides. Rocca held onto the arm rest. "Sam," Fred said, "is with a woman named Rachel Lane, and they are following another guy named Alex Smith who has some kind of sixth sense and can track El Fahd."

Rocca winced as they nearly picked off a bicycler on the shoulder. "Sixth sense? Are you guys still running those paranormal experiments from the '70s?" *Been better off with my guys back at the Broadmoor.*

"No, we didn't train this guy. He had an incident down in the Amazon and we've been following him since."

"The Amazon? What the hell were you doing down there?"

"I wasn't down there, but Sam was and… It's a long story. Let's say we have it on good authority that this guy will lead us to El Fahd. And El Fahd is very close."

Fred drove through one red light and turned into a quaint gas station where a man and a woman were standing next to a yellow Jeep Cherokee and a white pickup with a camper.

Fred jumped out and strode over to Sam, shaking his hand. "Good to see you, man. This must be the famous Rachel Lane. Sam Houston and Rachel Lane, meet S.S. Rocca, otherwise known as Rock. He's been chasing El Fahd for quite a while now, starting in Jakarta. He lost a good friend, Jack Dillon, to a bomb El Fahd exploded. So he has, shall we say, a personal interest."

Rocca nodded at them both and shook Sam's hand, then started getting into the Jeep. "We've been waiting too long. Let's go."

Alex used side streets to pick his way southwest of town, where he found a dirt road that was level and ran on the north side of the Arkansas River. He couldn't sense Jesse or El Fahd, but based on his prior feeling he was going the right way, so he ran, and ran hard. A part of him worried about his heart, like when he'd had that attack with Lora. But he had to get to Jesse. He poured on the speed and felt fine. The road ended and he dropped over to the railroad bed that ran beside the river. He still couldn't sense Jesse, so he kept running. The canyon deepened, and he started to worry he would never connect with Jesse. Then he saw the Royal Gorge Bridge and the connection to Jesse hit him again, and then became strong. But she was on the other side of the river, which was now a raging torrent. He would have to go for a swim.

He was swept away twice. Both times he lost his footing and had to grab onto rocks to keep them from braining him and crawl back to the shallows.

He looked back at the rapids. They weren't quite the Class 5 rapids of earlier summer that brought thousands of rafters every year, but they were still too much for him.

Dripping wet and gasping for breath, he rested a minute and studied the distant bridge he'd read about in the pamphlet Rachel had showed him. The tallest suspension bridge in the world, the Royal Gorge Bridge stood over a thousand feet above the river. From down here, it looked a lot further away. The Royal Gorge Train track glinted in the sun. The track climbed from the river up the side of the gorge all the way up to the top, ending at the park. If he could get to the train, maybe he could ride it to the top. But between him and the train were vertical walls, too dangerous to climb. Over here the walls up to the bridge looked steep but scalable.

Though he wasn't hungry or dizzy from not eating—weird for him— he was thirsty and it was going to be a long climb. He cupped a hand a few times and drank until sated, then started to climb. Once he was at the top he would cross the bridge, no drowning required. *But don't look down.* The thought made him dizzy.

He had done some wall climbing before, but this was a tad higher than a thirty-foot wall and much trickier to get handholds. Yet he moved easily, climbing the granite walls like Spider-Man. Resting infrequently, he forced himself to avoid looking down and moved quickly, up and up toward Jesse and her stalker. He could feel their signals, stronger and stronger. Once at the top, he ran around boulders and through gradually thickening groves of cedar trees and scrub pines. The Royal Gorge Bridge wasn't far. Hopefully the park caretakers would let him pass through without incident.

Jabril ran out of the house and peered around for Jesse. Her car door was open. It had been a wise move to take the keys. On foot she would not last long. He'd walked these hills many times, so he knew the terrain. Jesse didn't. The night was coming and the fading light would make it even harder for her. He had no doubts he would find her. And he had another advantage: he could smell her.

He raised his head and sniffed slowly, breathing in fully, wanting every odor.

It was there, but very faint. Maybe I was out longer than I thought.

A cough racked his body, bringing him to a standstill, bending him double while he tried to catch his breath. Wiping his nose with his sleeve, he shivered. The virus was taking hold fast. He had to find her quickly. He saw her footprints. and started running after her.

Jesse had been running up and down red sandstone hills, dodging piñon and juniper and sage without a problem until she fell, barking her knee on a rock. She swore, got up and tried to clear her mind as she had been taught by her father in order to sense what was ahead. Soon she was moving between the obstacles faster and more sure-footed. She could see the distant shadow of the canyon. She could escape Jabril there.

Before that, she had to get to an open space. Maybe the cell phone would work and she could call Alex back.

She heard something and stopped, listening. There, no doubt about it: a distant cough. Jabril was coming.

Hurry!

Down the hill the trees disappeared into an open space. She opened the cell phone and hit redial. Two beeps sounded. *No Service* flashed on the screen. She ran another fifty yards onto a rocky clearing at a bend in the river and tried again. It was ringing.

A woman answered. "Jesse, is that you? This is Rachel."

"Where is Alex? I need to talk to him."

"He's trying to find you. Where are you?"

"I don't know. Jabril is coming for me. I have to go."

There was some speaking in the background, and then a man's voice came on. "Jesse, this is Sam. Leave the cell phone on. We'll get a fix on you and be there soon. We're not far."

Jesse twisted her head back at the sound of another cough. Closer. But she had to explain so her parents wouldn't think she was a traitor. "Listen closely. Jabril and I have been friends since college. I never knew he was this…crazy. He recently told me about a plan to bomb the major reservoirs in the U.S., including the Hoover Dam, Lake Powell, and several others in Arizona and in Texas. Anyway, he's infected himself with a virus like the ones we were using in the Amazon. He sent vials of the same infected blood to several other sites. These are nuclear bomb shelters around the U.S. The sites are located—"

She stopped talking. There were footsteps in the woods behind her.

She kept the phone open in her hand and sprinted across a small creek.

Rocca had gotten out of the Jeep when Rachel's phone rang. She mouthed, "It's Jesse." They all crowded close to her.

Sam heard her say the word *Jabril* and said, "That's our guy. Let me talk to her." He held out his hand and Rachel hesitated, then gave it up.

Sam held the phone tilted away from his ear so Fred, Rocca and Rachel could hear. He was about to put it on speaker, when he started getting more static. He pushed the receiver to his ear. But her words were still disconnected: *"He recently told me about a plan to bomb...reservoirs... and several...sent vials of infected blood to other sites...nuclear...the U.S. The sites are—"*

Static.

"Jesse, where are the sites of infection?"

A garbled word.

"Jesse? We need to know *where*."

His reception ended with static.

"Can't you get a fucking trace on her cell phone?" Rocca yelled.

"Take it easy, Rock," Fred said.

Sam held up a hand and pulled out ear buds from his pocket and plugged them into the phone so he wouldn't miss anything. He wanted to tune out Rocca, yeah, but he also didn't want everyone to hear what he thought he'd heard. *Nuclear.* He dialed her number. "Jesse, please come back."

Static...no discernible words...*End Service.*

Rocca and Fred were having words and Fred had his hands on Rocca, keeping him back.

Sam tried twice more to call her. The second time, he got some static and the word *nuclear* again.

If they had nukes, Sam had to report it. And now. Then they would have to find a bomb shelter. The closest would be Cheyenne Mountain, about forty-five minutes away.

Sam felt a cold prickle run up his back and he leaned against the Jeep.

Rocca shouldered through Fred and Rachel and grabbed Sam by the shoulders. "What is going on?"

Sam turned around quickly, eyes boring into Rocca. "I can't hear anything if you keep bothering me!"

Rachel put a hand on each of the two men's chests. "Come on now, fellas. We gotta get along, here. Sam, give us a quick update. Okay?"

Sam held up a hand and tried calling her again. Nothing but beeps. The power on the cell phone was out. He pulled out the ear plugs. "Rachel, you got a car charger for this thing?"

"Yeah, sure, but tell us what she said first." She took the phone from him.

He glanced from one to the other, debating. They had a right to know. "She said something about nukes."

"Nukes?" Rocca beat a fist into a palm. "Holy shit! This guy is planning on nuking someone? I knew he was bad news when I first laid eyes on him. So he's going to nuke the reservoirs, then what?"

Sam knew he'd heard the word *nuclear*, but couldn't put it together. He looked at Rocca, then Fred. If he could just think about this for a minute.

Rocca took a step towards him.

Fred put a hand on Rocca's shoulder. "Give him a chance, Rock." Then he eyed Sam. "You want to elaborate?"

Sam shook his head. "I didn't say that, Rock. She said they were going to *bomb* the reservoirs, then *infect* other sites. I don't know where the nukes come in."

"I heard that first bit," Rachel said, "Didn't she say Jabril was going to infect other sites with the same virus he had contracted?"

"Yeah."

"If we could get a sample of his blood, maybe we could figure out how to combat it."

Fred started back to his car. "If there are nukes involved, I gotta fill in some people at Peterson, and in person. Keep me informed." He slammed the car door behind him and laid rubber peeling out of the station.

Rocca watched him go. "What? No good-bye hug?"

Rachel fixed Rocca's gaze. "Once we find him, I want you to promise not to blow him to pieces before we get a good blood sample."

"If I get a chance to blow him away, I'm gonna take it. He's bad news, and we should wipe him off the face of the earth as soon as possible. You can scrape any blood you need off the rocks when I'm done."

Rachel looked at him like he was from another planet. "It would be best if he was still alive. Fresh blood. Some of those viruses don't live too long in a dead host."

Sam's own cell phone chirped. He took it out and listened for a few seconds, then cracked a big smile. "Great job. You guys are the best."

He ended the call. Rachel and Rocca were staring at him. "From the minute Alex left San Antonio, I put a tracer on all his calls and asked them to update me after each one."

He paused and smiled at them. "I've got a location for Jesse."

CHAPTER 51

Alex made pretty good time initially going up the gorge wall, but then slowed. He had run over five miles before starting and fatigue finally set in. Darkness fell and he had to slow even more. Couldn't hardly see the next place to put a toehold. He was never going find Jesse in time at this rate.

Then a change occurred. His eyes adjusted and he could see again, though only in black and white. His fatigue seemed to vanish and his pace quickened. He felt like he had in Brazil, as fluid and quick as a leopard. *That's more like it.* With each step Jesse's presence grew stronger, but so did Jabril's.

The bridge was just over the next craggy stack of dark rocks. Yeah, had to be. Alex was sure it would materialize. But no. More trees and rocks.

He ran faster.

There were the occasional heavy footsteps and scrabbling over loose gravel behind Jesse. She was able to keep Jabril about a quarter-mile behind her as long as she kept running. As a little girl she had developed the ability to move quickly and quietly through the woods. It came in handy now as she cruised effortlessly around trees and over rocks. After running in almost total darkness for an hour, a half-moon rose and gave her more illumination through the pine and cedar shadows. Jabril would also be able to see better, and the thought made her run faster.

For a while.

She was not in the shape she had been in as a girl, so after an hour she had to slow considerably, her muscles pushed to the limit, lungs burning, the taste of copper in her mouth. She walked, then ran, then stopped to listen and to keep her bearings using familiar stars.

A distant cough and she started jogging again.

Jabril was also pacing himself, breathing hard and coughing even at a slow jog, stumbling over a dark sage bush, his face lashed once by a piñon branch. He was tiring too quickly. Nothing left but his will. If he could bring on anger, that had helped in the past, especially with his new…powers. He thought of his mother and tried to will his body to overcome the sickness. *I can rest in a few hours.*

If Jessibelle was not there to turn him over to Cheyenne Mountain generals, what would he do?

He could hear his mentors in Afghanistan urging him on. *Run faster. Allah and Muhammad are waiting!*

He slipped on a sandy rock and pitched forward, slamming his forehead onto a hard object. Everything went dark.

Alex was running hard when trees ended abruptly at a cliff.

His boots slid on the broken rocks and his feet came out from under him. His hips crossed the edge of the precipice, and instinctively his right hand did a backstroke, grabbing for any purchase. A lone pine saved him, its roots clinging to the small bits of soil wedged into a crack in the rocks. His heart pounded. One pine needle gouged a finger.

His feet flailed over the edge as he clutched the small, scraggly pine in his right hand. Charlie Brown's Christmas tree was going to save him. His other arm flapped like a wing. He wanted to scream, but instead he concentrated on searching for something else to grab besides this tiny twig that would surely snap any second.

But, as small as it was, the tree held.

Alex managed to turn over on his stomach, embracing the little sprig with both hands. With a few deep breaths, he grunted and strained and finally pulled himself up over the edge.

After sitting for a few minutes, he examined his savior. That fact that it was growing out of a small crevice in the rocks was miracle enough, but having a root strong enough to support him and his momentum? He might come back and water it himself for the next decade.

The half-moon shown on the gaping gorge—a seemingly bottomless crack in the earth. How the hell had the river cut through all this rock? The pamphlet he'd read said it had taken three million years. Yet it also said the river had only carved away ten inches since the birth of Christ. If Christ had been in this same place, with the same moon and sky, he would have seen the same thing. There must have been some sudden change to get through all this rock.

He looked out at the vista, the moon revealing every detail like midday. No, Christ could not have seen the same thing Alex's new improved eyes could see. He thought about evolution, about the river and realized he could be a sudden change in man's evolution.

After a few more minutes he dared a peek over the edge. A thousand feet below, the white and dark slashes of the river seemed a trickle, the only clue of its power the barely audible rushing sound. He jerked back, nausea and dizziness enveloping him. It would have been nice if that change had taken away his fear of heights.

He gazed across the chasm. *Jesse, I know you're over there. If I could jump over I would.*

A loud noise behind Jesse made her run. At top speed she came out of the forest to an open space. Too open. She skidded, twisting onto her stomach, her hands wind milling, grabbing for a purchase, anything. But she was not as lucky as Alex: There was no Charlie Brown Christmas tree for her to grab.

Floating over the edge, she felt weightless. Panic and darkness were her only companions.

CHAPTER 52

They were finally on their way. Sam had grabbed a large duffel of gear out of the camper, then parked it on the side of the station, locked it, and told the owner he'd be back. He tossed the gear in the back of the Jeep and hopped in. Alex's phone was plugged in to the car charger and sat in the center console drink holder. Sam held his phone in his left hand. Rachel drove west on Highway 50, the tires squealing around each curve. Rocca was in the back seat, breathing slowly and methodically, readying for battle and trying to calm his nerves against Rachel's swerves. With help from Cheyenne Mountain, Sam used Jesse's phone signal to triangulate her location.

In the dimming twilight, dark clouds were massing to the west. Then it was dark and all they could see were the headlight beams ahead. They crossed over the Arkansas River, then turned south at Parkdale on Highway 3.

Sam's phone chirped and he answered it. The voice on the phone from Cheyenne Mountain said, "Sam, we lost it."

"What do you mean, you lost it?" Sam shouted at the phone.

"Sorry, partner. Signal's gone. We'll see if it comes back and let you know right away." The connection ended.

Sam closed his phone. "Fuck!" He beat the side of the door with his right hand. "Fuck! Fuck! Fuck!"

"Sam?" Rachel said, "Uh, can you give us a clue?"

Sam took a breath let it out slowly, then another. "They lost Jesse's cell phone signal."

"Now what?"

Rocca squeezed her shoulder with a big hand. "We continue to the last location of the cell phone. If El Fahd got her, we can only hope he's not far."

"But if he got her, wouldn't he just leave?"

"Yeah," Sam said, "but Rock's right. It's all we have." Sam looked at his GPS unit. "Turn left at the next dirt road. We'll have to hoof it."

Rachel turned left onto a rocky, bumpy dirt road that headed mostly east and north, back towards the Royal Gorge. Dust clouds flew in front of the headlight beams. After a jerky fifteen-minute ride through taller pine trees than they'd seen previously, the road ended at a turnaround on a hill, the beams shining over the hill into darkness. She skidded to a stop. Rocca jumped out, ran to the back of the Jeep, opened it and grabbed the gear: flashlights, ropes, flares, water, and breakfast bars.

"Where's your gun, dude?" Rocca said.

Sam gave Rocca a wan smile and shrugged his shoulder. "I lost it in the Amazon Lab. Got an extra?"

"All I've got is my .45."

Sam looked at Rachel. "You said Jerry gave you a gun?"

She pursed her lips and shook her head in a slow exaggeration. "You're not getting my Glock."

A westerly wind whooshed through the tree tops, creaking the trees, though it was calm where they stood.

"Someone has to stay with the cell phone at the truck," Sam said.

Both men looked at Rachel.

She folded her arms and her jaw muscles flexed. "I can probably out-hike both of you."

"We'll draw straws then. Or in this case, twigs." Sam made a big show of taking three twigs and breaking off the ends, making one much shorter.

Rocca put his hand out, did a little eeny-meeny-miny-moe with his index finger, then plucked out the middle one. Long.

Rachel grabbed one quickly. It was short. "Shit." She stuck her open palm out. "Give me the phone."

"Take this walkie-talkie, too," Sam held it out. "It has a range of about five miles. If my calculations are correct, Jesse should be about three miles east of here. Her coordinates are marked on both our GPSs. If they call and change the location, revise the coordinates and radio them to us."

"Got it." She put the cell phone in her pocket and took the walkie-talkie. She looked at him, sighed, then reached around her back, pulled out the Glock and held it out to him, handle first. "Here. No telling what you'll run into out there. I'll sit tight inside the truck."

Rocca turned the flashlight on and adjusted the rope on his shoulder.

Sam grabbed the gun, but she held onto the barrel. "Sam."

"Yeah."

"When you find Jesse, bring back Alex, okay? He should be roaming around out there with his doggy sniffer on full power, so be careful with those guns. Don't just shoot *anything* that moves."

Rocca smiled. "You like this Alex guy, huh?"

"You could say that." She let go of the gun.

Sam nodded his head at her and stuck the Glock between his belt and butt.

Rocca's head nodded once at her, as if he were tipping a cowboy hat, and he and Sam headed out into the night.

The moon helped them initially, but storm clouds soon ended that. There was no trail, the trees so close together and the brush thick so that even with flashlights it was slow going. After a half-hour of dodging trees and tripping over brambles, Sam called a halt.

He looked at the GPS unit. "At this rate it'll take hours to find her. And that's only if the terrain doesn't get any worse. If this wind dies we could call in a chopper in the morning and be there and back in an hour."

A gust of wind rushed above the trees. Rocca's flashlight beam went up at the tree tops, then straight ahead. It only penetrated about twenty feet into the bush. "Yeah. Maybe. But if we keep looking tonight we might have El Fahd in custody in three hours." He glanced back where they'd come. "And we'd have Alex." He shown the light up at the bending tree tops. "Besides, if the wind keeps up, there'll be no choppers flying tomorrow."

They pushed on. The occasional strong whooshes above them became almost constant. The temperature got colder. They came to a clearing and Sam was literally blown off his feet by a gust. Rocca picked him up and the two leaned against the wind, making it to the next grove of cedars, gaining some relief.

They moved on cautiously.

Rocca yelled over the din, "I wish I had some night-vision goggles."

Another gust of wind and a loud crash in the pine trees ahead. They both stopped.

"What the hell was that?" Sam yelled. He shown his flashlight ahead. "I can do sharks, eels, and stingrays. But bears? At night? No fucking way!"

A weird sound drifted to them: the scratching of dry paper.

Rocca reached out and grabbed one of the tree branches. It snapped off. When he opened his hand, Sam saw dead brown needles, like a Christmas tree left without water past New Year's.

Rocca was barely audible over the wind. "These are all dead trees. Probably beetle-kill. That crash must have been one getting blown down."

Two more crashes came, one up the hill to their left and one ahead of them. Then a rolling, crunching sound came from their left. Both of their flashlights beams shone on a boulder the size of a small bear, rolling over the sage and finally smashing into a tree twenty feet ahead. A wave of sleet pelted them.

"Let's go back." Sam yelled. "I'm not up for death by bashing."

Sam's flashlight beam fell on Rocca. His hands were gripped in fists, the one holding the flashlight quivering. He looked at Sam for ten seconds. "God damn it! As soon as this shit dies down, you call your chopper friends. And if this wind doesn't go away by first light, we hit it again."

"Sorry, buddy. But if we die now, El Fahd will likely be gone forever. Anyway, he won't be going anywhere in this stuff either."

They gradually picked their way back. The Jeep was there but no Rachel. The door was unlocked. No keys inside, and the walkie-talkie and cell phone were gone.

"Great." Sam pulled his gun and motioned for Rocca to go around the back of the truck.

CHAPTER 53

Earlier that afternoon, sixty-four miles west of the White House at the Mount Weather Emergency Operations Center, the senior staffer in charge of computer maintenance, Jeffrey Messmer, made a call. The Xerox copier/fax machine wasn't working again, the second time this week, and this time he was going to make sure the damn thing got fixed.

Mount Weather was well hidden in the Blue Ridge Mountains. Even though the 600,000-square-foot center was like a small underground city, with its own emergency power plant, living spaces for several thousand people, hospital, and radio and television studios, it didn't have a Xerox repair technician. It was late, but the maintenance woman who lived in nearby Berryville, Virginia, had told Jeffrey to call any time they had another problem. It didn't hurt that she was a looker. He hoped she was feeling a little better. Last time she had the sniffles and turned down his offer for lunch. Maybe this time he'd get lucky.

Rebeca answered the call and forced herself to keep from coughing until the staffer hung up; then a paroxysm brought her to her knees. She was getting sicker by the hour. Though she felt bad and did not want to leave her bed, it was important to infect as many as possible, which was why she had rigged the fax machine to break down again.

Rebeca was not her real name, but being known as *Jasmine* along with her dark complexion would never do, especially now, after the Great Event. She took two gulps of cough medicine: she didn't want to raise any alarms by having a coughing fit. She would merely produce a few strategically placed coughs into the fax machine and between several reams of copy and fax paper. Then everyone who handled the paper would be infected. She was also the main repair technician for the multitude of computers inside. Over the last two days she'd contaminated every machine. Allah would be pleased.

She drove through a gate and waited while the thirty-ton, five-foot-thick blast doors opened to the main complex. In a few days, after the next disaster, hundreds of important government officials would be swiftly and secretly dispatched here to run the U.S. government.

One of her cousins, Juan, lived in small rural town an hour and fifteen minutes north on I-81: Waynesboro, Pennsylvania. He was a computer repairman at Site "R," another emergency underground command post. Located at Raven Rock Mountain astride the Maryland/Pennsylvania border, it was much less secret, with multiple antennae and satellite dishes adorning its exterior.

As in any typical rural town, nothing happened in Waynesboro without everyone knowing it five minutes later. Like all the helicopters and buses around Site "R" after the September 11 attack. His reports of this to Al Qaeda led to the "Next Day" plan.

Last week, Site "R" had had many computer and fax problems. Of course Juan had been called in to fix them. The model of politeness, he'd apologized profusely each time he had to reenter the secret facility. His coughing and sneezing had kept most of the workers at bay, but the computers hadn't minded.

Tonight he had been called again. After wiping his phlegm on machines for two hours, all he wanted was go home and crawl into bed. A shaking chill suddenly gripped him and made him drop the screwdriver he was using. The sound echoed off the bare tunnel walls like a gunshot. In a few days it would be filled with crowds of people. The virus needed company.

Allah would be pleased.

Jabril had made it, so Khan was happy. All his plans had been set in motion, and he would be out of the country in a few hours. He started his usual computer scan before he logged off and noticed someone had tried to access his computer from a different site. At first he thought it was another one of those hidden cookies from porn sites, but it was too subtle for porn. This was sophisticated: CIA or NSA.

He made another reservation under another name for a flight that left three hours earlier. It meant a connection in Houston first, then on to L.A., but it had to be done. Unfortunately, he had to depart from the same airport as the prior flight, Colorado Springs. He went to the bathroom, put in green contacts, fit on a bald pate and slightly bigger earlobes, and stuffed cotton in his cheeks.

A thought hit him: he glued on a soul patch, added a tie-died Grateful Dead tee shirt, white bell bottoms with a rope belt that hung down in front, and dark glasses, then took off the longer earlobes and put on an earring. The more garrulous he looked, the more likely they would ignore him.

Once inside the airport, he was a little nervous. Security had been hyped up: extra patrolmen, dogs sniffing packages. He sauntered by them, swaying his hips. No sniffs from the dogs. Not even a glance from the patrolmen.

Once he got to L.A. he got a call from one of his friends at the Colorado Springs airport. Apparently, an hour after his plane took off, a cadre of agents in gray suits and sunglasses arrived. They searched everyone, even the outrageous bald black man with gold incisors, a muscle shirt, and a tattoo of the American flag on his shaved pate.

She had worked on the CIA director's floor at Langley for nearly five years—mopping floors, vacuuming, emptying the garbage. Everyone knew her as Evelyn the cleaning lady. Even though her background had been thoroughly checked, no one was really worried that she had immigrated from Iraq nine years ago. She was obviously mentally retarded, or "arithmetically challenged," as some of the computer geeks joked. Everyone felt even sorrier for her when she had got that cold a few days ago. Some offered lozenges and tissues so she could blow her nose. They didn't have the heart to tell her it was rude to cough without covering her mouth. Nobody noticed when she rubbed her nose with her hand, then rubbed that hand all over the computer keyboards in each room.

What no one knew was that she had lost her children and sister in the Israeli bombing at Lebanon. Then she had lost the rest of her family after moving to Baghdad just before the American bombing in 1991. That's when she had joined the jihadists. After a year of training, she was sent to the States and manipulated into her job as a janitor. Nine years of patience, and she would finally get her revenge. Though she knew the disease would kill her, it was worth it to see her children in Heaven. Tonight, she added a few extra prayers for them.

CHAPTER 54

Two days earlier, Lieutenant Goloff, head of security for the Hoover Dam, had had a decision to make over lunch, in between bites of pizza. Earlier that afternoon, one of his roving patrols had found a small remote-controlled submarine and called the bomb squad. Funny thing though—the "bomb" barely had enough explosives to blow off a trash can lid. All it had inside were a few small packets filled with simple chemicals: muratic acid and potassium hydroxide, normally used as pool additives and drain cleaners.

One of his men asked, "Lieutenant, do you want us to cancel the tours?"

"Tours? Heavens, no! This was just kids fooling around." He thought for a minute about the recent planes flying into the World Trade Center and Pentagon. Surely those terrorists were not dumb enough to think their little bomb and chemicals could take out the six-hundred-foot thick walls of the Hoover Dam?

"We still have the extra patrol on the inside sector of the buoys and an extra guard on the external walls, right?" He had instituted those watches himself after the September 11 attack. It was called initiative.

"Yes, sir."

He dismissed the man and took another bite of pizza. The crust was excellent.

Rocca's flashlight beam came around the front of the Jeep and he saw movement at the edge of the trees. He pointed his gun at it. "Put your hands over your head and walk into the light."

A figure walked slowly towards him, raising a hand as a shield from the flashlight, but it also covered their face.

"Point that fucking gun somewhere else," Rachel said. "I had to go. Can't a girl have privacy?"

Rocca lowered the flashlight and gun, and Rachel lowered her hand. She walked right up to Rocca and said loudly in his ear. "Back so soon? Wind scare you big boys?"

Sam had come from around the Jeep and now he shook his head. "We thought someone took you and the cell phone! Next time leave a note or something."

"Jeez, aren't we touchy. If I would have had paper and a pen, I might have left a note. But then again, maybe not. You're kinda cute when you're mad."

"Give me the phone."

Sam snatched the phone from her and quickly tapped in a number. Walking to the Jeep with his back to them, his conversation was inaudible.

Rocca smiled at Sam and then back at Rachel. "Nice one." He held out his gun. "Hold this. I gotta piss, too. And don't be turning the flashlight on me."

"You guys are always comparing. Why can't I?"

Rocca walked off behind the nearest tree, chuckling. *Alex, you lucky son of a bitch.* Another tree bent in a wind gust and whacked his tree. Branches fell onto him. A coyote howled in the distance.

Rocca and Rachel walked to the Jeep. Sam sat in the driver's seat.

"What's up?" Rocca said. He piled in the back seat and Rachel got in the front. They both had to pull hard on the doors to shut out the biting wind.

Sam said nothing. His head rested on the back of the seat, eyes on a distant thought.

"Come on," Rachel said. "I'm sorry already. I had to pee and didn't want to miss any calls. Didn't think you'd get so worried."

Sam twisted around in his seat to face them. "When the higher-ups heard the words 'nuclear bomb,' this entire exercise changed. Tomorrow morning, the government will move from D.C. to our major nuclear bomb shelters." His jaw muscles flexed a few times, and he puckered his lips out and relaxed them, looked at the ceiling and sighed. "And, oh yeah, we've been ordered to go to Cheyenne Mountain as of 0800 hours tomorrow." He closed his eyes. "No helicopters will be helping us."

Rocca beat a fist into the back of Rachel's seat, sending her bouncing forward.

Rachel's eyes were wide. She kept shaking her head over and over. "What about Alex?"

"Guess it never hit me until now. A nuclear holocaust in the U.S.?" Rocca said. He thought about his sister, her new baby, fly fishing on the St. Vrain. All gone. "We gotta find Jesse. Now."

"Yeah," Sam said, "But we're getting nowhere with this wind."

Sam had been here before, many a mission put on hold at a critical time. It worked out, one way or the other. He settled in his seat and tilted it back. "Maybe we should try to get a little sleep. One of us can keep watch. If the wind lets up, we go."

"Sounds good to me," Rachel said. "You and Rocca get some shuteye. After all, you're the ones who are going out to look for Jesse as soon as things calm down. I'll take my gun and a flashlight and patrol outside to stay awake."

Rachel paced around the Jeep while they slept.

Wind rushed like a freight train. Trees crashed. The temperature dropped to the low twenties. Sam's friends at Cheyenne Mountain would have told them that an Arctic low-pressure system had moved over the Sangre de Cristo Range, colliding with moist air from the Gulf of Mexico. Snow was already blowing at 9,000 feet, and a winter storm watch was being posted for the eastern foothills.

Rachel pulled her coat closer and paced faster around the truck. She screamed at the howling wind, "Come on, God! All we need is a little break!"

Sleet pelted her like God throwing pebbles.

CHAPTER 55

At the edge of the Royal Gorge, Jabril awoke slowly, cold and in total darkness. Sniffing, he felt a crinkling sensation on the left side of his nose, like dried milk. He lifted his head and thought his forehead would explode. He touched a swollen, tacky lump on his left temple.

"Aagh!" He cried out. More gently he probed the sticky center and traced a trail of what must be dried blood down to his nose.

Then he remembered. *Something hit me. But what?*

A gust of wind answered his question, rattling the limbs on the fallen tree three feet above his supine body. Scooting out from under the tree and sitting up gingerly, his head hurt worse, but he was thinking clearer. The wind must have blown down a tree that hit him.

Dried blood. He'd been here awhile.

Taking inventory of his body, he noted abrasions on his hands where he must have caught himself falling. There was a bruised feeling on his left thigh, and his neck was stiff.

He took a deep breath and gradually stood. The headache improved. Then he coughed.

It was like a bomb exploded behind his eyes. He grabbed his head in his hands. *Don't cough!*

He glanced at his wristwatch—4:05 a.m.

If I don't find that bitch soon—then he caught her smell, a trace of spice and fruit from her perfume and the sour of her sweat. He started walking slowly, warming, the aches lessening.

The area was much more rocky and jagged here next to the gorge. The wind had subsided. The eastern sky started brightening. He started running, pain forgotten. *Today's the day.* If he had to, he would kill not only Jesse, but the infidel who had been clouding his thoughts—although his headache seemed to blot out any feel for the blond man that Jesse had called Alex.

Alex's scraggly savior of a Christmas tree was a distant memory. For the last six hours he'd been maneuvering across the north side of the gorge. He climbed over a fist-shaped boulder, dodged a dead spruce branch, and pushed through some junipers that smelled like cat piss, all in total darkness and in wind that threatened to blow him over the side.

He finally came to the Royal Gorge Bridge and Park entrance. Sparse streetlights illuminated a parking lot with one car parked in a far corner. Looked like a Honda Accord. The visitor's center had some weird things going on with white clocks, one for the day, one for the month, one for the year, and the standard time clock. Kind of an Alzheimer's checklist. At least he knew it was 4:10 a.m. There was no one in the little booth to raise the gate, so he walked around it.

Cables the size of his arm, probably twenty or thirty of them anchored in the cement and rock, fanned out on this side, then converged into one sheathed bunch that served as a suspension cable curving up to the top of two derrick-looking things, then back down on the other side. A sign said *10 MPH*. Not a problem. Walking across the bridge would be a piece of cake. Except for the wind. Leaning against the wind at almost a forty-five degree angle, he started forward. Then he noticed that the bridge surface ahead of him was made of wooden planks placed crossways, like an old covered bridge. Whose idea was that?

He stepped on the planks and felt it jitter and sway with the wind. Maybe he should have tried that swim across the river. Over the side he caught a glimpse of the immense dark chasm below and his stomach fluttered. Lots of time to think before hitting bottom. Talk about your life flashing before you. More like a slow burn with a bang at the end.

He grabbed onto the guardrail. At least it was metal. With his eyes focused straight ahead, he walked forward, moving his hands one over the other, never losing grip on metal rail. It was a long bridge. It felt like an hour passed before he finally saw the other cable coming down, and then he no longer felt wooden boards but solid pavement under his feet. He wanted to kiss the ground, but instead he started running. Up a slight incline with diagonal parking spots, past a building on the left. He smelled the buffalo and bighorn sheep before he saw the fence that kept them in.

The road went southwest into taller pines, but Jesse and her joyful heart pulled him more northwest, following the jagged line of the gorge. He could sense Jesse's hope and joy and almost hear her kidding him, though she felt very weak. *Jesse, I'm close now. Hold on, kid.*

There was also the other guy, way too strong. He had a darkness that felt like hate and guilt and lust all twisted like the cables of the bridge into a strength that made Alex pause a step. Yet there was a fray in the cable, like he was sick.

The wind died and the sky behind him became a pale gray. His paced quickened over the jagged ups and downs of granite alternating with soft soil and sage. It was so much easier with light and no wind it almost felt sinful. He kept his head up, sure to see Jesse any moment.

In a small motel in Las Vegas, Craig and Danielle awoke, ecstatic. After their jet ski adventure with the backpacks yesterday they were ready for the next step. The first tour was at 9:00 a.m., and they would be there. They got ready. God was great.

Craig put his head through the hole in the center of a large, flat rectangle of molded plastic explosive. It hung on his shoulders like a poncho. He cinched the Velcro straps, snugging it to his torso. Another strip of Velcro was strapped around his waist. He added a gray wig, whitish mustache, and a loose-fitting Hawaiian shirt to create the appearance of a middle-aged professional wrestler, thick-chested but gone to pot.

Danielle's disguise was just as odd: a middle-aged, obese woman with Semtex molded around her waist to form a pear-shaped body hidden under a rather colorful muumuu. A bleached-blonde wig with some brown roots, a well-molded and blended silicone nose and cotton inside her cheeks made her the quintessential California grandma touring the West. The wiring and tiny electronic detonators were in what appeared to be money belts around their waists.

The plan was simple and well-rehearsed. On the tour into the bowels of the dam, she would feign exhaustion and shoo away the tour guide, saying, "I take a little more time than most. Go on ahead. We'll catch up." With the guide out of sight they would quickly disrobe, take off the Semtex, place it on top of the pipes that ran above the walkway, set the timer, don their clothes and return to the tour. They had timed it during practice—two minutes and forty-five seconds. By the time the tour guide got suspicious, the explosion would be over. Easy.

Upstream at the Glen Canyon Dam, a young couple with several small children was preparing a similar explosion on their tour. Having three children with little backpacks, toys, and a baby carriage allowed for plenty of areas to hide plastic explosives.

Downstream at Davis Dam and the massive Mojave Reservoir, an elderly woman was preparing to meet her son for breakfast. They had arranged a special tour to view the inner workings of the dam. She had professed to need her own special wheelchair, which they would bring along. Most of the foam in the pads and most of the motor housing had been replaced by plastic explosives. They were both prepared to die in the depths of the reservoir. Hot-wired jihadist visitors planning similar tours of other reservoirs downstream in a few hours. All of these massive bodies of water were key to the distribution of water and hydroelectric power from the Colorado River to the southwestern United States. And, over in California, jihadist hikers were planting explosives up and down the length of the L.A. aqueduct, including its hydroelectric plants. The southwestern United States would be crippled for years, perhaps decades.

In L.A. the lights would go out, showers would end, phones become useless. If you had gas and a generator, you could power the basics, like refrigeration, a few lights and the TV. If you had stored-up water, you could last a few days. But when the water ran out, so would your luck. All the major roads to the city would be closed, and all air carriers grounded due to the spreading sickness. The Watts riots would look tame compared to what followed. The City of Angels would soon become the City of Death.

All the "Dam Bombers," as they called themselves, had met periodically to review their plans. In three hours all the planning would pay off.

They were very surprised, actually, for they had planned it all right under the noses of the FBI. They laughed in their last meeting, as one said, "Hey, it's a free country. You can do whatever you want as long as your neighbors don't find out."

At the end of that meeting they prayed for a perfect world, their world, Allah's world, where everyone obeyed the Qur'an. Today it would begin.

CHAPTER 56

Rocca had been walking all day, carrying the heavy pack, and all he wanted was to get warm and rest. Now he'd found it. The bottom of the deep ravine held a gin-clear river, intermittently lined by willows and groves of aspens in full yellow-and-orange fall colors. The breeze fluttered, the leaves making barely audible rustling sounds, like a pompom shaking next to his ear. Another sound bothered him: a hollow tapping sound. A red-cockaded woodpecker's head ratcheted back and forth on a dead pine above him. The sound grew louder, drowning out everything.

The bird disappeared, replaced by Rachel's knuckles knocking on the window.

"Wake up, guys. The wind is gone."

Rocca sat up, his muscles quivering, skin prickling, breath steaming in the icebox of a Jeep. Sometimes two hours of sleep was worse than no sleep at all. Especially when a blanket hog takes yours. Rocca had been on the right back, Sam on the left, both with green Army blankets, Rocca's Army blankets. He punched Sam's shoulder. "Hey, blanket thief, we better get going before Rachel breaks the window."

The sky was gray and there was enough light to see Rachel, and she did not look happy.

Sam sat up quickly with his forearm up in a classic karate blocking move, still half covered in a green blanket. "Is that what that noise was? I dreamed it was dead trees falling from the wind." A corner of his mouth ticked up. "Really sorry about the blanket, but I'm a beach guy. Don't really go for cold."

Opening the door of the Jeep, Rocca swung his legs out and started around the back of the Jeep. Rachel stood solidly, arms folded, cheeks pink, cheery except for her glare.

"Good morning, Rachel," Rocca said. "Jeez, it's cold."

"Tell me about it. But the wind finally died. We should go." Only her eyes moved, tracking Rocca like he was the slowest turtle on earth.

Sam poked his head out the other door, the blanket around his shoulders, peering over the windshield at her. "Any calls?"

Her eyes moved to Sam like he was the rabbit she was about to eat. "Shit, no. They're probably still sleeping in their warm, cozy beds."

"Okay, Rachel. Chill. Let me have the phone and I'll see what's going on." Sam held out his hand over the windshield.

Rachel leaned over the windshield from the far side and slapped the phone into Sam's hand with an audible smack.

"Fine! Call them. And for the record, my ass is chilled. In fact, if I put my hands in my back pockets they might get stuck there, my ass is so cold. But you, on the other hand, need to get the lead out of yours so we can find Jesse and Alex."

"Okaay!" Sam took the phone, got back inside and closed the door.

Rocca came back with a green wooly pully on. He opened the front passenger door for her and gestured an open palm. "Why don't you get in the truck and warm up?"

"You think the cold bothers me? Well, it doesn't. What bothers me is Alex out there roaming around in this gale all night, dodging dead tree limbs, and risking his life to find Jesse while we were sitting here, waiting."

"He's probably holed up somewhere, too. I mean, if Sam and I couldn't manage to keep up the search with all our combined field training, what makes you think Alex could? He's only human."

Rachel stopped pacing. "Right," she said. But she looked like she was wondering about that answer.

In Langley, Virginia, a small cadre had been up all night in a room with easy chairs, a leather couch, some hi-end stereo equipment and computers. They'd been watching a large computerized map of the Royal Gorge area of Colorado. Almost at the center was a blinking beacon showing the GPS signal from Jesse's phone. It had not moved for hours.

A man with a headset sat back in an easy chair. He hadn't moved for several minutes and his eyes were closed, but he wasn't sleeping. His was the concentration of a world-class chess player pondering the next move. The others in the group were in a similar state of suspended animation, sitting or lying around the office in easy chairs, on the couch and a few on the carpeted floor. Many hadn't moved for the better part of an hour.

A few hours earlier, they had received information that had begun a process that had kept half of Washington, D.C., awake throughout much of the early morning hours. Even after the disaster of September 11, the possibility of a nuclear strike made everyone antsy. More like frantic.

The timing was also on the bad side of worst. Two weeks after the September 11 attack, and the crews had had no sleep during the first week, busy getting the underground government facilities running. Then, two days ago, they'd put everything back in storage and everyone had just gone home for a much-needed rest. And now this. They were all exhausted.

Just outside the isolated rural town of Bluemont, Virginia, the process of reopening Mount Weather had begun. They alerted the security personnel, turned on computers, ventilation, and reconnected power supplies, everything necessary to run the underground city in case of a nuclear strike.

The duty staffer called the computer and copier technician once again. Though he wanted to watch Rebeca's ass when she bent over to repair something, he didn't want to bring her in, after observing how ill she'd been last night. But it had to be done. She was by far better than the other techs, even when she wasn't a hundred percent. And he needed all the computers to be absolutely, one-hundred-percent ready today; tomorrow might bring a lot of semi-permanent visitors.

Rebeca waited to answer the phone until after she'd first coughed up a sticky string of white mucous. "Hello, I.T. Incorporated." She kept her voice cheery and without the last days' hoarseness.

"Hi, Rebeca. Sorry to bother you again. But we need to have a general check on the entire system."

To Rebeca that meant only one thing. It had begun. She smiled into the phone and willed her voice to sound even perky, with a hint of desire. "I'll be there in about an hour, Jeffrey. I need to do a few things at home first."

"No problem. Take your time. You have all morning, though it must be done by this afternoon. You sound so much better. My offer still stands for tonight."

Wonderful. He was still trying to get into her pants. Well, she was feeling a little better after that cold medicine. What the hell! Allah would surely forgive her for one small indiscretion. After all, she was going to give up her life.

"Sure! Where do you want to eat?"

Jeffrey answered quickly and, after she agreed, he hung up and thought, *This is shaping up to be some kind of day after all*. He walked outside and took a deep breath of cool fall air. Closing his eyes he let the wind blow through his hair and enjoyed the warmth of the rising sun on his face. Life was good.

CHAPTER 57

Jabril walked, this time slowly and cautiously, to the edge of the gorge, his breath steaming and a slight wheeze with each breath. Though it was light now, with the glint of sun in the east, Jesse was nowhere to be seen. Raising his head once again he breathed in deeply through his nose. He could not sense her via telepathy, but maybe he could smell her. Snorting slightly, he cleared his nasal passages and sniffed again, this time in short gentle bursts.

There. Peaches and cloves and…blood. He licked his lips and quickly moved upwind, over one car-sized pancake rock, and threaded through several piñon trees, their shadows hiding the ground. He slipped and slid on loose shale, catching himself on one of the pines as one knee smashed the loose rock. He took a minute to get his footing. The musty smell of peaches and blood overpowered the pines. She must be close.

After passing through the trees he looked up. On a rock ledge about thirty feet below the rim of the canyon lay Jesse's body, face down, one leg canted at an odd angle, a dark patch on the thigh of her jeans.

Jabril watched. Was she alive?

He waited. Yes, there it was again—the slightest ebb and flow of her rib cage. Breathing.

He called her name, "Jesse! Are you okay?"

No movement but her breathing.

Was it a ruse? After last night she wouldn't trust him. Might not answer, hoping he would leave. Her leg looked odd. Must be broken and bleeding. Impossible to climb out of this wilderness in that shape.

He started to walk away. Let the buzzards and coyotes have their feast.

After a few steps he stopped and slowly looked over his shoulder. She might have the phone. He could not let her speak to anyone.

Retracing his steps, he spoke very calmly as he walked, "Jesse, I'm so sorry. What can I say? I lost my head. But, you know, you're absolutely right. I will call them off. It is too much. Your mother would be endangered. My mother would want me to be more tolerant. Can you forgive me? Please. Raise your arm or move your head if you hear me."

Ten minutes earlier Jesse had awakened as if drugged. She tried to turn over and screamed in a whisper, "Shit!" The pain in her right leg was excruciating. Using all her inner strength, she rolled over and sat up, suppressing a scream and gritting her teeth.

She had to be quiet. Jabril was out there somewhere.

Nauseous from the pain, she waited for it to clear. As it subsided, she surveyed her surroundings. Fifteen feet up was a large spire of granite.

Then it came back to her, her accident in the dark, hours earlier.

Last night she had gone flailing over the edge, grasping for anything, tumbling like a kite without a tail, rocks and water waiting eleven hundred feet below. Her hands found the spire, and it saved her life. It changed her momentum from going over the edge to swinging her legs down into a wedge between the granite wall and a bent gnarled juniper tree. The ancient tree had grown almost horizontal, stretching for the sun and blown by the wind.

Had she been a trapeze artist, she could have slipped the tree trunk behind her bent knees and dropped down on her feet. Instead, her right leg had slipped down to mid-thigh, wedged between the granite wall and the tree, and her backward momentum had snapped her right femur, then dragged her loose. Most of the time she enjoyed being a tall, muscular woman, but the extra weight and momentum had probably contributed to her broken leg and would make it hard to move. At least she had good upper body strength.

Below the tree trunk she saw a soft pile of gravel and sand, with a groove the width of her body, apparently formed by her unconscious body sliding downward to where she was now. She needed to get out of here before Jabril found her. Looking around for the phone, she saw

movement out of the corner of her eye above the cliff edge. The gray
dawn light was faint, but enough to see one piñon jiggle hard and rocks
rattled out from under the shadow. Jabril.

There was no time to retrieve the phone. Frantically she looked around
for a weapon. Anything. At the base of the gravel and sand, something
glinted in the sun. Barely able to reach it, she quickly pulled grasped a
long, thin shard of flint and rolled over onto her stomach, covering the
hand and weapon with her body.

The new wave of pain was too much. She passed out.

CHAPTER 58

Sam drove through the twilight before dawn with the accelerator mashed to the floorboard, oblivious to pencils, maps, and Diet Coke flying. Rachel was in the front, navigating via the handheld GPS with one hand, the other holding tight to the four-wheeling bar on the dashboard. In back, Rocca leaned into the turns and held onto the back of the seat. Back west down the bumpy dirt road, Sam turned left onto Highway 3, south a mile then east on 3A over a paved but windy road surrounded by pines. A few miles west of the Royal Gorge Bridge, Rachel told Sam to turn left onto another rocky dirt road heading north toward the Royal Gorge. The Jeep jerked up and down, side to side; the headlights flitted between road and trees and bushes. Sam gripped the wheel and peered into the gray shadows, Rachel held the GPS in one hand, the other now white knuckled on the four-wheeling bar, and Rocca grunted, bumping against the side.

Sam stomped on the brake and the Jeep slid, barely stopping in time. A slight yelp came from Rachel. What must have been one of the oldest pine trees on the hill lay across the road. Judging from the jagged, cracked-off base, it had blown over in the night. With its easily three-foot diameter, the gargantuan was going nowhere without a crew of lumberjacks, chain saws, and a much bigger truck.

"Guess we walk," Rocca said as he got out and went around back.

Sam picked up his sat phone and connected to Cheyenne Mountain. "Any chance of a helo in the next hour?" He listened for a few seconds, then said, "You do know she's our best hope of finding out if the nukes are real?" He listened a few more seconds, then ended the call.

"And?" asked Rachel, leaning over the center console, eyebrows raised.

Sam clicked his tongue. "They said they might consider a helo if we find Jesse. But since Jesse's phone hasn't moved since last night, they're guessing she's dead, end of story."

From the back of the Jeep, Rocca grabbed supplies, including a .45 that he loaded and settled into a chest holster. He pulled out a large coil of rope, pitons, and rappelling gear, and stuffed them and a box of bullets into a day pack. "Guessing's a poor excuse for reality. What say we go and find out for sure?" He swung the pack onto his back.

Rocca kept the flashlight trained on the gear while the other two got ready. Sam grabbed another flashlight, his gun and extra ammo while Rachel rummaged around and found a butt pack. She sorted through the materials she'd brought with her in preparation of going to Cheyenne Mountain and settled on surgical masks, a black plastic garbage bag, silastic gloves, eye shields, syringes, needles, rubber tourniquets, and viral blood culture tubes. She stuffed them into the butt pack.

She gave Sam her Glock and extra ammo, and looked up at Rocca. "Don't kill El Fahd before I get blood."

Rocca shrugged.

Sam put a hand on his shoulder. "We need him alive for questioning, Rock."

Rocca swiped Sam's hand off. "We'll see."

Over the next hour they trekked and scaled over the hillside north of their truck until the eastern orb finally came up and illuminated what they'd been hoping for: a break in the trees.

The fatigue of the last twenty-four hours was settling in to Alex's body faster than he could run. Now that it was getting light, dodging trees and scaling up and down rock buttes was easier, though his legs burned and felt rubbery as he moved down a steep incline. He glanced up and he saw something ahead around another stack of flat rocks. On a ledge lay the outline of a body. Was it Jesse? He stepped forward to get a better look. Something crumpled under his foot, pitching him forward against the stack of rocks and sending a shower of rocks over the side.

—

Jabril stood on the hill overlooking the ledge where Jesse lay and sensed Alex getting closer, could feel his anxiety over Jesse, could almost hear his heartbeat. He also figured since Jesse had spoken to Alex, he must have alerted others who would be with him. Jabril had to make sure Jesse was dead, or she would spoil everything. He walked and jumped down the escarpment toward Jesse. Halfway there, the sound of falling rock made him snap his head up stop and look away from Jesse. Rocks crashed down the side of the chasm like a hammer hitting a cement wall. On the east side of Jesse, following the wall of the canyon was a deep ravine, and ten meters up from the bottom was a three-meter vertical stack of flat rocks, and fifteen meters up from that were piñons and granite spires. Even though there was no person to see, that stack of rocks could easily hide Alex and several others. Jabril must hurry.

When Jabril had turned his head to find what caused the rock slide, he'd missed Jesse's arm moving slightly. She was regaining consciousness. Even that slight movement sent a shock of pain to her leg, immediately reminding her that Jabril was close and she must remain quiet and still. And any more pain might cause her to faint again. She screwed her courage to stay awake for one final, swift turn. It would hurt, but she had to make it count.

Jabril ran down the incline and jumped the last two meters, both feet landing with a solid thud on a flat rock only a meter from Jesse. He eyed the stack of rocks on the other side of the ravine. Still no movement. He glanced back at Jesse. She did not move.

All he had to do was throw her over the side. He took a step forward.

When Jesse heard his full body weight land behind her, she reflexively opened her eyes halfway. A flashy reflection peered at her out of the gravel, inches beyond her grasp. *The cell phone!*

Then she felt his knee in the small of her back.

Jabril decided to kneel on her back, and snap her neck before throwing her over the side. She at least deserved a humane death. His mother's words hit him: *You must love others, Jabril.* Had he loved Jesse? Had she loved him? Certainly she had helped him and the cause. Perhaps his threat to her family was too much. Family was important. Maybe he should take her back to the cabin.

But Alex and the others were coming.

He put his knee on her back.

Instantly, she became a writhing animal. She twisted her head and those dark eyes stared right through him. If there had been love in them it was gone. He wanted to say he was sorry, reassure her that he could stop it all, tell her everything would be okay.

A sharp pain gouged into his stomach.

Jesse backhanded the point of the long, thick splinter of flint into the pit of Jabril's stomach, all the while holding his gaze with her furious hate.

His eyes were surprised but sad and remorseful and searching, as if he didn't understand.

"What'd you expect, asshole? You rape me and have no qualms in killing my parents and destroying my country. All for your precious fucking Allah!"

She forced the flint in further and twisted it, left it in him and pushed him and he fell back against a rock, eyes glazed. He hit the ground with a grunting sigh.

She turned and crawled toward the phone on hands and one knee, dragging her bad leg. Her heart hammered and she was surprised at how little pain there was. She grabbed the phone and flipped it open.

Sam slowed from his jog, stuffed the Glock in the back waist of his pants, and pulled the chirping phone out of his jeans pocket. Rocca bumped into his back and he slipped on a patch of gravel and almost dropped the phone.

"Hello? Anyone? This is Jesse. Is anyone there?"

Sam regained his footing, fumbled the phone, finally got it to his mouth. "Yeah, it's Sam. Where are you? You okay?"

"Listen, I need to finish telling you what Jabril had planned."

Sam sat down on a rock, concentrating. "Right. I'm listening. When and where are the nukes and biological weapons to be used?"

—

Jesse's vision was fading and she felt light-headed. *Nukes?*

She crumpled to the ground, onto her stomach. She strained her abdominal muscles, hoping to push some extra blood to her head for a few seconds. *One sentence. Get it straight for Sam. There are no nuclear bombs.* She took a deep breath and her vision cleared.

You can do this.

She started to raise the phone to her lips.

A boot stepped on her forearm, pinning it and the phone to the ground. The jagged flint shard pressed on the side of her neck, dripping onto her skin.

She twisted her head.

Jabril's angry face and remorseless, penetrating red eyes filled her vision.

CHAPTER 59

Jabril had felt the flinty knife surge and twist: a terrible cramp deep in his bowels. He fell to the ground, closed his eyes, thankful it was finally over. Her look of anger and resentment had filled him with doubt.

Am I someone to hate?

For as long as he could remember there was death and destruction. Perhaps now he could rest, maybe not with Allah, but rest nonetheless.

I am sorry, Mother, for what I have done.

Losing consciousness, he felt such comfort. Then a familiar voice echoed in the deep reaches of his fading mind. It was the voice of his mentor at the training camp in Afghanistan. *The jihad is our calling. Muhammad has prophesied that you are the one. You must fulfill your destiny. The infidels must pay for the death of your mother and the destruction of Iraq. You must be strong to the very end.*

He opened his eyes. Comfort had vanished, yet he felt no anger, no hate, no love, no pity. Nothing. It was as if all emotions left him like water out of a broken pot. The only thing left was a numb void.

Jesse stopped talking. She was crumpling to the ground.

Pushing himself up, he pulled the shard of flint out of his belly and stepped toward the unconscious woman. It was his destiny to fulfill Allah's wish.

Her right hand held a cell phone. Her eyes fluttered open. She pulled the cell phone to her lips.

He stepped on her phone arm, pinning it to the ground, then placed the bloody flint shard on her beautiful neck.

He peered into her wide and tearful walnut-brown eyes and saw fear. In a deep, emotionless robotic monotone he said, "You must die."

He slashed her throat and tossed her body and the phone over the side.

After slipping on the rocks, Alex got to his feet and saw a man bending over Jesse. *Jabril! No!* She rolled over quickly and stabbed him. Jabril fell backwards. Jesse crawled away, out of his sight.

Relief washed over him. Jesse had killed Jabril. *I'll be there in a minute, Jesse.*

He started down the ravine between him and Jesse, glancing down to avoid another tumble. A few careful steps later he looked up at her again and froze. Jabril stood on the ledge, arms outstretched, and Jesse was flopping like a rag doll over the side, her head akimbo, blood gushing from her throat.

"No-o-o-o-o-o-o!" Alex screamed and began running and slipping down the ravine.

Jabril heard Alex scream and saw him running towards him. Jabril wanted to stand his ground and fight this infidel. Yet his legs were like jelly, and he felt dizzy. He could not fight this infidel, let alone the others that must be with him. He must escape, though when he tried to run up the incline from which he'd come he could only limp and crawl. With one hand he palpated the abdominal wound. It was almost closed, healing. Then he felt his leg muscles swell, his breathing eased and he was able to run up the hill. He remembered the dream of being Al-Buraq, the winged centaur. It was Allah showing him he was destined for the gods. And now it was true. He could certainly outrun this mere mortal.

Over the phone Sam heard an eerie baritone say "You must die." The call ended abruptly. Sam was about to say something into the phone when a scream echoed outside of the phone.

No-o-o-o!

Every muscle tensed. Sam stowed the phone and took out the Glock. The yell seemed to have originated about a quarter of a mile to the northwest.

Rocca and Rachel, who'd stopped walking and leaned on a tree when Sam answered the phone, jumped to their feet at the sound of the scream.

"That was Alex," Rachel yelled. "I'm sure of it."

Rocca adjusted the pack on his back, ready to run. He took the .45 from his holster and clicked off the safety and frowned at Rachel in confusion. "I thought you were talking to Jesse, Sam. Wasn't Alex with her?"

Before Sam could answer a loud crashing, like someone running through the woods in abandon, came toward them. Rocca figured the runner was about two hundred yards in front and to their left, directly from the northwest, where the scream had been. Everything ahead was shadows of trees and rocks. They couldn't see anything moving, but the pines and cedar were pretty thick where the sounds came from. Whoever it was must be scared and moving fast. And they were getting closer.

Rocca leveled his gun at the approaching noise.

Rachel grabbed his arm, pushing it earthward and screamed, "What if that's Alex? You might kill him!"

"And if it's El Fahd," Sam said, "We need him alive to get the information."

Rachel held up the butt pack. "We need his blood, remember."

Rocca shrugged off Rachel's hand. "El Fahd in the leg. Anyone else I'll let go. But let me do my job!"

A man burst through a clump of cedars and tall sage two-hundred yards to their north. He wore a black tee shirt and dark pants torn at the knee. His face was dark and his eyes locked on Rocca for an instant, an instant of mutual recognition. Jabril El Fahd. Rocca's reaction was immediate. Against his better judgment, he aimed low, toward the thigh, not the heart.

He pulled the trigger.

Jabril vaulted a fallen tree between a clump of sage and cedar into an open area. Several yards to his left was the guard from Jakarta, gun raised, pointing at Jabril. How could this be? How could this man know he was here? Jabril jumped to his right into the gap between two cedars and ran, pain slicing into his left buttock. A gunshot echoed behind him.

He dodged pine trees and hurtled rocks and sprinted northeast toward the Royal Gorge Bridge.

He could hear footsteps of Alex chasing from the northeast, Sam and his group from the southeast. Soon Jabril would be at the Bridge. On the other side he would have more options. One of his compatriots worked there and had left his Accord in the parking lot. Always have an escape route.

But he did not want to escape. He wanted to finish it. If he drove to Cheyenne Mountain and turned himself in, surely they would take him, a wanted terrorist.

Though his cough had improved and his nose was almost dry, he should still be infectious. His immunity had always been strong, so it didn't surprise him he was feeling so well. More than well. Perhaps he would tear off the head of the general.

Allah's will be done.

Rocca gritted his teeth and thought about taking another quick shot, but El Fahd was gone. He screamed, "Goddamn it! That was El Fahd!" Mad at not having aimed at the terrorist's heart. He started running after him. Sam and Rachel's footsteps were right behind him.

"How can you be so sure?" Rachel said. "You only saw him for a few seconds."

"His eyes," barked Rocca over his shoulder, watching his step as the terrain degenerated into scrub oaks and pines, so closely spaced that he took two side steps to one forward.

They all slowed. There was a commotion in the bushes to their left where El Fahd had come from. Rocca stopped and wondered if El Fahd had an accomplice. He started to raise his gun for another shot.

CHAPTER 60

A blond-haired, solid man burst out of the thicket and grasped Rocca's arm tight and shoved his arm down with such force that Rocca thought his shoulder would dislocate. The man's rapid forward momentum forced Rocca backwards, slamming him against a log and knocking out his breath.

The guy's green eyes stared at Rocca without the anger Rocca had expected, but instead sadness. Tears tracked his dirt cheeks. His muscles bulged through a rip in what once had been a tan tee shirt, now almost red with mud and dirt stains. "Hey, buddy, who are you trying to kill anyhow?"

Rocca blinked and coughed and tried to sit up.

"Rock, meet Alex Smith," Sam said, gently separating Alex from Rocca's arm. "A new, improved Alex Smith."

Rocca stood, angry, but nodded acknowledgment at Alex. He rolled his shoulders feeling a kink where the pitons from the pack must have dug in. *A measly scientist pushed me down?*

Rachel shouldered in around Sam and grabbed Alex, spinning him around and embracing him. "Alex! What the hell happened to you? You look like you've been dragged behind a horse all night."

Alex seemed to melt into her arms for a moment, his rippling arms tenderly wrapped around her. Then he gently released her and wiped at his eyes. "Jesse's gone." He looked at the ground and put one hand over the other. "Gone."

He looked up at Rocca, eyes glinting with fresh tears. "Jabril killed Jesse. You did shoot him, right? Tell me you got him in the heart."

Rocca glared at Rachel and Sam and shook his head. "Wasn't aiming for the heart—leg shot, so we can interrogate him and get blood. I think I tagged him, but he took off so fast I'm not real sure." He gritted his teeth and glanced ahead to where Jabril had run. "Come on. Let's get after him." Waiting and explaining was not getting El Fahd.

"I'm with you. What's this about interrogation?" He eyed Sam, a suspicious gaze. Sam stepped between Rocca and Alex. "He's going to explode a nuclear bomb and deliver some type of biological weapon somewhere in the U.S. It's imperative we find out where and when. So yes, we definitely need to interrogate him. ASAP!"

Alex nodded. "Right. ASAP. Now. Pronto. So which way'd he go?"

Rocca moved his gun barrel in the direction of Jabril's retreat. "That way. In fact, if I did hit him, we might be able to track the blood trail. Although in this light it might be pretty difficult."

"You leave that to me. I'll lead. You follow." Rocca watched Alex start running through the trees like a deer and murmured, "How the hell can a bush idiot scientist expect to see the blood trail running so fast?"

Rachel patted Rocca on the back and chuckled as she started to jog. "You heard Sam. Alex is new and improved. He's developed beyond what a mere Army sniper can achieve."

Rocca sped up, tripped on a sage bush, and cursed.

The strength Jabril had felt began to wane quickly as he jumped and ran and dodged trees and rocks. He started coughing, his nose ran, yet his throat was dry and his head pounded. He figured he had a mile to the bridge, but he started doubting he could make it. If the river wasn't a thousand feet down he would have dived in and drunk a gallon.

His buttock felt wet where he'd been shot. It must be blood. The gut cramp had returned.

He'd been thirsty before in the desert, and they'd trained him how to put it out of his mind. But this was different. If he didn't stop soon he felt he would collapse. He was probably very dehydrated from the last twelve hours of running. And now he was losing blood.

Concentrate on something else. Cheyenne Mountain! Get to the car. Only a few minutes away now. There's the bridge.

The orange of the rising sun back-lit the frame of the bridge.

So beautiful. Slow down. Look at that! So many colors. And finally, warm.

No! I must move faster. Move faster, Al-Buraq. Fly to the sun. Save the world from infidels.

A jolt of energy forced him forward, fatigue forgotten. He realized that he could will his body to change into that stronger self. All he needed to do was think it.

An hour earlier, Cheyenne Mountain had become a beehive of activity. Some of the arriving civilian and military staff had received the heightened alert warning with an update expected at 0730 hours, a mere ninety minutes to get last-minute jobs finished. They frantically retrieved recall rosters and called name after name of essential personnel.

After September 11, no one was treating this like a drill.

They all had stern faces, but even in the midst of another potential disaster they maintained a sense of humor. One senior GS-14 engineering supervisor read the alert warning on his computer in his glassed-in cubicle then called his supervisor. "What the heck does *potential nuclear-biological threat* mean? Come on, Colonel, they could get nuked 'til they glowed in Colorado Springs and down here we'd be cozy and smokin' seegars." He knew the colonel loved his Cubans.

"Well let me tell ya what that means, Dick. It means get yourself ready for World War III. If those boys launch nukes, we're going to be sittin' here for a long-ass time."

"What about the biological threat?"

"Quit worrying your tiny brain and get your people ready for the long haul. Make sure you're ready with that recall list by 0715 hours. The final recall is at 0730. Got it?"

"Okay, sir. If I knew more I could prepare better. But I'll get things moving."

Dick hung up. One of his computer experts, Robert, was walking quickly away from Dick's open office door. The young blond man had a spiky hairdo and wore a Hawaiian shirt, and Dick liked the guy. He was a great programmer, though a bit nosy.

"Well, Robert, did you get all that?" The young man turned around, and his words came out as staccato as an M-16 machine gun firing on automatic. "Hi, Dick, um, I didn't hear any surprises, typical stuff, suspicions of nukes and biologicals. The colonel didn't tell you much, though, did he?"

"Yeah, well we'll probably know a lot more at 0730."

Robert didn't leave. He stood there, shuffling back and forth.

"Something else, Robert?"

Robert fiddled with a button on his shirt, then blurted another stream-of-consciousness speed sentence: "I heard rumors that Glendo Dam might have contamination of the water supply 'cause they found a homemade submarine with a paltry amount of explosives in it, and I surmised that there might be some kind of biological agent in the submarine that would be released into the water system, and now they got some high-class civilian lab looking into it, so I might be right."

Dick raised his eyebrows, astonished that Robert put all that together so fast, and that he probably was right. "You know, I actually got all that. Must be all the coffee I had this morning." Then he shook his head. "You've been hacking again, haven't you? The last time I got you off on a mere reprimand because I told them it was a security check. I don't know if I can do that again."

This time the words came even faster. "No, no! I was only browsing around some of our own e-mails from the upper echelons and happened on some interesting tidbits this morning, only did it after I saw the alert, haven't told anyone but you, wouldn't compromise security, figured you needed to know, right? You asked the colonel, so you must need to know."

Dick had been squinting and leaning forward, concentrating hard on getting all those words. It was like listening to Robin Williams on speed. "You're right, I did need to know. I'll keep it under my hat, and I suggest you do the same. Now why don't you get all prepared for staying here until next September? And no more e-mail eavesdropping, Robert."

"Okay, Dick, but I've been here since 4:00 a.m. so I'm all ready to go, maybe I could write a few programs for checking our water supply, just in case, you know."

Dick blew air out his lips in a frustrated raspberry. "Our water supply is fine. Why don't you write a few programs to prevent hackers for spying on everyone's e-mail?

"Right…" He looked like he was going to say something else, then his eyes flicked back and forth and finally settled on Dick with a look of resignation. "No one will hack *our* computer." He spun around and strode away as swiftly as his words.

Once he was out of earshot, Dick breathed a sigh of relief. Robert was good, but Jesus. His poor mother must have been crazy or ready to shoot herself by the time he was three.

He glanced at the glass of water on his desk and rubbed his cheek. Maybe he should have Robert write a program to "figure out" their water.

The phone rang and another two workers walked into his office. It was going to be a busy ninety minutes. Dick forgot about the water.

Outside Dick's office, the janitor was finishing up his morning clean-up. He wasn't wearing gloves, nor had he for the past three days. He wiped his nose with his finger and discretely wiped that finger on some of the computer keys and pens on the two neatly arranged desks. He murmured, "Lâ ilâha illâ allâh." *There is no God but Allah.*

He shuffled off, coughing and sneezing, not bothering to cover his mouth. He wiped the cold sweat from his forehead. The shaking chills had started last night. Today would be the best day for the virus. A little overtime in the headquarters offices would benefit all.

CHAPTER 61

In Langley, Virginia, the small team chasing Jesse's cell phone was depleted to four. Most of them had been moved to work on the threatened nuclear strikes.

One of the remaining, Gunnar, was casually watching the screen, then moved his head forward and squinted. He hit a few keys, and looked closer. The GPS fix on Jesse's cell phone that had been stationary all night at the edge of the Royal Gorge had finally moved, not far, but at least ten meters. A few seconds later, the signal disappeared.

He pressed redial on his phone, hoping Sam would answer fast. An annoying female voice repeated the message he'd been hearing intermittently all night: "I'm sorry, the Cingular customer you are trying to contact is not answering, please try again."

He tried again, twice. No change.

He called his supervisor. "Sandy, this is Gunnar. The GPS unit has moved and disappeared off our tracking unit… Yeah, I know we need to have more info, but I can't raise Sam… Thanks. Excellent idea." That was what he liked about working here. The obvious didn't have to be spelled out.

He hung up. The rest of the team was watching him. "Sandy said she'd send a flash message to Fort Carson requesting a helicopter be sent within the next thirty minutes."

Then he chuckled.

One of the other guys said, "Wanna share?"

"She said, 'I don't give a fuck how bad the wind is, we gotta find this woman if we want to prevent World War III.'"

The team all laughed, and Gunnar murmured, "My kinda lady."

He turned around and almost bumped into the cleaning lady, a frumpy dark-haired Asian who had always been friendly with him.

"Good morning, Evelyn. You're here a little early, aren't you?"

Evelyn sneezed and blew her nose on an old handkerchief. "Yes, sir. I thought I'd get everything done early so I could go home soon. I've got a bad cold."

She shuffled off to the next office, and Gunnar thought she should wash her hands before grabbing the doorknob.

"You shouldn't be working with that cold. Why don't you go home?"

"Sir, I just want to do my job, just like you. I'll be gone soon enough."

"You're a dedicated woman, but finish up and leave."

Turning back to his work, Gunnar sniffled and wiped his nose. He made a mental note to get some vitamin C from his locker at lunch. He hoped Evelyn didn't have the flu.

Jerry took Doc and M.C. straight to Rachel's lab in D.C. They walked briskly down a white-tiled, yellow-walled hallway, passing two offices on the left, one with the door open and a thin redheaded man in blue scrubs rummaging around. Jerry kept walking and turned into the next open door on the left, a small office across the hall from the glass-enclosed Class IV biohazard room. Harry wore green scrubs and was sitting at the metal desk, looking at a computer screen lit with multiple sites.

"Harry, I want you, Doc, and M.C. to check out these samples." He handed Harry two vials of blood in a sealed and padded red biohazard bag. "See if there are any signs of genetic mutations or viruses floating around." He wished Rachel were here, but Harry was damn good.

"Okay." Harry stood and nodded at M.C. and Doc, then looked back at Jerry, tilting his head as if he wasn't quite sure he should do this. "Can you tell me whose blood this is?"

"The one with the red dot is Jesse's. The other one is from Alex Smith. They were both exposed to some of our monkey viruses down in the Amazon Lab."

"What do you expect me to find that the San Antonio gurus couldn't come up with?"

"San Antonio?" Jerry tried to look puzzled.

"Come on, boss. You really didn't think I was a dummy when you hired me, did you? I have a few friends around the country. Besides, Jesse and Alex are friends. I'd do this no matter what. But, if you tell me what you're looking for, I might find it faster."

Jerry rubbed his jaw with his hand. "You're right. You three know a lot more about the specific viruses we've been working with. I couldn't tell them in San Antonio. Someone might blab it to the wrong person. Not that I don't trust the Feds." He raised an eyebrow and gave Harry a wan smile.

Harry squinted a pained look on his face and shook his head, tilting his head and widening his eyes looking over Jerry's shoulder.

Jerry glanced behind at the doorway and winced. The redhead had just walked by, though he kept walking down the hallway. Jerry closed their door.

"What do you want me to tell the boys in blue?" Harry said.

"I'll handle them. Get into your Class IV outfit and do your work in the isolation lab. No one will follow you there. If you need to send any work out, let me know. I have a few friends of my own. Oh, and for organizational purposes, Doc is in charge of this team. Yes, I want this done as a team, and I need the results yesterday!"

M.C. looked at Doc. "You always get to be the bigwig. But we all know who does all the work." He smiled and thumped Doc gently on the arm with his fist.

"Yeah," Doc said. "But if this turns out to be what I think it is, none of us may want to be acknowledged for the result."

Harry dropped the vials of blood into his inner lab coat pocket. "That sounds like something I could live with."

"Work fast, guys," Jerry said, "but get it right."

Harry nodded. "We'll get it right, but it *will* take time."

Jerry nodded. "Whatever time you think it will take, cut it in half."

Harry frowned.

"Get going!" Jerry said and left.

In the upper echelons of the CIA, people were beginning to worry. How had they missed a nuclear bomb brought into the U.S.? Or maybe someone had managed to manufacture or steal one right here under their noses. The one consoling fact about the latter would be that the FBI would take the rap for that. They were slated for a meeting with the Feebees this morning. Maybe they could find out something more tangible.

Greg Biscoyne had been with the CIA for over ten years and was now one of the senior administrators. He couldn't believe anyone could sneak a nuclear bomb into the U.S. without some kind of warning. There was no way. This was some kind of ruse, he was sure of it. During the last two-hour meeting with other CIA terrorist experts he'd argued that point, and now, with his jaw muscles jittering and stomach fluttering from so much coffee he would make one last try. "Biologicals are one thing. They're easy to smuggle. Hell, enough anthrax to infect the city can be carried in a woman's makeup kit. But nukes! There are so many inspection points for any nuclear fuel that alarm bells would have been ringing with only grams of the stuff not accounted for. I think we have bad intel."

A few of the others were finally nodding in agreement. Maybe Greg would get to go home to his sick daughter. With his wife's recent job loss, though, he had to keep this one.

"We need to verify this before we notify the president or start sequestering Congressmen at Mount Weather."

One of the nodding heads piped in, "A false alarm could do more harm now that the whole country was nervous."

Another man who had been frowning said, "The whole country doesn't need to know."

Greg countered, "What about press leaks? Not a mere possibility, more like a definite probability. Panic will certainly overcome rationality if civilians think they're going to be nuked in their homes. Shit, the 1960s era of bomb shelters will pale in comparison. We have to get this right."

He finished the meeting and walked out his door, bumping into Sandy.

"Greg, we've got problems." She quickly explained the disappearance of Jesse's cell phone, their one link to the nuclear question and their problem getting out a helicopter. He squeezed his eyes shut and pressed his index finger and thumb against them, and sighed. This was going to hell.

He went back in his office and made a call on the secure phone. He keyed in his ten-character code, there were three distinctive beeps and someone answered.

"Senator Cardwell, please," he said.

The senator was in the back of his personal limousine on his way to the office glad to be away from his wife and the breakfast argument over new floors for their house. That woman was going to bankrupt him. The secure car phone rang, and he smiled at the caller ID. Could be another break. "Mighty early isn't it, Greg? I haven't even finished my first cup of coffee. How's that little wife of yours? She can sure make the best chicken-fried steak. What do you have for me?"

"Senator, thank you for taking my call. Let me explain a situation of national security that you could prevent from becoming a major FUBAR."

"Fire away. I could use a little something to perk me up this morning."

Greg outlined the problem and potential solution. All he needed was someone in a fast helicopter to get to the Royal Gorge Bridge. He ended the call feeling like he'd done the right thing.

The cleaning lady was fooling with the doorknob outside his office again. He walked to the door and opened it. "Evelyn, no more. Please, go home."

"Yes sir, Mr. Biscoyne. But rumor has it that you might be here awhile. Let me empty your trash and clean your sink before I go?" She coughed and wiped her dripping nose with her sleeve.

He put his hand over his mouth. "Okay, but then please leave."

Greg Biscoyne hurried off to a meeting with the FBI.

Evelyn wiped her sleeve on the arms of his chair, spat on his computer keyboard, and murmured, "Only doing my job, like everyone else."

CHAPTER 62

Alex didn't need to see the blood track; he could smell it. He'd also gotten a second wind, and it was a beaut, allowing him to lope along like an antelope, quickly distancing himself from the others. The trees began to thin out and the dirt road teed into a paved road. He took a left and ran even faster.

A sign at the entrance to the Park said *Stop and Pay to Enter*. Sorry, he'd have to pay later. There was no one in the booth, anyhow. He slowed and walked another ten yards and saw the security guard lying on his back in the pen with the buffaloes, bent backwards much too severely, unless he was some kind of yoga freak. Jabril must have done this.

Alex's muscles swelled with blood, stretching against his clothes. The breathing of buffaloes sounded inches away. There were flies on the buffaloes' nostrils. Not only did the buzzing of their wings sound like helicopter rotors whopping above his head, but he could even discern the blood pumping in their wings. A newfound energy surged through him. He started running for the bridge.

The footsteps of Rachel and the others behind him now sounded like giants tramping on the pavement.

"Alex…if we're going to…help you, you need to…slow down!" Rachel's words came out between heavy breaths. It sounded like she was right next to him, but when he turned, she was twenty-five yards behind, and Rocca was no longer running in his direction, but off to the right, towards a viewing platform.

Alex shouted, "I'll hold him for you. But if I slow down, he's going to get away. Call 911 for the guard." He pointed to the buffalo pen but kept running. Rocca didn't slow down either, and Alex heard him tell Rachel, "Might as well call the coroner. I'm with Alex. We gotta get El Fahd. Today! Now!"

Alex turned and ran toward the bridge. There was a sound like a dead-bolt flipping next to his head, which made him flick his head right, but all he could see was Rocca walking onto a viewing platform enclosed by a low fence. He was carrying his gun in both hands, as if getting ready to shoot.

Rachel heard Sam's footsteps behind her come to a stop, and she glanced back. "I gotta make a call," he said. "This cell isn't working. There was a phone in the guard shack. You go with Rocca and get blood before those two pulverize El Fahd."

She nodded. "Better hurry. Rocca's not waiting for anything."

Sam sprinted off.

Rachel tried to run faster, but she was almost done. Pretty weird, chasing a terrorist at dawn through a zoo and amusement park, over the tallest suspension bridge in the world. Her lover was some kind of good-guy werewolf, chasing some kind of bad-guy monster, and the guy behind her was a CIA agent who happens to be a world-class surfer. Shit, Rocca was the only one approaching normal, but even he was some kind of Special Forces mercenary. She'd be glad to get back to photographing moose. At least she'd know they were real animals.

Jabril half ran, half limped onto the bridge, feeling like a huge duck in a barrel, an easy target. He wanted to crawl to limit his profile, yet he had to get across quickly.

Someone was yelling behind him about the dead zoo guard and getting El Fahd. The distinctive click of the safety on a .45 and Jabril knew he had to do something quickly. He glanced back. No one could see him yet. *Hide. Evade and surprise.*

Quickly he pulled himself up on the bridge's suspension cables and climbed over the side. Then down, down, down—he moved slowly, like a spider on a web. He had only a few hundred feet to descend, much shorter than the descent in that long canyon in Afghanistan. This should only take a few minutes.

—

Alex ran around the final curve of the road and stopped at the bridge. El-Fahd was gone.

The Royal Gorge Bridge looked like every other suspension bridge, two huge parallel cables anchored into the granite on either side of the gorge, looped up over towers that were also set into the earth, looped down to the middle and back to the other side in reverse. Much smaller vertical cables supported the bed of the bridge, from the long loops, spreading any weight out. El Fahd was not on any of the cables or the bridge. He must already be on the other side.

Alex had to get across the bridge and quickly, but he could not take a step. In the light of day, the wooden planks making up the bed of the bridge looked way too old fashioned, and way too fragile, and the bridge was way too high up from the water.

He blew out a quick breath through his nose and started walking slowly onto the planks. At least the wind had died down. He looked down. Some of the planks looked pretty old and there were gaps between many planks. Gaps! He snapped his head up and kept walking.

Stay in the middle. Don't look down through the gaps. He had to move faster but his legs felt like pieces of spaghetti in slow motion.

Rachel rounded the corner, her chest heaving. Alex was walking over the bridge, looking for all the world like he was walking a tightrope. No one else was in sight. Where was El-Fahd?

From behind her, Rocca yelled, "He's down there! Below the bridge!"

She twisted her head around. Rocca was standing on the viewing platform, both hands on his gun aiming his down below the bridge. She shook her head and blinked. How could El Fahd get below the bridge?

Alex was walking faster, feeling pretty good, keeping his head up, almost halfway across the bridge. He even enjoyed the state flags fluttering in the wind on either side above their name placards tacked to the waist-high mesh fencing on either side. Then he heard Rocca's, "Below the bridge," and stopped to look back. Rocca was motioning with his gun below the bridge.

Shit! No way around it, he was going to have to look over the side.

One small step, another. It was like he was in one of those dreams where nothing worked right, and he couldn't move any faster. Finally he was to the side of the bridge. He reached desperately for the side where the huge suspension cable had looped down on top of the meshed fence and grabbed it: metal, solid, much better than wood. His heart was rolling around in his chest like a pinball. Holding on with both hands, he eased his chest and head over, peering down.

His gaze latched on to only one thing—the river. A mesmerizing, olive snake flowing between walls of black and rust-colored granite. And it was way down there. Way, way down there. The bridge started spinning. He was going to vomit. He forced his head up and his eyes closed, but he started falling over onto the cable with nothing else to stop him from thin air.

Rachel was breathing more normally as she walked on the wooden planks towards Alex, her weight rocking some of the looser ones. She walked to the side of the bridge. A printed sign stuck to a cable announced: *Arkansas River 1053 Feet Down.* She leaned her upper abdomen onto the side rail and looked over the side. The river entranced her, deep, green water highlighted by the occasional white rapid. She had to force her eyes away from the hypnotizing sight.

She scanned the granite walls for a body.

Nothing.

The crack of a gun snapped her head back toward Rocca. He was holding his .45 in both hands, propping the gun on the fence top, aiming just below the bridge bed.

Two other cables ran below the bridge, mirror images of the huge suspension cables above but much thinner. Like silver rainbows, they started somewhere below the sides of the gorge, then bowed upwards to the middle of the bridge.

On one of the cables, a dark form moved toward the other side, like an upside down inchworm, legs wrapped around the cable, hands pulling himself forward, foot by foot.

El Fahd.

Rachel ran towards Alex, yelling, "He's on the cable under the bridge. You've got to get him before Rocca kills him! We need fresh blood!"

Another shot ricocheted off metal below the bridge, announcing Rocca's deadly intent.

Rocca gripped the handgun in both hands, the stock resting on the enclosures rail, and sighted down the barrel at the distant figure scooting on the cable under the bridge. He had bracketed El Fahd with the last two shots. The next one would get the asshole. Piece of cake.

He aimed for the heart, then heard Rachel yelling about fresh blood. He pulled the aim down to El Fahd's right leg. There was always the hope that a leg shot would make him fall. It was a long way down, too. Rocca grinned. A long-ass way to ponder smashing on those rocks.

He blew out a breath and slowly, gently started squeezing the trigger.

Something hard like a fist smacked his right shoulder. The shot went wild.

"Fuck!" Rocca swung the gun around intent on killing whoever had ruined his shot. But before he could get around and see, someone kicked him in the solar plexus. He buckled at the waist, unable to breathe, and dropped the gun. It skittered to the very edge of the precipice.

CHAPTER 63

Rocca came up like a bull, breathless but ready for a fight. Expecting an enemy but seeing Sam, he stopped.

"Whadja do that for? That asshole killed my partner, God knows how many others, and is going to destroy our country. I was aiming at his leg, anyhow."

Sam was crouched, ready for a punch. He stood up and put out his hand to Rocca. "Sorry, Rock. You and I both know if you even shot him in the leg he probably would have fallen. Yeah, we need blood, but the bigger picture is: We need information. We gotta find out what the hell he's up to or he may just do it. Blood will help, but information? That's our ticket to end this."

Rocca grabbed Sam's hand and shook it, reluctantly. "Yeah, you're probably right." He walked over to retrieve his gun.

Sam ran after him. "Maybe you should let me carry that thing for a while. At least until you cool off."

"I'm cooled off. Don't worry. I'll only shoot him if he tries something." He smiled. "And I promise it will be in the leg." He leaned down, the pitons rattling in his pack, grabbed his gun, flipped on the safety and stuck it in his shoulder holster.

They both looked at the bridge. El Fahd had stopped, one leg hanging down. Alex was climbing over the side, moving slowly down towards the terrorist.

"Come on, Rock. Let's go help Alex. The chopper will be here any sec."

"You convinced them to send a chopper?"

"Not really. Someone got their head out of their ass. Jabril is the only way to verify the nuclear threat. Gotta make sure before they pull out all the stops. So let's go verify."

They both ran.

Alex managed to grip the cable tighter and prevent falling over. He pushed away from the side, but kept tight hold of the cable. His head cleared. He blew out a deep breath and leaned his chest onto the cable, craning his neck and head, scanning under the bridge. El Fahd clung to a thinner cable as it arced close under the bridge, both arms hugging it, one leg looped over, the other hanging. Alex swept his arm out and back. "Come on up, dude. If you don't that friend of mine will shoot you."

El Fahd said nothing. The look in his eyes and the way he clung to the cable told Alex he was frozen in terror.

Alex swung one leg over, the other, and started climbing down, with only brief glances below for a hold on the underframe. He was twenty feet down, almost to the cable, with about thirty more feet to El Fahd when the distant chatter of an approaching helicopter made him look over his shoulder. The canyon walls started spinning like a merry-go-round, and his stomach lurched, everything started to go gray, and his grip loosened.

"Alex, we've got reinforcements, look!" Rachel's voice came from straight up.

Alex appreciated her enthusiasm, he really did. But no way was he looking anywhere but at his hands and feet, keeping them on the cable. He took another deep breath and looked up at Rachel. She was leaning over the rail looking down at him, eyes wide with worry. He smiled and gave her a thumbs-up and started back down, one foot, one hand, one foot, one hand. He'd give his left nut for a safety harness and rope.

He shot a quick glance at El Fahd and stopped. Now that he was closer he could see the guy's eyes seemed more of a glare than terror. The anger he'd felt back at Amazon Lab returned. Then he felt El Fahd's haughty, righteous hatred like a red hot poker, sticking behind his eyes. Alex started to pull himself back up to Rachel. *Let him fall. He deserves it after throwing Jesse off the cliff. Fucking psychotic Muslim asshole.*

He glanced up at Rachel and felt her love and knew their future depended on getting blood from this terrorist. He climbed down five more feet and straddled the cable, leaned over and started climbing the cable like the rope in grade school, arms sliding forward, pulling the rest of his body. Only he wasn't inching up—his head was lower than his legs as the cable arced down toward El Fahd. The blood started pulsing in his head. He kept his eyes on the cable for a few feet, then looked at El Fahd. He seemed more relieved. But Alex read something else in the man's mind and paused. A flash of a woman in a shawl on a ship. His grandmother.

The merry-go-round returned. He closed his eyes and breathed deeply through his nose, but his mind was fading and one leg slipped off the cable.

Jabril held tight with his arms and one leg, the other leg still weak from the gunshot in his buttock, but getting stronger with less pain. It would be healed soon. Alex climbed towards him, and Jabril waited, hating the blond, green-eyed infidel, looking forward to killing him.

The woman said something about getting his blood—they must think he was infected. Then he recalled the phone call he'd heard before he killed Jesse. They also thought Jabril had nuclear weapons. Perfect! They will have to take him to the nearest nuclear shelter and military base for questioning—Cheyenne Mountain. He must make them move faster.

He dropped his weakened leg even further down and moaned as if in pain, and tried to read the man's mind. Suddenly Jabril felt dizzy, his stomach twisted, he gripped the cable harder and he felt terror at possibly falling.

But there was something else. The man was somehow connected to Jabril's grandmother, Alexandra.

Pushing further into the man's thoughts brought the fear of heights screaming inside, so that Jabril did not have to feign terror in his voice: "Hurry! I am slipping. I have been shot in the hip, and I cannot hold on much longer."

Alex strained his abdominal muscles, shook his head, regained his grip. He looked back at El Fahd and saw his wide eyes, pinched face and knew he was telling the truth. He tried to make his voice soothing, "Don't worry. I'll be there in a few seconds." He had decided that if he showed anger this would take longer. Be nice and get the hell out.

He pulled closer and looked at El Fahd again. He stared into eyes that reminded him of what he'd seen in the mirror in the Amazon.

"So now you know," El Fahd said in a gentle baritone—musical, soothing, almost calming, but having a touch of a snake. Alex did not want to move any further. El Fahd continued. "We are the same, it seems; you and I, brothers in blood. I have been sensing you chasing me for several days. It is good to finally meet you, Alex. Jesse spoke highly of you. I am Jabril El Fahd. Thank you for being my American savior."

Alex could feel the falsity, the underlying hate still prodding the back of his eyes. "I'm not your God damn savior. I saw what you did to Jesse."

"You think I killed her? I could not. I loved her. I was helping her and she fell, cutting her throat on a rock. I tried to save her, but she slipped. Please, give me a hand or I am going to fall."

Jabril realized his words were not enough. He must convince Alex in his mind as well. He blocked his thoughts of hate and let his right hand slip off, throwing his body out toward the chasm. Though his left hand was tightly gripping the cable and one leg still curled around it, he felt the terror; he did not have to feign it. "Please hurry!" Suddenly Jabril wanted to quit this charade, end it all, let go and join his mother. Then other thoughts from his mentors tore at him, *Jihad! You must prevail.*

Alex had been one second from leaving the terrorist. *Let somebody else risk their life to rescue this piece of shit.* Then Jabril's right hand slipped off, and Alex saw the look of panic and pleading. *Aw Crap! Maybe he's telling the truth.* Alex hadn't seen him actually cut Jesse's throat. He could have been reaching out to save her. It had all happened so fast.

Alex felt fear and, at the same time, wanted to cry. It came from Jabril, a deep sorrow from Jabril's past, a loss that cut him deep. His mother. And then he felt something deeper, inside his chest like a band constricting. He realized Jabril's grandmother, Alexandra, had saved Alex's parents from the Nazis. He looked at Jabril and wanted to push thoughts to him, but saw his eyes glaze over. The poor guy was going nuts. "Alright, I'm coming." Alex pulled himself closer to El Fahd.

The helicopter whopping sound was getting louder. Rachel yelled from above him, "Alex, maybe you should wait. Rocca has rope. He'll be here any second." The fear in her voice was apparent.

Jabril reached out his right hand. "Please, Alex. I am so weak from being shot. Please, grab my right hand so I can move up a little."

Alex paused, looked up at Rachel, her pinched eyebrows and pursed lips, thought about Rocca and waiting for the rope. His head pounded with blood. The helicopter noise was deafening. A breeze had come up and the bridge swayed.

"Please, Alex." Jabril's voice had gone up an octave and a few decibels.

Alex sighed. If this guy fell and contaminated the Arkansas River, there would be no Rachel. Hell there might not even be a U.S. Plus Alex owed his grandmother. He pulled his body a foot closer to El Fahd and reached out his right hand while holding the cable in the crook of his left arm.

He was still six inches short.

He unhooked his left arm and gripped the cable with his left hand, pulled on the cable, testing his grip, felt his legs curled tight around the cable. He reached out, looking into Jabril's eyes, trying to calm his fears, pushing out a thought, *This is for your grandmother*. But Jabril's eyes stared over Alex's head, as if he was in a trance.

Rachel kept watching the chopper get closer and closer. Too close. She started jumping up and down, arms waving, butt pack flapping against her lower back. "You stupid asshole! Get the hell out of here! You're going to blow them off the bridge!"

The pilot looked at her and gave her the okay sign. The helicopter tilted as if to bank away, but a gust of wind must have caused it to drop three feet. The wind from it rotors increased. Rachel quickly looked over the side, hoping Alex was firmly holding on. But he wasn't. She froze, unable to speak or move.

Alex was not looking at Jabril's eyes or he might have done everything differently. The wind gusted and chopper downdraft made him close his eyes. The whopping noise blotted out all thought. He blindly reached out as far as he could.

His grasp was returned by a strong grip that easily should have been able to hold onto the cable. The grip turned into a pull so strong it forced him to open his eyes.

Jabril's eyes glowed red, and a fiery piercing jabbed behind Alex's eyes.

"Why do you hate me, "Alex yelled. "I'm only trying to help you." Jabril only pulled harder.

Alex strained and twisted his hand, trying to pull away.

Jabril brought his other leg up around the cable, then grabbed Alex's one hand with both of his and pulled even harder.

Alex let go of the hold on the cable with his left hand and tried to pry Jabril's hand off. It was like trying to pry open an oyster. Then he felt his muscles swell. It was time to end this.

The muscles in both of their arms bulged. They were like two sumo wrestlers struggling to throw the other off the mat, only there was no floor, only thin air. One wrenched right, the other left, each testing the other for a weakness.

Rachel watched from above realizing Alex was at a disadvantage. Gravity was on Jabril's side. He was lower on the cable and could use Alex's weight as she had been taught in her self-defense classes. She raised her leg to go over the side and help Alex, but the bridge swayed with another gust of wind and she put her leg back down. The chopper had moved off fifty feet, but the rotor noise was still deafening. She remembered Alex at Amazon Lab, his raw strength, and felt sure he could best Jabril. But Alex needed no other problems, like that damn helicopter. She started waving her hands again at the chopper pilot. But his eyes were glued on Alex and Jabril below.

Alex felt sure Jabril had never heard his thoughts of his grandmother or he would have reacted. It was all or nothing now. He gripped his legs tight around the cable took a deep breath and yanked hard.

Jabril's hands slipped an instant. Then something tore in Alex's jeans and one of his legs lost its hold. He thought he heard Jabril laugh. The terrorist seemed to have gotten a surge of strength and yanked Alex so hard both Alex's legs started to slip off the cable.

Alex made a last effort at holding on with his ankles, but they bounced off the cable.

He swung like a trapeze artist from the hands of the terrorist, each one grasping the other's wrists. Only air lay between Alex and a terrible death below.

Looking into Jabril's eyes Alex yelled at him, hoping to finally get through. "Your grandmother helped my parents. That's why I am named

Alexander. Please, let me help you. I owe that to your grandmother." His voice sounded weird to him, low, eerie, enveloping them both. "I know losing your mother is eating you up. I can help you, like your grand-mother Alexandra helped my parents."

Jabril flinched, like a current was passing through his body.

The red disappeared from Jabril's eyes and he frowned at Alex, as if he almost believed it. Then the red glow crept into his eyes and his thoughts berated Alex. *Sandra was a fool. You…a Jew. You can never help me.*

The sweat on their hands was a great lubricant.

Jabril smiled and loosened his grip. "Goodbye, Alex." He jerked his hands and severed their connection.

Like a game of slap the hands, Alex was too quick. He grabbed Jabril again: this time he had his wrists in a vice grip.

Jabril was just as quick, slamming his wrists together at Alex's knuck-les, releasing one wrist and smashing Alex in the face with a fist.

Alex still held on with one hand. The emotion Jabril saw surprised him again. It was not hate, but…

Love?

His mother's radiant face was there. He felt her arms cradle his head. Her voice soothed his fury. *Jabril, you must help him. It will be your true salvation.* All the alcohol, all the women, all the murders, everything would be forgiven? Her head nodded and she smiled. *Save this one man and all will be forgiven. You are connected. This is your true destiny.*

Alex dangled by one hand, but stared deep into Jabril's eyes, and his voice came out low and soothing, cutting through the rotor noise. "Why else would we be here together? Listen to her. All your torture will be over if you help me."

Jabril felt his whole chest relax and warm. No more hate would be so wonderful. He reached down to grab Alex's other hand.

The helicopter dropped and the wind from the rotors flung Alex sideways.

Alex reached up to grab Jabril's outstretched hand and touched his fingertips. His other hand slipped off Jabril's sweaty wrist.

Both men grabbed out, but missed.

Alex fell face up, and Jabril could only watch his eyes as he got further away.

Jabril saw no fear. Only acceptance, not acceptance of death, but Jabril was sure it was acceptance that Jabril had wanted to help, had really tried. Jabril closed his eyes. *Allah has spoken. My destiny is written. Goodbye, mother.*

Rachel stopped jumping and waving when she saw the pilot's eyes widen at the sight below. She leaned over the cable and looked down.

Alex was falling away from El Fahd. Everything else blurred.

His face filled her vision, calm, accepting, loving. Yes, he loved her. How could she have ever doubted him? Tears streamed down her cheeks. Then Alex disappeared into a mist that had formed over the river.

She threw a leg over. Someone's arms encircled her and pulled her back. They were gentle but strong. It was Rocca.

She squirmed and beat her fists against chest. "Let me go! I have to save him!"

Rocca's arms did not let go. They held her close and he took the blows but said nothing. Eventually she stopped beating at him. Her body went limp and she sobbed.

CHAPTER 64

Sam was jogging leisurely behind Rocca on the right side of the bridge, when he saw Rachel leaning over looking at El Fahd. Alex was falling. *Damn!* Yet Sam's gaze returned to the terrorist, hanging by his legs, flailing with his arms in midair, trying to grab the cable above him. Rocca had sprinted off and grabbed Rachel. But what about El Fahd? They had to get blood. They had to question him. He was the key, not Rachel. Sam sprinted across the bridge and yelled, "Rock, I need the rope!"

Rocca held Rachel, gun holstered, pack tight to his back. He looked at Sam coming to a halt in front of them like he'd asked him to stab Rachel. "That guy's a piece of shit. Let him fall. On second thought, here, take my gun and blow his head off."

Jabril hung by his legs, arms dangling, blood rushing to his head, mind spinning. Alex's look as he had fallen made Jabril wonder: *Should I just let go as well?* Then he gripped his legs tighter. This was his chance to finish it. They wanted his blood. They wanted his knowledge about nuclear bombs. But he had to play it right so they would to save him and take him to the generals.

Yet he was weaker, the blood pulsed in his head but no longer thrummed through his arm muscles. They felt like noodles. He used every muscle to reach out and grab the cable with his right hand.

"Help! Please help me!" Jabril's cry was high-pitched and desperate, truth made it convincing.

Sam unzipped Rocca's pack and tore the rope out, hearing Rachel's sobs, knowing he had to snap her out of it so she and Rocca would help. "Rachel, I know you hate El Fahd right now, but you know as well as I do there is more at stake here. We need El Fahd for questioning and blood or there may be a lot more people dead. I don't know what happened down there with Alex, but I promise you, if El Fahd is responsible for Alex's death, he will pay. Right now, though, I need you and Rocca to help me pull him up." He put a gentle finger under her chin and raised it up and held it there for an instant, hoping she would look at him.

Rachel opened her eyes, and her jaw muscles flexed, and Sam quickly took his finger away, afraid she might snap his finger off. She pushed herself away from Rocca's shoulder. Rocca stepped back and looked at Sam like he was scum. Rachel pulled her butt pack around to her front and unzipped it. Tears tracked a scant coating of red dust on her cheeks. "I want to question that son of a bitch myself. Right after I stab his heart for blood!"

She handed out surgical masks and eye shields and donned rubber gloves. "Put these on and avoid any direct contact with his blood. Once we get him up here, Rocca, you immobilize him, and I'll put on his mask and draw his blood."

Sam eyed her, raising his brows and the corners of his lips before he tied on the mask. "Not really his heart, right? We need him alive."

"Sounds good to me," Rocca said, grinning. He tied on the mask and put on the gloves.

But Rachel did not smile. She looked at Sam, eyes as flat as stones.

"Come on, Rache. We gotta know what he's really up to. You kill him now and everything, all the bullshit of the last week, Alex's life, all for nothing."

She put on her mask and gripped the syringe. A long needle was attached, very long. "All right." Her voice was steady, without emotion, and sounded distant, as if the words were without meaning.

Rocca stepped back a pace from them, pulled on his gloves and folded his arms. Sam and Rachel turned and leaned their chests onto the cable and peered over the side. They saw a contrite and weakened Jabril El Fahd. "Please, I am very weak. Your friend was truly brave. But I could not hold onto him when he slipped. I tried, but the helicopter...the wind...I was not strong enough."

Sam lowered the rope with a slipknot tied in the end. The loop framed Jabril's head like a hangman's noose and Sam hesitated. Maybe Rocca was right. One quick pull and...

He played out a more rope. "Slip the noose under one arm, then over your head and under the other arm and we'll haul you up."

Jabril did as he was told and Sam and Rachel started pulling, straining with their arms and legs and stepping back and back. When they got to where Rocca stood, Rachel said, "How 'bout it, Rock. I need to get his mask ready."

Rocca sighed and grabbed the rope and Sam hardly had to pull as the rope moved much faster. Rachel let go and readied the mask as El Fahd clambered over the side and stood facing them.

Rocca let go of the rope and pointed his gun at the terrorist. "Wait just a second, Rachel." Rocca moved his gun toward the planks. "You know the drill. Hands behind your head. Kneel and lay face down on the ground."

Jabril stepped forward, hands held out towards Rachel, eyes kind. "But I wanted to thank you."

Rocca fired a shot, inches above Jabril's head. "The next one will be in your heart. Down on your belly, now! Pretend it's your Morning Prayer. You can do that, can't you? Or don't you pray anymore, now that you've killed so many people, asshole?"

Jabril flinched, feeling the truth in the words, yet letting a breath go and knowing he was done with prayer. Despite feeling weaker, power still pulsed in his limbs. Allah had left him. He did not need Allah. All that mattered now was revenge for his mother. Kill them all. He lay prone, but eyed Rocca, anger returning. *You shot me once. You will never get that chance again.*

Rachel dropped onto his back with two knees like a professional wrestler—anything but gentle. "So you dropped Alex down there, huh?" She grabbed one of his hands and pulled it hard and fast behind his back in front of her knees.

Sam got the other hand and tightly bound both wrists with the zip tie, enjoying pulling them a bit too tight.

Grunting his answer with his right cheek pushed against one of the wooden planks of the bridge, Jabril kept all anger out of his voice. He had to play them right. "The helicopter blew him out of my grasp. I tried to reach him, but...I am truly sorry."

Rachel slipped a surgical mask onto his face and tied it behind his head. "You're going to feel a needle stick."

Still kneeling on his back, she drew blood from a prominent forearm vein that Sam would have never thought to do. She placed a piece of gauze at the site, securing it with tape wrapped around his arm.

Very professional, thought Sam.

Then she raised her hand high and brought it down hard, slapping the side of Jabril's head with her closed fist. She stood as if she were done, then jumped into the air and came down knees first onto his kidney area.

Jabril grunted. Sam caught Rocca's eyes. Rocca nodded at him. Sam nodded back. He might have done it a little different, but it would do for now.

Rachel stood again, her face flushed, breathing hard. "Okay, stand up now, motherfucker."

Jabril wallowed from side to side, feigning weakness.

Rocca stepped in and grabbed the zip tie between El Fahd's wrists and jerked him upright. "You need to listen to the lady."

Jabril, winced, and stood, making sure he had an obvious list, favoring his right side.

Rocca eyed the blood-soaked right butt cheek of El Fahd's pants. The dark patch covered most of the back pocket with a neat hole in the center. The exit hole was also visible in the outer right seam of his hip.

One side of Rocca's mouth twitched. "Guess I hit you after all. Too bad it didn't come out the middle and take out your balls. Turn around and start walking. We're going for a little ride."

"Wait a sec." Rachel grabbed a garbage bag, cut two holes for legs, pulled it onto Jabril like a big black diaper, then duct taped it to his waist and legs. "There!" She slapped his face. "That should keep you from getting the chopper all bloody."

A peach rose flared on Jabril's cheek at the edge of his mask. He eyed her curiously.

She glared and slapped him again.

The helicopter had landed at the parking lot on the north side of the bridge, rotors now slowing, a slight wheeze as they turned. A passenger climbed out and stood beside the helo. He wore khaki pants, green fatigue pants and dark mirror sunglasses. He motioned with his arm for the group to hurry.

Rocca prodded El Fahd in the back and they all walked a bit faster.

Rachel asked Jabril, "Where are the nukes going to go off? And—"

Sam elbowed her in the side. "Let's get him in an interrogation room before we start asking questions. After all, he needs to be treated fairly."

"Sorry."

Sam thought he'd never heard more sarcasm.

Jabril felt like laughing and celebrating. *They think I will release a nuclear weapon. Many will already be moving into the bunkers. But if they are looking too hard for nuclear weapons, they might find our bombs at the reservoirs.*

"There are no nuclear weapons," he stated flatly as they walked off the rocking wood slats onto solid pavement. He slowed, part of him worried about the man in the sunglasses standing beside the helicopter. There was something about his stance. Rocca's fingers prodded his back at each lame step.

"Right." Rocca said. "Next thing you'll be telling us is that you are not a terrorist and we should let you go back to helping old ladies cross the road."

"That is not correct. I am Jabril El Fahd, the Sword of Gabriel, the right hand of Osama bin Laden. I know what is about to happen and there are no nuclear weapons. We had plans for them, but they are too hard to acquire and move. If you do not believe me, I can give you an address where you will find the aborted plans for nuclear weapons." He paused thinking of how to make them believe him even more. "You will also be able to pick up a few of my comrades as a bonus."

Sam stared at Jabril. "Why would you come clean now?"

Jabril gave him a blank look. No answer would imply he had more.

"All right," Sam said. "Give me the address. We'll call and find out from the helicopter radio. If you're bluffing we will know soon enough."

Jabril gave them an address in D.C. His comrades in there would not understand, but Jabril had to stop the Americans from searching everywhere else for bombs or they would find those in the reservoirs. Besides, soon it would not matter for those in D.C. or anywhere else. They would all die of the illness.

They walked up to the man in sunglasses. He nodded at Sam.

"Sorensen." Sam nodded back.

The pilot was leaning over toward the passenger side, shaking his head. "What's with the masks? Nobody told me about needing masks."

Rachel reached around Sorensen and handed the pilot a mask. "He might have an infection." She stepped back and looked at Sorensen.

Sam stepped between Rachel and Sorensen. "He's with the Agency."

Sorensen sidestepped Sam, took one of the masks Rachel held in her hand, said, "Thanks," and got in the front passenger seat. Sam frowned.

The pilot looked at Sam. "Look. We need to get out of here. There's some top dogs waiting for this dude. They want Sorensen to come with him. There's only room for two more, the terrorist and one other. Make a decision so we can go."

Sam stood back, traded stern looks with Rocca, then pulled Rachel back. Sam would honor Rocca's desire to finish hauling in Jabril. Rocca pushed Jabril in, and got in behind him.

Agent Sorensen leaned into the back seat and buckled Jabril's seat belt and placed sound protectors over his ears.

"Where are you taking me?" Jabril asked.

Sorensen said nothing, but looked at Jabril. Jabril leaned towards him. "I am not infectious. But I know where and when the virus will be released. I will gladly give out that information, but only to someone who is in command."

"Don't worry," Agent Sorensen said, taking off Jabril's sound protectors. "You're about to see someone in command, and you might rethink that wish after you meet him."

Sorensen sat back down, then leaned out and gave Rachel a radio handset. "There will be another chopper here in a few minutes. Use this to direct them in."

The pilot leaned over and gave Sam a thumbs-up. The wind and noise of the rotor blades increased. Sam wanted to smash Sorensen in his pretty sunglasses and get some straight answers, but he grabbed Rachel's arm and they kept their heads low and ran back several paces as the chopped lifted off. They watched it tilt and fly east.

Rachel gave Sam the radio and yelled, "You seem to have a little more clout around here than I do. Ask the pilot to send someone to retrieve Jesse and Alex. They need a proper burial."

Sam keyed the radio and asked. The pilot said, "Roger that," but Sam didn't think he meant it. He watched the helicopter and wished he'd gone instead of Rocca.

—

Without ear protection, the roar of the chopper as it took off deafened Jabril. Peering out over the side he watched the distant plains grow closer. Though he did not have a good sense of direction, he knew they were taking him exactly where he wanted to go: Cheyenne Mountain.

The morning sun warmed his face and he closed his eyes. Soon he would be free.

He would see Mother again.

When he opened his eyes, the clouds to the west had abated. The treeless summit of a nearby mountain peak was dusted in white, stark contrast to the vivid blue sky. And then Sorensen turned around and pointed a gun at Rocca.

CHAPTER 65

M.C. and Harry were sitting at a lab table surrounded by numerous lab machines. They stared at papers on the table beside two vials of blood, their shoulders slumped. Doc paced in front of them, shaking his head. They'd been working all morning on those two damn vials of blood.

Doc stopped and looked at the vials. "Harry, run it through that DNA probe one more time. I want to make sure before I tell Jerry."

"You're the boss. But we've already done it twice."

"I know, I know. But this is pretty hard to believe. Humor me."

M.C. glanced over at Harry, who shrugged his shoulders and took a pipette sampling of each tube and carefully placed them in the machine.

"It'll be a little while," Harry said, dropping the pipettes into the red garbage bucket. "What about the viral analysis. You want us to do it again too?"

"No," Doc said. "Those results match San Antonio's analysis. I can accept that."

He squinted at the samples in Harry's hand and puckered his lips as if he already knew the answer. "But if these last test results are the same, we'll have to get Jesse and Alex back here for more tests."

M.C. rubbed his forehead with a finger and sighed. "I don't get it. How do you think this happened? I've known viruses to insert their DNA and cause mutations. But Alex's mutation was definitely not caused by the viral DNA. How could it be?"

"I don't know. In fact, there's lots of stuff we don't know about viruses and mutations and DNA. Maybe Mother Nature just decided it was time."

"That's a real scientific answer." Harry's voice carried a sarcastic edge. He flipped a switch and the machine hummed.

"You know what I mean—spontaneous mutation, not caused by the virus, but only related. This could be like the chameleon and changing body colors, only Alex's mutation affects his muscle and brain cells. Sometimes a mutation takes billions of years and other times—it happens overnight. Maybe the stress of the flu kicked off the mutation in Alex. Maybe he ate the wrong hotdog for lunch. Maybe the psychological stress of losing Lora did it. I don't know. And we'll probably never find out."

An iffy frown grew on Harry's face. "I thought you said both Alex and Jesse were acting like they had some kind of viral infection: fevers, sweats, upper respiratory symptoms. How can you be sure this wasn't caused by the virus?"

"I can't be sure yet. Jesse's tests are inconclusive. The virus could have caused the mutation in her DNA without inserting its DNA, or she was due for it, just like Alex. To be sure, I would need to reproduce the exact mutation by an infection with the specific virus that infected Alex and Jesse. But you see," he pointed to the results on the paper in his other hand, "the virus we isolated couldn't have caused that mutation. That is why I wanted to have our lab check the viral proteins again."

M.C. raised his eyebrows at Harry. "Doc, uh, I hate to break this to you, but viral protein identification is not the standard for specifying viral types. We need to culture the virus before we can be sure."

Doc put his hands on the lab table and leaned over at the other two. "I don't seem to have any live virus or fresh blood to culture in my back pocket. Unfortunately the blood we have was not properly transported."

"Unless," Harry said, "we could get fresh blood from Alex or Jesse."

"Exactly." Doc stood and started walking toward the door. "So I'll be getting a shower and breakfast and coffee while the final test runs. Then I'll try to reach Alex and Jesse."

"Harry can handle this. Mind if I tag along, Doc?" M.C. said.

"No problem."

They walked through out of the lab door, closing it behind them, then down the corridor beside the glassed in Class IV lab, turned right and down the long hallway leading to the main door to the lab. The left wall was mostly windows, viewing a park beside the building.

Doc stopped several feet before the locked door and stared outside a window.

"You okay, Doc?"

"Yeah, it's interesting, though."

"What do you mean?"

"Blue sky, water, green trees, beautiful birds, insects, animals—they all know their place. Mother Nature, God, Allah, evolution, or whatever, created a wonderful world that meshes and works well together."

"True."

Doc held up an index finger. "Then there's man, the screw in the works. What effect will we have on the world in twenty years, or better yet, in a century?"

M.C. shrugged. "Not really my area."

"Could depend on what we do in the next twenty-four hours, M.C. Will we be the screw that holds everything together? Or will we rattle around and break all the teeth on the gears of life?"

Without waiting for an answer, he strode on down the hall. M.C. looked out the window.

Rachel had been busy in Cheyenne Mountain making sure a fresh tube of blood was being transported to Doc in D.C. the correct way, absolutely no mistakes. This tube held Jabril's blood. Doc should have it in hours, thanks to a special flight arranged from Cheyenne Mountain. The pilot understood Rachel perfectly when she told him about the possibility of biological warfare: get there quick, but make sure you get there.

After arranging that, Rachel went back to the intake area to find Sam.

He was sitting on a bench against a wall in a spacious room filled with machines and bustling people, looking like a converted plane hangar, though there were not just Air Force personnel. Suited men, women, Army, Marine Corps and even the occasional Navy uniformed personnel bustled through. There was a buzz of conversation and computers beeping. The noise of arriving and departing jeeps and Humvees resounded through the large entrance door at one end.

She found Sam sitting on a bench next to the wall close to the entrance, elbows on knees, head between palms, his fingers rhythmically rubbed the back of his neck as he stared at the floor. He seemed to be ignoring a middle-aged man who stood in front of him gesticulating with his hands like a conductor of an orchestra.

As she walked up, the man threw up his hands. "…so, basically I don't have a clue."

"Don't have a clue about what?" she asked.

The man spun around, surprised, and Sam abruptly ended his floor gazing, sat up and looked at Rachel.

"Who's this?" The man said. His eyes were large, brown and peered at Rachel as if she was a spy. Wispy blond hair was combed back over a pale pate, and…

Rachel looked away, trying not to laugh. The guy could fly with those ears.

"This is Rachel Lane," Sam said. "She's the scientist that came in with me. Rachel, this is Richard Herbert. He's in charge of all incoming air traffic here. He tells me they have no record of any other helicopter with El Fahd or anyone else landing in the last hour."

"So, Mr. Herbert, where did you direct your pilot to take Colonel El Fahd?" Rachel locked her gaze on his big brown eyes. If she looked at those enormous ears she would have to touch them.

Sighing, Mr. Herbert—or, she could not help thinking, *Big Ears*—looked at the floor. He closed his eyes, shook his head, then looked at her. "We only sent one pilot and he brought you two in. We've had no communication regarding another helo. I thought there would be a couple of other passengers with you, so I came down to find out where they were. And that's when Sam told me this bizarre story about someone taking El Fahd in another helicopter with your friend Rocca. I have no idea where they took them. Not a clue."

He paused. "However, we already knew about there being no nukes."

Rachel stared, first at Big Ears, pursing her lips to avoid smiling, though she felt angry as hell; then her gaze locked on Sam, then back at Big Ears. "So you're telling me that one of the worst terrorists in the world just got rescued? Sam, I thought you knew that guy on the chopper. And what do you mean you knew there were no nukes?"

Sam scratched one eyebrow, averting his gaze, and his reply was almost inaudible, "Yes, I did, I do—"

Rachel interrupted, her eyes widening. "And what about the bodies. Is someone going to look for Alex and Jesse? Or do I have to go back there myself?"

Big Ears answered, "When Sam told me about them I immediately called to get a search party started. I'm afraid with this whole scare it will be at least twenty-four hours."

He looked embarrassed, his large ears turning a flame red, and his brown eyes moistening.

Rachel breathed easier. "At least we have Rocca out there with El Fahd. Wherever they are, they have to deal with him and his .45."

Staring at the business end of a .357 Magnum was not allowing Rocca to do anything but be quiet and think about how stupid he'd been. He'd been forced to surrender his .45 and was now a passenger like Jabril.

Agent Sorensen was in control. He took off his mask and looked at Jabril with those mirror sunglasses and a smirk on his face. "Thought you'd be bigger." He reached back and pulled Jabril's mask down. "Yeah, no mole. Guess you were right, Rock." He shrugged and tilted his head at Rocca. "Sorry, Rock. But you know how it is, a guy's gotta pay the bills. And God knows working for the CIA has been a real pisser the last three years, one with a poor stream of cash. Cardwell pays really well."

Rocca said nothing. He studied the countryside below. They were headed east onto the plains. *Where the hell are we going*?

Jabril was jubilant. The man Sorensen was not only greedy, he was a fool. Jabril's mask was off so he could spread the disease, and his nemesis, the man who had hunted him across the globe, was powerless.

He looked below and saw farm fields going by. This was not where Cheyenne Mountain was located. He leaned forward and glared at Sorensen. "Where are you taking me? I demand to talk to someone in charge!"

Sorensen grinned and jabbed the muzzle of his gun at the deck.

Jabril was pushed back into his seat by the helicopter tilting forward as it started to descend.

CHAPTER 66

The chopper made its approach to land on a dirt road fronting the small, single-story, red brick house where Robby waited outside with five other men. All Robby's men filled out their old grubby sweats and fatigues like NFL linemen. The air smelled of anticipatory sweat and vibrated with their jitters. The house, built circa 1963, was perfect for their purpose: brick walls for sound insulation, a dirt basement for easy cleanup, located in the sticks but still only a twenty-minute drive east of Colorado Springs. A very "safe" house. A poor farmer named Luther who couldn't make ends meet had given it up for a good price to a friend of a friend of the great and powerful Senator Cardwell. Only the house was no Emerald City palace, and the real wizard of this house, at least in Robby's mind, was in the basement, preparing. Robby elbowed one of the newbies, a big guy with a thick neck, chest like a bull, arms as big around as one of Robby's calves. "Hey, Thomas, how do you spell information?"

The man stopped moving from one foot to the other and looked puzzled. For someone who insisted on being called Thomas instead of Tom, Robby thought, he was slow on the uptake.

"T-O-R-T-U-R-E."

Thomas's face pinched as if the answer was distasteful.

"This should get us back in the graces of the senator. Can't wait to find out El Fahd's breaking point. Maybe we can stretch it out, you know, just a little."

"But the senator said—"

"I know, not too long. The senator made that clear. Too many people are looking for this guy. Crack him quick, and give him up tonight."

Thomas went back to shuffling his feet. His eyes darted back and forth like he'd been caught at a poker game with stakes he couldn't front. "What are we going to tell the Feds?"

Robby slapped the man on the back of the head and Thomas's face grew flat; his eyes stopped moving and landed steady and hard on Robby. *Finally got the dope's attention.* "Don't you listen? We'll say El Fahd took a gun from one of us in the air and forced us to land. Fortunately we overcame him once on the ground, and brought him to Cheyenne Mountain."

Then he added, "Anyway, after we're done with El Fahd, he won't be telling anybody anything."

The chopper landed in a dusty swirl. As the engine powered down and the blades slowed, Agent Sorensen got out of the helicopter, .357 still pointing at Rocca. Thomas and one other man ran out and took Rocca's .45 from Sorensen, and with their own handguns "escorted" Rocca to the rear entrance. Two other men grabbed each arm of El Fahd and dragged and pushed him toward the front door where Robby stood, hungrily watching. El Fahd's eyes were piercing, angry dark orbs that seemed to penetrate Robby's deepest thoughts.

Robby stepped back into the house, averting his eyes. *This might be a bit harder than I thought.* Robby opened the front door and let them pass.

Jabril counted six men outside, minus the pilot and Sorensen and the two who had taken Rocca. There were two cars, a new gray Camry and an old, red American car. The man at the front door initially looked excited and confident, but one look from Jabril was easy enough to make him cower. He opened the front door, and Jabril was shoved inside. There were electric cables and wires running along the floor of the first hallway from his right to the stairwell in front of him. He had seen houses and men like this. He had run them. *Prepare yourself.*

The men pushed him down the stairs. The cables and wires ran down the stairs on either side of his feet. He stumbled into the musty, dirt-floored basement. One light hung over a high-backed dental chair, and there was a small wooden table beside it. On the wall behind the chair was a large gray panel with one hand-sized switch and a round rheostat beside it. One man with small pig eyes stood beside the panel, his arms folded and a flat smile on his lips. The thick electric cables ran up from the floor into the bottom of the panel.

Jabril was immediately strapped into the chair with Velcro around his arms, legs, torso. Another bank of lights came on, momentarily blinding him. His head was forcibly pulled back and secured to the headrest with another Velcro strap, too tight to move. His shirt was cut off and electrodes were attached to his nipples and earlobes. His shoes were taken off, feet lifted up, a pan of cold water placed under them, then his ankles were strapped to the legs of the chair, securing his feet under the water.

A thin man with a massive head, pasty white skin, and deep, sunken eyes walked into the room from behind a wall. He placed a small case on the table beside Jabril and opened it. Out of the corner of his eye, Jabril saw it was a small power tool, the same American Dremel tool Jabril had used in making bombs. The large-headed man looked with pleasure at the tool, touching each attachment and accessory as if saying hello to a friend. He placed each accessory neatly on the table.

Robby wanted Landon get on with his work, but not before Robby had his say. He sidled in front of the thin man and stood directly in front of Jabril. He had rehearsed this speech last night, and he was determined to give it.

"So, you are the famed terrorist, Jabril El Fahd. You are an enemy of the United States. You are responsible for numerous deaths and acts of terrorism, and now you apparently are trying to spread some kind of disease in my country. Well, all we want is to know where the disease is going to be spread and when it will happen. If you tell us that, then you can avoid all this." He ended with a flourish of his hands towards the table and Landon, as if introducing the stars of the show.

Jabril's eyes seemed to look right through Robby, unblinking. "I will be glad to tell the commanding general at Cheyenne Mountain." His voice was a deep baritone, the slow calm of a man who felt no danger. "That is the only person I will speak to."

"You'll get to Cheyenne Mountain. It's not far. But…" Robby smiled thinking of how much the senator would enjoy military rank. "The general wants a few answers first. Then he'll talk to you. So give me a little for…the general, and I'll get you what you want. Let's start with when. When are the biologicals going to be released?"

"What time is it?" Jabril's response was so flat and quick Robby flinched.

"It's 0730 hours."

"In ninety minutes, the weapons will be released."

The answer and the matter of fact tone in Jabril's voice unnerved Robby. But at Jabril's slight crinkle of a smile, he collected himself quickly.

"Okay, that was easy. Now, how about where?"

"I will only reveal this to the general. Take me there and I will reveal all."

"Sorry. Not what I was looking for."

Robby nodded to the man standing by the switch. He adjusted the volt regulator knob, then pulled down the handle to complete the circuit.

The voltage shot through the wires connected to Jabril's earlobes and nipples, exiting his feet via the water. His body jumped and strained, and his back arched in a tetanic contraction, lifting his butt off the seat.

It should have been excruciating, but Jabril's eyes remained focused on Robby, calm, steady and confident, a red tint to his irises.

The lights dimmed. The wires hummed.

Jabril never blinked.

Robby made a cutting motion with his hand at his throat, and the man flipped the switch off.

The muscular contractions immediately ceased. Jabril's butt slapped down onto the chair and he continued his gaze at Robby: no blinking, no twitching, only the laser look.

Robby nibbled at his upper lip and blinked several times, a nervous habit he had years ago. This was not the way it usually went.

He stepped back. "Okay, Landon. Do your thing."

The balloon-headed thin man stepped forward, donned a mask, gown, hair net, gloves, and goggles, then plugged his Dremel tool into an extension cord. He attached a small burr and turned on the machine. The man smiled at the little whirring noise. His hands caressed the housing like he was petting a purring cat. Then he revved it to a high whine and his smile widened, revealing yellow teeth.

Jabril knew his kind. They loved to inflict pain.

Jabril's comfy-cozy dental chair was leaned back so Jabril was almost supine. A man placed an instrument over his left eye that kept his eyelid open. It was a simple device that was used in ophthalmologic surgery, and it worked very well. No matter how hard Jabril tried he could not shut his eye. Though he did not try, for he knew what was going to happen, to him and all the men here. Yet even with this knowledge, the sight coming at him made his heart trip, his breath quicken. All he could see was the hideously pale Frankenstein looming over him with a whirring drill.

Jabril had heard of this form of torture. The cornea had the most nerve endings per surface area of any organ in the body. Even a small scratch could cause enough pain to require narcotics. But what Landon was about to do, it was not a mere scratch. He would create pain that even high doses of morphine would not relieve. It would fill Jabril's brain with only one message: *Do anything to stop!*

Landon spoke, a shrill grating voice above the whir of the spinning Dremel. "I will start at the periphery of your left eye, abrading the cornea with this burr. I will then work my way around and end at the pupil. You will not be blinded until I thoroughly scar the cornea over the pupil. If you decide to talk, say *No more* and I will stop. But if it is a ruse, I warn you, I will place a chemical on the abrasion that will improve on my work by another fifty percent. That is what the animal studies say, but most of my human subjects say it quadruples the pain. This is not opinion or boast; it is fact, based on my considerable experience. Do you understand?"

Jabril did not answer. His one artificially-widened eye stared at Landon.

Landon had seen calm before in these tough guys. He shrugged and leaned forward, drill only inches from Jabril's eye.

Jabril started to brace himself. Then the balloon-headed man backed off six inches and smiled broadly, yellow incisors touching his lower lip. "Oh yes. The beauty of this is that you must remain perfectly still, stare straight ahead, or the burr will pierce your eye."

It truly was ingenious, thought Jabril. The tortured man had to contribute to his own torturing.

Jabril's first scream was involuntary. It had taken all of twenty seconds, and a trip halfway around the cornea from the whirring burr. But it was a horrifying howl, filling the room and making even the unflinching Landon pause and pull back.

A guttural whisper followed.

"No more," was heard by every man in the room.

Robby stepped forward.

"What do you have for me?"

Jabril's artificially wide-opened left eye was tearing. The searing pain had a direct connection to his brain.

He wretched, choking, unable to catch a breath. His other eye opened wide, his inhalation attempts a mere croak.

Landon looked at Robby and shrugged as if to say *I told you so*. Ideally he would have liked the suspect to have had nothing to eat for eight hours. He'd warned Robby about the higher risk of aspiration, but Robby had been insistent: They had to do this quickly.

Robby, clearly panicking, yelled, "Unstrap him! Do the Heimlich! Do a tracheotomy! I don't care. Whatever it takes. I want him alive and talking in two minutes. Move!"

Jabril's body went limp. Two men unstrapped Jabril. One of them took off the eye spreader and peered into his mouth while the other started forcibly pushing on his upper abdomen, doing the Heimlich maneuver. Landon held a scalpel, ready for a tracheotomy. Robby and the third man stood watching.

Jabril became a writhing animal. The man peering into his mouth was first. Jabril grabbed his head, twisted, felt the neck crack, then shoved the limp body aside. The second was the man doing the Heimlich. Jabril smashed the heel of his hand into the man's nose, an enjoyable crunch as the nasal bone spiked into his brain. The body started twitching. Jabril stood, pulling the twitching body in front of him as a shield.

Robby stood paralyzed, his eyes wide, mouth parted.

The man beside Robby started shooting. Bullets thudded into the dead-body shield. Jabril shoved the body forward, toppling the gunman onto his back under the corpse.

Jabril snatched the scalpel from Landon and jammed it into his eye while with his other hand jabbed a fist into Landon's trachea, crushing it. The torturer's one eye bulged, his mouth wide in a soundless scream.

Robby started reaching for his gun.

Jabril wrenched the scalpel out of Landon's eye, dropped his lifeless body, and charged forward, lashing at Robby's throat, cutting all the way to the spine through the trachea, both carotid arteries, and the jugular veins.

Robby grabbed at his throat, eyes blinking over and over. Blood poured through his fingers.

The man that Jabril had pushed the corpse on top of was crawling out from underneath it, bringing his gun around. Jabril stomped on his gun hand with one foot. The shot went wide.

With his other heel, Jabril smashed the man's head, a melon cracking and giving way underfoot. The man's gun arm shuddered, then was still. Jabril grabbed the gun.

Robby fell, his head knocking into the packed dirt like a coconut falling. The dirt floor darkened under his neck. Fifteen seconds had elapsed since Jabril had snapped the first neck.

Jabril ran towards the stairs. He must get to the helicopter. One of the men from upstairs was peering around the door. Jabril shot him through the door. The man dropped and Jabril ran up the stairs. That was the fifth man from outside. There was one other and Rocca, and Jabril had no time to find them. He sprinted up the stairs and burst out the front door onto the dusty road. Momentarily blinded by the sun, he shielded his eyes and looked around: Allah was testing him. The helicopter was gone. But Sorensen must have gone with the pilot.

He sprinted to the new gray Camry, not wanting to risk the older car's state of repair or stand out like blood on sand.

CHAPTER 67

Rocca was being a good boy, lying prone on a cot in the back ground-loor bedroom. The door was locked and a guard was outside. Shots were fired in the basement. He thought that might be okay, then jumped up from the cot and kicked the door open, splintering the door jamb. His guard was already moving down the hallway, a window to the right revealing the area where they'd landed. Rocca saw El Fahd getting into the Camry.

He yelled at the guard. "Go check the guys downstairs. And give me my gun back. El Fahd is getting away. I'll go after him."

The guy was built like a professional wrestler. He shrugged and tossed the gun to Rocca. "Take my car. It's the only one left. Keys are in it."

Rocca checked the magazine. Full. *Smarter than he looks.* "Thanks."

Thomas nodded and started down the stairs. Rocca ran out the front door. Outside, the Camry pulled out, front wheels spitting gravel and a cloud of dust. Rocca aimed, but all he could see was dust.

He shoved the gun into his belt and ran for the cherry-red '65 Chevy Impala SS. The V-8 cranked easily and purred. The car jumped forward with a mere touch on the accelerator. How cool was that?

The SS ate up the dirt road between the two cars quickly. The ride was smooth despite the bumpy road. Sweet, Rocca thought. Special shocks and power.

He made a mental note to find out who'd hopped up the car. Rocca's 442 Olds in his sister's garage in Longmont could use the same treatment.

Gravel thrown up by his speed and spinning tires pinged off the buffed sides of the Impala. Rocca winced, momentarily letting up on the accelerator. A shame to damage such a sweet finish.

Couldn't be helped, though. He pushed down the accelerator and fishtailed around the next turn. The Camry was now within shooting range. He pulled his gun.

The Camry turned onto a two-lane blacktop.

Jabril kept the accelerator mashed to the floor. He had to get to Cheyenne Mountain.

His damaged eye was tearing so much he could barely see, but the pain was almost gone. Healing fast. The tears and the dusty road almost made him miss the paved road.

Allah is merciful! He sends a magic carpet. It was an automatic thought and he despised it. Allah should have left him the helicopter. It was not Allah who left the keys in the car but an incompetent guard at the torture house, a guard he had killed. Jabril was more than Allah. The blood of power still rushed through him and the engine roared.

He turned the Camry onto the blacktop. The car leaped forward on the pavement, and as the dust cleared behind him, he saw the red car in his rearview mirror. The driver waved and yelled something.

Rocca!

Jabril stomped on the accelerator.

Fate has given me the better car. That relic will never keep up.

The road was a straight shot west, an arrow to Pikes Peak.

I will be there in the next hour.

Rocca got a good look at Jabril when he turned right onto the two-lane. He waved and yelled, "Yeah, it's me, asshole!"

The Impala's tires squealed when they hit the pavement. The car lurched forward: the four-hundred-and-twenty-five horsepower engine and special fifteen-inch tires were now on home turf.

Within thirty seconds Rocca was only fifty feet behind the other car and closing fast. The road was straight, flat, and he'd have a clear shot in another twenty seconds.

If it hadn't been for the pickup.

—

Luther had been a dry-land farmer most of his seventy-four years and still enjoyed driving the old pickup. Yesterday he'd finished planting the winter wheat and was on his way to Colorado Springs for supplies and one of them fancy pepperoni pizzas. The old 1980 Ford F-150 had served him well for 389,000 miles, but it was prone to overheating, so he was taking it easy, babying her along at forty-five miles an hour. It was only ten under the speed limit, no big deal.

Then he saw the two cars approaching in his rearview. They were coming fast. To avoid them he decided to turn left at the Hampton's Place road and wait for the cars to pass. He pressed the accelerator to get off the road.

The carburetor flooded and the engine died. The truck stopped in the middle of the two-lane, an effective diagonal obstruction to most of both lanes.

Jabril had decided to pass the slow truck on the left and had switched lanes when the truck moved to the left and stopped. His training made him turn the steering wheel to the left and then to the right, then pump the brake. He should easily swerve around the truck to the left.

The truck jerked forward, now a complete barricade to the left.

With the third turn of the key the old truck started and Luther, concentrating on getting out of the way pushed on the accelerator. But in his excitement he had forgotten to shift into first. The truck was still in second gear and bucked forward about five feet before dying again.

Luther looked up to see where the cars were. The headlights of a Toyota Camry were a few feet from his door.

Rocca had seen the old truck about a mile back. He was used to these old country roads. Farmers drove slow. So when he saw the Ford pull onto the blacktop, he let up on the accelerator. When the truck started turning left, Rocca was already steering right. Why was El Fahd still trying to pass on the left? The Camry never slowed. Rocca was almost past the truck when the Camry T-boned the F-150.

It sounded like nails on a chalkboard with hammer blows thrown in. The truck's front end came off the ground about a foot as the Camry submerged its hood under the driver's side door.

El Fahd was ejected out the windshield of the Camry, hurtling past the cab and over the hood of the truck.

Rocca's raised his eyebrows and smiled. "Someone didn't obey the seat belt law."

He slammed on the brakes stopping on the near side of the truck, and jumped out to check on the driver. The old man's head was twisted at an odd angle with an abrasion on his left temple and sightless eyes. His frail neck had probably snapped after smashing against the side window. But his seat belt was on.

Jabril had thrown his arms in front of him when he saw the truck looming. Like a diver splitting the water, his arms took the brunt of the blow going through the windshield. He landed on the far side of the truck on his left arm and felt a sharp pain and clunk in his left shoulder.

He lay in the dirt, momentarily unsure where he was, but the piercing pain from his left shoulder quickly reminded him. He could not move it, and touching it with his right hand he knew it was dislocated. Pushing up with his right hand, he got to his knees and forcibly threw himself onto his left shoulder. *Clunk.* He screamed. But he had effectively relocated his shoulder and now could move his arm.

Rocca stood by the truck, shaking his head at the poor farmer and wondering how to contact his next of kin. He was about to check the glove box when he heard the scream from the far side of the truck. *El Fahd! When's this guy gonna die? Maybe he has a lot of Egyptian blood and is half cat like the pharaohs.*

He went back to the car for the .45.

Jabril lay prone in the dirt, arms bleeding, but his shoulder almost normal. *I must kill him now and complete the mission.*

Yet even though they felt better, his arms were barely able to push himself up, and his legs almost gave out when he stood.

Why had he weakened so?

He walked around the back of the truck, already feeling his legs grow stronger, the cuts on his arms with less pain and visibly knitting together.

Rocca was walking toward the shiny red car, his back to Jabril.

Jabril took a deep breath, reached down and grabbed a fist-sized rock, then ran towards Rocca, willing the speed of Al-Buraq into his legs.

One hard blow, take his car and get to Cheyenne Mountain. Perfect.

His right arm cocked high, the rock gripped tight, he ran in for the kill.

Rocca saw movement in the reflection of the slightly dusty mirror finish of the Impala's door. El Fahd was running and had a rock raised. Reaching in his pocket Rocca fumbled for the smooth handle while he turned to meet his attacker.

Jabril saw Rocca turn, and changed the direction of the swing of the rock in anticipation of Rocca stepping back. But Rocca moved toward him instead of away, so all he could do was collapse around Rocca's shoulder, the rock flying out of his hand, banging off the side of the shiny red car.

A bystander would have thought Jabril was hugging Rocca like a long lost brother, face to face. But it did not feel like a hug to Jabril.

Rocca always carried the backup switchblade. A Tijuana special, it had a full six-inch blade and an unfailing mechanism. It snapped open perfectly now and locked in an instant. Unfailing.

He jabbed the blade under Jabril's ribs, up into his heart, and flicked and stirred the end of the blade like he was trying to get a cherry in the bottom of a milkshake, or in this case to do the absolute most damage to heart, lungs, and major blood vessels.

He glared into Jabril's eyes. "I don't care if you are part cat. This is your last life."

Rocca could feel the life ebbing out of the terrorist when he realized he needed an answer.

He lay the terrorist onto his back, but kept the knife stuck in to the hilt. "Maybe you could tell me when and where the biologicals are to be released? Allah might forgive you for all your prior sins."

Jabril felt his arms and legs getting cool. His vision was tunneling. Yet even now he thought of a way to gain Allah's pleasure and continue his mission to kill all the infidels, starting with Rocca.

He whispered, "I will tell you."

Rocca leaned forward, eyes wide, trying to read El Fahd's lips in case he didn't hear him.

Jabril spit into Rocca's eyes. "I am the Sword of Gabriel, the angel of Allah. And now I will join Muhammad."

Rocca blinked at the sting of saliva, but held the knife steady.

El Fahd's body went limp and Rocca made a couple of final zigzags with the end of the blade before taking it out. He wiped it on El Fahd's shirt, wiped his eyes, and chuckled.

"Had to get the final word in, didn't you?"

He started to get up but paused and kneeled. He rammed the blade under the soft part of the terrorist's chin into his upper spinal column, twisting and slicing with the end, mixing Jabril's brain like a milkshake, pulling up so hard on the blade that he lifted Jabril's upper body off the ground. *No more lives for you, cat or not.*

With a quick twist of his wrist, he pulled the blade out. Jabril's body flopped onto the ground, dust smoking out from the sides.

Rocca walked with a slow, deliberate pace back to the Impala, wiping the blade on his pants, frowning at the ding on the side caused by the rock meant for his head. He'd have to get that fixed for the big guy. He popped the trunk, making sure it was empty. Trudging to the F-150, he pulled out a tarp from the bed. Dust puffed up from each tired step as he plodded back to the terrorist. He rolled El Fahd up in the tarp and dragged him back to the Impala.

Hefting him in, he closed the trunk with authority. "I'd leave you to rot…but somebody will probably want proof."

CHAPTER 68

Rocca interrupted his drive to Cheyenne Mountain only once, to stop at a pay phone. He was glad to find Sam and Rachel still at the underground fortress. On speakerphone he also spoke to another man there about cleaning up the mess left behind at the senator's safe house.

"Oh, we've already got somebody out there." The man was almost chipper.

"Okay, I won't ask how you know about that, but I will tell you that I have a certain colonel in the trunk of a beautiful Impala and would like to deliver him to someone who cares. Unfortunately, I never got anything out of him, except some spit in my eye."

Sam's voice came back online. "He spit in your eye?"

"Yeah, pretty funny, huh?"

Sam didn't answer, but instead gave instructions on where to drop the car.

"Oh, yeah," Rocca added, "tell the big guy at the safe house that his car is really sweet and to call me. I got a '65 Olds four-four-two that I need a little work on."

"You may be able to tell Thomas yourself. He'll be there for your debriefing."

Rocca sneered at the phone. *Always a debriefing.*

"How long is this going to take, anyway? My eyes feel like they could use two days of sleep and my stomach is about seven meals behind."

"It won't take long, Rock. They already know most of it." He paused. "Hey, after you get some chow and shut eye, how'd you like to come back to D.C. with us? Rachel needs to check in at work. You could crash at my place and we could go fishing for sea bass in the Chesapeake."

"Thanks, but I try to stay far away from D.C. Don't like making decisions by committee. Long time ago I swore an oath that if I ever got a job in D.C., I'd slit my throat. Besides, I need to catch up with my sis in Longmont. I'll see you in a few."

After skirting just north of Peterson Air Force Base and weaving through southern Colorado Springs, he drove south on Highway 115, up the winding NORAD road past the brown sign announcing that NORAD lay ahead. He slowed at the guard shack, unrolled his window, and prepared to get out for the usual body search, but the guards in green camouflage fatigues waved him through to follow a Humvee. They all held M-16s and wore light blue surgical masks. Another Humvee pulled in behind him from the nearby parking lot. Rocca didn't really have a choice but to follow, though he thought this overkill.

Through the north tunnel entrance, down the lighted tunnel, the front Humvee stopped and several men got out. They wore white scrubs with tight fitting hoods over goggles, blue gloves, and surgical masks, and surrounded his car.

Rocca started to get out and tell them how stupid this was when one of the men stepped forward with his hand out. "Please wait right here, sir. We need to get the body."

"Okay, okay." Rocca threw him the keys.

They carefully opened the trunk, placed the body into a zippered bag, and wheeled it off on a gurney.

Rocca was immediately masked, and given a suit and gloves and goggles. He garbed up just like everyone else as requested, knowing he had no choice. Then he was escorted to a vehicle like an enclosed golf cart, one suited man with a gun behind him. The door locks clicked shut and the cart took off, zooming through a brightly lit, hanger-like room, through two other lighted tunnels, then stopping at the end of one of them. Another cadre of surgically suited men waited by an open door to a lighted hallway. The locks on the cart's doors clicked open.

"This is your stop," the man behind him said as he got out and opened Rocca's door. Rocca took a deep breath, sighed out his nose in resignation, got out, and walked down a hallway that looked like it had been steam-cleaned. It had gleaming white tile and semi-gloss beige walls and bright fluorescent overhead lights. There were no doors except at the end of the hallway. No secret where he was going. His footsteps echoed. Thirty steps later he walked through the open doorway into a small room. It had beige walls, a white floor and bright fluorescent overhead lights. At least the decorator was consistent. After he went in, the escort left and closed the door. A deadbolt clicked.

All the furniture was gray and black aluminum, including a bed, chair, bed stand and lamp, and a small chest of drawers and closet stocked with clothes his size. A TV hung high in one corner and a bookshelf was loaded with best-sellers.

He sat on the bed and took off the surgical garb, tossed it into a corner, and blew out a long breath. "Okay. It's not D.C., but Jesus Christ this is bullshit."

His words bounced off the beige walls, no reply expected.

Sam's voice came over the intercom speakers flanking the TV. "Sorry about this, Rock, but they pretty much insisted we had to do it this way. We had to get you in here to do tests. They wouldn't let me say anything else on the phone."

The TV flickered on. It showed Rachel and Sam in another room surrounded by computers and several white-suited men and women. Sam waived a hand and smiled.

"You might remember El Fahd was infected with a virus. Problem is, it's related to HIV, and you could have been infected when he spit in your eyes."

"Perfect. So he really did get the last word." Rocca chuckled, then laughed until tears came to his eyes.

"Easy, Rock. We should have answers in a few days. You said you were hungry and tired, right? Food's coming and you can sleep all you want."

The screen went blank.

A few minutes later a key unlocked the door and a steaming tray of food was handed in by a zoot-suited guy. Everything a growing boy needed: medium-rare T-bone, baked potatoes, Caesar salad, lasagna, red wine, and New York cheesecake with fresh strawberries on top.

"Well, at least you got the food right." He dug in. After the meal he lay down on the bed and slept for sixteen hours.

Over the next three days he stuffed himself, read, watched reruns of football games he'd missed, and slept. He watched the news and got the same old political and bad weather roundups. The real news, he found out from his captors. The CIA and FBI had picked up some terrorists wired with bombs at many of the Western reservoirs. A security guard had also found a small submarine at Hoover Dam filled with marble-sized chemical packets.

Rocca laughed when he heard the lieutenant in charge of security at Hoover Dam had ignored the guard. Typical officer weenie. Fortunately the guard hadn't trusted his lieutenant, so he'd contacted the CIA anti-terrorist unit himself. All reservoirs were ordered to promptly stop tours. Security was doubled. They apprehended several terrorists before they triggered the bombs. One old lady blew up herself and her son in a getaway car.

All that news was easily squelched, hushed by the FBI using bribes or told it was for "national security" and their "their patriotic duty" to avoid panicking the masses. Not many lived around the reservoirs, so very little bribe money was spent.

The lieutenant in charge of security at Hoover Dam was transferred to a desk job in D.C. where he could be observed daily and quietly kept out of any further positions of authority.

The only bad news was that most of the workers in Cheyenne Mountain were getting some kind of flu. Other underground shelters were also reporting an epidemic of flu symptoms. The CDC sent a team to look into it. They were nervous it might be a strain similar to the 1918 bug that had killed millions. The FBI was there, too, of course.

On day three, Rocca was finishing breakfast and reading a local paper, when it hit him. He buzzed Rachel and Sam. "Rachel probably thinks I'm an insensitive ass, which maybe I am for not asking this sooner. What about Jesse and Alex? Did they ever find their bodies?"

On the TV screen, Rachel looked down and said softly, "No, not a trace. They said the Arkansas River could have taken them a long ways downstream. They did search the Pueblo Reservoir and come up empty. They'll probably call off the search in a few days if they don't find anything."

"Sorry, Rachel. It would have been nice to have a funeral to say a final goodbye to them both. You guys were pretty tight."

Rachel covered her eyes, stood up, and left the room.

Rocca swore under his breath. "Guess I screwed that up."

Sam was at the screen now. "Don't feel bad, Rock. I don't think anything you said would have been right. Not sure Rachel wants them to find the bodies, at least not Alex's. Slicing, dicing and dissecting in a postmortem from hell doesn't seem like much respect. Anyhow, there will be a ceremony at the end of the week at the Air Force Academy chapel. I had to pull some strings, but I thought it would be appropriate since they died trying to save their country from another terrorist attack. You're getting an award, too. So you'll have to be there."

Rocca shrugged. "I'll think about it."

The next day, the door to his room opened and Sam and Rachel came in without masks. Rocca was lying on the bed reading a copy of the latest Fly Fisherman magazine.

He raised one eyebrow at them. "What's up?"

Sam carried a bottle of champagne in one hand and put his other up in a fist. "You're free, Rock. It was only a very pale version of the flu! Several viral cultures were confiscated from the network of jihadists that tried to infect Cheyenne Mountain and other sites. On interrogation, one of the them confessed they were supposed to be sent some kind of lethal mutant virus from the lab at Jakarta. But it looks like someone sent the wrong cultures. So instead of the mutant viruses, all they got was a fairly meek version of the flu virus. Let me tell you, there are some pissed off terrorists. They thought they were going to die for a cause and all they got was a runny nose and a cough."

Rocca sat up, shook his head and drew air through his teeth. "I can't believe El Fahd would have made a mistake that big."

"It wasn't him. Some guy named Jorge assigned another guy and they apparently had a vial marked with blue dots but didn't know that there were about ten other vials marked with blue dots."

"What about Jabril? Did he get the flu too, or did he have something different?"

Rachel, who stood beside Sam, said, "You're not infected, so don't worry about it."

"Got it. Above my pay grade." He put the magazine on the bed, pursed his lips and squinted at her, almost afraid to ask, but knowing if he didn't it would be worse. "When's the memorial service for Alex and Jesse?"

Rachel looked at the floor, her eyes welling up, and walked out the door.

Rocca was still looking at where Rachel went. "Damn. I did it again. Somehow I keep saying the wrong things around her."

Sam answered quietly, "Since Jesse and Alex have most of their friends and coworkers in D.C., Jerry and I talked it over with their family, and okayed a funeral service at the Naval Academy Chapel in a couple of weeks. The families are being flown out by the government. The press doesn't know due to the nature of their work, so it won't be a big deal. But the CIA decided a little formality would let the families know how grateful the nation is."

Rocca rolled his head on his neck, blew out a breath through his nose in frustration at not hitting it right with Rachel. He looked at Sam. "Well, Annapolis is a damn sight better than D.C. I guess I can go."

"Jerry has a cottage on the Eastern Shore. Or—I'm going back to see friends in Virginia Beach and you're welcome to come with me. But if you're going, you better get packed."

"Wearing everything I brought. I'm ready now, but I think I'll hang around here for a while and catch up on some fishin'." Rocca stood and walked out the door.

"You might want to take a left at the end of the hallway. That's the way out."

Rocca gave the thumbs-up sign and kept walking.

CHAPTER 69

Two weeks later, Rocca had decided he should go to the services, if nothing else to repair some of the damage with Rachel. The morning before the ceremony, Jerry arranged a tour of the Naval Academy for Rocca, Sam, and Rachel. First they went to Bancroft Hall, the dormitory that housed over four thousand midshipmen. Then they saw the noon meal formation, an elaborate but by-the-numbers parade of white-uniformed men and women. After every battalion and regimental commander shouted "All present or accounted for, sir," the band played Sousa and the middies all marched inside and downstairs into the fifty-five-thousand-square-foot King Hall, the dining room that, at one sitting, fed all of the midshipmen.

After lunch they attended the service for Alex and Jesse at the Naval Academy Chapel, a gold-domed stone building with exquisite stained glass windows that rivaled French chateaus Rocca had seen. The playing of the huge pipe organ at the service reminded Rocca of the Phantom of the Opera.

It was a touching service to the families, Rocca was sure; each family got a tri-folded flag that had been flown by a helicopter over the Royal Gorge. There wasn't a dry eye in the place, except Rocca's.

The day before, the Director of Central Intelligence had called Rocca, wanting to set up an awards ceremony. Rocca politely declined, asking for them to mail him the award. Once he got home he would put it with the rest, in the attic trunk.

Inside the church, Rocca stood just inside a side entrance, and at the end of the service he slipped out, walking downstairs to John Paul Jones's crypt.

See the big guy himself. Then I'm outta here.

The ornate gray casket sat in the middle of a circular, tiled room with plaques and busts on the side walls telling the history of the famous man. Rocca's rubber soles squeaked on the buffed marble floors. He read the famous words on one plaque: "'I have not yet begun to fight.'" He paused "And that's the name of that tune."

A voice behind him echoed in the marble-floored room. "You played it so well, too."

He turned and saw Rachel smiling at him, cheeks still wet.

"Hi, Rache. Sorry I left. Never been much for funerals. No disrespect for Alex or Jesse."

"I know, Rock. I understand." Rachel looked toward the exit. "Would you like to take a little walk? I hear the view across the Severn River is pretty good. I could use some fresh air."

They walked by Mahan Hall and Nimitz Hall, exchanging small talk, and gradually meandered down to the seawall that separated the Academy from the Severn River. On the opposite bank of the river were beautiful homes that must have had a spectacular view of the Academy.

To their left, a footbridge crossed a creek to the "O" course, or "obstacle" course that every midshipman had to run many, many times before they graduated. A squad of middies in white shirts and navy blue shorts was just finishing the course, with a few stragglers finishing up well behind the others.

Rachel stared across the Severn River. "In a way, I'm glad Alex died."

"Excuse me?" Rocca frowned and stepped back a pace, wanting to take back the accusatory tone, but unsure of what to say.

Rachel turned and looked him, a slight quiver to her lip, but her gaze steady as if she had to get this out. "You know those blood and tissue samples we took from Alex and Jesse?"

"Yeah?"

Rachel sighed as if she was confused, too. "It's possible there were strange mutations in their DNA."

Rocca waited.

"Anyway, that would explain what happened back in the Amazon Lab."

"Sorry Rachel, you're losing me. Possible strange mutations? Amazon Lab?"

"Alex and Jesse did some…unusual things, possibly related to some strange mutations in their DNA. The military is salivating. Wants to recreate those mutations. Would make great soldiers. They believe the viruses we were studying caused those mutations. Problem is, they don't have a live Jesse or Alex, and all the viruses seem to have been destroyed. They're not even sure what viral combination got it started. It may take years, or maybe they'll never know."

Rocca nodded. "Well, I feel better now."

"What do you mean?"

He tried to hold back the grin, but it was there. "At least there was a good reason why some egghead scientist could outrun me and beat me to the punch. I thought I was getting too old for this stuff."

"Oh, right." The sides of her lips and eyes started to turn up, and Rocca thought maybe he had actually said something right.

"But there is another reason I feel better."

"What's that?"

"Now you've really got job security. From what I've seen, they'll need your talents even more."

Rachel watched as one of the midshipmen was helped off the obstacle course, limping. "I'm not so sure I want to do this stuff anymore. After getting shot at, hunted, and almost infected with several lethal viruses, I might skip it. Besides, I've got a couple of other problems to think about."

"What's that?"

"First, Jabril had mutations in his DNA as well as being infected by the flu. The military is ecstatic. They think another viral-induced mutation caused him to heal very quickly and to have incredible strength. Though, once again, which virus is responsible is a mystery."

Rocca smiled more broadly, getting into it. "So now it's in me, this virus, and I get to be an X-man like Wolverine?"

Rachel's near grin now showed teeth and she chuckled. "Not exactly. As it turns out, the virus he got is not contagious." She looked at him, serious now. "While he's alive. The virus lives deep inside the organisms cells until the organism starts to die. But there's no danger of that."

Rocca frowned. "He's still alive? No way! I pithed that guy."

"He is a brain-dead organ donor now and we've been studying him for the last two weeks and will probably study extensively into the foreseeable future. Another reason I may quit this gig. I hate Jabril…but I'm not sure I like how the military is going to study him."

Rocca stared into space wishing he would have cut El Fahd's head off.

Rachel should have looked serious, but her lips were pursed like she had something else she was holding back. "You mentioned a couple of problems? I'm almost afraid to ask about the other one."

"Oh, it's a good kind of problem. I'm pregnant."

She scratched her temple and there was still a gleam in her eye.

"Something else?" he said.

"Maybe later."

EPILOGUE

It was a small, hundred-year-old stone cabin deep in the High Sierra wilderness. The man who had built it was a mason and knew his craft, carefully laying each hand-picked stone, using fine brown sand from the nearby riverbed for grout. Even now, a candle could easily stay lit inside while the wind of the harsh winter blew through the surrounding four-thousand-acre wilderness property.

After the mason died, no one ever inhabited the cabin. He'd secretly willed the property to a distant relative. But she was very busy, and no one else knew about the land.

Over the years, wild berry bushes and aspen had taken root around the cabin, hiding it from view. The hearty roof gradually succumbed to the harsh winters, and on the north side a hole had attracted dirt, pine needles, and a few small animals.

During the last four months things had changed. The roof was repaired, the berry bushes and aspen trimmed away, and the inside cleaned out. Now a plume of gray smoke snaked up from the stone chimney. A stack of wood grew outside each day, piled neatly next to a newly built corral that held two horses, a roan and a pinto.

The distant relative had decided to move in.

Rocca took in the bucolic scene as he rode the huge black stallion towards the corral. The horse stopped with a little pressure on the reins, and Rocca eased down. He walked the horse to the corral, stretching his legs. It had been a long ride. His sleeping bag and clothes flopped when he took off the saddle. The horse drank from the water trough, and Rocca opened the feed hamper where fresh hay waited. He shouldered the saddle and was closing the gate when the door to the cabin opened.

Rachel stepped out, nursing a beaming, diapered infant. "How was the ride?"

"Long, as usual. Why couldn't you live a little bit closer?"

Rachel breathed in deeply, enjoying the crisp air. "Oh come on, Rock. A little two-day horse ride too much for you? Maybe you *are* getting old."

"Yeah, well, I am only human. I don't sprout wings like Pegasus, or heal up in minutes. And I don't do this every day like you guys."

Rachel eyed him as he made his way to the cabin. He was graying a little at the temples, though it was hard to see because he kept his hair clipped so close.

He stopped when he saw her looking at him. "Have you decided on a name?"

It was a beautiful child, already with a head full of golden hair and twinkling green eyes the color of spring aspen leaves shimmering in the wind. The baby looked at each of them when they talked, as if she understood every word and was about to interject her own comment.

"We have."

Rocca looked at the infant, then chuckled and gazed up at the blue sky. "So are you going to tell me, or do I have to guess?"

"It's Alexis, after her father."

"Alexis. Yeah, that fits. Say, where *is* Alex, anyway?"

"Oh, he's out hunting, as usual."

—The End—

DAN'S WAR

 Dan's War is about the end of world oil…in two weeks. Abdullah El-Hamain, a high-roller OPEC member, hates Big Oil for polluting earth and killing his wife. His solution: sink or swim—end global warming by destroying the entire world's oil supply in two weeks, using spiders and nanobacteria. Drawn into his apocalyptic scheme is Dan Trotter, a CIA computer savant without equal, but with an Asperger's-like syndrome that makes him a social goof. If Dan can only become a field agent in a real war he will become a hero like his father, breaking out of his geek job, and gain the respect from his wayward son and roaming wife. Dan soon finds himself in the middle of an oil war, a war that his own computer program helped start.

Dan's War is a sister novel to *The Next Day*, sharing some characters, including Sam Houston.

ABOUT THE AUTHOR

 Milt grew up in Colorado, then spent most of his adult life as a Navy doctor. After graduating from the Naval Academy and medical school, he travelled all over the world with the Navy, the Marines, and a Navy Security Group, finally coming back to rest in Colorado. He's worked as a fly fishing guide and currently is a primary care doctor for the VA.

Other published works by Milt include the novels *The Guide* and *Dan's War* and the short stories "Thanksgiving with Riley" and "The Dry-Land Farmer." He lives with his wife in Colorado.

Milt's website is www.miltmays.com.